DISTORTION

A Phobos novel

VICTOR DIXEN

Translated by Daniel Hahn

First published in French by Éditions Robert Laffont, S.A. Paris, in 2015

First published in Great Britain in 2018 by
HOT KEY BOOKS
80–81 Wimpole St, London W1G 9RE
www.hotkeybooks.com

*This book is supported by the Institut français (Royaume-Uni)
as part of the Burgess programme.*

ROYAUME-UNI

A CIP catalogue record for this book is available from the British Library.

ISBN: 978-1-4714-0706-2
also available as an ebook

1

This book is typeset using Atomik ePublisher
Printed and bound by Clays Ltd, Elcograf S.p.A

Hot Key Books is an imprint of Bonnier Zaffre Ltd,
a Bonnier Publishing company
www.bonnierpublishing.com

For E.

1 teaspoon white Karo
1 big can evaporated milk
equal part boiled water or distilled water
1 egg yoke
mix and chill
Don't feed him meat or formula cold
1 drop vitamin solution per day

Last words written by James Dean (1931–1955)

GENESIS PROGRAM

Dowry Values on the final day of the *Cupido's* journey
Six girls on one side. Six boys on the other.
Six minutes to meet. An eternity to love . . .

The girls

Kirsten, 19, Germany [Biology Officer]	$370,234,008
Elizabeth, 18, United Kingdom [Engineering Officer]	$222,345,457
Léonor, 18, France [Medical Officer]	$200,234,890
Safia, 17, India [Communications Officer]	$171,123,987
Kelly, 19, Canada [Navigation Officer]	$151,345,091
Fangfang, 20, Singapore [Planetology Officer]	$132,215,067

The boys

Alexei, 19, Russia [Medical Officer]	$202,234,351
Marcus, 19, USA [Planetology Officer]	$197,867,341
Tao, 18, China [Engineering Officer]	$186,667,008
Mozart, 18, Brazil [Navigation Officer]	$177,890,334
Samson, 18, Nigeria [Biology Officer]	$151,222,306
Kenji, 18, Japan [Communications Officer]	$78,999,013

ACT I

1. Genesis Channel

Saturday 9 December, 12:13pm

WE APOLOGISE FOR THE INTERRUPTION TO THIS SERVICE.
WE ARE WORKING TO RE-ESTABLISH THE CONNECTION WITH THE
CUPIDO AS QUICKLY AS POSSIBLE.
THANK YOU FOR YOUR PATIENCE, AND FOR YOUR LOYALTY TO YOUR
FAVOURITE CHANNEL:
THE GENESIS CHANNEL!

2. Shot

Twelve.

We are twelve, gathered all together for the first time in the Visiting Room, the glass bubble that has seen us parading in, two by two, over these past five months: us, the participants in the Genesis programme, the greatest TV game show in all history – and the cruellest lie of all time.

We are twelve people thirsty for glory, who were persuaded that by setting off for Mars we would become immortal.

We are twelve people hungry for love, convinced that everything would have a fairy-tale ending – *they were married, had lots of children and lived happily ever after.* Isn't that what we're always reading at the end of a good story?

There's Kris, the German girl, my lifetime friend (even though we only met a year and a half ago), whose big blue eyes gleam beneath her crown of blonde braids, like those of a Sleeping Beauty waking up from a too-long sleep.

There's Kelly, the Canadian, the hot-head of the team, all dishevelled from the struggle that set us against each other a few moments ago, when the girls thought I was some kind of lunatic having a total paranoid breakdown.

There's Safia from India, the youngest and wisest among us, who I hurt in my frenzy and who has a purplish mark around her neck from the scarf I nearly strangled her with, though I'd never meant to.

There's Liz the English girl and Fangfang the Singaporean, our top model and our intellectual, each of them supporting one of the injured girl's arms.

All five of them are looking at me in amazement – and in terror. Even Louve, the on-board dog who looks like a poodle, gazes at me with her shining black eyes as though she understands the terrible deception of which she's been a victim, her every bit as much as the rest of us.

'They've sent us to our deaths,' I say for the third time, feeling like I've got razor blades scraping my throat. 'Serena and the instructors. They led us onboard the ship knowing there would be nothing waiting for us when we got here, nothing but defective habitats unable to keep us alive for more than a few months. The whole thing is explained in here. Look.'

Saying nothing, the girls slide towards me across the Visiting Room they burst into just moments ago. Here at the heart of the *Cupido*, there's no artificial gravity – we seem to be floating in the middle of a void. Outside the window, the Earth is just a glimmering dot among so many millions of others. Resting in my palm is a bright object that never should have come into my possession, but which destiny allowed to fall into my hands: a cellphone with a photovoltaic screen, recharged by the light of the cosmos.

7

It was the stars that finally lit up the screen, illuminating the truth. It would be a lovely image, if it weren't such a tragic one.

'What does it say on that thing, that's got you so worked up?' asks a voice full of doubt and anger.

It belongs to Alexei, the Russian, once the most highly sought-after boy on board, before he became engaged to Kris.

He's standing on the other side of the unbreakable glass that splits the Visiting Room from top to bottom. His voice reaches me through the audio system that allows communication between the two perfectly airtight hemispheres. His steely eyes look daggers at me as though I were the guilty one, the criminal, the shatterer of dreams. Can I blame him? I've had weeks to nurture my suspicions, to believe the unbelievable, to name the unnameable. But them? They suspected nothing, and here I am hurling everything in their faces, all eleven of them, like a slap. They thought they were the lucky ones chosen for the greatest adventure anybody has ever experienced, and they discover they're just victims, destined to die wretchedly.

The faces of the boys, pressed up against the reinforced glass, make them look like men on death row in their final session in the visiting room. Not the Visiting Room of our sensational courtships, no, the real visiting room of a real jail, where the prisoners receive their final visitors before setting off down the corridor that leads to the electric chair.

The forehead of Samson from Nigeria makes a pool of ink against the glass, and Kenji's from Japan a pool of milk. The powerful hands of Tao, the Chinese acrobat, press against the glass as though he wants to shatter it, which is certainly impossible. As for the last two, Mozart from Brazil and Marcus the American, they aren't looking at the small telephone screen – they're watching me.

My freckled face, still soiled with dried blood.

My red mane of hair, tangling with the shreds of my torn chiffon dress.

My bare shoulder, from which the Salamander leaps out, that long scar I've spent my whole life hiding. It took just seconds to reveal it to the entire craft.

'*Noah Report*,' reads Kris, her voice trembling, as she leans over the telephone screen. 'That's what it says, Alex: *Noah Report.*'

She clears her throat so as to be able to speak more loudly, so that everyone can hear.

'*Report Summary: The sensors indicate that the six pairs of rats, lizards and cockroaches that were sent secretly to the seventh habitat of the Martian base survived for eight months, and reproduced at a pace comparable to terrestrial conditions. But at the end of the ninth month, every one of the organisms died suddenly, for reasons unknown.*

'*Conclusion: As things stand, and until there is a better understanding of what caused the inexplicable loss of the trial animals, the habitats are considered not capable of sustaining life in the long term.*'

Alexei thumps his fist hard against the glass, interrupting Kris's reading.

There is a crease across his usually smooth, high forehead.

His elegant white outfit with the grey seam does appear to be encumbering him all of a sudden, and there's something incongruous about his perfectly combed hair, like a movie

9

star's. In the movie he's currently a part of, whether he likes it or not, there's no juvenile lead ready to save the day, no superhero who can rescue the world, and, most importantly of all, no Prince Charming. There are only losers, and all of them are at breaking point.

'It can't be true!' he cries – his Russian accent, usually so mild, rolls as furiously as a swell in the midst of a storm. 'The report's a fake!'

'It's signed by Gordon Lock, Archibald Dragovic and Ruben Rodriguez,' whispers Kris, still trying to make out more of the writing on the telephone screen. 'The names of the technical director of the programme and my own Biology instructor are right there, in black and white.'

'You'll believe anything!' Alexei cuts her off. 'There's no evidence they're the ones who actually wrote that web of lies.'

I can't help thinking his tone of voice sounds more like a father speaking to his daughter than a fiancé addressing his bride-to-be. But Kris says nothing and, standing behind me, Fangfang nods vigorously, clinging to the hope that all this might be no more than a bad dream.

'Alexei is right,' she says. 'It's definitely a hoax, some kind of mean joke. You must have gotten it wrong, Léo.'

She so wants to believe what she's saying.

I can see a silent prayer in her eyes; she's begging me to answer her with something like *Oh yes, of course, I got it wrong, now you mention it it's obvious, thank goodness you're here, Fangfang, right as always!*

But the words that come out of my mouth are the opposite of what she's hoping for.

'Fangfang, Alexei, this is no joke. I did not get it wrong. Crazy as it may seem, Serena has sacrificed us all for money. This is the truth. She launched the show despite the flaws in the installations, to rake in the billions from the advertising, the sponsors and the viewers' gifts. She didn't even try to deny it. She knows that she hasn't got time for that. The only thing that matters to her is that we tell her that we'll land nicely on Mars tomorrow, Sunday, as set out in the protocols and announced on the TV broadcast, without making waves. It will then be up to us to try to fix the habitats once we're in place. In exchange, she commits to not depressurising them remotely.'

'Hang on,' murmurs Safia, looking horribly pale, as though all the blood hadn't yet returned to her head after the terrible accident that almost ended her life. 'That's unbelievable. That would mean she wants to buy our silence in exchange for the tiny hope that we just might pull through?'

'That's right, Safia. That's the squalid deal that Serena offered me, after she'd confessed everything. That we should keep playing the game, as if there was absolutely nothing wrong.'

But Alexei is no longer listening – or rather, he's only hearing what he wants to hear.

'*Serena confessed everything to you?*' he spits. 'You're kidding, right? You want us to buy that? That Serena *confessed everything* in front of billions of viewers?'

'The transmission was cut off. There are only six viewers watching us at this moment: Serena, Gordon, and the instructors, minus Roberto Salvatore who ran away when he learned that

I had this telephone. It belonged to Ruben Rodriguez, the third signatory to the report, who was in charge of NASA's animal collections where they got the guinea pigs that went before us. The guy tried to warn me at the last minute, on the launch platform. He must have been overcome with remorse when he saw us about to board the rocket. Unfortunately, his intervention came too late. I didn't understand what he was trying to tell me. Now he's been murdered, like Sherman Fisher before him.'

'Murdered? Yeah, really?' retorted Alexei. 'And you were there to witness that? You've got some proof? It's funny, I could have sworn you'd spent the last five months with us on this craft, not on Earth playing Sherlock Holmes.'

'Alex, I'm begging you, stop this,' says Kris.

But Alexei doesn't stop.

His shouting gets louder and louder.

He fires off questions that sound like accusations.

'What's your game, Léonor? Do you find it entertaining, all this bullshit? And anyway – what the hell is that *thing* behind your shoulder?'

I feel all eyes on my back like laser beams. Here in this bubble of transparent glass there's nowhere for me to escape to. My dress is now no more than a shredded rag on my defenceless body. My long red hair floats in the zero gravity and cannot hide me. My eighteen years of camouflage are nothing more than a useless memory. Now I am the Salamander. The Salamander is me.

'Are you sick, is that it?' Alexei rages. 'You've got some disgusting disease that's going to kill you and you want us to believe we're all going to die with you?'

Mozart gives a quiet groan.

'Will you just *shut it?*'

Head down, he charges at Alexei, who takes the blow in the middle of his chest. But with absolutely no gravity, the impact meets no resistance: the Russian is thrown across the Visiting Room, against the glass wall that looks out over the emptiness of space.

'You're the one who's going to shut it,' he shouts. 'Scumbag! What difference does it make to you, anyway, to know that you're going to die? If you'd stayed on Earth you'd only have taken an overdose in your shitty favela anyway!'

Mozart doesn't bother to answer; instead he spins like a torpedo towards Alexei, striking him an uppercut. With his back already to the wall, the Russian can't step back: the fist crashes against his jaw with a dull thud.

'I'll make you pay for that!' he spits, wiping his bloody mouth with the back of his hand.

Ignoring Kris's shrill cries, he presses against the wall and propels himself, in turn, at Mozart. They cling to each other, each fighting the zero gravity as much as they struggle against their opponent. You might mistake it for a dance, some strange synchronised swimming in the infinite sea of space. Except for the murderous gleam in their rolling eyes. There are thin trickles of blood coming from Alexei's mouth and spreading slowly through the air; each time Mozart turns, his brown curls rise up, revealing the little metal ball shining in his neck: the *death's egg*, that capsule filled with poison, grafted onto every member of the Aranha gang.

'Dying . . .' murmurs Kenji.

He unsticks his forehead from the glass to pull the hood of his futuristic grey kimono back over his head. It's lined with wave-shielding sheets of aluminium, which are supposed to stop the cosmic rays that are filtering through the glass bubble of the Visiting Room. With this protection – which is pretty ridiculous when you think of the deadly danger we're *actually* in – Kenji is looking at the moon Phobos. It's as though this huge, battered black rock was hypnotising him. He is repeating the same words, unrelenting, this boy so gifted with a phenomenal memory, so phobic and so unsuited to this mission, like a machine that's frozen on an algorithm and going round and round on a loop, an obsessive watching his obsession becoming a reality.

'Dying . . . I suspected it . . . There's no escape . . . There never has been . . . The cosmos has never wanted the human species to live on Mars, and now we're all going to die . . .'

Samson and Tao are trying in vain to part the fighters.

Warden, the boys' Doberman-cross mutt, starts barking loudly, and is instantly imitated by Louve, while the girls throw themselves one after another against the glass barrier crying out the names of those they'd expected to spend the rest of their lives with – long, happy lives, full of thrills, laughter and wonder.

Only Marcus remains apart from the throng.

It's as though the rest of the boys, tearing each other apart in his hemisphere, don't exist to him. He doesn't take his magnetic grey eyes off me, as though there were no one here but us. A vein is throbbing in his forehead, tense with the stress. At the wide opening at the top of his shirt, where his heart is, the wound he inflicted on himself with the point of his penknife has clotted. An L, an E and an O: the first three letters of my name. As it's dried, the blood ink has changed from scarlet to the deepest purple, almost black, the colour of the countless tattoos that tangle across the rest of his skin.

The idea that I might never get to touch that skin if we were to turn the ship around suddenly grabs hold of my guts, wringing them like a dishcloth.

It hurts like hell!

'Shut up,' I barely manage to mutter, my belly clenched.

The shouts graze my ears.

'Shut up.'

The barking crashes through my eardrums.

'Shut up.'

The more the girls shout themselves hoarse, the more the boys yell, and the more the dogs bark, the more I realise how pitiful this scene is, both huge and tiny; the Visiting Room is a bubble of life in miniature, just a few cubic metres, in the middle of an ocean of death that goes on for ever.

As fragile as a soap bubble.

'Shut up!'

This time I've shouted so loudly that they can't help but hear me.

See me.

Their eyes all turn towards me, some misted over with tears and distress, the others shot through with blood and fury.

'All the way down there on Earth, fifty-five million kilometres from the *Cupido*, Serena and her gang of psychopaths are watching us,' I murmur, breathless, gesturing with my chin towards the transmission dish perched at the top of the Visiting Room. 'In three minutes, taking account of the communication latency, they're going to hear us tear each other apart. They'll hear the insults, the blows and the tears. I can picture the smile creeping onto the face of that botoxed witch, and that gets me so furious. It makes me want to throw up.'

I take a deep breath.

Nobody else is moving a muscle at this moment – not even Alexei.

'This woman has offered us a deal. She's waiting for an answer. She wanted me to decide on behalf of the whole *Cupido* crew, but I refused. Do you know what I told her, before opening the hatch to the girls' quarters and demanding that she re-establish audio contact with the boys' side?'

I can feel my heart racing, like when I had to go up to the front of class when I was a student, terrified at the thought that my back might be visible through my clothes.

'I told Serena that she was all *alone*, but not us, we were *twelve*. I claimed it was a strength. Please let's not make it a weakness. We need to stick together, all twelve of us, stay united in order to make our decision. We don't have dozens of options, only two: land on Mars, as Serena has asked us, and try everything we can for nine months to fix the habitats, without letting any of our circumstances be visible on screen, so it goes without saying we also have to be damn good actors; or turn the *Cupido* right around and bring Serena down the moment we get back on the air, knowing that we will die of hunger, of thirst or asphyxiation before we reach Earth.'

It's ironic: these eleven pairs of eyes trained on me are really stressing me out, even though for the last five months I haven't given a damn about being ogled twenty-four / seven by billions of total strangers. Why am I so worked up? Because I care about these eleven, that's why, and I'm afraid of losing them!

'I don't know if we'll be able to get out of this,' I say. 'I don't know how we'll manage to survive on Mars if we do land there, and how long it'll be before we die if we turn around.

'Deep down, I don't know anything at all. Except one thing: we are twelve.

'Twelve lives.

'Twelves voices.

'I suggest we take a vote.'

3. Reverse Shot

'*All the way down there on Earth, fifty-five million kilometres from the* Cupido, *Serena and her gang of psychopaths are watching us.*'

Léonor's face, dotted with the freckles that make her look so catlike, appears in close-up on one of the windows in the digital wall, at the back of the dark bunker where the organisers of the Genesis programme have gathered.

'*In three minutes, taking account of the communication latency, they're going to hear us tear each other apart. They'll hear the insults, the blows and the tears.*'

Three minutes have indeed passed since Léonor spoke these words, the time it took for the laser transmission from the *Cupido* to make its way to Earth – and to the ears of the six allies of silence.

Their six pale, moonlike faces look ageless in the dim light of the digital wall.

Geronimo Blackbull, the Engineering instructor, is nervously twisting his long crow-black dyed hair around his ring-covered fingers, while Odette Stuart-Smith, the Planetology instructor, clutches her little crucifix, muttering prayers.

The disturbing face of Archibald Dragovic, the Biology instructor, is troubled with nervous tics, in contrast with that of Arthur Montgomery, the resident doctor, whose mouth looks like it has been sewn on beneath his grey moustache.

Completing the circle around the table, Gordon Lock, the programme's technical director, dabs at his damp forehead.

'*I can picture the smile creeping onto the face of that botoxed witch, and that makes me so mad. It makes me want to throw up.*'

Despite Léonor's predictions, the woman in the green suit who is standing at the digital wall is not smiling. Her face, beneath her grey bob of hair, is as rigid as a block of ice, a perfect mask of concentration. She is totally tense, eyes fixed on the window occupied by the girl who is talking, the girl she had expected to sweep away like a speck of dust shortly after their touchdown on Mars, dispatch her as if it were no more than a formality – like all twelve passengers whose deaths she has decided on without a moment's hesitation.

These twelve are currently all that stands between her and absolute wealth, total power, the spoils of a whole life of lies and manipulation: the gold mine promised by Atlas Capital, and the position of vice-president of the United States of America.

'And what if they refuse the deal?' says Gordon Lock suddenly. 'What if they decide not to land on Mars, but to turn right around and reveal the Noah Report? I'll be the first one to be brought down: my name appears on the last page!'

He holds his bald head with his paddle-sized hands. His trembling voice, high-pitched all of a sudden, is in contrast with his vast body.

'I should never have agreed to destroy the report in exchange for the money Atlas offered. I should have made it public, even if it meant cancelling the programme, giving up on conquering Mars, going into early retirement without ever hitting the jackpot. I don't know how I've got myself here, me, who used to be a real NASA man, a top-level scientist. I don't want to end my days in prison. I've got a family, a wife and kids.'

'Oh, stop whining!' Serena cuts him off sharply. 'It's starting to sound like all that sickly snivelling from Ruben Rodriguez. And it did not save him. As for your childish fear of prison, open your eyes: if the Noah Report is discovered, I can assure you the investigation will quickly lay the blame on us for the murders of Ruben and Sherman, as well as of the twelve participants. It's not prison that's in store for us six, it's the death penalty for premeditated murder.'

A terrified murmuring echoes through the bunker.

But the programme's executive producer herself, as is always her way, betrays no signs of emotion.

'What a poignant irony!' she says. 'Our lives are in the hands of these nobodies, these bits of garbage I chose from out of the most repellent slums of all humanity. They were supposed to die after having put on a show, as oblivious to their fates as the insects on the Noah mission. But the cockroaches have discovered what awaits them – who'd have thought it? And now they're refusing to let themselves be crushed without putting up a fight. Fascinating.'

'How can you stay so calm?' babbles Gordon Lock, somewhere between astonishment and disgust. 'You aren't human. You're an android, like those things Atlas uses for their spokesmen.'

'An android? No. Just a realistic woman. And a far-sighted one. If it's any reassurance, the private jet that Atlas have placed at my disposal for getting about since the start of the programme is currently waiting directly above us, on the tarmac here at Cape Canaveral. If things go *really* badly, we can always try a hasty escape abroad to some neutral country that will be happy to welcome us in exchange for hard cash. For now, however, I'm going to draft a brief message to give our viewers. Something to keep them busy . . .' – she runs her finger across the digital screen and calls up a touch keyboard – 'I do need to deal with the PR, after all. We haven't had a comms person in our little team since Sherman left us in the lurch.'

4. Off-screen

The Villa McBee, Long Island, New York State
Saturday 9 December, 12:53pm

A girl is sitting on the edge of a bed that is heaped with silk cushions. She is wearing a long-sleeved dress made of grey lace. The delicate embroidery disappears beneath the layers of woollen shawls over which spreads her near-white hair. Opposite her, set into the wall between two Impressionist paintings, there is a black screen on which white letters appear, at the rhythm of the invisible hand that is typing them:

MY DEAR VIEWERS, LADIES AND GENTLEMEN,

THIS IS SERENA MCBEE.

I CAN IMAGINE YOUR WORRY

AT THE SUSPENSION OF OUR BROADCAST,

BUT THERE IS NO CAUSE FOR CONCERN.

THE *CUPIDO* IS WORKING PERFECTLY,

AND THE PARTICIPANTS ARE WELL.

THEY JUST NEED A LITTLE TIME

TO RECOVER OFF THE AIR,

JUST A FEW HOURS

FROM THEIR HISTORIC LANDING ON MARTIAN SOIL.

THEY HAVE LEFT YOU ONLY SO AS TO RETURN TO YOU
ALL THE BETTER.
WE WILL EXPLAIN EVERYTHING VERY SHORTLY.
UNTIL THEN, STAY ON YOUR FAVOURITE CHANNEL:
THE GENESIS CHANNEL!

No more letters appear.

The screen is fixed on this message, its millions of viewers left waiting expectantly – the girl sitting on the bed perhaps more than any of them.

'Mom . . .' murmurs Harmony McBee.

She doesn't get a chance to say any more before a sudden noise echoes around this huge room, this prison with its barred windows, beyond which the December snow is falling.

She turns quickly towards the door.

Yes, that's where the noise is coming from!

She hears it again.

Someone is knocking at the double-locked door.

Harmony gets up, glides across the waxed parquet floor and presses her cheek against the thick wooden panel.

'Is it you?' she whispers. 'Are you that young man I spotted in the garden?'

'Yes,' comes the muffled reply. 'Thank you for not telling anyone I was there.'

'Have you brought me my hit?' asks Harmony feverishly. 'It's too cold to send the pigeon out, and that's why you had to come in person, right? They sent you to bring me what I need?'

'What hit? What pigeon? I don't understand. I'm not whoever you're expecting.'

A terrible expression passes across Harmony's pale face – a mask of disappointment, an emptiness that nothing can fill, as she despises herself and her own weakness.

'What are you doing here, then, and who are you?' she shouts, her voice furious, as she collapses at the foot of the door. 'A ghost who's come to taunt me? A hallucination from the withdrawal? Or just some stupid draught of air? I can't open the door to see!'

'Don't shout, I beg you!' says the voice on the other side of the door. 'I'm not a draught of air. I'm going to come in to talk to you. To explain it to you.'

The door handle turns, but there's something obstructing it.

Turns again.

Bumps again.

'Are you locked in?' murmurs the voice. 'Why? Who are you?'

A shadow passes across Harmony's face.

She furrows her colourless eyebrows, as though this question – the simplest, the most pressing of all – was an enigma to her: *who are you?*

'You've said it, Ghost,' she answers at last, reluctantly. 'I'm the girl who's locked in . . . The girl who's walled in . . . The girl who's so fragile the tiniest bit of nothing could break her . . . Or at least that's what my mother, Serena McBee, says.'

There's a silence of a few seconds broken only by the echo of Harmony's words.

'*Serena McBee?*' repeats the young man from the other side of the door. 'Serena doesn't have a daughter!'

'She does, she does have one. She's had one for eighteen years.'

'But who's your father?'

'I don't know.'

Silence, once again.

Then – all of a sudden – some hurried words: 'I can hear someone coming up the stairs! I have to get away. I have to hide.'

'Don't leave, ghost, don't go!' cries Harmony, flattening her frail body against the door.

'I'll be back, I promise. To free you. If you want. If you'll guide me.'

Harmony talks fast, without bothering to catch her breath.

'Balthazar, the butler. He has all the keys for the villa. In the drawer of his desk. First floor. At the end of the right-hand wing . . . Are you still there?'

This time the girl receives no answer but the monotonous rustle of the snow, which is still falling, beyond the bars.

5. Shot

D +159 days, 23 h 24 mins.
[23rd week]

'Did you feel that?' cries Liz.

Yes, we all of us – boys and girls – felt it: a strange sensation of emptiness, cutting short the fiery arguments that had kept us so agitated on both sides of the Visiting Room for several long minutes.

'Could we have broken down?' murmurs Fangfang.

'No,' says Kelly, 'it's not a breakdown. If the engines have stopped, it's because we've reached our destination: the *Cupido* has aligned with the orbit of Phobos.'

Our Navigation Officer is right.

We can no longer hear the nuclear booster, nor the braking retrorockets. The subtle, constant hum of the craft, which has cradled us these past five months, has fallen silent, giving way to the impenetrable silence of space.

We've stopped getting closer to Phobos, positioning ourselves in its wake. We can see it more clearly than ever, through the glass bubble in front of the spacecraft: bloated and shapeless, it drags us along behind it the way a comet drags its tail. From this close, it's possible to make out its horrible surface, pitted with craters. From out of one of these rises a small metallic tower, attached to the rock.

'What the hell is . . . ?' asks Kris, her voice trembling.

'It's the main communications antenna, which was placed on Phobos by the unmanned missions that have come before us,' replies Safia grimly. 'With the help of extra satellites put into the Martian orbit, it captures the radio data emitted from the New Eden base and converts them into laser rays for sending across space at the speed of light. The images for the Genesis channel, each of our communications with Earth, the rest of our lives: all of that will be transmitted via Phobos, if we decide to go down.'

The Indian girl points at the huge red sphere of Mars, which seems to be drawing us in like an abyss.

'We've got to do something!' cries Fangfang suddenly, in a panic. 'At once! Before it's too late, before the planet grabs us once and for all into its gravitational field!'

'As long as we stay at this distance, we've got nothing to fear,' replies Kelly. 'The *Cupido* won't be going any further. Don't forget, anyone who wants to go to Mars will do it on board the capsules, according to the protocol. Personally, I won't be one of them. I vote to go back.'

These words from Kelly, the first to vote, fall like a cleaver.

Because that's really what it is: a guillotine blade, a death sentence – turning ourselves around means choosing death without reprieve.

'Are you serious?' asks Fangfang.

The Canadian nods, her long peroxide hair floating around her Barbie-doll face.

'I've never been so serious in my life. For as long as I can remember, my family and I have been treated like the dregs of society, and I've had enough. I can't take any more of it. My junkie brothers have spent their entire existences being exploited by dealers, trampled on by cops, despised by respectable people. By heading off to Mars I hoped I'd give them the chance to look up into the sky and think about their little sister, to feel something they'd never known before: pride. But it turns out I'm the one who's been most humiliated of all! The Martian guinea pig! Could it be any worse? The only thing that matters to me now is revenge. Whether we go down or whether we stay on board the *Cupido*, I can assure you we're all going to perish. The difference is that on Mars we could croak at any moment. Yes, it's true, we might manage to hang on for a few days, a few months longer, in constant fear of Serena pressing the depressurisation button – but what kind of life would you call that? Here on the ship we can at least calculate how long we have until the resources run out, and use that time to toss that foul witch Serena down the garbage chute.'

'Eighty-three days.'

It's Samson who just spoke, from the other side of the glass partition.

He's holding his tablet in his hands, the light from the screen reflected in his emerald-green eyes. As the boys' Biology Officer, he has access to all the ship's life-support statistics.

'The two compartments of the *Cupido* share the same

recycling network,' he explains, 'which produces the drinking water by treating a proportion of the used water, and oxygen by electrolysing the rest. If we recycle comprehensively, every single drop of urine, again and again, while remaining totally immobile for weeks so as to avoid any loss of moisture through sweat, we can expect to produce a thousand litres of water and the equivalent amount of oxygen. Now, one litre of water a day, that's the absolute minimum. So working it out's easy enough: a thousand divided by twelve, which makes eighty-three. We'll die of thirst in eighty-three days . . . or a little earlier, if we factor the dogs into the equation.'

At these words, Warden flies over awkwardly and snuggles up next to Samson.

'That's bullshit!' cries Alexei.

His jaw bruised where Mozart's fist struck him, he looks the Nigerian up and down.

'You want us to believe we'll be able to hold out for eighty-three days without eating? Let me remind you, our stores are almost empty, and we can't live on only air and clean water. If we turn the ship around, we'd have to start off by sacrificing the dogs. First to minimise the number of useless mouths to feed, then to take back their tins of food, and finally to turn them into steaks.'

Alexei's stare takes us all in, as though challenging us.

'Is that what you want?' he asks. 'For us all to start eating dog, before we finally end up on each other? For us to become subhuman, to become shapeless, rickety woodlice? Because in Samson's scenario there's no question of our being able to do any physical exercise at all in order to fight against the muscle wasting that comes from the weightlessness. No, I don't want to end up like that!' He spits, a mixture of saliva and blood that stretches out in space, forming a strange reddish arabesque. 'I took a lot of blows, back in Moscow. I often felt the disgusting taste of blood in my mouth. And I've had to make some terrible sacrifices. But there's one thing I never gave up, even when suffering the worst of it: my honour! I want to land on Mars with my head held high, and with Kris beside me!'

His steel-blue eyes pierce my friend's sky-blue ones.

'Tell them, Kris. Tell them you'll come down with me. Otherwise you and I will never be able to touch, to kiss. And I will never be able to kneel down in front of you and place this on your finger.'

He gestures towards the ring hanging from a chain around his neck – the ring he promised Kris the day they decided to get engaged, three whole months ago.

'Yes,' murmurs Kris, never taking her eyes from Alexei's. 'I say yes. I'll go down there with you, out of love . . .'

'Thank you, my angel.'

'. . . on two conditions. You, too, must make a promise – and an apology.'

Alexei's eyes flash, but he nods without a word.

'You must promise to respect the group's decision, just as I will,' Kris continues. 'If the majority votes to turn around, we have to decide to do the same.'

'And why not break off into two groups?'

'You really think Serena will allow that? You think she'll allow some of us to return to Earth, ready to turn her in, the

moment the broadcast is resumed, while the rest of us go down
to land on Mars? Either we all land, or we all turn around.
We have no choice but to remain united. We should leave it
to the choice of the group, and to the hands of God. You too.
Promise me.'

'I promise. And the apology? You said I had to make an
apology.'

'Please – ask Léo's forgiveness for what you said to her. Her
scar is no disease, it's a burn. And it's not contagious.'

Once again, all attention is on me, and it makes me uneasy.
I put my hand on my darling Kris's arm and say: 'Let it go.'

But Alexei is also turning towards me.

'Léo, forgive me,' he says, lowering his eyes. 'I didn't . . .
mean it. I was angry. I lost my cool. I spoke without thinking.
I'm so sorry.'

'Forget about it.' I wave away the offence, and all those eyes
that are boring into me. 'We haven't much time. Let's get on
with the voting.'

A tally has been started in my head, as I'm sure it has in
everyone else's. One vote for staying on board – *Justice*; two
votes for setting down on Mars – *Hope*.

'I vote to turn around!' Safia cries all of a sudden.

Her face is still so pale. But her black eyes are as lively as
ever, shining with determination.

'What do you think is going to happen?' she explains. 'You
really believe Serena's deal is like that *Serenity* package my
sponsors Karmafone offer to all new customers – guaranteed
network coverage, billing transparency and free technical
assistance twenty-four / seven? Wake up! We all know Serena

will press the depressurisation button at the first possible opportunity! And we also know that this way we stand at least some chance of testifying to the world about what's happened to us; if we pass up that chance, it may never come again. Those bastards will sacrifice us for the cash. Serena McBee – *the* Serena McBee who is running for vice-president of the United States – is deliberately sending twelve teenagers to their deaths, and we'll let that happen without a word? Don't you understand? Well, I say no! Because it's no longer just about us, can't you see that?'

The Indian girl's nostrils, one pierced with a tiny gold stud, flare each time she breathes in; with such strength of spirit it's hard to believe she's the youngest of the group, who might not even make it to her eighteenth birthday.

But the thirst for justice has transformed the girl who received acid burns from a rejected fiancé, only then to be disowned by her parents. She continues making an argument in a voice that is unwavering, and each word she speaks sounds painfully fair.

'Listen to me. We twelve – us orphans and exiles – we thought the Genesis programme would offer us a second chance. We thought somehow the programme would make up for the injustice of our lives. I know it's hard to admit, but we've been cruelly deceived. And that's not all. Today an even more serious injustice is about to happen, and it's a monstrous one. If it's allowed to go ahead, it will have not twelve victims, but millions. Serena, that foul snake, is about to be confirmed as vice-president of the United States. Imagine what will become of the world if someone like her gets in to that position! Let's stop that happening – we can do it! We must do it! Who's with me?'

From the other side of the reinforced glass, Samson is watching Safia admiringly. He makes a kind of gesture with his hand, never taking his eyes off her; she nods, seriously. What's this – a kind of sign language? But there's no time to ask.

'I agree with Safia,' says Samson. 'I vote to turn around.'

And so the scales tip: three votes for Justice, two for Hope.

Liz and Fangfang pull sharply away from Safia, as though she were suddenly infected with the plague.

'Voting to turn around?' murmurs the English girl. 'I really don't know . . . I don't know any more . . . I had so many expectations! I so often imagined myself treading on the Martian soil in my ballet shoes . . . Doing two-metre high entrechats in such a light atmosphere . . . I wanted to be the first star dancer in space, to win immortal glory . . .'

Liz's pupils are dilated, lost somewhere far away, as though she's watching a film unspooling before her eyes – of a dream she doesn't want to give up.

'. . . There's still time,' she murmurs, her voice trembling. 'Still time to write my name in the firmament. In the life of a dancer, the number of performances isn't what matters: the only thing that counts is managing at least one sensation, to do at least one single thing that nobody has ever done before. Even if I die tomorrow, I want the world to remember me as a great artiste, not as a poor victim crammed to the very end in a sardine can hurtling into the middle of the void. I want my last dance. I've deserved it. I vote to land!'

33

Liz lets her body drift towards Kris's, which is stuck to the glass opposite Alexei; in an opposing movement, Kelly and Samson move closer towards Safia. Two groups have formed. Half the crew have voted. The scales are in balance again: three votes on each side.

'And how about you, Fangfang?' asks Safia. 'What do you choose?'

The Singaporean girl nervously straightens her square-framed glasses.

'I need more d-data,' she stammers. 'I can't make a decision like this, emotionally. I've never done things like that before. Even when I was applying for the Genesis programme, I analysed everything for weeks before submitting my application – each of the mission's technical parameters, every one of the selection criteria – everything!'

'And yet you fell for it just like me, who signed on a whim,' says Kelly, with ruthless clarity.

But Fangfang doesn't hear her.

'May I see the cellphone?' she begs me.

I hand it to her.

She starts scrolling through the pages of the Noah Report, saved in the phone's memory. Her eyes run across the lines at speed, like a metronome on its fastest setting. She's clinging with every fibre of her being to Reason, the one thing which up till now has never failed her – the brainy one on our crew, the maths PhD, the Planetology Officer.

I realise all of a sudden that each of us has their own lifeline: a final value to give meaning to whatever time is left us, before death erases everything.

For Fangfang, it's reason.

For Liz, glory.

For Safia and Samson, duty.

For Alexei, honour.

For Kris, love.

For Kelly, revenge.

And what about me; what's going to help me decide, when my turn comes to vote? Which will be stronger, my hatred of Serena, who I dream of stabbing, or Marcus's skin, which I dream of touching?

'Hey!' shouts Fangfang all of a sudden.

She holds out the telephone. The girls all come closer to get a better look, and the boys cluster up against the glass partition.

There is a chart on the screen, three curves that rise steadily before plummeting down, all at once, like cliffs after a precipice.

'I think I've found something interesting,' says Fangfang. 'Look – these are the demographic data for the seventh habitat.'

She touches her glasses again, the way she always does when she's nervous, and pushes a curtain of shiny black hair behind her ear. I can tell she's trying to control the trembling in her voice, to demonstrate the pedagogical qualities one would expect of a Planetology Officer, not least one who's also the oldest girl in the group.

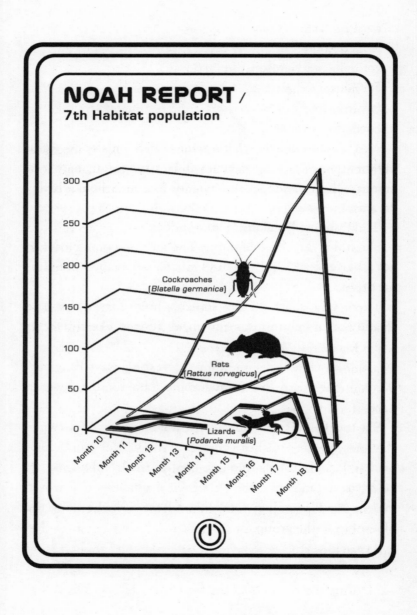

NOAH REPORT /
7th Habitat population

Cockroaches
(*Blatella germanica*)

Rats
(*Rattus norvegicus*)

Lizards
(*Podarcis muralis*)

300

250

200

150

100

50

0

Month 10
Month 11
Month 12
Month 13
Month 14
Month 15
Month 16
Month 17
Month 18

'These lines show the development of the three populations of trial animals, month by month: the cockroaches, the rats and the lizards that went up before us.'

'Why does the graph start at *month ten*?' asks Kris. 'Did the journey to transport these animals up to Mars take ten months?'

'No,' replies Fangfang. 'Remember that time is measured differently on Mars: the days are replaced by *sols* that are forty minutes longer, and there are twenty-four months, not twelve like we have on Earth. Which means the guinea pigs arrived in month ten of the Martian year . . .' She glances nervously at the vast red planet, which takes twice as long as the Earth to rotate around the Sun. '. . . and it means they died in month eighteen.'

'No news so far,' Kelly interrupts her. 'We've known all along that it took them nine months to die, it hardly matters if they were Martian months or terrestrial months. The length of a pregnancy – how ironic is that?'

'You don't understand!' says Fangfang, unable to contain herself a moment longer. 'Month eighteen isn't just any old time! It's the perihelion!'

'The peri-*what*?'

'The moment when the distance between Mars and the Sun is at its shortest!'

The Singaporean's eyes shine with excitement, as she describes a phenomenon she has never seen but that she's spent so long studying she must have dreamed about it many nights.

'During the perihelion, the temperatures rise. The hot air

spins up and begins to blow at the kind of speeds we've never seen on Earth. Millions of tonnes of particles are lifted into the atmosphere, stretching a thick red cloak over everything. Month eighteen is the month of the Great Dust Storm that's raised up over Mars every year!'

Everybody exchanges glances that are filled with questions. Except Marcus, whose gaze is still on me.

I'd give anything to see the thoughts behind his furrowed brow.

'So it was the Great Storm that killed the guinea pigs?' murmurs Kris.

'The document doesn't say,' replies Fangfang, continuing to scroll through the pages of the Noah Report, scanned into the phone's memory. 'The New Eden base was built to withstand phenomena like that. As far as I can see, the life-support infrastructure did continue to function normally during month eighteen and beyond; the oxygenator continued to provide the base with air, the well continued to extract water from the frozen Martian sub-soil, the greenhouse plants continued to grow. No failures are recorded in the on-board log. But hang on . . .'

Fangfang's eyes widen behind her square-framed glasses.

'. . . the report states that contact with the base was lost for an hour, just over one Martian year ago, on sol 511, month eighteen, between 10:27pm and 11:29pm: just before the population curves suddenly fell!'

'What do you mean, *contact was lost*?' asks Samson from behind the glass.

'The people who wrote the report believe that as the

penultimate Great Storm began, it temporarily disturbed the signal between Mars and the Earth, before the transmission systems were restored to normal . . .' Fangfang takes a deep breath before continuing: '. . . but I think there was something more than an interruption in communications. The death of the trial animals, which took place during this hour of silence, is somehow connected to the perihelion . . . I've just got this hunch . . . It's too much of a coincidence.'

A *hunch*.

It's the first time I've heard this word coming from Fangfang, the ultimate rational one who usually trusts nothing but her equations.

'Which month are we in now?' I ask impatiently. 'I mean, which month are we in *on Mars*?'

'We're right in the middle of the twentieth Martian month.'

'Meaning another Great Storm has just happened down there, right? The second one since the deaths of the guinea pigs?'

'Yes, that's what it looks like.'

Fangfang turns her attention back to the surface of Mars, displayed beyond the glass of the Visiting Room. The red planet is perfectly visible, the Sun illuminating its contours, its canyons, its mountains and craters. On the whole hemisphere that's facing towards us, we can't see the shadow of a single cloud, or the least atmospheric disturbance.

'The sky is totally clear,' murmurs Safia. 'Hard to believe a terrifying hurricane of dust was unleashed here not long ago.'

'Each Martian summer, the Great Storm takes a different form,' explains Fangfang, uncertainly. 'Sometimes it covers the entire planet, and sometimes only a small part. Sometimes it lasts months, sometimes it only takes the winds a few days to disperse it. That must be what happened this year. We'd have to check the meteorological archives in Cape Canaveral to be sure.'

Alexei claps his hands, interrupting the Planetology Officer.

'To hell with the archives!' he exclaims forcefully. 'The past isn't what matters, it's the future, and we should be thinking about that. Look!'

He puffs onto the glass partition, his warm breath forming a patch of white mist, across which he draws a line with the tip of his index finger.

'The guinea pigs died during a Great Storm, long before we got here,' he says, marking the line with a number one – he's written it in reverse, so we can read his diagram correctly from our side.

'Fangfang tells us that a second Great Storm has just taken place, twenty-four months after the first . . .' he continues, putting a second notch on the line. He also adds a cross to mark the *Cupido*'s arrival in the Martian orbit: '. . . and here we are, at S + two months.'

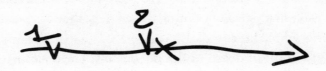

'That means we have twenty-two months left before the third Great Storm,' he concludes, marking the line for a third time. '*Twenty-two months!* And we thought we had only nine months ahead of us! All the more reason to land here and take our chances!'

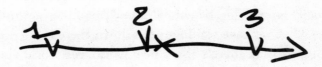

Alexei lifts his blazing eyes from the timeline to look at us.

His enthusiasm falls flat: on both sides of the glass, there's silence.

'Nine months or twenty-two, I don't see how that changes anything,' murmurs Kenji at last, white as a ghost beneath his hood, his eyes lost in the void. 'We have no idea what happened to the guinea pigs. There's no discernible breakdown in the systems, no shadow of a clue. If we decide to land on Mars, the months we spend there will be months of terror. I'd rather turn around now and face death serenely.'

There's a strange calm to Kenji's voice. It's more than just resignation: it's relief. As though the certainty of the imminent end was paradoxically calming the anxiety that has petrified him his whole life.

But not me, it doesn't calm me one bit. The scales tip one way again: towards returning, towards agony in the middle of space, ending the journey in two separate vaults. I feel my belly clenching at the thought, as though my guts were being sucked in. Does this mean that, deep down, I've already chosen to land? No, I'm not sure: the prospect of being at Serena's mercy appals me just as much.

'I vote to . . .' begins Fangfang, who I'm sure is about to add her voice to those of Kelly, Safia, Samson and Kenji.

Tao doesn't give her a chance to say any more.

'Kenji's wrong!' he cries, his big hands pressed up against the glass. 'What we have waiting for us down there is not terror, or not only that: there's also a new world, the world you've been studying so passionately!'

Fangfang half-opens her lips to reply, but once again Tao is too quick for her.

'I don't have a hundredth of your education, Fangfang, or a tenth of your intelligence,' he says. 'That's what you made me feel each time we've met in the Visiting Room.'

'Me? But I . . .'

'Each time, I would come out feeling lower than ever, with my heart in my boots and the same one question going round and round my head: *what could a girl like her see in a boy like me?* You've got a doctorate in mathematics; the only studies I've done are that single year of Engineering training in Death Valley. You were a ward of the state in Singapore, selected out of everybody and placed in a school for gifted students; I'm just an unknown circus acrobat, one Chinese man among hundreds of millions, and now I've even managed to fail in the goddamn school of life.'

'*The school of life?*' repeats Fangfang. 'You mean this mission? But that's not your fault, we all fell for it.'

Tao takes a deep breath, which swells his athletic chest, so well developed from his time as an acrobat.

'I'm not talking about the mission,' he says. 'You know, when I chose to set off to Mars, it wasn't my first fall. I've fallen before. And from a great height. From the highest point of the big top. I didn't catch the trapeze in time, during my last acrobatic number, and there was nothing on the ground to catch me, as acts are more impressive to an audience when they're done without a net. I broke my legs.'

'What are you saying? Your legs healed afterwards, didn't they? They're strong and powerful, just like your arms and that whole amazing sports-star body of yours, I can see them through your trouser-legs.'

'My trouser-legs are just holding two slabs of useless meat. In the weightlessness of the Visiting Room, I can make it seem as though these dozens of kilos of dead flesh don't exist – that's what I've tried to do, during all our meetings. But once we're on Mars, my legs will have weight again; even if they weigh less than on Earth, it'll be enough to confine me to a little wheelchair. The *sports star* will be transformed into an old man. Yeah, like Cinderella, after the clock has struck midnight.'

The eyes of everyone on board, which had previously been burning into my spine, are now drawn towards Tao's legs. The fact that this great, strapping, muscular lad is comparing himself to the fragile orphan from the fairy-tale is pretty surprising, and moving.

'I never thought I'd have the courage to tell you all this,' Tao adds. 'I thought I'd land on Mars without having dared to talk to you about my disability. I'd resigned myself to the idea that you'd discover it at the last moment and you'd reject me twice over: as a cripple and as a liar. But our circumstances have finally given me the courage I was lacking before. Léo's example really affected me. Her bravery has inspired me. Her burns have freed me.'

Tao's eyes meet mine. They are full of candour. And his words echo in my head.

My burns have freed him.

I never would have thought that the Salamander, to which I've been a prisoner my whole life, could free anybody.

'I feel lighter than ever, now that I've spoken, and it's nothing to do with the weightlessness,' Tao goes on. 'I'm no longer afraid of going down to land on Mars, Fangfang. The fact that I'm stuck in my chair no longer scares me. Even if it's just for twenty-two months, I want to roll it across Mars's red plains, I want to inscribe the furrow of my wheels in Mars's red sand. And I want to hold you in my arms, which still have all their old strength – if you still want me, without my legs for walking, and even without the time to make all eight of the babies you'd dreamed of.'

Fangfang blinks behind her square-framed glasses.

She hadn't expected any of this – not Tao's confession, not how much those words move her, a girl who's always planned out everything in her life with such care.

'The eight babies . . . can w-wait,' she stammers. 'But I can't wait any more. Of course I still want you. I want to feel you, to hug you, to touch you. You're right, twenty-two months is not nothing. It's precious time to try to understand why the penultimate Great Storm wiped out the trial animals, and to prepare ourselves for the next one. I vote to go down and land here on Mars, Tao. With you.'

Kris claps. 'Five votes to land on Mars!' she cries. 'Two more and we'll have a majority!' She turns towards me: 'You want to go down with us, don't you, Léo? Like Alex and me, like Fangfang and Tao: you're also going to go down there, you and . . .'

She stops dead in the middle of her torrent of words, the palms of her hands frozen between claps.

You and . . . who?

She can't say.

None of the girls know who I'm going to choose, not even my best friend. How could they? The whole journey I've been doing everything in my power to delay the deadline, even in the recent weeks when I've been meeting Marcus and Mozart in turn so as to remain impartial. But while I managed to persuade the world that there was still everything to play for, while I was feeling a tenderness steadily increasing in me for Mozart, something other than tenderness was taking root in my heart, getting a little deeper each time I saw Marcus.

Now that I have them both in front of me, together for the first time, one darting his black eyes at me and the other his grey eyes, I can no longer deny the existence of that thing – even if I try, just one last time, as a reflex, to dodge the question.

'The couples, the Heart Lists, the whole damn happily-ever-after, it no longer means anything,' I say in a strangled voice. 'It's all meaningless, now that we know what really awaits us on Mars.'

The moment the words leave my lips, I realise how false they are, how cowardly, even. The others must sense it, too, and Kris is the first to speak.

'You know very well it does still mean something!' she says forcefully.

Her crown of braids seems to glow, fine blonde hair escaping in every direction to dance in the weightlessness.

'It still means something to all of us, and to the millions of viewers of the Genesis channel! Remember Serena's conditions: she'll allow us to continue down to Mars so long as we keep playing the game to its conclusion – as if it were that simple.'

Liz joins in at once.

'Kris is right. If we go down to land, we all have to stick to the rules of the programme; we must form six couples, to fill the six Love Nests in the New Eden base. To the eyes of the viewers, it has to look like a perfectly choreographed ballet. And no missteps, or it's death. It's time for you to choose, Léo.'

The girls, who have now all voted, circle around me.

'First, whether you want to land here on Mars . . .'

The circle tightens, there's no escape.

'. . . and then, with who.'

6. Off-screen

The Villa McBee, Long Island, New York State
Saturday 9 December, 1:05pm

There is a very quiet click in the lock.

The porcelain handle turns silently.

The bedroom door opens slowly onto a corridor lit by pale December half-light.

The young man whom Harmony spotted in the gardens of the Villa McBee, who spoke to her through the door, is now standing right in front of her. He's dressed all in black, apart from the last white flakes that are melting on the straps of his backpack and the hood of his anorak. His face is pale with cold, his lips chapped by the wind, but behind his black-framed glasses, his eyes are burning.

'You found the key,' Harmony whispers. 'You aren't a ghost.'

She is standing on the threshold, shivering. The current of air blowing down the corridor and through her grey lace dress is giving her goose-bumps, in spite of the shawls she has wrapped around her shoulders. Her colourless, almost white hair, is lifted slightly by the draft. The only touch of colour in her spectral appearance is the small golden locket she wears around her neck.

'Yes, I found the key,' murmurs the young man. 'Just like you told me, down on the first floor, in the drawer of the last office at the end of the right-hand wing. That's where it was – along with all the others . . .'

He lifts his hand to show her a metal ring from which dozens of keys are hanging.

'. . . and no, I'm not a ghost, even though it has felt lately as though I've been living in a different dimension, cut off from the world. But I'm sure I don't need to explain what that feels like to you. The best-kept secret in the whole U.S. of A. The daughter of Serena McBee. You have the same colour eyes, your face is the same shape as hers, you look so like her, but at the same time I can see something in you that makes you completely different.'

Harmony shivers a bit harder, and wraps her arms around her shoulders to protect herself from the cold – or is it from something else? Every distant noise that rises from the bowels of the villa makes her jump. The empty expanse of the long corridor, behind the young man, almost makes her dizzy.

'You should leave, now you've got the keys,' she says quickly, blinking her water-green eyes. 'Yes, that's right – leave. No, first explain to me what . . . No, don't. No – leave. I haven't seen you. Disappear.'

'What?'

'Go!'

'But . . . I thought you wanted to run away?'

'I don't any more. I'm too cold. I shouldn't leave my room. Run away; I won't say a thing. I don't even know your name. I don't want to know it. All I want is to forget all about you.'

She is about to shut the door, but the young man blocks it with his leg.

'Andrew,' he says. 'There, now you know my name. And I know yours, Harmony.'

He holds up the first key on the key-ring, which bears a small typed tag: HARMONY'S ROOM.

'I know your name,' he says again, 'and I'm not going to forget you. The world should know you exist. The electors should know they've voted for someone who keeps her own daughter shut up in a dungeon!'

'I shouldn't have told you where to find the keys,' she says. 'I'm warning you, I'm going to scream.'

'Fine. Scream.'

But Harmony does not scream.

Her pale face in the doorway is quite still, her lips half-open over teeth that look as white and fragile as chalk. It's no longer the breeze from the corridor that makes her hair flutter slightly, but the breathing of Andrew, who is so close, his eyes fixed on hers.

'The outside world isn't for me,' she says at last with a sigh. 'If I stay safely sheltered inside, I'll end up being happy. My mother has promised me that.'

'My father also made me promises. He didn't keep them. There's only one way to find out whether the outside world is for you: go and meet it!'

Andrew closes his hand around Harmony's slender wrist – delicately enough not to break it, but firmly enough to pull her towards him. The girl's light body slips out from the other side of the door; she steps onto the hallway floor without having been given permission, for the first time.

For just a moment, they remain standing there close together, like a prince and princess from the olden days, whose kiss might be the only way to break the evil queen's spell and free the world from the darkness into which she has plunged it.

But all of a sudden, the sound of footsteps echoes from the stairs leading up to this floor.

'It's that security guard who almost caught me a moment ago,' says Andrew, closing the door again. 'Quick! It's time for me to go and find what I came for. Where's Serena's study?'

He's about to dash down the corridor, but Harmony doesn't move, her eyes fixed on him.

'Your father,' she says softly. 'You referred to him in the past.'

'He's dead! Come on!'

'I don't even know if I'm supposed to talk about my father in the present or the past. My mother never told me . . . she never . . .'

Andrew's eyes sparkle.

'Perhaps the answer to that question is in your mother's study. All the more reason to go there.'

The heavy footsteps are getting closer and closer.

But Harmony is still uncertain, her face frozen in doubt, her body paralysed by the mental bars that Serena McBee has put between the girl and her freedom. Her right fist grips the locket that hangs around her neck, as though, in this storm of indecision, it is the only rope to which she might cling.

'If I do come, do you swear not to abandon me like . . . like *the other boy*?'

'The other boy?' repeats Andrew, trying to keep his voice calm despite the anxiety that is starting to overwhelm him. 'I don't know who you're talking about. But I swear I'll never abandon you, Harmony! And I'll help you track down your father!'

That pledge is the thing that clicks.

It's the bolt that slides open.

Harmony launches herself down the hallway like a suicide throwing herself off a bridge, like an explorer flying off into the unknown.

'That way!' she says, pushing the first door they come to, which opens onto a hidden staircase.

The two teenagers disappear into the spiral staircase, which swallows them up like a gullet. Beneath their feet, the flights of stairs awaken clouds of echoes, that bounce around the pitch-black stairwell.

They emerge into a narrow corridor lit by white bulbs.

'Ah . . . it's the servants' corridor,' says Harmony, breathless. 'It's used by the staff to connect the different rooms to the kitchen, the days when there are guests . . . I used to play here when I was little . . . Today I'm sure we won't run into anyone . . . That's . . . that's the service door to my mother's study.'

Harmony stops at a smooth, closed door.

While Andrew is frantically sorting through the key-ring in search of one with a tag identifying it as being for Serena McBee's study, the girl struggles to recover her breath.

'You haven't told me . . . ah . . . what you've come looking for . . . looking for in here?'

'The truth,' replies Andrew, inserting the key he's finally identified into the lock.

'The truth? I don't know what you mean.'

Andrew quietly turns the key.

'I don't think you and your father are the only secrets Serena McBee is keeping from the eyes of the world,' he says. 'I think she's got a lot of other things to hide. Like what happened to my father, for example.'

Harmony blinks.

'What do you mean? I thought he was dead? I don't understand. Mom would be furious if she knew I . . .'

Andrew turns the key a second time, furious himself now.

'I'm the son of Sherman Fisher, who was head of Communications for the Genesis programme. They said he was the victim of an accident, just like Ruben Rodriguez, who kept the programme's animals, not long before him. But I'm convinced these two "accidents" were anything but. Dad was killed behind the wheel, though he never took any risks when he was driving. A member of the Genesis team wiped Ruben's hard drive during his funeral. Coincidence? No. What I'm sure of is that they were both silenced to stop them speaking . . . but to stop them saying what? What secret is hidden at the heart of the Genesis programme? Perhaps the answer is to be found in this study. That's what I've come to find. Some sign of your father, and the memory of mine: my truth and yours.'

Andrew gives the key a third turn.

The door opens, creaking on its hinges.

As a reflex, Harmony turns around quickly, expecting to see a servant appear, alerted by the noise. But the corridor is deserted. Then she takes one last breath and enters the forbidden room, close on Andrew's heels.

7. Reverse Shot

A flashing red message appears at the top of the digital wall, just above the window showing Léonor's doubt-stricken face.

INCOMING CALL FROM THE EDITING SUITE

'There it is!' cries Gordon Lock, gripping the table with his powerful hands, as though he wanted to drag it across the concrete floor. 'We're done for, and all because of those kids who waste their time talking about Martian meteorology and don't get around to making a decision! The police are already on their way to arrest us, before we've even had the time to get back to ground level to escape in Serena's jet!'

The executive producer merely shrugs.

'Don't talk nonsense. The police have no reason to come and arrest us – at least not for now. The secret of the Noah Report hasn't yet been revealed, after all.'

She lightly touches the blinking message with the tip of her index finger, with its green-polished nail that matches her suit and her jewellery – the colour of President Green and the Ultra-libertarian Party.

Another window opens immediately on the digital wall, this one showing Samantha, Serena's young assistant, an earpiece fixed to her temple.

'I'm so sorry to disturb you, Ms McBee,' she hastens to apologise. 'I know you asked for peace and quiet to edit the end of the journey yourself, but . . .'

'But?'

A flush of shyness comes to Samantha's face, turning her cheeks red.

'. . . but it's been nearly two hours since we stopped transmitting. We've tried to reassure the press, telling them you've got everything under control, as you explained in the brief message you scripted for the Genesis channel.'

'Well, then, as you say, I've explained it already. We'll be back on the air shortly. Just let me have another thirty little minutes, just enough time to finalise one last detail with our participants.'

'It's just that . . . I don't know if we've still got thirty minutes left.'

'What do you mean?'

'The base is under siege, Ms McBee. A huge crowd has swarmed onto the Cape Canaveral peninsula. People are worried to death! Unfortunately, your message wasn't enough to reassure them. They want to know what's *really* happening.'

'What nonsense is this? The peninsula is private property, protected by fences, checkpoints and extremely highly paid security guards!'

'The fences have been breached. The checkpoints have been smashed open. And as for the guards, well, I'm afraid there just weren't enough of them to contain a surge like this. You can see for yourself on the security camera images.'

The window splits in two: to the left, Samantha; to the right, Armageddon. The peninsula, which was practically deserted just a few hours earlier, is now overrun with vehicles, so many of them it's impossible to see the tarmac of the road or the heather of the moorland. The TV vans can be identified by the antennae on their roofs, but most of the vehicles belong to private individuals. They continue to arrive in their thousands from the mainland on the west, as do the motorbikes, the mopeds, whole coaches laden with stools and ladders, and fans who will do anything to find out the next instalment in the programme. In an extraordinary funnel movement, all America is gushing towards the last piece of land before the great emptiness of the Atlantic Ocean.

Down in the bunker, there is panic.

The allies of silence are jumping to their feet, knocking over their chairs, as though the human tsunami were about to surge right out of the digital wall into the little concrete room and sweep all away before it.

'I see, Samantha,' says Serena calmly, as usual the only person in the room keeping her cool. 'Indeed, we do not have thirty minutes. But you could probably manage to buy us a mere twenty, could you not? Make all these people wait.'

'Make them wait, Ms McBee? But how am I supposed to . . .'

With the touch of a finger, the executive producer makes the window disappear, along with Samantha and an entire country she has been holding spellbound for months.

'Call to the passengers on the *Cupido*: this is Serena,' she says, taking hold of the microphone that allows her to communicate with the craft fifty-five million kilometres away. 'You have had long enough for your deliberations. The moment for us to resume our show is approaching. We only have about twenty minutes left. We already need three for my message to reach you, and another three for yours to come back down to me. That means you've got fourteen minutes from the moment you hear me to make the right choice – which is, of course, to go down to land on Mars tomorrow, which is in your own interest and in mine.'

Serena brings the mic a little closer to her lips.

'You have fourteen minutes to agree, finally, all twelve of you, and to convince those who want to turn around to give up on that morbid plan. There is no room for doubt. The viewers *must* see twelve radiant smiles on your faces. They *must* see twelve young people burning with desire to touch one another, impatient for marriage. We can always continue our discussions in private once you've touched down, from the seventh Love Nest. The cameras there aren't connected to the broadcast, as it's supposed to be uninhabited. I'll get the audio-visuals streamed directly here, to the bunker from where I am currently speaking to you, and here alone. The viewers will never see those images. I'll tell them that these occasional moments of one-to-one consultation are necessary for your psychological well-being. I'm sure they'll understand, if it's explained to them properly. We've rechristened the *Vasco da Gama* the *Cupido*, the Martian base the *New Eden*, the six habitats the *Love Nests*, so why not find another name for the seventh? The *Offline Pod?* The *Rest Hall?* We'll see. For now, I need your answer. Don't forget, at the slightest sign of treachery, the smallest attempt to turn me in, all I need is the touch of a finger to depressurise the habitats and the entire base. You're under my thumb now. Prepare yourselves to go back on the air. It's 1:25 – we resume the broadcast at 1:45 sharp.'

8. Shot

D +159 days, 23 h 58 mins.
[23rd week]

'*Don't forget, at the slightest sign of treachery, the smallest attempt to turn me in, all I need is the touch of a finger to depressurise the habitats and the entire base. You're under my thumb now. Prepare yourselves to go back on the air. It's 1:25 – we resume the broadcast at 1:45 sharp.*'

Serena's voice chills my blood.

'Quick, Léo!' cries Fangfang. 'Tell us that you want to go down onto Mars, and who with, so we can finish the voting before the Genesis channel starts back up. Serena was very clear: once the viewers are watching us, we can't allow for the least bit of doubt!'

I open my mouth, but Kelly grabs hold of my shoulders before I'm able to say a word, making the bracelets on her wrists clink.

'Don't let yourself be influenced by them,' she says, looking at me from so close that I can smell her strawberry chewing-gum. 'I know deep down you think like me, and like Safia, like everyone here who wants justice to prevail and our deaths to mean something, rather than nothing at all. The moment we're back on the air, we'll have Serena tossed down the garbage like the stinking old piece of trash she is.'

'You're the one who's trying to influence her, Kelly!' Kris butts in, pulling me away from the Canadian girl.

Now she's the one putting her hands on my shoulders, forcing herself to control the trembling in her voice.

'You've always told me we must never give up,' she says. 'All the way through our training in Death Valley, that's what you kept hammering into me. That's what you've taught me. And are you going to give in now, pass up our one chance for survival . . . and for love?'

'Open your eyes!' Kelly responds. 'The *one chance* we'll be passing up if we land here is to bring Serena down! As for loving . . . remember what you used to say at the start of the journey, Léo, that you didn't care about that, about love! So forget about love and save the truth! That bitch Serena must be made to pay!'

Kelly's words pierce through me.

But she's right, those really were my words. *I don't care about love!* I repeated them often enough during training, so all the girls remember them.

And the boys?

What do they think about it?

I don't dare look over to the other side of the glass partition. I know Mozart and Marcus won't have taken their eyes off me. There's enough chaos in my head already – if I look at them just once I'm scared I'll lose any ability to think at all.

'You said love was dumb nonsense!' Kelly is furious. 'You

said it was all a fraud, hollow! The only thing that mattered to you was glory. Remember that! And now glory is within reach. All you need to do is reach out and grab it. You only need to say the word, Léo, and you'll go down in history as the girl who saved America – no, make that the whole world – from the biggest utter cow ever!'

Liz sticks her arm out between us, showing her elegant wristwatch.

'It's already one-thirty!' she cries. 'Just a quarter of an hour before the channel starts back up, and twelve minutes to give our answer! I don't want to die! I want to go down to Mars!'

'And yet you've kept your watch set to the time on Earth,' comments Safia, still pale. 'I think that's a sign. A sign that Mars isn't for us and that we ought to turn around.'

'No!'

Liz gives a terrible scream; she turns towards the other half of the Visiting Room, the half I won't let myself look at.

'Mozart, Marcus, say something!' she begs. 'Léonor is starting to zone out, but you two, you can save us! You haven't voted yet. If both of you decide to stay here, we'll be in the majority, seven votes, and a victory for survival!'

'A few weeks ago, I told Léo she'd be the one to lead our dance . . .'

The warm tones of Mozart's voice make me shiver.

Yes, he said he would obey my rule.

Yes, he said he'd follow me to the ends of the universe.

But that was before, when he didn't yet know my heart was leaning towards Marcus. When he discovered it – I have no idea how – he flew into a ferocious rage. So why is he back on this old promise today, when it no longer makes any sense?

'. . . and I say it again. It's Léo who will lead our dance. If she stays, I stay. If she turns around, so do I.'

'But you c-can't . . .' stammers Liz. 'Our future on Mars . . . I thought you and I . . .'

'If there had been just you and me, Liz, I would have voted to follow you the moment you announced your decision. Except this is how things really are now. There isn't just you and me. There's also Léonor. I swear I've tried to forget her, to act as though she no longer existed, to turn the page. But it's not possible. I can't do it.'

This time, it's too much for me, and I look up.

First I see Mozart's face, trembling with emotion, behind the reinforced glass.

Then Liz's, bathed in tears, just a few centimetres away from me.

'The tablet . . .' she just manages to say, turning towards Mozart. 'You remember the sketching tablet I showed you? It wasn't you that Léonor drew there. Remember those pages and pages, all filled with Marcus's tattoos?'

The sketching tablet?

My sketching tablet?

All of a sudden, everything becomes clear – Mozart's sudden change of heart towards me, the way he went for Liz, everything! She took my tablet without my permission, she went into my secret garden without being invited, and she gave the key to Mozart without my knowing.

'Don't look at me like that!' she spits between sobs, her

61

face distorted by a mixture of fury and guilt that makes her unrecognisable. 'It's not like I've committed a crime! I just opened Mozart's eyes to your true feelings. Can you explain to him why you spent all those hours drawing Marcus's tattoos?'

'Because I thought they were beautiful, Liz. Because I wanted to remember them.'

'Because you prefer Marcus! At least admit it!' She glances desperately at her watch. 'Oh God! It's 1:31! I can't believe we're all going to die, just because the three of us can't tell each other the truth to each other's faces!'

But on the other side of the glass, Mozart merely repeats what he's said before.

'I've already told you my truth. I've already made my decision. My choice will be Léo's choice. Perhaps today she does prefer a rival, but all that might change tomorrow.'

As a last resort, Liz turns to Marcus.

'You've won!' she yells. 'You're the one Léonor is going to choose, who she's already chosen. She's crazy about you, she copied every one of your tattoos into her tablet, you've just carved her name into your skin. Tell her you want to go down onto Mars with her, and she'll go down there, too, and we all will because we'll be in the majority. For God's sake, Marcus!'

'I vote to turn around.'

My heart skips a beat.

Turn around?

Did I really just hear that?

Is that really what Marcus just said?

Were those really the words for which he's just opened

his mouth for the first time since communications were re-established between the two halves of the Visiting Room, to add his voice to Kelly's, Samson's, Safia's and Kenji's? To restore that terrible balance once again, five votes on each side, five weights in each dish of the scales? To say that we will *never* be together?

'Marcus . . .' I say.

'I'd never have thought I'd get to this point,' he says with the ragged breathing of a cornered animal. 'I'd never have thought I would turn down what I most wanted in the world, at the very moment I was about to get it. Aargh!'

He bangs the glass with his fist and all his frustration.

It doesn't even shake. The reinforcement is perfect, it seems.

'It kills me to admit it,' he goes on, his face contorted in pain, 'but those who want to turn back are right. If we give up this chance to get rid of Serena, right here and now, it might never come again. And you, Léo, you'd blame me for each of the days you have left to live, which will have come at such a high price. You'd see something in me that has made you fail, that made you weak, that deprived you of your revenge. You'd hate me – and worse than that, you'd despise me. I could never bear that! If you really do want to land here tomorrow, with all the risks that go with that, I don't want it to be because of me.'

Little shining pearls of red are rising around Marcus's face. The violence with which he punched the wall has made the scarring on his chest start to bleed again. The drops of blood float like rubies before his grey eyes, where a storm is brewing. His beauty hurts me. His cruelty kills me. I want to beg him and to curse him, to kiss him and slap him, all at the same time.

'We've only got ten minutes to give our answer,' says Liz, her voice cracked from so much screaming, so much begging and so much weeping. 'Five apiece, we're just where we were when we started. But you, Léo, you hold the power over two votes, Mozart's and your own. And over twelve lives.'

9. Off-screen

'It's like being in a TV studio,' whispers Andrew, as he enters Serena McBee's study.

On one side there is a magnificent desk in precious woods, positioned in front of a large pair of French windows that look out over the snow-covered gardens; opposite this there is an aluminium gantry adorned with spotlights, light filters and cameras on articulated arms.

'This is where Mom does her commentaries for the Genesis channel when she's here at the villa,' explains Harmony.

'I do recognise the view, actually,' says Andrew, walking over towards the French windows. 'These have got to be the most famous gardens in America – no, the world! Viewers have been able to watch them change over the seasons, behind Serena's back, each time she speaks live to the *Cupido*. But the spotlights are switched off today. The cameras aren't rolling. No one can see the gardens. No one can see *us*, Harmony.'

He presses his hand to the icy windowpane.

On the other side, the snow falls more and more heavily, like a curtain shrouding the bushes, veiling the bare trees, blurring the views. You can't see the fences around the property, or the men in charge of keeping the place under surveillance – maybe they've returned under cover, to take shelter in the warm, to wait for the return of the Genesis channel, or at least the TV news.

'This silence,' murmurs Andrew. 'It's like nothing else exists, don't you think? Not the enormous media machine that has kept the Earth spinning for nearly six months, not the billions of viewers glued to their screens, and definitely not that spacecraft that suddenly disappeared off the radar the moment it had aligned itself with the orbit of Phobos – as though it had never even taken off.'

'What do you think's happened today?' asks Harmony reluctantly. 'Was the crew wiped out by some accident? Does it have anything to do with your father's disappearance?'

'I don't know. But my gut tells me all these mysteries are connected. I feel it in my bones. I'm like a compass needle going crazy in this place.'

Andrew moves away from the French windows to sit in the chair from which Serena McBee has for weeks been orchestrating the game of seduction. A control panel is set into the wood of the desk, invisible to the cameras.

Andrew takes off his backpack and pulls out a laptop, and a cable with which he connects it to the control panel.

'What are you doing?' asks Harmony.

'I'm trying to make the silence talk.'

He taps away at speed, the lines of code appearing on the screen of his laptop, reflected in the lenses of his glasses.

Suddenly there is a humming sound from the ceiling.

Harmony jumps.

Instinctively she grabs hold of Andrew's wrist, suspended over the keyboard.

He closes his fingers over hers.

Like this, hand in hand, their pulses beating in unison, they watch an enormous black screen, two metres by three, descend from the ceiling, moved by an invisible motor. The screen ends up coming to rest in the middle of the aluminium gantry, which forms a kind of frame around it, bristling with its cameras. A message appears on the dark, glassy surface:

ESTABLISHING CONTACT WITH THE *CUPIDO* . . .

'Oh!' cries Harmony, fiddling nervously with her gold locket. 'What have you started? You've got to stop, before it's too late! If the connection goes through, we'll be broadcast on the ship and on the Genesis channel and then the whole world will know we broke in to my mother's study!'

But Andrew does nothing to halt the process.

'The Genesis channel signal goes out from Cape Canaveral in Florida,' he says, 'not from this villa in the Hamptons. For some reason I'm not aware of, the people in charge of the programme decided to stop the global broadcast. If we manage to get in contact with the *Cupido*, the viewers won't know anything about it. Only we will discover if the passengers are still alive – and if they know anything about my father's disappearance.'

A spotlight comes on abruptly, followed by a second, then a

third, and so on until all the firepower of the gantry is trained on the two intruders.

A new message appears on the giant screen:

CONNECTION MADE, AWAITING RETURNING IMAGE . . .

All the cameras come to life at once and start to pivot towards Andrew and Harmony. They are like the multiple black, round, shining eyes of a gigantic spider, the aluminium supports its spindly legs.

All of a sudden, the screen lights up.

And splits into a digital wall, divided into twenty-seven windows.

The thirteen windows on the left represent views of the girls' quarters; the thirteen on the right, the boys'; the twenty-seventh, in the middle, the largest of them all, shows absolutely nothing: it's the black screen of the Genesis channel.

'The p-programme's editing wall,' stammers Andrew. 'Right here, before our very eyes.' He brushes his fingertips against the buttons of the control panel set into the desk. 'Beneath our very fingers!'

'Look! They're safe and sound!' cries Harmony, pointing to the topmost windows on the digital wall, which are showing the footage from the Visiting Room. 'There they are, all twelve of them!'

10. Shot

D +160 days, 00 h 02 mins.
[23rd week]

'Did you hear that?' asks Fangfang suddenly.

'Hear what?' replies Kelly. 'You're hearing voices now? We're in the middle of an interplanetary void, the engines are off, there's nothing to hear. Nothing but the last vote to be cast. Come on, Léo, let's have your verdict!'

There's a terrible weight crushing my chest, heavier than I felt from the acceleration of the rocket that tore me away from the Earth, five whole months ago.

'You are alone, but I am one of twelve!': those were the words I hurled in Serena's face, when she made her disgusting proposition. I thought that by giving each of us a chance to speak, we'd decide our common destiny together. But now everybody has spoken, and now things are even more complicated than before. There was no consensus. There was only a breaking up. Even Marcus has dissociated himself from me, offering me a poisoned chalice, a venomous gift: the freedom to choose. I don't know if I should love him even more or hate him for giving it to me.

I glance across the glass bubble, over the heads of the girls and boys who are hanging on my words. I don't stop to look at Marcus's face. My attention is fixed on the monstrous silhouette of Phobos and its communication antenna pointing like a threatening dart. Despite the vertiginous speed at which it's travelling around Mars, the black moon seems to be suspended in the void, because we're travelling exactly as fast ourselves. Speed is a relative concept. Like life itself.

The witch Serena was right after all.

The final decision will be up to me.

Me, and me alone.

Alone!

That thought fills my heart with rage and my lips with fire!

I open my mouth to say I've made my decision!

That I'm also voting to turn around!

That I . . .

'And what about now? You can't say you didn't hear it this time!' says Fangfang just as I was about to speak.

This time nobody thinks she's crazy, nor that she's hearing voices. Because we've all heard the sound coming from the hatch behind her.

'. . . *calling the passengers . . . on the* Cupido . . . *do you . . . read me . . . ?*'

We all pounce on the access tube that leads down to the gym; on the other side of the Visiting Room, the boys do the same, as they've heard the voice coming from their own quarters.

My heart is beating in my temples.

My elbows and knees bump against the rungs of the ladder.

The ten per cent gravity seems to pin my legs to the floor

of the gym, after so long spent in the weightlessness of the Visiting Room.

There's a face there, on the twelve screens set into the exercise machines. For the first time since setting off on our journey, it isn't Serena McBee's. It belongs to a young man who looks about our age, with brown hair and an anxious expression behind his black-framed glasses.

'Do you read me?' he asks over and over. 'You need to leave the Visiting Room and go down into the living quarters so that we can communicate. Can you see me?'

The girls around me answer him with an explosion of screaming.

'Yes! Yes!' they cry, as though by shouting loudly enough they might be able to eliminate the communication latency with Earth. 'We've come down! We can hear you! We can see you!'

There's something stopping me from sharing in their delight, doubtless a fear that we are being deceived once again. 'Wait,' I say. 'Maybe it's a trap. We don't know who this boy is. Look behind him – those are the gardens of the Villa McBee.'

The shouting stops abruptly, replaced with a tense silence. But the young man on the screens keeps on talking, as though he could guess my thoughts from a distance.

'You'll be hearing this message three minutes after I've sent it,' he says. 'And I suspect the organisers of the programme will hear it, too, from their HQ, since Cape Canaveral and the Villa McBee are connected to the heart of the secure Genesis network. So we've got to escape from this place before they make us stop.'

Escape?

We?

A second face is outlined behind the young man. It's that of a girl, so terribly white and with such light-coloured hair that she seems to blend in with the snow-covered gardens, as though she were their living incarnation.

'Harmony,' murmurs Liz. 'That looks like Harmony McBee.'

She's right.

There are only two people with those water-green eyes: the executive producer of the Genesis programme, and her daughter who we met briefly more than a year ago at the small reception held in our honour at the Villa McBee.

'What's she doing there?' asks Kelly nervously. 'Serena's darling little girl, who she cossets like a mother hen in her lovely villa, while she sends other people off to the slaughter . . . I'm sorry, girls, but if you ask me, I'm suspicious.'

Kelly's doubts are understandable enough. The one time we saw Harmony, she trailed her mother the whole afternoon. Like her reflection. Or her shadow. And such a discreet shadow that nobody could see it: Serena explained to us that, like a rock star, she wanted to keep her daughter sheltered from the dangers of celebrity, and that nobody knew of her existence apart from a handful of staff and close friends. She told us she had taken the decision to introduce her to us because she considered us, too, to be like her own children – the worst part is, I believed her at the time.

'We've just seen you leave the Visiting Room to go into the gym: that's when you heard us!' exclaims the young man in the black-framed glasses, all of a sudden. 'You might even have replied to us already, but we don't yet know.' He glances feverishly at his watch, then immediately continues: 'There's no way to make the three minutes separating us any shorter, so we just have to manage. No doubt you've recognised Harmony McBee on your screens. And my own face might be familiar. I'm Andrew Fisher, the son of Sherman Fisher, the Genesis programme's head of Communications.'

Safia gasps. 'Yes!' she says. 'He looks just like my old instructor, who died at the start of the summer! I didn't know he had a son our age. Sherman's son and Serena's daughter. I wouldn't believe it, except there they are, right in front of us.'

A bitter thought pierces me like a knife: there they are on the screen, pressed against one another – the children of those who've ridiculed us, deceived us, condemned us. They're nice and safe on Earth – Mum and Dad were careful not to send *them* on the mission! What a surprise! While we're lost in the depths of space, hanging by a thread between life and death. I feel a ball of rage forming in my belly. But the moment this bomb is about to go off, the girl on the screen opens her pale lips slightly and, for the first time, speaks to us.

'I don't know what our parents have done to you, but I'm begging you, don't blame us,' she says in a trembling voice, dispatching her entreaty across the void of space. 'We don't know why the people in charge of the Genesis programme have been keeping you off the air for two hours. We have no idea what secret they're trying to hide from the whole world, us included. You see, there's something I've only just realised: despite what I've been led to believe all these years, and even though we look as alike as two drops of water, though I carry her name and her coat of arms, I . . . I'm *not* my mother. And

73

Andrew is *not* his father. Any more than you are the parents who abandoned or rejected you in the past.'

The argument strikes me to the heart. The very idea that I might one day be capable of dumping my own kid in a trash can seems so revolting, so repellent, it takes my breath away. I'm nothing like my parents, who I can't remember at all, and I never will be! Nobody should have to carry the weight of the crimes committed by their family. Not even the daughter of the most despicable creature ever to have trodden the face of the Earth.

'For the two months before his death, my father kept me distant, like a stranger,' adds Andrew Fisher, following the plea of his strange neighbour. 'For years, Harmony's mother has kept her locked away in the Villa McBee like a prisoner. We can't take any more of this silence. We broke into Serena's study. We need to understand the guilty secret hidden at the heart of the Genesis programme. What is it our parents have been shielding us from? Why has the broadcast been interrupted? Do you know the answers to these questions? It's so difficult not being able to communicate with you in real time! If you know anything, please, tell us!'

Unable to hold back any longer, Fangfang raises her arm towards the black dome of the on-board camera, which is filming continuously. She is still holding the cellphone.

'Wait!' yells Kris. 'They seem to be telling the truth, but if we reveal the existence of the Noah Report to anybody, Serena will depressurise the base!'

No sooner has she spoken these words than she covers her mouth with her hand as though to swallow them back up.

But it's too late. Under all this stress she has said too much. Her words are already travelling through space, towards the mysterious intruders in the Villa McBee, and there's nothing that can erase them.

'It's 1:35,' groans Liz, eyes fixed on her watch. 'No more than seven minutes to give Serena an answer.'

Seven minutes . . . This countdown, which ought to chill me to the bone, makes me feel neither hot nor cold. It's as though there's something in me that has decided we can trust these two new interlocutors of ours. Because once again, in this poker game we're playing with Serena McBee, the cards are about to be re-dealt.

I swiftly turn towards the camera dome, my eyes stinging, my throat burning, and the words tumble over each other out of my lips.

'I do want to believe you! No, better, I *do* believe you! I believe you, truly, completely, absolutely!'

And that's it, I'm crying.

I cry my eyes out, but it isn't because of weakness, or defeat, or for any of the reasons why I've so often forbidden myself from crying my whole life.

These tears gush like a geyser from my very depths.

I get my breath back and force the words to come out in an orderly fashion, to address the girls as intelligibly as I can.

'We think we're so different from the monsters who signed our death warrants before they'd even met us, don't we? Well, what kind of monsters would we be if we condemned these two in advance, without even knowing them? Have our murderers made us so suspicious we can no longer recognise people like us? So suspicious we can't tell the difference between wolves and lambs? Just look at them, for God's sake!'

I point at the closest screen, the one above the treadmill.

'Look at them!' I say again, softly.

The girls step over towards the screen. Their own faces are reflected in its smooth surface, mixing with those of the two intruders who are looking at us without really seeing us, because all they can see is the image of the girls we were three minutes ago.

Andrew's pale forehead suddenly creases. Hesitantly he repeats our first replies, which have finally reached him and which are gradually outlining the terrible secret he snuck into Serena's study to uncover.

'*Sends other people off to the slaughter? Depressurise the base?*' he stammers. 'Is that really what Kelly and Kirsten said? I don't understand . . . Or I'm afraid I may understand all too well . . . Oh God!'

Time is slipping through our fingers as quick as sand, but nobody is trying to stop it now.

'They're . . . they're like us,' murmurs Safia in a thin voice, after a moment of silence that feels like an eternity.

Tears begin to fall from her beautiful black eyes, tracking thin furrows of kohl down her cheeks.

'They've been deceived, as well,' says Liz.

'They've been lied to, as well,' adds Kris.

'You mean they've been had? Ha!' roars Kelly. 'Welcome to the club!'

A smile lights up Andrew's face all of a sudden, banishing the distress for a moment: he's just heard the words I spoke a few minutes ago; my tears have just started to flow.

'Léonor,' he says, holding his hand out towards the camera in a touching gesture, as though trying to reach me across the abyss that separates us. 'Léonor, you believe us? Thank you! We aren't responsible for what's happening to you, I swear it! Do the other girls believe us too?'

'I think they do believe you,' I say, touching Andrew's hand on the screen over the treadmill. 'Don't you, girls?'

My friends nod.

'Do they believe us?' Andrew says again as he and Harmony are held expectantly in the cruel communication latency, not knowing whether we have yet answered them. 'They have to believe us, because we are like them! We don't have a spacecraft, or fans, or a Dowry. But we are also disgusted by the legacy our parents have left us. Even if we're at opposite ends of the solar system, we're with you! Tell us everything you know and we'll do everything we can to help!'

'Andrew, Harmony, listen carefully to what I'm going to say.' I look straight at the camera, wiping away my tears. 'By the time you hear this I will have left the room. Yes, there's a terrible truth and we will tell you what it is. Yes, our lives are in danger. Yes, we're counting on you. Your craft will be whatever vehicles you can use to escape as far as possible from Serena McBee. Your fans will be us, the twelve of us on the Genesis programme. Your Dowry will be our infinite gratitude and, perhaps, also the triumph of truth at the end of the adventure. There are still two roles to fill in our crew. Twelve plus two equals fourteen: you will be our Survival Officers. Because you really can save our lives. The Genesis people will do everything in their power to muzzle you, just like they've tried so hard to silence us. The difference is that you aren't at their mercy, locked in a prison the far side of space. You are free. Do whatever you can to stay that way. And if we do die one day, reveal to the whole world what we are about to reveal to you now.'

I give Fangfang a nod. She is still holding the cellphone in her trembling hands.

'You can show them the pages of the Noah Report, Fangfang. You can explain to them that we have twenty-two months to the next Great Storm. I'm going back up to the Visiting Room to give Serena our answer: it's time. I'm sorry about the doubts, girls. This old Determinator had stalled, but it's started up again, and voting to go down to Mars. We will all go to Mars, and with a *Serenity* contract as good as anything you can get from Karmafone, thank you very much!'

11. Reverse Shot

Fallout Bunker, Cape Canaveral Air Base
Saturday 9 December, seven minutes earlier, 1:35pm

'What's going on? The ultimatum has almost run out and they still haven't given their answer. Why are they all leaving the Visiting Room?'

Puffing like an ox, Gordon Lock staggers towards the digital wall showing the images from space on a three-minute delay. Around him, all the allies of silence are on their feet: they're so stressed they couldn't sit still.

'Look!' cries Odette Stuart-Smith in her shrill voice. 'The screens in the gym have come on. Are we being broadcast to the *Cupido* right now?'

Like wild spectres, the conspirators slowly gather round Serena McBee at the foot of the digital wall. And they realise it isn't the bunker that's being shown on the screens above the bicycles and treadmills.

'That looks like the g-gardens of your villa, Serena,' stammers Geronimo Blackbull. 'Who's that on the screen?'

'I recognise him,' squeaks the Planetology director. 'That's Andrew Fisher, Sherman's son. And he's not alone. Look, there's someone behind him.'

The normally imperturbable Dr Montgomery lets out an astonished 'Oh!'

'Serena!' he says, grabbing the executive director's arm. 'It looks like . . . like . . . your daughter!'

Serena McBee takes three seconds of silence, as though the information was struggling to reach her brain. The first second, a wave of doubt crosses her face; the next, something like sorrow seems to make her eyes shine; but by the time the third second has been and gone her features have resumed their usual mask of cold determination.

She yanks her arm from Dr Montgomery's grip.

'You're mistaken, Arthur,' she replies to him, icily. 'You thought you'd seen Harmony, but that is not her.'

'Are you quite sure?' the doctor insists. 'The resemblance is striking.'

'My daughter would never betray her mother in such a way!' Serena cuts him off.

She presses the bee-shaped brooch pinned to the collar of her jacket.

Her orders come out as fast as pistol bullets.

'*Serena to Balthazar.* I repeat: *Serena to Balthazar.* Two criminals have infiltrated my study. A boy with glasses and a girl made up to look like Harmony. They are dangerous criminals, and they have broken in. They must be rendered harmless. Legitimate defence. The law allows it. Destroy them both. *That is my will!*'

Serena lets go of the brooch.

The other allies of silence stare, but no one dares to question her.

Serena looks at the digital wall in front of her, still as a corpse.

All of a sudden, a red flame tears across the screen. It's Léonor throwing herself onto the ladder, disappearing from the window that shows the girls' gym and reappearing in the Visiting Room. It's like a tiny will-o'-the-wisp facing off with an ice giant.

'Listen to me, Serena,' says Léonor, staring into the camera, panting from her run. 'You are receiving this message just before the channel is restarted. We have made our decision. The decision is to go to Mars.'

Léonor's chest rises and falls haltingly. She is visibly overwhelmed by the situation, by being the chosen spokesperson for the twelve passengers. Fire colours her freckled skin; her red curls are clinging to her cheeks, which are gleaming with perspiration; the edges of her eyelids are still wet with tears. But however great her emotion, she does everything she can to keep control of herself: her bronze eyes barely blink. They look straight into the camera, pupils dilated by tiredness and excitement.

'We have decided to go to Mars,' she continues, 'but not on your terms. On ours. Going down there and blindly putting our lives in your hands – that idea is intolerable. But going down there knowing that the moment we die, the secret of the Noah Report will be revealed to the whole world, that's a much sweeter idea. You and your allies are not the only people on Earth to know of its existence. There are two other cards in the game. Two trump cards. And they are not in your hands.'

Léonor takes a deep breath, like a swimmer inhaling for the last time before a long, deep dive, who doesn't know when she will get the chance to breathe again. She looks so fragile, suddenly, and so young.

'You like deals, bargains, contracts,' she begins, trying to control the tremor in her voice. 'Well, then, listen carefully, Serena, as these are our terms . . .' She stumbles over her words, hesitates, then continues: '. . . no, I should say, these are your *commitments. This is . . . the* Serenity *contract.'*

Once she has spoken those words, 'the Serenity *contract', all the rest flows from Léonor's mouth with miraculous ease. She's suddenly galvanised by the intensity of the moment, as if infused with some force that has come from far away: the will to survive.*

'First, a commitment of Coverage: *you will never take us off the air again.*

'Second, a commitment of Transparency: *you will tell us everything that happens on Earth in real time, with no filters, no delay.*

'Third, a commitment of Assistance: *you will supply us remotely with any technical or logistical support we need to repair the habitats.*

'At the slightest failure to meet these commitments, we will talk. At the slightest attempt to get rid of us, our friends will share the evidence that damns you. So it's really in your interest that we live on Mars for a long, long time.'

12. Off-screen

'They've lied to everyone on Earth,' mutters Andrew.

He is opposite the digital wall of the Villa McBee, which is identical to the one in the fallout bunker in Cape Canaveral. Eyes wide behind his black-framed glasses, he is looking at the pages of the Noah Report, which Fangfang is scrolling through on the window showing the girls' gym.

'They knew they were sending the participants to their deaths, but they said nothing. They acted as though there was a bright future waiting for them on Mars, when they knew they were really going to die like rats. All that just to keep the programme going, to make the sponsors' and audience's cash machine keep paying out! And my father . . . He lied to them, too, didn't he, Harmony? But he was a good, decent guy. He never would have agreed to be a part of this organised murder, even if he'd been in debt, even if without the salary that Genesis paid him he wouldn't have been able to make the payments on our house in Beverly Hills.'

Andrew looks imploringly up at the girl beside him, behind the desk. She is hypnotised by the screen, and paler than ever.

'I'm sure your father was innocent,' she murmurs in a voice so fragile it seems to be made of glass. 'I want to believe it with all my heart. And how I wish I could convince myself that my mother was also the victim of a plot, or at the very least a terrible misunderstanding.'

She tears her eyes away from the digital wall and looks straight into Andrew's.

'But the proof is there,' she concludes in a breath. 'Everything suggests my mom really did unleash this horror.'

The two are still for a moment, facing the muffled silence of the snow falling beyond the window, unable to speak another word. For them, nothing will ever be the same again. They are alone in the world now, even more isolated than the twelve up there in the furthest reaches of space: cut off from the rest of Earth's inhabitants by the discovery they have just made.

All of a sudden, there is a muffled noise from beyond the French windows.

A distant crunch of trodden snow.

'What's that?' says Andrew.

A black figure appears in silhouette behind the curtain of flakes.

There is a man approaching across the freshly fallen snow, leaving a heavy imprint of his boots on the virginal white.

'It's the guard doing his rounds!' cries Harmony. 'Quick, we've got to get out of the study before he passes the window!'

She grabs Andrew's arm to lead him towards the service entrance through which they entered the study a few minutes earlier. But the young man resists.

'Wait,' he says, pointing towards his laptop, which is still connected by a cable to the control panel set into the desk. 'Just a minute. The screen captures of the Noah Report are already saved in here, but I have to finish copying the data from the desk's central unit.'

'What central unit? What data?'

At that moment, the main door to the study is flung open to reveal a man of about fifty, wearing a morning coat, with an earpiece on his temple and a revolver in his hand.

'Balthazar!' cries the girl. 'It's me, Harmony! Don't shoot!'

But the butler doesn't lower his gun.

His eyes stare, unmoving as a robot's.

His face is locked shut like a safe.

'Balthazar?' says Harmony again, her voice quavering. 'Don't you recognise me? It's me: Harmony. You've taken care of me since I was little . . .'

There's no sign on Balthazar's long, smooth face to suggest that he understands or even hears Harmony's words. She doesn't know it, but the only thing he can hear is coming from his earpiece, which is whispering orders he cannot but obey.

'You remember, Balthazar,' says Harmony insistently, almost shouting now. 'The day of my tenth birthday, you chased off a crow that came into my bedroom and gave me such a fright! Every spring you've brought me the first roses from the garden to decorate my dressing-table! Balthazar! Balthazar! It really is me!'

'Watch out!' yells Andrew, throwing himself at the girl at the very moment the butler squeezes the trigger.

The explosion bursts through the silence.

The boy and girl roll onto the floor.

One of the panes of the French windows breaks with a great crash.

Balthazar is already preparing to shoot again. But his movements have been slowed by the daze in which he seems to find himself. Andrew is quicker than him and leaps to his feet, grabbing a huge quartz paperweight from the desk and hurling it with all his strength at the head of the butler, who collapses, stunned.

The icy winter air rushes into the study through the smashed French windows, the wind whistling furiously against the glass shards.

'Oh God! Balthazar!' cries Harmony, unable to tear her eyes away from the body spread across the Persian rug covering the study floor. 'Is he . . . dead?'

'I d-don't think so,' stammers Andrew, 'I don't know. I . . . I acted on impulse . . . but I do know he almost killed you. If this man who knows you was ready to fire, I'm sure those mercenaries paid to guard the villa wouldn't hesitate at all.'

He glances nervously towards the smashed windowpane.

But there's nothing beyond it now except the white snow, so thick that it's impossible to see even two metres outside.

'Maybe the storm muffled the gunshot?' asks Harmony.

'Let's hope it keeps going this time, to hide our escape. We'll have to cross the gardens and scale the railings to get back to my vehicle – that's the only possible way out.'

He pulls down the screen of his laptop, yanks out the cable linking it to the control desk, throws the whole thing in his backpack and gets ready to jump over the splinters of glass.

At the last moment, he turns to check that Harmony is following him.

But she is standing totally still in the middle of the study.

'You've changed your mind? You don't want to come any more?' says Andrew, alarmed, bringing his leg back down onto the floor.

The wind is tousling his hair, transforming his brown locks into straps that whip his forehead and his glasses.

'I don't want to stay in this place a moment longer,' replies Harmony. 'But I can't leave till I'm sure Balthazar isn't dead.'

She throws herself down beside the lifeless body, and presses her cheek to his morning coat.

'I can feel his chest rising,' she says, relieved. 'I can hear his heart beat. I can hear . . . my mother's voice?'

Harmony sits up abruptly and looks around at the floor.

Balthazar's earpiece came off as he fell.

There it lies, on the rug, buzzing like a little bee lost far from its hive, in the heart of winter – a little buzzing creature – with the voice of Serena McBee.

'*Serena to Balthazar . . . I repeat: Serena to Balthazar . . . Did you find them . . . ? Have you killed them . . . ? Reply at once,* that is my will . . . !'

Harmony jumps to her feet, as if the winter bee had pierced her with its sting, and rushes after Andrew towards the French windows and out into the cold.

13. Reverse Shot

Fallout Bunker, Cape Canaveral Air Base
Saturday 9 December, 1:50pm

'Well?' asks Gordon Lock, with an imploring look at Serena McBee. 'Have they been neutralised?'

The executive director takes her index finger off her brooch-mic.

'Well, I don't know,' she says quietly. 'Balthazar isn't answering. He is under hypnosis, however, and mentally conditioned like everyone on my staff, so he ought to fulfil every order I give him with the precision of a machine.'

The allies of silence barely have time to complain; a flashing red message is already appearing at the top of the digital wall, shedding faint ember-like lights around the tiny bunker:

INCOMING CALL FROM THE EDITING SUITE

Serena touches the smooth screen with her index finger; the window showing the editing suite at the surface of Cape Canaveral appears at once. Samantha is there, reliably at her post, but she is not alone. Hundreds of people have invaded the sanctuary of the Genesis programme, and are spreading utter chaos – teenagers and elderly people, solo travellers and whole families, supporters dressed head to toe in the programme's colours and total strangers in ordinary dress, in formal wear, in sweatpants – in whatever state the sudden suspension of the Genesis channel happened to find them.

'When the assailants breached the final defences, the guards decided not to fire . . .' explains Samantha. 'The social networks have exploded. Word is going around that you've suffered a full cardiac arrest in the middle of live editing. That you've dropped dead. Some people are claiming that the message posted on the channel was written by someone else. The craziest conspiracy theories are starting to circulate, we're hearing things about the C.I.A., the K.G.B., the Illuminati . . . Faced with these rumours, the White House itself no longer knows how to react and is pestering us with questions about the new vice-president. Ms McBee, the twenty extra minutes you requested, and which we announced on the channel, have expired. If we put it off any longer, I can't be answerable for what happens. Will we be able to resume the broadcast?'

A young black man, twentyish, wearing a red jacket and a matching helmet with a *Mario's Pizza* logo, bursts roughly into the frame.

'Am I dreaming?' he shouts. 'You're really talking to Serena McBee? I was in the middle of delivering a pizza to Port Canaveral when the show stopped. I immediately changed course and raced over here, such a feeling of terror in the pit of my stomach.'

'Sir, please.' The assistant tries to defend herself. 'You have no right to be here.'

'Hey, everyone, listen to this!' the young man shouts, smiling as brightly as a sun. 'It wasn't a bluff. Serena is still alive, and she's going to save the participants, the craft, the whole programme!'

A clamour of relief overwhelms Samantha's protestations like a fire consuming wisps of straw.

'Hooray! Long live Serena!'

In the bunker there is consternation, in violent contrast with the jubilation breaking out on the screen.

'Well, then. It really is time to get back on the air,' says Serena. 'Samantha is right: we can't wait any longer. We have no choice.'

'Get back on the air?' says Gordon Lock, in a strangled voice. 'Knowing there are two individuals walking around out there in the middle of nowhere with a copy of the Noah Report?'

'When I think back to that nosey little kid, Andrew Fisher,' groans Odette Stuart-Smith, wringing her hands. 'His ridiculous snivelling at Sherman's burial! Spawn of the devil! We've escaped the father, only to end up in the clutches of the son!'

'This time it really is all over,' concludes Geronimo Blackbull sombrely. 'The three commitments that redheaded devil is imposing on us are a real diktat: *Coverage*, *Transparency*, *Assistance*! And why not *Breakfast in bed* while she's at it!' He gives a bitter laugh, dissonant as the cawing of a crow. 'It was originally in our interest for them to die so they would never be able to speak, and now we need them to live on Mars for as long as possible! And the kamikaze participant

Serena programmed is of no use to us at all; on the contrary, we absolutely have to ensure they never act. But make no mistake, even without the kamikaze, the participants will end up dying when the habitats fail them, and then that goddamned report will be brought to the attention of the public. We're like rats in a trap!'

As usual, Archibald Dragovic merely rolls his mad eyes, his body seized by a nervous trembling.

Serena gives a small, uncomfortable smile.

'I admit the situation is awkward at best,' she says reluctantly. 'And I take my share of responsibility, as captain of this expedition. *Like rats*, you say, Geronimo? But when the ship is wrecked, rats always have a chance to leave it, don't they? Only the captain is obliged to remain on deck.'

The executive director emphasises her words with a look at each of the allies of silence.

'In a few moments, I am going to go back on the air,' she continues. 'But you, my friends, you can make a run for it if you wish to. The Atlas jet, which is always waiting on the Cape Canaveral tarmac, is at your service. You've heard as well as I: the participants have decided to land on Mars. Atlas Capital will transfer our bonuses into our bank accounts once the capsules have touched down on Martian soil, in a few hours, as predicted. With those tens of millions of dollars, you should be able to buy political asylum in the country of your choice. Honduras, Panama, Guatemala, El Salvador, Nicaragua . . . You need only to pick one of these dream destinations for an early retirement beneath the coconut palms.'

Serena extracts a powder compact from her snakeskin

handbag, to even out her make up, which recent events have slightly smudged.

Director Lock opens his eyes wide.

'You mean to tell us, you'd sacrifice yourself, to give us cover while we escape?' he asks, articulating each syllable carefully.

'Yes, my dear Gordon,' Serena answers without stopping powdering her nose. 'You might put it like that, with your famous sense of melodrama. *I will sacrifice myself for you.* But don't just stand there: stay or go, there's not much time.'

'It's just that . . .' begins Gordon Lock, struggling to find the words. 'I never expected . . . Thank you, Serena.'

'Not at all. And here, take this, while you're here. It might help you persuade the jet pilot to go to the destination of your choosing, in the event he proves reluctant.'

Serena casually clicks her powder compact shut and replaces it in her bag, only to extract a revolver which she holds out to Director Lock. He takes it from her, babbling his thanks. Then he quickly arranges his things in his leather briefcase, followed immediately by Odette Stuart-Smith, Geronimo Blackbull and Archibald Dragovic. Only Arthur Montgomery remains standing at the foot of the digital wall, straight as a post.

'Don't fancy going on safari, doc?' asks Geronimo, as Gordon positions his big, sweat-dripping face against the retinal identification box that controls the bunker door.

'I'm no rat,' says the doctor. 'If safaris have taught me anything, it's that man is at the top of the animal kingdom. I still have my honour!'

The Engineering instructor shrugs and tucks a lock of black hair behind his ear.

'Honour?' he croaks in his incorrigible smoker's voice, a smile at the corner of his dry lips. 'I'm not sure that's very healthy, these days. But health is your department, after all, doc!'

He disappears into the neon-lit corridor towards the lift that leads to the surface.

ACT II

14. Genesis Channel

Saturday 9 December, 1:59pm

BACK ON THE AIR IN 30 SECONDS . . .
29 SECONDS . . .
28 SECONDS . . .
27 SECONDS . . .

15. Off-screen

Hotel California, Death Valley
Saturday 9 December, 10:59am

'Mr Bill, it's a miracle!'

Cindy, the waitress at the little Hotel California that clings to the edge of Route 190, wipes her hands on her apron and hurries over to the TV set to turn up the volume.

'What's up, darlin'?' murmurs the old man settled behind the bar, not bothering to raise his tired eyes from the newspaper he's reading.

The blades of the fan attached to the ceiling lift his sparse grey hair and make the edges of the paper shiver.

'Is there someone wanting a room? At this time of year, with the crisis we've got going on, that really would be a miracle.'

'HEY!' shouts Cindy, pointing at the ancient cathode-tube screen. 'The Genesis channel is coming back on! We're going to be able to see the participants again, at last!'

The manager lifts his head. His heavy eyelids open wide, all of a sudden, and his eyes start to shine.

'Yeah,' he cries, 'I think you're right!'

At the back of the restaurant, the only two customers drop

their forks onto their beans. They're brawny lorry drivers, slaves of the road, covered in sweat and the red dust of Death Valley, but their eyes shine as brightly as Bill and Cindy's; at this moment, sitting opposite the TV set with the numbers counting down, they have turned back into the children they used to be, wonderstruck.

'I was so scared!' says Cindy, wringing her hands. 'So scared! I thought we'd lost our participants for ever. I never would have gotten over it. But now, praise the Lord, everything will be back in order again.'

She gives a sigh of relief, then a second sigh, this time of regret.

'I do so wish I could be at Cape Canaveral tomorrow evening,' she says, 'to watch the marriage ceremony conducted via link-up with Mars.'

Mr Bill bangs his fist on the bar.

'Then you should go!' he says with a big smile.

Cindy looks at him, astonished.

'Mr Bill?'

'You only live once, Cindy! Pack your bags! Quick! There's still time for you to jump on a plane!' He turns to the room and calls out to the drivers: 'Might one of you gentlemen be able to escort a lady to the airport?'

16. Genesis Channel

Saturday 9 December, 1:59pm

BACK ON THE AIR IN 23 SECONDS . . .
22 SECONDS . . .
21 SECONDS . . .
20 SECONDS . . .

17. Off-screen

Railings of the Villa McBee, Long Island, New York State Saturday 9 December, 1:59pm

A horn sounds, piercing the curtain of silence and snow that is falling on the Hamptons, four thousand kilometres from Death Valley. A few dozen cars, vans and caravans are parked there, outside the frozen railings of the Villa McBee, where the Genesis programme's most devoted fans are gathered. It looks like a village whose houses cluster feebly against one another so as to better resist the winter. Fine ribbons of smoke rise up from the exhaust pipes of the mobile homes, over the whitened roofs. Behind the frost-covered windscreens, it's possible to make out the trembling brightness of the screens lit by the Genesis channel.

Another horn blare , this time from several vehicles at once.

By the third time, the whole village is resounding with the noise: every driver is pressing in time on their steering wheel, marking the countdown towards the resumption of the programme. The sounds rise up in unison towards the heavy sky, once per second, like a bell ringing in a church tower, like a universal prayer.

At that solemn moment, nobody pays any attention to the black campervan with the tinted windows that moves apart from the huddle and launches at full throttle onto the whirling snow-covered road.

18. Genesis Channel

Saturday 9 December, 1:59pm

BACK ON THE AIR IN 18 SECONDS . . .
17 SECONDS . . .
16 SECONDS . . .
15 SECONDS . . .

19. Off-screen

Times Square, New York City
Saturday 9 December, 1:59pm

Not far from the improvised village in the Hamptons, the snow is also falling on the heart of the great World City. Despite the wintry weather, Times Square is still teeming with the crowds who gathered two hours earlier to watch the final speed-dating.

A million faces, blue with cold, have turned towards the giant screens fixed to the sides of the glass and steel buildings, across which the countdown numbers are scrolling.

A million mouths exhale a cloud of steam and chant with one voice:

'Eight . . . !'

'Seven . . . !'

'Six . . . !'

'Five . . . !'

20. Genesis Channel

Saturday 9 December, 1:59pm

BACK ON THE AIR IN 4 SECONDS . . .

3 SECONDS . . .

2 SECONDS . . .

1 SECOND . . .

Open to black.

Static shot on Serena McBee, sitting in her padded leather armchair. She is smiling generously, revealing her perfectly aligned, sparkling teeth. Her silver bob is impeccable, as though she has spent the last two hours in the hairdresser's salon, while the rest of the planet has been plunged into an abyss of doubt, distress and confusion.

Serena: 'My dear viewers, it's such a pleasure to see you again at last! I've missed you. You've touched me. All these messages of sympathy we've received on social networks, all the signs of affection, the fear that I might have suffered some accident . . . Please reassure yourselves, I'm quite alive, readier than ever to serve you, and to serve our brave space heroes.'

Serena's smile widens – or tightens? 'Our dear boys and

girls are quite alive, too. Did you doubt it? And just about to complete the final stage of their extraordinary journey: their descent onto a new world! Who would not be moved by such a sight, the most dizzying view Mankind has ever contemplated? We are moved by it down here on Earth, at our screens – so imagine what it's like up there, hanging right over Mars? After five months of live broadcasting, the tension on board the *Cupido* was at its height. Yes, Léonor did make a small slip-up, but let those among you who have never faltered cast the first stone. Just don't expect me to do it! Yes, Léonor has a striking scar on her back, but how is she to blame? I chose her despite this imperfection – and who among us doesn't have one? And I'd choose her again today if I had to! That dozen, they are my selection, and I take responsibility, one hundred per cent. I wanted to leave the craft offline for a moment, to take the pressure off them, to allow them to spend some time together without the cameras. Don't try to find anybody else to blame for the momentary pause in transmission, it was me and me alone. I take full responsibility.'

A new image is embedded into the screen, to Serena's right.

It's an aerial view ringed by tall buildings, which is clearly being filmed by a TV camera attached to a drone, with red letters superimposed: TIMES SQUARE, NEW YORK CITY, LIVE.

'SERENA!' yells the frenzied crowd, lit up by the giant screens on which the executive producer's apologetic smile is widening.

The camera swoops down, gliding just a few metres above the thousands of arms holding up pieces of cardboard bearing hasty scribbles in marker pen: *You were right Serena*; *We R all with U*; *America is proud of you.*

The image shifts to a view of Paris, likewise overflowing with gratitude and enthusiasm.

Serena: 'I infringed the Genesis programme regulations, which stipulate that the cameras will never stop filming. I deprived you of two hours of watching, without any warning. I thought the programme's participants needed a rest before the great leap. The pressure was too onerous for them, as I'm sure we can all imagine! Two hours' respite was the greatest gift I could give them. I just listened to my heart. I confess. Even if it meant disappointing you. Even if it meant losing the money from the broadcasting rights. If you are angry, my dear viewers, I'm the one you should blame, not the participants.'

The picture from Berlin, which follows on immediately from that of Paris, shows the explosive relief of the fans all rigged out in the famous hairdo shaped like a crown of blonde braids, which has become the rallying emblem of Kirsten's supporters; girls but also grandmothers, men of all ages and children wear it proudly, shouting out their delight.

Serena: 'The good news is that this brief moment of respite has borne fruit – harmony reigns once more aboard the *Cupido*! Our young friends have recovered their serenity and their confidence: the qualities for which they were selected for the Genesis programme. Let us return to them, without further ado – roll credits!'

Fade to black.

21. Shot

D +160 days, 00 h 31 mins.
[23rd week]

The panoramic screen opposite the fireplace comes on suddenly, exploding into the starry space-scape of the Genesis credit sequence.

We have come back down to the living room, all six of us and Louve, for the restoration of the channel. I did just think to run a damp towel over my cheek to wipe away the dried blood and hastily stick a bandage over my eyebrow. No time to sew up my torn skin. Kris has tied knots in the tatters of my dress in order to more or less cover my chest and my right shoulder. The rest of my back is still uncovered. But it isn't my bare skin that's making me shiver, it's the opening notes of *Cosmic Love*, the official anthem of the Genesis programme, which are bursting into the compartment just as they did on that first day – as if nothing had changed!

'*Six girls on one side . . .*' announces the pre-recorded voice coming out of the screen, like the voice of a ghost from beyond the grave.

The *Cupido* appears. It looks so small all of a sudden, so puny in the middle of the interplanetary void. A real rat trap! And twelve human beings were crazy enough to board that thing!

But isn't going down to Mars even crazier? whispers the Salamander's voice in my ear, as it just now awakens.

It remained mute during all our overheated discussions, but now that the decision has been taken, when we have all fallen silent, now at last it speaks. Even if I know that we've made the right decision, that we have two allies on Earth who are ready to denounce Serena McBee if she doesn't adhere to her three commitments, I can't help having doubts. Especially when I see the silhouettes of the girls appearing on the screen, our own portraits shot before the start of the voyage, glowing with joy, with naïveté . . . with such stupidity!

Title: FANGFANG, SINGAPORE (PLANETOLOGY)

Title: KELLY, CANADA (NAVIGATION)

Title: SAFIA, INDIA (COMMUNICATIONS)

Title: ELIZABETH, UNITED KINGDOM (ENGINEERING)

Title: KIRSTEN, GERMANY (BIOLOGY)

Title: LÉONOR, FRANCE (MEDICINE)

I glance nervously at the girls, who are huddled together opposite the screen. Their pale faces no longer look anything like those in the opening credits, when they thought they were living out the dream of their lives. Because now they have woken up. And they know that death awaits them just around the corner.

'*Six boys on the other . . .*' announces the voiceover.

The girls' quarters on the screen are replaced by the boys'. The six boys' silhouettes scroll past at top speed, lined up like men awaiting a firing squad.

Title: TAO, CHINA (ENGINEERING)
Title: ALEXEI, RUSSIA (MEDICINE)
Title: KENJI, JAPAN (COMMUNICATIONS)
Title: MOZART, BRAZIL (NAVIGATION)
Title: SAMSON, NIGERIA (BIOLOGY)
Title: MARCUS, UNITED STATES (PLANETOLOGY)

Marcus.

My Marcus . . .

The boy I thought I knew so well, after just a few sessions in the Visiting Room. The truth was, maybe I didn't know him at all. And what if that magical thing I thought I felt between us was only an illusion, like the rest of the programme, like the model of the spacecraft in the opening credits, like the doll's-house silhouettes, cut out in 2D? Did he really vote to turn around in order to allow me to make my choice without being influenced, or . . .

(. . . or was he really gripped by doubt when faced with the prospect of spending the rest of his days with a girl who is mutilated?)

I clench my fists inside the folds of my dress, till my nails make imprints in my palms.

Marcus has accepted me as I am, I'm sure of it!

He engraved my name in his skin, even after he had seen my scar!

I won't let the Salamander spoil everything we have!

The voices of Jimmy Giant and Stella Magnifica, the performers of *Cosmic Love,* swallow up my thoughts in the final crescendo of the opening credits, as the Genesis programme's foetus logo appears on the screen. Once it didn't used to bother me especially. But now, knowing everything I know, it horrifies me – a child dead before it's even been born, a mission aborted before departure, the very image of the Genesis programme itself.

The torment of the opening credits finally stops, which brings me no relief because it's replaced by an even more painful sight: a smiling Serena McBee. I never would have thought it before, but today her smile makes me think of a sickle. Yes, that's how I'd draw it: a long, well-sharpened, white ivory sickle, ready to mow down a dozen lives, the rictus grin of Death itself. Now, I know only me and my fellow passengers can see this; in the eyes of the millions of viewers Serena's smile is still that of a kind of teasing, doting grandma, a model of good will and humanity – the very opposite of what she really is.

'Oh, my dears!' she cries, in a voice that almost makes my ears bleed, her sweetness conceals such calculation and hypocrisy. 'We meet again at last! It's such a delight seeing you all reunited, all six of you, after the small difference of opinion that set you against each other. Something to do with the boys, I'll bet! But tell me, why do you have those funereal expressions on your faces now? You're fretting about the spectacle you've made of yourselves, is that it? Don't worry, I suspended the broadcast until your reconciliation. You can smile again.'

I can guess from the tone of Serena's voice that this isn't just another banal phrase, but an instruction – we are meant to understand it not as 'you can' but 'you should'. The cameras installed in the living-room wall, pointed at us, are taking careful note of our grim faces, the furrows that tears have marked on our cheeks, our stress-wrinkled foreheads. We mustn't remain like this. From this moment on, we need to become actors performing our own lives – feigning joy when we feel only distress, imitating carefreeness when the one thing that drives us, from here on in, will be the furious desire to survive.

I focus all my energy on forcing the corners of my lips to turn up – it feels as though I have a hundred-kilo weight attached to each cheek.

I draw my lips back to show my teeth – it's like all the muscles in my face are clenching in a grotesque grimace.

It's horrible, transforming my face into a mask like this, but I have no choice: I need to follow Serena's example, hiding what I truly feel and, just as she always says with her appalling cynicism, 'put on a show'.

'Thank you for being so understanding, Serena,' I say.

My voice sounds like an untuned violin – so totally wrong! You must do better than that, Léo.

'You're right, it's time for us to celebrate,' I continue, forcing my smile wider. 'But at the same time, it's all so intense, so . . . intimidating. We're about to get what we've always wished for, what we've been dreaming about for months: Mars, and everything it represents. We do, in a sense, have a *commitment* to be happy.'

I really emphasise that word, *commitment*, staring into the camera, and through it at the woman from whom I'm awaiting a sign that she'll fulfil her part of the deal.

Then I turn to the other girls, who are looking at me as if I'm an alien.

'Isn't that right, girls?' I ask, my voice a bit too cheerful, a bit too loud. 'It's all making us a bit crazy, the little scares, the final Heart Lists, the great leap, the marriages . . . the wedding nights.'

Kelly is the first to join in.

'You can say that again!' she exclaims, bursting out laughing – however does she manage to laugh in these circumstances? Where does she find the strength? 'We're about to find ourselves face to face with six horny males, who've been caged up for the last five months: we're going to have to get our whips out if we're going to tame them, girls!'

She goes back to chewing her piece of gum spiritedly (or furiously), and it's Liz's turn to lighten up.

'Oh, it's all so emotional!' she says, fanning herself with her hand. 'I just can't believe the best day of my life has arrived!'

The enormity of this lie is such that – this time – we all burst out laughing too. A deep, wild laugh, that grabs hold of all six of us and shakes us like washing machines on spin cycle. It seems nothing will be able to stop this laughter that twists our bellies, that takes our breath away, that draws burning tears from our eyes. Louve contributes a jerky barking, strangely like a human voice. The minutes roll by. Six in total: three for the echoes of this monstrous meltdown to travel down to Earth, three for Serena's reaction to make its way back up to us.

'There we are!' she cries, on the panoramic screen. 'That's more like it! '

Finally, we manage to recover our breath, while the executive producer continues to spool out her monologue.

'If it helps to reassure you, the *horny males* are just as freaked out as you are just now, at the prospect of really meeting you. And they have been fighting too, because of you.'

Such a skilled liar! If the boys' nerves are also frayed, it's not at the prospect of meeting us – it's because they know what awaits them on Mars; if Mozart's fist has left a nasty bruise on Alexei's jaw, it's not our fault – it's because of the terrible choice Serena has imposed on them. But that's something the viewers will know nothing about . . . as long as we hold our tongues.

'From a psychological point of view, these little bursts of passion were entirely normal, indeed necessary,' Serena explains, now wrapping herself in her authority as a psychiatrist. 'They have allowed our brave heroes to relieve the tension accumulated over the course of the journey. And what a journey! The journey of the century, no less! But now that these entirely understandable concerns are behind us, the Genesis programme is going back to normal; I solemnly commit to that. And what's more, I make a three-fold commitment. If it's true that the boys and girls, who have been blessed by God, have a commitment to be happy, I myself have a triple commitment to make *you* happy, my dear viewers.

'First, *Coverage*: I will never take the participants off the air, so you never lose sight of them again.

'Second, *Transparency*: I will tell them everything that happens on Earth in real time, so that they receive all your kind messages without the slightest delay.

'Thirdly, *Assistance*: I will supply them remotely with any support they need, in the event that some little psychological crisis or other happens to take place in the future. On that subject, any participant who requests it may benefit from a private fifteen-minute consultation with me in the seventh habitat, which I have renamed the Rest House for the purpose. These consultations will be private, the first exception to my commitment to total *Coverage*; the second exception relates to the night-times, which will no doubt be torrid, and which will of course take place off camera, as privacy demands.'

Serena underlines her speech with a meaningful look. She's so ingenious – and such a liar. It's really to us that she's addressing these final words. By going back point by point over the three commitments I imposed on her – inspired by the Karmafone *Serenity* contract – she's telling us she has understood the deal and there will be no cheating. She doesn't really have a choice; one false step and Andrew and Harmony will publicise the screen captures of the Noah Report.

'To sum up, I wish our friends *very, very, very long lives* on Mars,' she concludes, hinting at the very words I used myself when the two of us were talking off camera. 'Those long, happy Martian lives will begin tomorrow, with the forming of the definitive couples and their descent to the base at New Eden, where they will be officially married. My dear young men and women, you have just one evening and one night left to think about your final rankings, before the publication of the final Heart Lists: tomorrow at 11am, like every Sunday!'

22. Reverse Shot

Fallout Bunker, Cape Canaveral Air Base
Saturday 9 December, 2:10pm

Serena McBee presses her manicured finger to the *OFF* button of the small control desk set into the round table in front of her armchair.

'There you go, those brats now have a few hours ahead of them to rack their little brains, to set up their final pathetic rankings . . . and we're going to make the most of that time, to act.'

'We?' says Arthur Montgomery.

He is the last of the allies of silence still in the fallout bunker. Sitting up straight in his chair, he looks more than ever like an expressionless wax model.

'Yes, *we*,' she says again. 'I've always known I could count on you, Arthur. What we have between us . . . is so strong.'

'I th-think so too,' stammers Arthur Montgomery.

His thin white moustache trembles imperceptibly. His blue eyes shine with the harsh beams of the halogen spotlights.

'The others took the first chance to run away,' Serena goes on. 'But not you – you're a man, not a wimp. You've hunted wild beasts all over Africa; you're able to look a lion straight in the eye without blinking. Whereas I, despite appearances, deep down I am just a weak and feeble woman.'

'Serena . . .'

'When I'm with you, Arthur, I can let my mask slip. I can tell you – and only you – how vulnerable I feel, how fragile. Imagine if one of our former allies were to decide to talk, to save his skin, trading in their testimony that will have me up in court, in exchange for immunity? The thought terrifies me. But what else could I do? How could I have held them back? They have all abandoned me, you saw it for yourself; all of them, except you.'

Serena's voice cracks. She buries her face in her hands and begins to sob.

'Oh God! I think I'm going to lose my mind!'

'Serena!'

The doctor gets up quickly, trembling under his Genesis jacket. His arms hang uselessly down at the sides of his stiff body. He doesn't know what to do now he's confronted with this woman falling apart (or appearing to, at least). He ends up putting his hand clumsily on the executive producer's shoulder, as she lies back prostrate in her armchair.

'Serena, my love . . . I beg you. Don't be scared. I'm here. I'll never let anyone hurt you. Those others who abandoned you, they're all traitors!'

Serena looks up at him, her face crumpled with distress – so far as the botox will allow, which in her case translates into a light creasing of the eyebrows.

'Traitors? You really think so?'

'Yes, vile traitors, who deserve to die! I'd strangle them with my own hands if I had the chance.'

Serena rearranges her hair with an elegant gesture. Her eyelids immediately stop trembling, like those of a dramatic actress recovering in the wings after her great monologue, and return to their usual sharpness.

'There might perhaps be a way of administering justice,' she says, taking a small box out of her handbag.

'The remote control for depressurising the Martian base?' says Dr Montgomery. 'I don't understand.'

'This is something different,' says Serena. 'This remote control was also given to me by Geronimo Blackbull, but it isn't connected to Mars.'

Serena runs her polished nail over the logo in the casing of the remote control. Beneath the little digital screen it says, RAPAX 5.

'One of the fighter drones you deployed to defend the Cape Canaveral base!' says Arthur Montgomery.

'Quite so. Except the drone that responds to this control hasn't been on the base for several days. I hid it in the cockpit of the private jet that Atlas put at my disposal, which brought me here from the Villa McBee. Why? Because my instinct told me to. And my instinct, my dear Arthur, never lets me down.'

'That's why you encouraged the traitors to run away on that jet!' exclaims Dr Montgomery, smoothing his moustache nervously.

Serena nods.

'And that's why I gave my revolver to Gordon Lock. When

the drone, which I'm operating remotely, shoots the pilot dead with a laser and the plane plummets into the sea, we will simply have to explain how the Genesis programme's technical director was overtaken by a severe attack of paranoia. Look at this . . .'

Serena taps on the control desk set into the table, calling up a window in the digital wall at the back of the bunker. It's the view from one of the base's surveillance cameras, framed to show a deserted runway.

14:12:45 reads the counter at the top of the window.

Serena presses *fast rewind*. The counter and the recorded images start racing backwards, until the Atlas jet reappears on the tarmac some fifteen minutes earlier, at *13:57:01*. Four small silhouettes appear suddenly on the screen, flattened by the low-angle shot. They run across to the jet, visibly in the grip of panic. Serena zooms in on the last of them: Gordon Lock, covered in sweat, his eyes bulging, brandishing the revolver in his fist. He pushes the others into the plane, throws one final glance behind him – a madman's glance – before disappearing inside himself. A few moments later, the jet takes off with a deafening racket.

'So tell me, Arthur, what have you just seen?' asks Serena, stopping the footage.

'What I've just seen? The allies of silence running away like rats, trying to escape justice?' ventures the doctor.

'No – come now – what you've just witnessed is the taking of hostages by a maniac capable of anything, even of killing a pilot mid-flight. Remember, you've just gone up to stretch your legs in the fresh air, you and the other instructors for the Genesis programme, while I remained behind in the bunker to wait for the restoration of the channel. That was when Gordon Lock sprang into action. He forced the others to board the plane, threatening them with his revolver – you alone managed to escape, and I of course don't know a thing about it because I was here in the bunker the whole time. That's what you'll have to say when the police question you.'

The doctor is fiddling with his moustache so furiously now that it's frizzing between his fingers.

'The story about the hostages is brilliant, and the images really are disturbing, but . . . there's one thing I don't understand: why would Gordon have done such a thing?'

Serena throws her head back with that little crystalline laugh only she can produce.

'Why?' she repeats, as though it were the funniest joke she'd ever heard. '*Why?* Oh, I haven't the faintest idea, my dear Arthur, and that couldn't matter less! Only novelists need to worry about credible motivations for their characters! In reality journalists will willingly do the job themselves. All you need to do is supply the journalists with facts, real or presumed. They'll invent what follows perfectly well, I can assure you. Don't deprive them of that pleasure.'

'Serena, you're a genius!' says Arthur Montgomery, his eyes sparkling with admiration.

'A genius?' she simpers. 'I just know one or two things about life, that's all, and in particular that pictures don't mean anything in themselves – they merely mean whatever we want them to mean. But enough of this chitchat. I'll unleash the drone attack when the jet is above the Caribbean, which should be soon enough. I'd really like it to disappear into the waves, so it's not too easy to recover the bodies or the black box. As for you, Arthur, it's time for you to go up to the surface to raise the alarm and bear witness to the madness that has overtaken Gordon Lock, whom you only managed to escape after a fierce struggle. Let me mess you up a bit, to make your story more believable.'

At this, Serena McBee gets up from her armchair and bounds catlike towards Arthur Montgomery. Her polished nails become claws that loosen his tie, yank out buttons from his shirt, scratching her lover's torso to a peak of excitement.

'Serena . . . Oh, Serena . . .' he pants.

She doesn't allow him time to say any more: she gives him an uppercut to the jaw, the stone of her signet ring acting as a knuckleduster. Then she plunges her long fingers into the doctor's white hair, messing up its perfectly neat parting, and grips his neck with her other hand, to stifle his protests with a ferocious kiss.

23. Off-screen

Interstate 80 West, State of New Jersey
Saturday 9 December, 3:15pm

'We now have confirmation: a private plane belonging to Atlas Capital, the firm known for their financial involvement in the Genesis programme, disappeared a quarter of an hour ago over the Caribbean, between Cuba and Nicaragua. Our air security expert, Ralph Bennet, joins us via link-up from Washington to tell us more . . .'

Above the car radio from which the crackling voice is emerging, through the tinted windscreen, stretch the kilometres of highway bordered with snow blackened by exhaust pipes. It is far away from the Caribbean, and the campervan is getting further every moment – it's heading due west, as indicated by the signposts punctuating the road: INTERSTATE 80 WEST.

Andrew Fisher takes his hand off the wheel to turn up the volume.

In the rear-view mirror, he briefly catches a glimpse of Harmony McBee. But she does not see him. Wedged into the passenger seat, she is paler than ever. Her wide eyes are fixed

122

on the strip of tarmac that races before her at a hundred kilometres an hour, and her nails are plunged into the stuffing of her seat. She is petrified. She has no experience of speed, having spent the first eighteen years of her life in a prison cell.

'*The jet was identified while it was still in American airspace,*' says the expert via the radio, his voice puffed up with excitement. '*It was travelling without authorisation, and its itinerary can be traced back to Cape Canaveral, where it would appear to have taken off at approximately fourteen-hundred hours.*'

'*And are we certain that it does indeed belong to Atlas?*' asks the presenter.

'*We sure are, Silvia. According to what we have learned, the ground log at Cape Canaveral has no record of any other aircraft of this kind. Beyond question, it's the plane put at Serena McBee's disposal by her employers, Atlas Capital.*'

'*But Ms McBee was not herself on board, right? Because she's still presenting the Genesis programme at this very moment.*'

'*Correct.*'

'*Who was on board this plane, that so mysteriously disappeared, then, Ralph? Who?*'

The expert mutters something in embarrassment.

'*At present I'm not able to answer that,*' he admits at last. '*All attempts by those on the ground to make contact with the plane, while it was still in flight, failed. Neither the American government nor the Cuban authorities seem to have received a reply from the pilot or the passengers. It's as if their radio weren't working . . . or they were refusing to communicate with anybody.*'

'*An equipment failure or a refusal to communicate? Those are two pretty different scenarios!*' The presenter lowers her voice, adopting a confidential tone. '*Just between us, Ralph, what do you think happened?*'

'*The fact that Atlas have not released a statement, and nor has the White House, doesn't exactly reassure me. This silence feels a lot like the kind that precedes a media storm, when the emergency communications committees gather before releasing some shock piece of information to the public. The sudden disappearance of the craft over the Caribbean leads us to fear the worst. Certainly it's the tail end of hurricane season in this region, so you could imagine there might have been an emergency landing on some isolated atoll in order to escape the poor weather conditions, but I don't really believe that. This whole thing smells like airline terrorism to me. Was this plane hijacked and headed towards some unknown destination in Latin America? Did the unfortunate hostages bravely attempt to retake control of the craft, but in vain, causing their deaths and that of their kidnappers? We can't say with any certainty just yet. Only time will tell.*'

'*Thank you, Ralph,*' the presenter concludes, gravely. '*We'll be staying in contact with you. Don't hesitate to let us know any time there's anything new to report, to keep our listeners up to date with the situation. For now, though, we travel to the other end of the solar system, where the twelve passengers on board the* Cupido *are getting ready to complete the final phase of their journey. Today, even more than usual, the Genesis programme is making news, and it's an opportunity for us to remind ourselves of the journey being undertaken by our twelve space heroes.*'

Andrew turns down the volume, as the car radio starts to spit out extracts from the soundtrack recorded on board the

Cupido, to remind listeners of the extraordinary adventure of the past five months.

'Who was on that plane, do you think?' asks Harmony, without taking her eyes off the road, as though she were the one driving and a second of inattention might send the vehicle flying off the road. 'Do you think there *were* hostages?'

'I have no idea,' replies Andrew. 'It's another mystery, and perhaps also another piece of the puzzle. But those twelve up there, who the radio are calling "space heroes", they're the ones who really *are* hostages. We're the only ones who know it. The only ones who can help them. Except a rescue mission for a craft at the far end of space is completely different than for a jet lost in the Caribbean, especially when nobody even suspects there's been a hijacking.'

Suddenly a tune strikes up in the cab.

Harmony sits up with a start.

'*Star Wars*: *Episode IV*?' she asks. '*A New Hope*?'

'Yes,' says Andrew, reaching for his ringing cellphone. 'A new hope . . . and a call I've been expecting for a long time. Hello, Cecilia, is that you? Did you get my message?'

'Andrew?' answers the panicked voice of a young woman, with a rolling Spanish accent. 'Yes, I just got your message. I was at work, my phone was switched off. What's going on? Are you –'

Andrew doesn't let her finish her question.

'I'll explain later. For now, you need to do what I say, to get yourself out of danger. You and the little one.'

'Out of danger? What do you mean?' In the background, a baby can be heard starting to cry. '*Madre de dios* – I'm listening, Andrew!'

'Leave at once; don't bother packing a suitcase. Only take with you what's absolutely necessary. Withdraw the maximum amount of cash you can from the first ATM you come to, because after that you'll have to avoid using your credit card so as not to be identified. You'll have to leave the country without going through an airport: checking in to a flight would be too dangerous. Do you know anyone who can get you out of the country by sea, secretly?'

Cecilia tries to hold firm, but Andrew's words only serve to increase her panic.

'Secretly? I'm a totally legal immigrant! I don't understand what you mean!'

'You are, but maybe you've got some friends who know the right networks, in the Cuban community in Miami? When Serena McBee comes to power, I can assure you, we're all of us going to become illegals, and worse, we'll be criminals sought after by every police force in the land. You have to trust me.'

The young woman's breathing wheezes from the handset.

'I might know someone,' she admits finally.

'Good. Contact that someone right away.'

'OK. But what about you, Andrew, where are you right now?'

'On the road,' replies the young man laconically.

'Are you also going to seek refuge abroad?'

'No, my family's here. I have to protect them. I think I can do it. I have information that could sink Serena McBee for ever. But I can't reveal it now, not without risking the lives of some people who are counting on me. Forgive me if I don't tell you any more. I'll stay in touch. Not by phone, as I imagine my number will be cut off soon. Set up a new anonymous email address, and write to me at sisyphus077@gmail.com. I swear to you, sooner or later justice will be done. And promise you'll stay strong, Cecilia.'

The handset wheezes again.

'I promise.'

Andrew hangs up

'Who was that?' asks Harmony.

'The widow of Ruben Rodriguez – the guy who ran the NASA animal store.'

'You didn't tell her I was with you,' replied the girl, her voice heavy with reproach.

'I'm not sure that would have reassured her, knowing that I'm travelling with the daughter of the woman who most likely ordered the murder of my father and her husband.'

Realising how upsetting these words might be, Andrew continues at once: 'No, OK, that wasn't what I meant! You're on our side! I mean, your mother tried to have you killed too!'

'Maybe,' says Harmony, eyes still fixed on the road. 'But you aren't telling me to flee the country to put myself out of danger.'

'How could you do that? You have no passport.'

'And no say in any of this? I'm just supposed to follow you and not ask any questions, the way I just obeyed my mother these last eighteen years? I don't even know where you're taking me.'

Andrew gives a slight cough.

'You're right. I can tell you. We're going to cross the whole country to Death Valley.'

'Death Valley? Isn't that where the Genesis participants did their year of training, before lift-off?'

'Yes. Also the place my father died.'

'I thought it was a desert.'

'Exactly. It's the last place anyone would think to look for us. Thousands of square miles of nothing, which I know like the back of my hand, having spent all last summer there. There's this one place, Dry Mountain, where I camped out for a whole month without seeing another soul. We'll be well sheltered there. And we won't be too far from my family. An anonymous Cuban immigrant might fear for her life, but Serena wouldn't dare to openly attack the wife and daughter of one of the directors of the Genesis programme. For now, they're relatively safe. At least that's what I want to believe with all my heart.'

The two passengers fall silent for a few moments.

The radio broadcast continues on low volume beneath the purring of the engine. The voices of the Genesis participants seem so terribly far away, so faint that it would take only the tiniest thing to silence them for ever.

'*The boys, the game, that whole thing, in a way it's just there to divide us,*' says Liz's voice, recorded five months earlier, right at the beginning of the journey. '*But what unites us today is stronger than what will try to separate us tomorrow. It's not the individual dancers who determine the quality of the performance, it's how well the whole* corps de ballet *coheres. We're sisters. Mars sisters. Let's never forget it. One for all . . .*'

The other five passengers pick up the chant in chorus, with a yell that crosses space and time, from the belly of the *Cupido* in the early summer right to the inside of the campervan on this December afternoon: '*. . . and all for one!*'

'I remember those girls,' says Harmony all of a sudden, curled up in her seat. 'I remember the afternoon when Mom invited them for tea at the villa. It was July, a month after their training started at Death Valley. They were glowing with happiness. They had such hopes. I was dazzled by their beauty, by their energy, by their . . . desire to live.'

The girl takes a deep breath.

'I'm ashamed to admit it, Andrew, but I was jealous. Jealous till it made me sick to the stomach, till I couldn't eat a single mouthful of the red-berry Bavarian cream that my mother had ordered in the shape of the planet Mars. Those six strangers represented everything I didn't have, everything I was not. You might think of them as orphans, children from deprived backgrounds, but they had already had so much life, while I was their age and had no memories apart from those I'd stolen from my novels. They were being promised a dazzling future, full of adventure, love and glory, while my own horizons went no further than the garden railings. I felt such injustice I wanted to scream. But I held my tongue, as usual. I smiled, I curtsied, I did everything my mom told me to do. *My mom, who I just heard in Balthazar's earpiece ordering him to kill me!*'

Harmony gulps painfully, as though she were struggling to swallow this appalling, unimaginable idea, a mother's murder of her own child. But she cannot erase her memories. She cannot forget what she has heard.

'I thought I was the most important person in the world to my mom,' she manages to say. 'I was convinced she would always do anything to protect me. I remember the way she made the participants swear not to reveal my existence to any journalists, explaining I was too precious, too fragile to bear the world's attention and the glare of the media. I could read the pity in the eyes of our guests as they nodded, and at the time that made me feel ill, too. It wounded my pride, that these deprived kids felt sorry for my poor little rich girl fortunes. When I watched them leave through the bars on my bedroom window, my thoughts were all poison, and secretly in my heart I cursed all six of them. And now, what's happening to them . . . They are surely going to die in twenty-two months, when the next Great Storm comes . . . and it's as if my curse were coming true. I'm the daughter of a murderer, you said so yourself. I'm just like my mom: her eyes, her chin, her cheekbones, her cruelty. I'm a monster, like her!'

Harmony's voice cracks.

Still clinging to her seat, she starts to tremble.

Once again Andrew lets go of the wheel, this time placing his hand over Harmony's.

'Don't talk nonsense,' he says. 'There's no curse. I also felt jealous and bitter when I saw the participants leaving. I also made myself ill. Why hadn't my father supported my candidacy? Why hadn't he favoured my childhood dream? These questions were eating away at me, but now I see he was doing it to protect me. And now it's our turn to protect them. We're their Survival Officers! Because they will survive, for as long as we threaten your mother with revealing the Noah Report screen caps! She's the only monster, for what she's done to the twelve of them, and for what she's done to *you*, Harmony.'

For the first time, Serena McBee's daughter dares to take her eyes off the road, to meet Andrew's in the rear-view mirror.

He stares at her from behind his black-framed glasses.

'I have a hunch you're an even more fascinating, more dangerous mystery than the Noah Report,' he says, his eyes alternating between the road and the girl he's talking to. 'Why did Serena McBee keep you in a cage like a precious bird for all these years, only to have you killed just like that? I'd like to get to the bottom of that one. An enigma to solve. I told you when I opened the door to your room, to your jail: I want the truth. The naked truth.'

Harmony shivers.

She pulls her hand back sharply from under Andrew's.

'Let go of me,' she says coldly.

Her voice is hard all of a sudden. Chilly and piercing like a shard of ice. And her water-green stare, in the rear-view mirror, chills him too.

Andrew hesitates, then finally brings his hand back to rest on the steering wheel.

'I just want to help you.'

'To help me, or unravel me like a mystery? Or solve me like an enigma?'

'It was just a m-manner of speaking . . .' stammers Andrew. 'I promised you we'd find your father.'

'Yes, you promised me that so I'd come out of my bedroom and guide you through the Villa McBee. We hardly know one another. What made you think you have the right to strip me bare? You think I'm a toy? A doll to dress and undress at will? In that case, you're no better than my mom and no better than . . .'

Harmony bites her lip to prevent one more word from coming out of her mouth. She lets the necklace of her locket slip between her fingers, as though it had suddenly become a convict's chain too heavy to lift.

'I'd rather do my searching on my own!' she says.

Andrew's jaw clenches; he grips the steering wheel harder. His cheeks flush red – shame? Anger? He no longer dares look in the rear-view mirror.

'My computer, on the parcel shelf,' he says quietly. 'I uploaded all the files I could access in Serena's study. You'll find her correspondence there, her emails, everything. Do your searching, Harmony. Have a rummage through that. And find it all on your own, your truth, if that's what you want!'

24. Reverse Shot

Editing Suite, Cape Canaveral Air Base
Saturday 9 December, 3:20pm

'Well? What do the security cameras show for the rear runway, where the jet took off? I've got a warrant from the F.B.I. to access all the tapes.'

'We're in the process of breaking down the footage to locate the period of the take-off, Inspector Garcia,' replies Samantha.

The protestors who a few hours earlier had stormed the editing suite have now been removed. A pack of tensely frowning men has replaced the colourful throng of Genesis fans. One of the older ones, with greying temples, is deep in conversation with Serena McBee's young assistant.

'Perfect,' he says. 'Let me know when the pictures are ready for viewing.'

'Leave it to me, Inspector Garcia.'

'While we wait, I'd like to request an interview with the witness, Arthur Montgomery. Is he in a position to talk?'

'He's in the infirmary, still in shock, but I think he'd be ready to talk to you. But your colleague has already been to question him anyway.'

'My colleague?' frowns Inspector Garcia.

'Yes, a gentleman from the C.I.A. He showed up about fifteen minutes ago. If you'd just like to follow me.'

A few moments later, the young woman and the inspector enter the white-tiled room where the Genesis programme's infirmary has been set up. The man in charge of the infirmary is there, but not in his capacity as a doctor: today he is the patient. Stretched out on the bed, Arthur Montgomery is looking totally dishevelled, his hair tousled, his jaw puffy, his shirt torn and blood on his chest. While a nurse bandages his wounds, a man in a black suit, seated at his bedside, is busily questioning him, Dictaphone in hand.

'Larry Garcia, F.B.I.!' announces the inspector, his voice piercing the room threateningly. 'This is a domestic security matter, which falls under the jurisdiction of the Bureau: we're leading on this investigation, kid, so don't even think about bypassing us!'

Click! – the man in the black suit pauses his Dictaphone and turns towards the newcomers. He's younger than the F.B.I. man by some thirty years; he has a triangle of fabric covering his right eye, a patch as black as his suit and his slicked-back hair.

'It *was* a domestic security matter,' he corrects the inspector calmly, seriously. 'But the plane disappeared over international waters. The C.I.A. is totally as justified as the F.B.I. in investigating its hijacking. I'm Agent Orion Seamus, by the way.'

He holds his hand out to the older man, who takes it grudgingly.

'Hijacking . . .' mutters Inspector Garcia. 'Seems to me you're being a bit hasty, young man. Jumping to conclusions prematurely. You're showing a troubling lack of process – just what I've come to expect from those C.I.A. hooligans, always sinking other people's investigations! You sure you wouldn't rather audition for the next *Pirates of the Caribbean* and leave me to handle the Caribbean accident on my own? For starters, who do you think could have hijacked the plane?'

By way of response, Agent Seamus turns to Dr Montgomery. 'Doctor, please . . .'

'Gordon Lock,' says the doctor, wincing as the nurse passes a piece of alcohol-soaked gauze over his wounds. 'It's Gordon Lock who stole the plane.'

Inspector Garcia's eyes widen.

'Gordon Lock?' he repeats, incredulous. 'The technical director of the programme? But why? And how?'

'It happened while the broadcast was paused. We came up to get some air – the five of us, four instructors and Director Lock. Some of us wanted to smoke, others just wanted to see a bit of daylight. Only Serena McBee stayed down in the bunker, to keep talking to the participants, to calm them down a bit before the broadcast resumed. She's so committed to her job, you know, always putting her duty before any personal enjoyment. She's taken those girls and boys under her wing, and she'd work herself to death rather than see any of them unhappy. Even though Gordon Lock insisted that she come up for a breath of fresh air with us, she wasn't having any of it; she stayed faithfully at her post.'

The nurse puts a bandage across Arthur Montgomery's

chest. Beneath his aristocratic moustache, his jaw tightens. It is evidently the pain that makes him clench his teeth – at least that's how it looks to the eyes of an outside observer like Inspector Garcia, who is drinking in the doctor's words like a man dying of thirst in the desert.

'You don't need to persuade me,' he says. 'I've been a great fan of Ms McBee since her talk show, *The Professor Serena McBee Consultation*, and needless to say I voted for the Green-McBee ticket in the recent elections. But let's get back to your testimony – you wanted to get a bit of air, the five of you came up to the surface, and . . .'

'. . . and it all happened very fast. No sooner had we reached the ground floor than Gordon Lock pulled a revolver from inside his jacket and ordered us to head along the corridor that leads to the rear airstrip, without passing the control room. We thought it was a joke at first, but he didn't seem to be finding it funny at all! The moment I realised it was serious, my heart skipped a beat, but doubtless all my experience hunting in Africa taught me to keep a cool head in situations like these. I jumped onto Lock to try to disarm him. But that devil of a man was worse than any wild animal I've ever had to face. I was just lucky he didn't shoot me at point blank range – maybe he was saving his bullets, or he didn't want a gunshot to attract attention. He punched me and grabbed hold of my shirt – I felt his nails sinking into my skin, the moment he lifted me off the floor and sent me flying along the corridor. I think I briefly lost consciousness. I almost certainly blacked out. I guess I'll have to book myself in for a cranial X-ray. Anyway, when I came to, the corridor was deserted. I ran out to the airstrip – but the plane was no longer there.'

Just as Inspector Garcia is about to unleash an avalanche of questions onto the witness, Samantha takes his arm.

'Excuse me, Inspector. I gather the images are ready. Have a look.'

She touches the screen set into the infirmary wall, beside the illuminated panels used for reading X-rays.

A static shot appears on the screen.

The runway . . .

The four silhouettes hurrying towards the plane . . .

The shape of Gordon Lock following them, waving his revolver like a madman . . .

'Sweet Jesus.' Inspector Garcia whistles, stunned. 'Three-quarters of the leaders of the Genesis programme, disappeared! The vice-president elect only barely escaping the attempt! Director Lock transformed into the worst kind of thug! What could have made him do it? Was he acting alone? I can't imagine that. He must have had accomplices. Has Serena McBee been kept up to date with this tragedy?'

'I don't think so,' says Arthur Montgomery. 'Her passion for her work has saved her. She's still down there in the bunker, watching over her protégés' well-being, coaching them before their great leap into the unknown . . .'

'. . . and she's got to keep doing it. The whole of America has its eyes glued to the Genesis channel just now – what am I saying, the whole world has! That gives us a bit of time to decide how to announce the news of this terrible, unexpected tragedy.'

The old F.B.I. inspector turns his wrinkled face towards his C.I.A. junior.

'You're right after all, Jack Sparrow. It no longer falls within my jurisdiction. Nor yours, by the way. It's up to the White House to decide now.'

25. Genesis Channel

Sunday 10 December, 3:32am

Wide shot on the girls' room, plunged into near-darkness.

It's the middle of the artificial night on board the *Cupido*, synched to the Eastern US time zone since the start of the journey, so that North American viewers can wake and sleep at the same time as the boys and girls on the spacecraft. But the channel doesn't stop broadcasting, since a good number of insomniacs watch even at night, not to mention the countless viewers at other longitudes where it is currently day.

Stretched out on the bunk beds, the girls' bodies can just be made out by the light of the safety lamp.

Close-up on Safia's sleeping face. Her curiously serene expression makes her look like a statue.

Cut.

Close-up on Alexei – the camera has now slipped into the boys' bedroom. Deep breathing raises the cashmere blanket that is attached to the mattress with velcro strips and stretched over his broad chest. His blond hair glows in the half-light like gold.

Cut.

The camera slips back to the girls' side, to focus on Fangfang's face – or rather, on her thin, catlike chin, because her eyes and forehead have disappeared under the velvet mask she wears every night to sleep.

Cut.

Close-up on Mozart. His sleep is uneasy. He tosses and turns against the pillow. His brown curls rise over the back of his neck, revealing the little ball implanted in his skin, whose metallic surface catches the gleam of the safety lamp.

Cut.

Close-up on Kirsten. She has untied her crown of hair for bed. Her long, blonde, wavy locks stretch around her like the waves of an unmoving sea.

Cut.

Close-up on Tao. His impressive body is so huge that his broad shoulders don't quite fit on the upper bunk. In contrast, his smooth, high-cheekboned face has something childlike about it.

Cut.

Close-up on Elizabeth. Even asleep she is supermodel beautiful, with her perfectly smooth jet-black hair, her long eyelashes at the end of her closed lids, and her perfectly proportioned face.

Cut.

Two heads appear in shot, and they couldn't be more different. To the right, the handsome face of Samson, who

140

looks sculpted out of obsidian; to the left, just beside him and resting on the same pillow, the fearsome mouth of Warden, the half-Doberman, half-gargoyle mongrel. The dog and his master have fallen asleep together.

Cut.

What appears on-screen next is not a face, but a mass of blonde hair: it's Kelly's, her face buried in her pillow.

Cut.

Close-up on Marcus. The upper part of his bare torso, just above the blanket, reveals another edge: that of the forest he's had tattooed onto his skin. His thick eyebrows frown slightly, and there's a faint crease across his broad forehead. It's impossible to know whether he's sleeping or thinking in silence, enigmatic as a sphinx.

Cut.

The frame is overwhelmed by a red wave. Even in the dusky light, Léonor's extraordinary hair sets the screen aflame. It catches the tiniest glimmer of light in its bright curls and distils it, transforming it into a flash of rubies. Léonor's naturally red lips are slightly parted, as though about to say a word, a word that is wrested out of sleep, but which never comes.

Cut.

The final pillow is empty.

In the place where Kenji is supposed to be, there is no one. The camera pulls back, hesitates, rotates around the room.

141

But there are only shadows and silence.

Cut.

The living room, on level two of the boys' quarters. Half-packed travel bags are lying around here and there. The boys started preparing them the night before, in anticipation of their departure, and left everything out when it was time for bed. No sound amid this chaos. No movement.

Cut.

The upper level. Kenji is here, in the gym. All he is wearing is a pair of sweatpants and a white bandana tied around his forehead like an ancient Japanese warrior. His shoulders and arms are better developed than one might have guessed, going by the wide, hooded kimonos he usually wears. It's possible to make out his muscles tensing under his skin as he performs a series of extremely slow, carefully choreographed moves, like a mysterious kind of t'ai-chi. But the strangest thing is not what he is wearing, or how he moves.

It's his eyes – frozen perfectly within their sockets, as empty as a statue's.

26. Shot

D +160 days, 21 h 45 mins.
[23rd week]

The revision tablet trembles slightly in my hands.

Although I did sleep last night – our final night on board the *Cupido* – I feel more shattered than ever. It's as if the stress that's built up over the last few days, when I alone suspected the horrific truth, doubting each one of my friends, was now landing on me all at once. We're all up to speed now, and all united against Serena: me, the other girls, the boys, Andrew and Harmony. But I'm still stressing out. Ever since I got up this morning, I've had a knot in my stomach stopping me eating even a crumb of our last meal in space. And now here I am, sitting with my tablet, alone once again, alone to decide on my final Heart List.

My face is reflected in the smooth glass surface, as I lean over it. I can see my pallor, the hollow bags under my eyes, the bruises left by the violent events of last night. But above all I see the names of the boys inlaid in my transparent skin as though engraved there.

23RD HEART LIST: RANK FROM 1 TO 6, it says at the head of the page.

For now, the names are arranged neutrally in alphabetical order, as they are for every Heart List. ALEXEI and KENJI appear over my forehead; SAMSON and TAO over my chin; and as for the two names in the middle . . . The six letters of MARCUS are spread across my eyes, those of MOZART are positioned over my mouth. Maybe because my eyes are burning to read the rest of the story on Marcus's tattooed body, and the melodies hummed by Mozart come to my lips when I think of him?

'Has everyone finished their rankings?' asks the sickly-sweet voice of Serena McBee, coming from the panoramic screen in the living room. 'It's 11:15. You've had fifteen minutes to input your choices, which you'd already been considering carefully for a long time, I'm sure. The moment has come to compile your final Heart Lists!'

Go on, Léonor.

Play the game.

Because that's what survival is all about.

I touch the name ALEXEI, Prince Charming to my darling Kris, the boy who in the Visiting Room yesterday looked at me with such revulsion and talked about my 'disgusting disease'. The number 6 appears beside his name, which automatically positions itself at the bottom of the screen.

Next I touch the name TAO. Not that I don't think he's great. On the contrary, the boy's a total sweetheart who would always go out of his way to help others, and the discovery of his disability has made him even braver in my eyes. But he seems to be truly in love with Fangfang, and she'll need to get support from that love in the coming months.

For the same reason, I rank SAMSON at number 4. The handsome green-eyed Nigerian has been bound to Safia since the start of our journey – I'm hardly going to take him away from her, having come so close to taking her life!

With the tip of my index finger, I allocate KENJI to position 3. The youngest in the team isn't spoken for by anyone, as far as I know; nobody will object to my putting him in third place on my personal podium.

The two final names remain . . .

MARCUS and MOZART . . .

My eyes and my mouth . . .

If I could keep just one of these organs, which would it be?

Without my mouth, I would never again be able to speak, taste, kiss.

But without my eyes I'd never see the world again, never be able to draw it – I'd be in eternal night, as though I were already dead.

It's Marcus I've chosen deep in my heart, why deny that? Even if he voted to turn the ship around, he's the one I want to put at the top of my Heart List. Him, and no one else!

Without hesitating a moment longer, I touch the two final names, one after another. A small number 2 appears beside MOZART, and a small number 1 beside MARCUS.

A button appears on the screen: CONFIRM YOUR RANKINGS?

I press so hard I could break the glass of the tablet – but no, it holds, and the names of the six boys disappear, swallowed into the bowels of the software that will determine the final couples.

Only now do I look up from the screen.

The other girls are all there, staring at me, their tablets on their knees. They've already published their own final Heart Lists, a moment ago, but they allowed me to do mine in silence, without disturbing me, offering me the only gift they possess – and, in fact, the most precious of all: *time*.

'So is that it?' asks Kelly, with a little smile. 'Has the Determinator made her final choice? What rule did it choose to follow this time?'

The Canadian is referring to my psychorigid side, the rule I set for myself to meet each of the boys in turn over almost the whole journey and which I know seems totally pathetic in hindsight.

'Give me a break. Don't laugh at me, please. We've all done our share of dumb things in our lives.'

'I'm not laughing at you at all!' says Kelly. 'On the contrary, I love your dictatorial side!'

'Dictatorial?'

'Like, the way I'm always dictating commitments to myself and the others. You do it so well, I think it's amazing!'

Kelly gives me a wink. She really shouldn't say another word, shouldn't say too much in front of the viewers. In any case, she doesn't need to: the other girls have all understood what she's referring to.

I sense from the way they're smiling at me that the commitments we've imposed on Serena do reassure them. Their gratitude warms my heart. I hope I truly deserve it.

'Well, there we are!' Serena McBee's voice cuts into my thoughts, six minutes after I sent my Heart List into the system.

She's here in front of us once again, in the living room, via the panoramic screen opposite the fireplace.

'All the rankings have been transmitted to Earth by laser,' she says. 'Our computers have used an algorithm to combine everything, the boys' Heart Lists as well as the girls', in order to establish the final couples. My dear boys, my dear girls, if you only knew how moved I am by all this today.'

Serena's voice pauses mid-phrase, apparently cracking in the intensity of the moment. Her chest rises with the rhythm of her hurried breathing, beneath her elegant suit pierced by her bee-shaped brooch. Her eyes go moist right on cue, like a jet of water cleaning a windscreen. This woman is a deception machine, yes, a deadly machine. The way she feigns emotion, good will, it's perfect – a mother leading her daughter to the altar would look exactly like that. If any further proof were needed of Serena McBee's gift for manipulation, this would be it. An icy chill runs up my spine. Even though I know we hold the advantage over her right now, even though I know we have two Survival Officers on Earth who could bring her down at any moment, I can't help being afraid.

A pre-recorded drum-roll sounds in the living room, as thunderous as a breaking storm.

I feel a hand closing on mine.

It's Kris's, just like on the day of the lift-off ceremony that feels so long ago, just like each week when the successive rankings have been announced on board the craft. She's here at my side, my Kris – so pure, so angelic – and yet her innocence has been stolen from her and she will never get it back. The fairy-tale she hoped for so fervently has become a horror story.

How long will she survive, once she's down on Mars? Will her ice prince be able to bring her the happiness she deserves, even if it's only for a moment . . . ?

A double image appears on the screen, replacing Serena's face: on the left, the rankings made by the girls; on the right, those by the boys.

Fangfang (SGP)	Kelly (CAN)	Elizabeth (GBR)	Safia (IND)	Kirsten (DEU)	Léonor (FRA)
1. Tao	1. Kenji	1. Mozart	1. Samson	1. Alexei	1. Marcus
2. Mozart	2. Samson	2. Marcus	2. Mozart	2. Tao	2. Mozart
3. Marcus	3. Marcus	3. Samson	3. Marcus	3. Samson	3. Kenji
4. Samson	4. Tao	4. Tao	4. Kenji	4. Kenji	4. Samson
5. Kenji	5. Alexei	5. Alexei	5. Tao	5. Mozart	5. Tao
6. Alexei	6. Mozart	6. Kenji	6. Alexei	6. Marcus	6. Alexei

Tao (CHN)	Alexei (RUS)	Mozart (BRA)	Kenji (JPN)	Samson (NGA)	Marcus (USA)
1. Fangfang	1. Kirsten	1. Léonor	1. Léonor	1. Safia	1. Léonor
2. Léonor	2. Elizabeth	2. Elizabeth	2. Kirsten	2. Léonor	2. Kelly
3. Safia	3. Safia	3. Kirsten	3. Kelly	3. Kirsten	3. Safia
4. Kelly	4. Kelly	4. Safia	4. Fangfang	4. Kelly	4. Kirsten
5. Kirsten	5. Fanggang	5. Fangfang	5. Safia	5. Fangfang	5. Fangfang
6. Elizabeth	6. Léonor	6. Kelly	6. Elizabeth	6. Elizabeth	6. Elizabeth

I have a huge feeling of relief, as if a hundred-kilo weight has been lifted off my chest. My fears were unfounded: even though he did choose to turn back yesterday, Marcus kept me as his number one! Two participants, meanwhile, have collapsed in the rankings since last time, and the spectators must surely be wondering why. Alexei, the young man in first place ever since the start of the journey, is now floundering at the bottom of the rankings, and I have an idea that the way he violently laid into me in the Visiting Room is something to do with it. The same goes for Elizabeth, who managed the feat of being second on every Heart List last week: she's now the least well-scored of all, presumably because she stole my sketching tablet, which she admitted in front of the whole crew. Beside the joy of having been chosen by Marcus, beyond the fierce will to survive once on Mars, I feel a strange impression taking shape within me – of having a kind of debt towards two other human beings among the eleven who should all be my indestructible allies. *Note to self: remember to set my ego aside and make some kind of gesture towards them as soon as possible, so we can make up. It's really so dumb staying angry.*

I don't have a chance to think any more about it, as Serena's voiceover resumes.

'*We can now see the results from the algorithm that has determined the final couples,*' she announces. '*The system has also totalled up the Dowries collected by the members of each couple over the course of the journey thanks to your generous donations. Ladies, gentlemen, it is my pleasure and honour to introduce you to . . . the first couples on Mars!*'

The two tables merge to form a third which, thanks to the Genesis software, is arranged as a list of couples, ranked 1 to 6 according to their earnings.

Couple	Him	Her	Combined Dowry	% of Total
1	Alexei (RUS) $202,403,002	Kirsten (DEU) $378,596,876	$580,999,878	25%
2	Marcus (USA) $199,009,876	Léonor (FRA) $205,908,543	$404,918,419	18%
3	Mozart (BRA) $179,567,098	Elizabeth (GBR) $223,789,065	$403,356,163	18%
4	Samson (NGA) $152,568,093	Safia (IND) $172,456,890	$325,024,983	14%
5	Tao (CHN) $188,567,890	Fangfang (SGP) $134,567,900	$323,135,790	14%
6	Kenji (JPN) $79,098,567	Kelly (CAN) $155,678,097	$234,776,664	10%

Once again, I feel Kris's hand take mine. 'Marcus and you, Alexei and me, just as we've always dreamed,' she whispers in my ear, her voice trembling. Her face is radiant with joy beneath her crown of blonde tresses. At this moment I can see, I can feel, she is utterly fulfilled – as if the trap of the Genesis programme, our deal with Serena McBee, none of that existed. I'm surprised to notice my own smile is just as unforced. I'm no longer playing a game. I'm really me. Truly.

Yes, I'm on the edge of the abyss, about to fall six thousand kilometres onto a red hell from which I will never return, and yet I do feel it's the happiest day of my life!

'Aren't they glorious, our space fiancés?' cries Serena McBee, bringing me back harshly to the reality of the broadcast. 'Aren't they magnificent? Aren't they worth their weight in gold?

Over the past five months, you have sent them more than two billion dollars – two billion, two hundred and sixty-nine million, four hundred and fourteen thousand, eight hundred and ninety-seven dollars and ten cents, to be exact. An amount which – I might remind you – will make it possible for Atlas to recoup all its initial costs of buying the equipment from NASA and so contributing to the conquest of Mars!

'On the girls' side, the overall champion is the adorable Kirsten, whose incredibly impressive Dowry has just been added to that of Alexei – himself also the wealthiest (by just a smidgen) on the boys' side. Between them they have one quarter of the gifts, with which to rule the auction that will take place once on Mars for purchasing the equipment for New Eden! Two couples follow them with eighteen per cent of the total apiece: Marcus and Léonor, with Mozart and Elizabeth hot on their heels. Samson and Safia are likewise almost exactly neck and neck with Tao and Fangfang, each couple holding fourteen per cent of the total sum. Far down in last place, Kenji and Kelly have ended up with a ten per cent share, suffering from our youngest crew member's somewhat subdued performance as far as fundraising is concerned.'

There is a popping sound behind me; I turn to see Kelly who has just burst her bubble gum.

'Don't worry about it, Serena,' she says. 'I've always thought Kenji was adorable, with his antisocial side and the wildcat look in his eyes. And as for being skint, I'm used to that. *I'm not the kind of girl who'd kill her whole family just for money.*'

My heart skips a beat. Ever since we went back on the air, hot-headed Kelly has been playing with fire. The provocation is obvious in the way she speaks these last words. Is she already starting to crack up, ready to throw everything away in the heat of the moment?

No, her face is hard and determined, totally controlled. Her dig was aimed at Serena, and only her. The viewers could have no way of knowing – Kelly's well aware of that, otherwise she never would have allowed herself to make it.

'I'm just like you, an incorrigible romantic,' she concludes with an irony only we can detect. 'The most important thing for both of us is love.'

While that irony of Kelly's travels across time and space, Serena continues to remind the viewers what will happen next in the programme. For several minutes, she shows the on-screen views of the Mars station, and describes the final steps that need to be taken to reach it.

'The *Cupido* is currently in orbit around Mars, following the trajectory of Phobos, which completes seven-hour-and-thirty-minute cycles of the planet. According to the data I've been receiving from the control room, the next window for uncoupling to land in the canyon of the Valles Marineris, where the New Eden base is set up, will take place at 6pm Eastern time. The moment is approaching for our fiancés to finish packing their bags, to put back on the suits they wore five months ago for the take-off, to get back into the capsules and to . . .'

Serena's voice stops abruptly.

Her face freezes, still as a statue – she's still smiling, but it's an ambiguous smile, revealing slightly too much of her gums.

She's just heard Kelly's reply, I'd bet, after the three minutes' delay, and it took another three for her reply to return to us.

'. . . take the great leap into their new world,' she manages to say in a single breath.

Her features are moving again and her pupils dilating slightly, as she leans towards the camera – towards us.

'Yes, Kelly, you're absolutely correct,' she says in an unctuous voice. 'Love is the most important thing of all to me. And I do love you, all twelve of you, as if you were my own little ones. What a wrench it'll be, watching you flying off towards your glorious destiny, even if I know that the next logical step in the programme is the fulfilling of your dearest dream. Because once you're at the bottom of Mars's gravitational well, nothing will ever be able to bring you back to Earth again.'

27. Off-screen

'Nothing, nothing, nothing! I can't find a single thing!'

Harmony McBee's face is lit up by the screen of the computer she is holding on her lap. Outside, beyond the windows of the campervan that is still continuing on its route west, the end of the day is so dark, so blurry with the snow, that all the cars on the road have their headlights on.

'I've been combing through these emails since yesterday, all night and all day long!' she groans. 'All I can find are lists of supplies for the Villa McBee, orders for bee-keeping equipment, staff salary records and, most of all, emails supporting her candidacy for the presidential election: hundreds, thousands of them. But nothing about my father. Nothing about me. Not a line. Not a word. It's as though I didn't exist.'

She sighs, desperate.

'I can't believe my mother knows all these people who are writing to her, while I can count everyone I know on the fingers of two hands.'

'You have your whole life ahead of you to get to know

154

the world,' says Andrew, who looks just as pale and tired as Harmony does. 'But you'll need to allow the world to get to know you, too.'

His voice is somewhat distant. He is still wounded by the way Harmony put him in his place the night before. But she's too absorbed in the emails scrolling up the screen to notice.

'*It was an honour to perform the Genesis programme anthem, and I'd be delighted to sing the national anthem on the day of your inauguration – as I'm sure you're going to be elected with flying colours!*' she reads aloud. 'It's signed Jimmy Giant.

'*Here at our company we congratulate ourselves daily for having invested in handsome young Marcus, as a diamond sponsor: our sales of frozen "astronaut meal" specials have gone through the roof, and I should tell you we even ran an internal campaign to get all our employees to vote for you!* Signed: Henry K. Delville, CEO of Eden Food International.

'*Dear Ms McBee, in anticipation of your being confirmed vice-president, we are pleased to inform you that you have already been selected as Person of the Year by our magazine.* Signed by the *Time* magazine editorial board.

'There are so many important people who're convinced Mom is a saint. Who's going to believe us when the time comes for us to speak and reveal the truth? Who?'

'Stop torturing yourself, Harmony,' says Andrew, his voice gentler now. 'You should get some rest. You haven't shut your eyes since we left! Look, I'm going to stop at the next gas station, the tank is almost empty. And I need to sleep a bit too.'

He points through the windscreen at a light on the side of the road.

'We'll get a hot drink. And I'll make the most of the stop to run search software on your mother's files to see if your name appears anywhere.'

She isn't listening. It's as though she's on automatic pilot, obsessing over the emails as she continues to scroll through them, unable to take her eyes off the screen. Under the fine skin of her temples, a network of blue veins throbs to the rhythm of her increasingly frantic litany.

'*It's our honour to inform you that thanks to your efforts at bringing peoples together by means of wholesome entertainment, you have been shortlisted for the next Nobel Peace Prize.* Signed: the Nobel committee.

'*If you are elected, may your term of office begin an era of hope and prosperity for the United States of America and the whole world. In the meantime, Cardinal Giacomo would be happy to represent the Catholic Church at the ecumenical marriage ceremony.* Signed: The Holy See.'

'Harmony? Harmony, can you even hear me? Do you feel OK?' Andrew is seriously worried now. 'Listen, you've really got to turn that laptop off and get your strength back. Look, this is the exit. I'm going to park.'

He turns the wheel to pull the van off the highway, races for the first parking spot, and brakes the vehicle with a great crunch of anti-snow salt.

'Let it go, Harmony,' he says, taking the laptop from her hands and putting it down on the dashboard.

He turns on the roof light.

A harsh yellow glow strikes Harmony's distraught face.

'You're really shivering! And you're so pale! What's the

matter? Is it just exhaustion?'

'No, withdrawal . . .' she stammers.

Andrew frowns.

'Yesterday when I showed up at the door of your room!' He suddenly remembers. 'You asked me if I'd brought your hit. You're . . . on drugs? What are you on? Answer me, Harmony – what?'

The girl's fine eyebrows rise and fall, over and over. Her eyelids with their long transparent lashes blink involuntarily, and her eyes roll back. Her whole body is trembling now, making her locket roll back and forth across her chest, like a pendulum out of control.

She finds the strength to answer him. 'Zero-G.'

'No! That's the worst of all!'

Andrew himself is starting to tremble, out of sheer panic. This young man with such a gift for machines and codes finds himself totally helpless when faced with a girl on the edge of an abyss.

'What should I do? Should I call the emergency services?'

'We shouldn't . . . show ourselves . . . said so yourself . . . just need a sleeping pill . . .'

With trembling hands, Harmony extracts several pills from the pocket of her dress and slips them between her lips. Her breathing speeds up. Her nostrils open and close like the gills of a fish suffocating out of water. A trickle of blood starts to flow from each of them.

'Harmony!'

'I'm cold . . .'

The driver quickly twists round in his seat, to grab the rug that's lying on the back seat among the technological gadgets that litter the campervan.

He wraps Harmony's trembling body, as she continues to stammer.

'It'll pass . . . it really will . . . it's not a real withdrawal crisis, just a brief moment of weakness . . . it's happened before . . . in this condition, sleeping pills still work . . . they'll take effect soon . . .'

Her words are getting further and further apart, leaving long silences between each scrap of a sentence.

'. . . keep driving, please, don't stop too long . . .

'I want to be as far as possible from my mother when the crises really kick in . . .

'I want to be at the other end of the world when I beg you to bring me to her to ask for money . . .'

She breathes two more words – '. . . keep driving . . .' – then closes her eyes.

Bit by bit, her trembling stops.

Her eyebrows stop their rise and fall.

Her breathing recovers its rhythm, becomes that of someone who is sinking into sleep, totally defeated.

Andrew sits still for a moment, distraught. He watches his passenger's sleeping face, above the thick blanket. She looks more than ever like a porcelain doll. He takes a handkerchief out of his pocket, and with a hesitant hand wipes away the two strands of still-fresh blood that are dripping onto her diaphanous lips.

He restarts the ignition with infinite delicacy, as though the key were made of glass, and touches the accelerator gently with the tip of his toes, to slide the campervan over to the nearest gas pump.

Without making a sound, he opens the door and fills the tank, barely taking his eyes off the girl dozing behind the windscreen.

'I'll take you to the end of the world, Harmony, I promise you,' he murmurs. 'And my own sleep can wait a few hours more.'

He heads over to the little neon-lit gas station, and pushes open the glass door, setting off an electric bell.

'Pump number five,' he says, taking a coffee cup from the self-service counter and filling it to the brim. 'And a coffee. I'll give you cash.'

But the cashier isn't paying him the slightest attention.

Nor are any of the three customers dotted around the aisles of the little minimarket.

All four have their eyes glued to the big TV screen hanging above the counter.

'News just in!' yells an overexcited reporter, positioned in the snow-filled gardens of the White House. 'The identities of the passengers on the plane that disappeared in the Caribbean yesterday at approximately 3pm have just been confirmed by Washington! They were a pilot from Atlas Capital plus four of the most distinguished team members of the famous Genesis programme! Gordon Lock, Odette Stuart-Smith, Geronimo Blackbull and Archibald Dragovic are reported missing. They most likely died when . . .'

Andrew lets go of his boiling-hot cup, which hits the floor in a great brown splash.

28. Shot

D +161 days, 02 h 35 mins.
[23rd week]

'My biggest regret is that I can't take this wonderful thing with me.'

Kris contemplates the screen that's set above the bunk we've shared these past five months. It's showing a picture that looks like her, like a reflection of her in a magical world where she is omnipotent, with the power even to break spells, to banish curses. It's the digital portrait I made for her nineteenth birthday. I portrayed her as an ice princess, a real fairy-tale character, or someone out of one of those novels she likes so much.

'It's just a digital file, Kris,' I say. 'You can upload it onto one of the screens in your new home once we're down there. I could even do a portrait of Alexei in the same colours, the same shades, if you like. That way you'll be immortalised together, the prince and princess of ice, the best-looking couple on Mars.'

Immortalised . . . I'm well aware it's a lie, because digital pictures are no more than a heap of data that can be erased with a click, and because what's waiting for us down there is anything but immortality.

'Maybe I could even do a *real* portrait of you both,' I add hurriedly, to disguise my unease. 'I learned to draw on a screen, and that's always been enough for me up to now. But ever since I've been using the Rosier make-up, all those lipsticks, those shadows and powders – all that stuff – I've wanted to have real sheets of real paper, too. Like artists used to, back in the day. To feel the colour spread, to feel it physically, not only in two dimensions, but with all its thickness. Does that make any sense?'

Kris stops removing the last outfits from her closet for a moment, and looks at me.

'Yes, I understand what you mean,' she says. 'At least, I think so.'

She smiles.

'It's sweet of you, saying that about Alex, that you'd like to do his portrait and all that. He's sometimes a bit direct when he talks, but it's because he's so passionate. He's good deep down, you know that.'

'Yes, I know,' I say, understanding that she's referring to an episode the viewers are unaware of, my argument with Alexei when we were off the air.

'I think he's lived through some things in his life that weren't easy. That gang he hung around with for two years in Moscow, before submitting his application . . .'

'I thought they were idealists, dreamers. Isn't that what he told us, each of us, when we first met him in the Visiting Room? The whole story of modern-day knights going off

161

to seek adventure in the urban jungle – don't say he never told you?'

Kris looks up from her things again, to fix her eyes on mine. They are filled with tenderness and goodness.

'Yes, that's what he said,' she murmurs. 'He might have softened the reality a little. But it's all in the past, all that. Whatever his wounds, I'll help him to bandage them, with all my love.'

Alexei's angry words, yesterday in the Visiting Room, come into my mind. Summoning up his past, it was no longer a question of knights and noble causes, but punches, sacrifices and the foul taste of blood in the mouth.

'You chose him, and that's enough for me,' I say. 'All that matters, for me, is that you're happy with him.'

Happy . . . Another word that rings so totally false in my ears.

But Kris doesn't lose that optimistic smile, a smile that could disarm an entire regiment. She really is a great actress, much better than me. Because she is mainly smiling for the cameras, isn't she? Or is she really managing to relish this moment, the delicious eagerness of a bride-to-be getting ready to marry the boy she loves, as if the rest of the world didn't exist, as though the future really was going to be brilliant? Either way, I think she's amazing.

As for me, I find it hard to tear my thoughts away from Andrew Fisher and Harmony McBee. Where might they be now? How long will they manage to stay free? Can we really trust the secret daughter of the woman who has condemned us all? My gut keeps telling me, yes, because Harmony has a secret of her own, a suffering that echoes our own destinies.

Kris lays her final dress in her bag gracefully, as though none of these questions mattered to her.

'I must confess, I was just about starting to get fed up of cooking with only Eden Food preserves,' she says. 'Apparently, down there in the greenhouse on the base, the machinery they've sent down before us has managed to grow cereals and fruit. Guess what – there are even apples! I'm finally going to be able to make my famous strudel – I can't wait for you to taste it!'

She removes the picture she Velcroed to her closet door at the start of the journey, Botticelli's *Virgin with Child*. And now her locker is empty, as bare as the first day. It makes me shiver to see it, this corner of our craft depersonalised, anonymous, just as it was when we first came on board . . . as it will be when it turns around without us, to head back to Earth.

'I'm all done,' says Kris. 'Want me to help you sort out your things?'

She delicately takes hold of the tatters of my red chiffon dress, which I removed yesterday in order to put on my undersuit, that black figure-hugging second skin that covers me completely – including the Salamander.

'I'll mend this dress for you, I promise,' she says. 'You're a master of design, but it turns out I've got pretty nimble fingers for sewing.'

'I'm the one who's going to be condemned to mending the socks and underwear of the whole of New Eden, given the way our Dowries have turned out!' cries Kelly, who's walking past dragging her bag behind her.

She's just crammed her entire multi-coloured wardrobe and dozens of pieces of costume jewellery together into a big ball, so it's not surprising she is first to be ready. It's funny seeing her in the undersuit again, just her bleached hair standing out against the black material. It's like looking at a surfer in the middle of the ocean, paddling up against the current.

'It's me, the Oliver Twist of the cosmos,' she says, making a begging-bowl shape with the hollows of her palms. 'My guy and me, we're really gonna be on the streets. Please, fine ladies, spare a coin or two, out of the kindness of your hearts. Just a million or two so we can take part in the auction and have a roof to crash under tonight.'

There are people who try to resist the tides of destiny, beating back against the waves, but Kelly manages to make do with mischievous little jokes.

Her performance does get a smile out of me. Even Fangfang herself can't help burst out laughing at the clowning around of the girl who has so often set her nerves on edge. Kelly's morale really is unbreakable. This is the girl who only yesterday wanted us to turn around, and now she's getting overexcited at the idea of completing the mission for which she's been trained. The fact that we're active at last, after all this waiting, does her a world of good – and it's infectious! Her energy warms my heart, just like Kris's smile does.

Half an hour later, the airlock that leads to the space capsule creaks open in the floor of the bedroom. The six customised seats, made according to our measurements, are waiting for us. We lower our bags into the hold as carefully as though they were filled with crystal glasses – they contain all our souvenirs of our lives before, those fragments of Earth we want to take with us to our new world. As we pack in the last bag, all the screens in the bedroom which had previously been deserted come on at once. It isn't Serena, nor any of the other organisers, but a view of the surface of Mars, filmed from the camera affixed to the top of the *Cupido*. The vast red planet turns slowly, and with it the long gash of the canyon of Valles Marineris, our destination. Large digital numbers are flashing at the top of the screens, like the countdown that preceded our departure five months ago, on the launch platform at Cape Canaveral.

D -75 mins.

'Hey, girls,' asks Safia with a tiny note of concern. 'Is it just me, or is the Valles Marineris getting further away?'

'You're right, hon,' says Kelly.

'But I don't understand. Just when we're supposed to be about to land there . . .'

'Because you thought we were just going to drop down there in freefall, like a bungee jump? You're in such a hurry to meet your Samson? Oh, those hormones, when they get going!'

Safia's cheeks flush – how nice to see her getting some colour back in her face!

'We'll be going down to Mars, *deorbiting*,' explains Kelly. 'Don't look at me like that! It's not a dirty word! Just look at this . . .'

She holds up her revision tablet, on which she has been doing her pilot practice for months.

'You remember this diagram, which we saw during our training in Death Valley? Or have five months of speed-dating cleared your brains out once and for all? OK then, *whoosh*, revision session!

'*One*, deorbiting. The capsules detach from the *Cupido* and the orbit of Phobos to spiral down into Mars's gravitational well, for a period of two hours, during which time you'll be able to enjoy uninterrupted views of our new neighbourhood.

'*Two*, atmospheric re-entry. We slide over the thin atmosphere of Mars to start our braking, a bit like a curling stone on the ice – and we pray hard that the capsules' heat shields withstand the impact so we don't end up as popcorn.

'*Three*, landing. OK, now it gets really technical . . . At twenty kilometres above the ground, a hypersonic balloon will inflate beneath the capsule for a hell of a deceleration, a kind of giant airbag. At ten kilometres above the ground, the parachute will deploy; finally, just a few metres before our arrival, the retrorockets will give a final burst of juice to reduce our speed to zero or close to it. And there we are, at the Valles Marineris! And who can tell me what will happen to the *Cupido*? Safia? Kris?'

It's Fangfang, the good student, who raises her hand in a Pavlovian response. She replies without pausing for breath.

'I know: the *Cupido* will do a circuit of Mars and switch to automatic pilot for the voyage back to Earth where it will pick up a new team of astronauts for season two of the Genesis programme.'

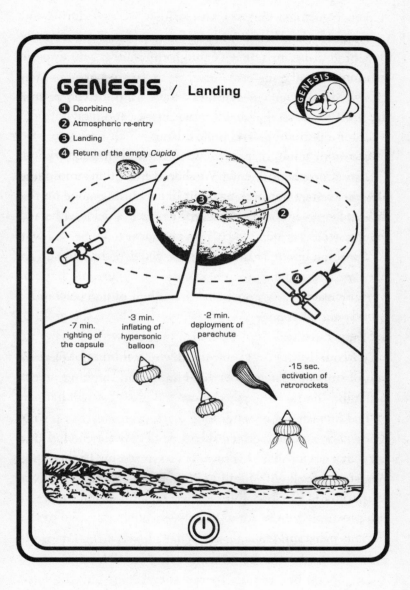

'Correct, gold star for you,' says Kelly.

Then she claps her hands, playing teacher all the way.

'Come along, girls, that's enough chitchat! It's time to put on our suits and transform ourselves back into Michelin Men. I know, it's not very pleasant. But there's a positive side to it all: it makes us all the same on the scales, even Liz!'

The English girl gives a hollow laugh.

We're all tense, of course, but Liz more than any of us. It wasn't just the boys who lowered her in their rankings after her scheming was revealed: the girls have got something against her now too, she must sense it. But I've decided I'm not going to hold a grudge, and it's now or never to let her know it.

'Spacesuit or not, I can't wait to see you dance on the surface of Mars!' I say, giving her a big smile.

Her closed expression, beneath her hair pulled back into a bun, opens all at once.

'You . . . really?'

'Of course. And . . . I want to ask you something. What are you planning to dance? Not that I understand anything about ballet, but I'd be curious to know.'

The English girl bats her long black eyelashes, but it's not a pose, not a studied effect: she's just deeply touched, and so am I. 'It's not a ballet,' Liz says. 'It's a symphony. The one Neil Armstrong took with him in 1969 on the Apollo 11 mission to the Moon. I've loaded it onto my tablet. I wanted . . . to be the first to dance the *New World Symphony*.'

'The *New World Symphony*? What a lovely title! I'd love to draw you while you're performing it, if you'll let me.'

Liz opens her mouth to say something, but she's too

overwhelmed, and the words don't come.

Then she catches me by surprise, taking me in her arms.

I can feel her head resting on my red curls, her hot tears on my neck. And I can see my own on her long jet-black hair.

My throat is too tight to speak; all I have is the misted-up look in my eye to tell the other girls to come closer: *if I'm forgiving her, you can forgive her too.*

D -59 mins.

It's all done; with some contortions we've finally managed to get our kit back on. The kilos of my spacesuit seem to have turned into tonnes. I've just gotten used to living in light clothing, in low gravity, over the last five months. And besides, this time we also need to lug around not just the suit but a unit for extra-vehicular survival, a kind of large backpack full of cryogenised oxygen, that should allow us to survive when we set foot outside the capsule. In short, at the moment of our descent to Mars, it's as if we are weighted with lead to be totally sure we make it right down to the bottom and never come back. But I couldn't care less. Liz's sisterly hug has lifted a weight off me that was heavier than any spacesuit in the world.

Because it's only together, united, that we'll be able to survive on Mars.

D -37 mins.

We're now crammed into our seats, our bloated bodies wedged as firmly as eggs in a box. Kelly, Safia and Liz are up in the

169

front row, as they were for take-off, and the other three of us are in the second. Louve is installed in her own little seat, her worried black eyes blinking over the muzzle that Kris has tied around her neck. The slow rotation of the planet Mars continues beyond the capsule's reinforced windshield, and on the transmission monitor the countdown continues.

'All good. I've established contact with the control room,' says Safia, our Communications Officer. She adjusts the headphones over her ears. 'But wait, they're telling me Roberto Salvatore is unavailable.'

'He's too stuffed with one of his carbonaras?' grumbles Kelly. 'No great loss.'

We're all well aware that Roberto actually ran away when the programme started to derail; Serena admitted that to me when I discovered the Noah Report. Right now, she must be too busy plotting the next way to screw us, alongside Director Lock and the four remaining instructors. They don't have time to get back on the air, and it's for the best. I'd much rather not see their filthy traitors' faces.

'There's another navigation expert who's going to be helping with our manoeuvres,' says Safia.

'Pff, I don't need help from anyone!' Kelly brags. 'I can do this with my eyes closed.'

She pretends to cover her eyes, but it's basically impossible, of course, with the bulky astronaut gloves she has on, and her whole face disappears. One thing is for sure: Kenji isn't going to get bored with her. It's more a question of whether he'll be able to keep up.

That thought of the couples getting ready to meet brings

Marcus's face to mind. We've spent five months alongside each other on the same craft, but only eleven sessions together in the Visiting Room (almost all concentrated in the later part of the journey, when I'd finally given up on my ridiculous rule). Eleven times six: that makes sixty-six minutes. Barely more than an hour to become crazy about a guy. Does that make me too easy? Well, that's the least of my worries right now. When I think about what I was like before leaving Earth, with my heart armoured like a bank vault! So totally wrong. And to think that tonight, after six kilometres of spinning between Phobos and Mars, I'm finally going to touch Marcus – that heart I thought impenetrable is getting swept away as if our plummet down to the ground had already begun.

D -30 mins.

The airlock closes slowly above our heads. The light from the vessel, carefully regulated to recreate daylight, disappears. It's replaced by the gloom that reigns in the capsule, pierced by dozens of LEDs on the dashboard and the red glow of the planet Mars behind the reinforced windscreen.

'Belts on,' orders Kelly.

Following protocol, it's Kelly who is in control of the crew during the navigation phases.

'Helmets on.'

Well, we're doing it now, I think, as I slip my thick red curls under the rim of my helmet. *We're going to enter the gravitational well of Mars.*

With the touch of a finger, I engage the radio relay that allows us all to communicate with one another.

'Capsule separation in thirty minutes,' Kelly's voice sounds slightly distorted through my helmet, as if heard over a walkie-talkie.

The die is cast.

29. Reverse Shot

Fallout Bunker, Cape Canaveral Air Base
Sunday 10 December, 5:39pm

'If you only knew how proud I am of you, Arthur! The police believed every last detail of the testimony you fed them yesterday. The allies of silence are no more than a bad memory now, bits of confetti scattered across the Caribbean Sea, and Gordon Lock is the leading suspect. At this very moment, dozens of junior staffers from the White House communications team are answering questions from journalists the world over, doling out our little tale over and over. And the best part of it is, the press has started constructing some story about terrorism to explain the unexplainable, just as I predicted! Washington is putting me under army protection, as if I'd been the victim! You've handled the whole thing masterfully, Arthur, with the manly composure I knew you had, and which seduced me from the first day we met.'

Serena McBee presses her chest, which is generously emphasised by the low neckline of her jacket, against Arthur Montgomery's torso.

'Mmmm . . .' he moans.

'Oh, was I hurting you?'

'It's just that yesterday you scratched me with your nails, and the skin is still raw under the bandages. You tigress, you!'

'I can't help it if you drive me crazy with desire, my intrepid savannah hunter . . .'

Serena brings her lips close to the doctor's moustache.

'The Genesis participants will be travelling down to Mars in a few minutes, as anticipated,' she whispers. 'And if it really is the Great Storm that threatens the base, as they assume, that means we have twenty-two months ahead of us – that is, nearly two years – half a presidential term! A lot can happen! Once I have been inaugurated to the vice-presidency, I will set the forces of law and order to track down the two sneaks who're wandering around in the middle of nowhere with a copy of the Noah Report. The families of the victims have already been put under close police protection, Andrew Fisher's mother and sister among them, including a ban on leaving U.S. territory in case they are needed for the enquiry. That presumptuous kid has me in his grasp, but I've got him in mine too! We'll just see who lets go first.'

'And the other runaway, that girl I mistook for Harmony?' asks Arthur Montgomery.

'Her? I'm looking forward to getting my hands on her! A usurper! An impostor! Who knows where that tramp is, where she comes from, and what got into her head to make her break into the house? In the meantime, it's my duty to guarantee the safety of my daughter during this troubled time. I've had her sent over to my sister Gladys, in the Scottish Highlands, the place of my ancestors. So you needn't worry, Arthur, if you don't see her at the Villa McBee.'

The doctor nods, too captivated by Serena's assurances to question her.

'In other words,' she says finally, 'it's all under control. Once I've neutralised the informers, I'll give the order to the programme participant whom I've unwittingly hypnotised to carry out their carnage among the twelve of them up there. The very thought that they dared impose their three ridiculous conditions on me, Serena McBee! I've never in my life signed a contract where every word of the terms and conditions weren't personally drafted by me – appendices included!'

'Serena, you're remarkable!' breathes Arthur Montgomery, delighted. 'Oh, Serena, Serena, eat me alive! Tear me with your claws! I'm your prey, my silver cougar!'

But the moment he leans towards her, to close the last few centimetres between his mouth and hers, Serena pushes him roughly away.

'Later,' she says. 'No harm in waiting. For now, I need to make a small speech – it's time for me to announce the sad news to the participants. I'd rather do it now than when they're on Mars; if I wait too long, they might take it badly, complain I'm keeping things from them, accuse me of not respecting their ridiculous *Serenity* contract. Yes, better to do it now. Not least because my boss-to-be, President Green, has invited himself into this broadcast. Then I'll go speak to the journalists up on the surface; they're working so hard for us, without even realising it!'

The executive producer curls herself into her padded armchair. She takes a small black ribbon, folded into a V-shape, out of her pocket, and pins it to her lapel, right beside her bee-shaped brooch-mic. Then she opens her python-skin handbag and extracts a phial of saline solution, before tipping a few drops into each of her eyes.

Then she glances at her watch, batting her eyelids to get the artificial tears flowing.

'5:45 pm! It's time!'

She turns her tearful face towards the camera hanging from the ceiling of the bunker.

30. Shot

'*Pressurisation?*' asks Kris via the relay that connects our six helmets, repeating the words she spoke five months ago when we used the capsules for the first time.

'*One hundred per cent,*' replies Liz, her voice slightly deeper than usual in the audio system.

'*Ambient oxygen levels?*'

'*Optimal.*'

'*Ventilation?*'

'*Activated.*'

'*Electronic viewfinder?*'

'*Set to target: latitude – 7.38°, longitude – 84.39°; Ius Chasma canyon, extreme southwest of the Valles Marineris.*'

Liz touches the screen of the viewfinder, a sort of GPS for space, which in the blink of an eye shows us the key data for our destination.

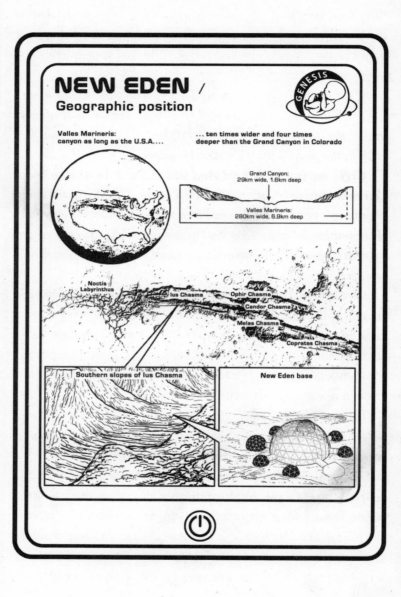

'*The total length of the Valles Marineris is as great as that of the United States of America,*' says Liz, '*and we're aiming for a very precise point, to the nearest few hundred metres. We have no intention of missing.*'

'*It's a piece of cake!*' says Kelly. '*Or maybe a slice of pizza? I don't know about you, but when I hear* Marineris *it always makes me think of* Marinara.'

'*Uh, the pizza with the seafood?*' asks Kris.

'*Urgh, no, you philistine! And you claim to be able to cook! You're confusing it with the Frutti di Mare. The Marinara is the poor man's pizza, the only one I could afford in Toronto – the one with nothing interesting on it at all, not even cheese, just tomato sauce and* basta!'

I hear the girls all burst out laughing simultaneously through the earphones in my helmet, which fills the radio waves and creates a funny feedback loop. We can always count on Kelly to make the most random comments at the most unexpected moments! Although . . . Mars as a space pizza? That could make a pretty cool drawing.

'It's nothing to do with Marinara,' explains Fangfang, who always starts right up whenever we talk about anything connected with planetology. 'Valles Marineris was named after the probe that discovered it in 1971, Mariner 9.'

'Still,' replies Kelly, 'when I see that red surface, what it reminds me of is a huge, delicious pizza. Fortunately, Serena, the pizzaiola of reality TV, is about to chuck out some crunchy new ingredients: us. Hey, talking about Serena, we haven't seen her pretty little face for ages. I hope she's not dead, poor thing. All that sadness at watching us fly away from her for ever; too much grief can kill, you know.'

No sooner has Kelly said this than the transmission monitor starts to crackle. The black background against which the countdown had been running is torn open, to reveal the space pizzaiola herself, proving she's still entirely alive.

At first glance, I can tell there's something fishy going on. Her *mater dolorosa* expression, the moist tear-tracks that shine on her cheeks . . . The whole thing stinks to high heaven of trickery.

'*My poor, dear friends,*' she moans into our earphones. '*I'm sorry to have left you to yourselves for the final preparations for your landing. It's just that here on Earth there's been a terrible tragedy.*'

My whole body tenses up in my spacesuit, as though I'd stuck my fingers in a socket. The faces of Andrew Fisher and Harmony McBee appear in my mind's eye, pale and tired, so vulnerable, just as they appeared to us yesterday on the screens in the gym.

(*She's killed them! She's found them and killed them! And you're next on her list!*)

No! I force myself to drive back the morbid thoughts the Salamander is whispering in my ear. If Serena really had killed the two people on whom our fate depends, she would hardly be announcing it to us in a live broadcast just as we are about to begin our descent onto Mars.

'*You must have been wondering why you haven't had news of your dear instructors, over these past hours,*' says Serena. '*They were supposed to be by your side for this final stretch, those people from whom you learned so much, who treated you like their own children.'*

The hypocrisy turns my stomach.

But the relief at learning this isn't about Andrew and Harmony is much stronger than the nausea.

I breathe out slowly, waiting for whatever Serena will say next.

'*I was worried about their absence myself, but I kept hosting the channel as I was duty-bound to do, as our viewers expected, as my employers Atlas Capital required. As I sat alone behind my editing desk, I kept telling myself that perhaps my colleagues were preparing a surprise for me, a little party to celebrate the success of the programme. I never could have imagined what the police have just this minute reported to me. It grieves me terribly to have to break to you the news that's just shaken the whole of Earth, and that you also should know. Gordon, Odette, Geronimo and Archibald were kidnapped, yesterday afternoon, from Cape Canaveral. The plane that was carrying them disappeared into the sea. The authorities believe there was a crash . . .*' Serena's voice cracks. '*. . . and that there were no survivors.*'

I hear the girls' breathing accelerate in their mics, jumbling together in the headphones in my helmet, and mingling with my own.

After Sherman and Ruben, Serena's done away with four more of her 'allies'. Because she's behind their disappearance, I'd bet my life on it. Her crocodile tears don't fool me one bit. Deep in her moist eyes there is an unstoppable determination, a supreme contempt for those who died and for whom she's pretending to grieve.

181

But her voice trembles, and the quavering is the only thing that will be remembered by the viewers, who have no idea what she's capable of.

'*I can't imagine how upsetting this must be for you,*' she goes on. '*It's as if you've been orphaned a second time! I don't know what else to say, except that we've had the families of your dear instructors put under police protection, since we don't know what the terrorists' intentions are, or whether they're getting ready to strike again. With the exception of Archibald Dragovic, who as far as we know had no family in the United States, the relatives of all the others are under guard at this moment: the Locks in New York, the Blackbulls in San Diego, the Salvatores in Chicago, the Montgomerys in Boston, the Stuart-Smiths in Beverly Hills. And their local neighbours the Fishers, of course!*'

At the same time as crying, Serena keeps her eyes fixed on the camera. Behind her compassionate façade, I know we need to hear a warning. The family of Andrew Fisher is under police protection . . . in other words, under the surveillance of the woman who's about to become vice-president of the United States! This information is aimed at us in our capsules, as well as at Andrew and Harmony on the road.

'*I beg you,*' Serena goes on. '*Don't let this break your resolve. I may be shaken to the depths of my soul by this tragedy, but I refuse to allow someone else to take my place. That would just be giving the terrorists what they want. I'll continue to fly the Genesis programme flag high, even if I now display this symbol of mourning, the Remembrance ribbon.*' She points at the black ribbon pinned to the lapel of her jacket, then adds: '*But the show must go on!*'

The show must go on – the exact same words she spoke five months earlier, when she informed us of the death of Sherman Fisher, who she subsequently confessed to me she'd killed! I can sense a new admission here: it really was her behind this apparent attack. Why? No doubt so she'd be left as the sole captain on deck in the delicate situation where she finds herself.

'*It's just you and me now,*' she continues, confirming my suspicions perfectly. '*We must be strong and united if we are to overcome adversity. Nothing and no one will come between us. And we'll keep moving forward, just as your instructors would have wanted. It's our duty, in the name of America and of the world.*'

At this moment, the screen splits in two, to show a second person via link-up. I immediately recognise President Green, with his green tie and orange tan. However, he isn't wearing his famous ultra-bright smile that we're used to seeing on the posters and the TV debates. He is sitting, sombre, at a huge oak desk, behind which a heavy star-spangled flag is hanging. He has the same ribbon as Serena attached to the lapel of his jacket.

'*This is a black day for America, and for all those of us down here who love freedom,*' he says gravely. '*But all the more so for you, my young friends, this is a day of mourning. Today you have lost more than just instructors: you've lost tutors, mentors – dare I say, parents? We do not yet know who is behind this vile attack. We haven't yet had anyone claiming responsibility. But one thing is certain now: the Genesis programme does not have only supporters. There are barbarians on this Earth, who have decided to set themselves – in the most violent way imaginable – against the conquest of space, against friendship between peoples, against everything the twelve of you represent.*'

President Green fixes the camera with his piercing eyes, as though addressing each of us directly, as if he knows us personally, even though we have never met. It gives me a certain thrill, I'll confess. I know that at this moment the *billions of viewers* he's talking about are watching us too, and that it would take one word, just one, to dispose of Serena live on TV.

Wake up, President Green! I suddenly want to shout. *The queen of the barbarians is on air with you at this moment!*

But I say nothing.

Because if I spoke, I would be condemning us all.

Because we voted to travel down to Mars.

Because I've got to pretend.

'*I would so much rather you'd learned this news at some other time, rather than now, just as you're getting ready for your descent,*' Serena continues from the other half of the screen. '*But it's the second commitment I made when we restarted the Genesis channel, after the commitment to* Coverage: Transparency. *You have the right to know everything at the same time as the rest of the world. Yesterday, terrorists succeeded in destroying some of the Genesis programme's finest – but tomorrow? Will they attempt to harm you, even across the millions of kilometres separating us? I, Serena McBee, swear to you that I will do whatever I can to prevent them. That was my third commitment:* Assistance. *Unconditional assistance. You can count on me. You must count on me. I will protect your lives as though they were my own, like a little guard bee defending her hive!*'

What a dizzying double meaning!

To the viewers, Serena sounds like a cornered mother, ready to stop at nothing to defend her offspring.

Only we know that if she wishes for a long life for us, it's just because the moment we die, she too will fall. Yes, she has the Fisher family in her clutches, but it would be the easiest thing in the world for Andrew to disseminate the screen caps of the Noah Report. Yes, she's got us under her thumb, but we've got her too, on the tips of our tongues: we need only say a few words to reveal the terrible truth to the viewers.

Serena's allies may have disappeared, but not the deal that connects us to her. That hasn't changed at all.

'*Serena McBee is correct,*' President Green concludes solemnly, unable to understand the real meaning of his future vice-president's words. '*A guard bee – what a lovely image! This is a real war we're engaged in. We need to forge ahead. We need to keep building the future without allowing ourselves to be intimidated by vile attempts to drag us back into the past. Alexei and Kirsten, Tao and Fangfang, Kelly and Kenji, Samson and Safia, Elizabeth and Mozart, Marcus and Léonor, I'm counting on you. America is counting on you. The world is counting on you. Oppose the terrorists' language of death by responding with the language of life: offer us the first babies on Mars. God bless you. God bless America.*'

The image on the monitor fades to black, leaving nothing but the countdown.

D -1 min

D -59 secs

D -58 secs

On the screen in front of us, the numbers are still scrolling past.

All around the capsule, the on-board cameras are still filming.

Beyond the reinforced windscreen, the planet Mars is still turning.

Suddenly a button on the dashboard lights up.

'*It's the boys' capsule,*' says Safia from deep inside our helmets. She presses the button with the tip of her finger.

'*I'm connecting them in to our relay, so all six of us can hear them.*' She also adds a warning in coded language, to avoid any slip-ups: '*And I should remind you that our friendly viewers can also hear us right now, as we're still live, so . . . um . . . no swearing, OK?*'

The voice of Kenji, the boys Communications Officer, sounds in our earphones.

'*Hello, is that the girls? We're not totally calm about this, over on our side. I'm not just speaking for myself – it's normal for someone phobic like me to be afraid – but the others are pretty scared too. The viewers will understand, I'm sure. And they'd also understand if we decided to do one or two extra orbits around Mars before landing. What do you all think? What does Léonor think?*'

By way of an answer, Kelly, Liz and Safia swivel their front-row seats around; to my left and right, Kris and Fangfang also turn towards me.

D -41 secs

Me, who revealed the existence of the Noah Report to them.

D -40 secs

Me, who organised the vote for the twelve passengers.

D -39 secs

Me, who feels much too small to fit the role of leader they want me to take on.

D -38 secs

The reputation of the Determinator clings to my skin closer than the Salamander, while deep down I'm as full of doubts as anyone else, if not more.

But doubts aren't what the others need just now.

And if there's one thing, just one, that I'm sure of, it's that Serena McBee hasn't yet regained the upper hand. By revealing the death of her former allies to us at the same time as the rest of the world, she really has acted with Transparency. Because the *Serenity* contract requires it of her. Because she had no choice. And as for us, the sooner we get to Mars, and the sooner we can start trying to repair whatever's wrong in those crappy habitats, the better!

'*What do we do?*' I say. '*We resist fear and intimidation. We show how strong we are, and that anyone who wants to wipe us out will never do it.*'

My own words come back to me through the mic, with a slight echo. I try to articulate them as clearly as I can, so that my friends receive all the positive energy they contain, so that the viewers can sense all the determination, and so Serena gets the blast of irony full in the face.

'*We will do as we were told by President Green, who is counting on us to make freedom victorious.*

'*We will do as we were asked by our dear Serena, who will protect our lives as though they were her own.*

'*We will go straight down, right now – without wasting a moment – if Kelly and Mozart are up for doing some piloting!*'

There's a crackling in my helmet, and the audio feed switches towards the boys' capsule.

'*Received loud and clear,*' Kenji's voice answers. '*Here on our side, Mozart is confirming that he's good to go. We're following you, girls – descending now.'*

Kelly gives an excited little whistle, that unleashes a new bit of feedback.

'Tell that amateur Mozzie to hang on tight!' she says. *'Last one on Mars is a pile of moose dung!'*

The helmets move away from me, as one by one the girls return to their positions.

The moment of hesitation has passed, and now everything is full speed ahead.

D -25 secs

D -24 secs

D -23 secs

'Braking of the central rotor?' asks Kelly, back to her professional self.

'Underway,' says Liz.

My body is getting lighter and lighter in spite of the spacesuit: there's now nothing keeping me in the seat but the safety belt – otherwise I would fly away. I'm not turning into a helium balloon, it's the rotation of the *Cupido*'s wings that's stopping, and with it the artificial gravity we've benefited from these past five months.

The notes of *Cosmic Love* pour out of the capsule speakers as a background – as usual, at every key moment in the programme, we get violins.

D -15 secs

D -14 secs

D -13 secs

'Electronic viewfinder?' asks Kelly, like a surgeon at her operating table.

'*Set to target.*'

'*Propulsion system?*'

'*Engaged.*'

'*I've got* Cosmic Love *coming out my ears! I might be the biggest Jimmy Giant fan, but enough is enough!*'

Liz reaches under her seat and pulls out her tablet.

'*Can I?*' she asks.

'*Do anything you want so long as you can stop this torture.*'

Liz connects her tablet to the sound input marked URGENT COMMUNICATIONS, short-circuiting the Genesis theme music.

The synths stop abruptly, to be replaced by a great silence, and then, a few moments later, the first notes of a melody that is at once very sweet and very powerful. No need for anybody to tell me what it is – I can guess it's from the *New World Symphony*.

D -3 secs

D -2 secs

D -1 sec

'GO!' cries Kelly, gripping her joystick, the moment the countdown comes to an end on the transmission monitor. '*Here we come, Pizza Marineris – with all the extras!*'

I close my eyes and allow myself to be carried away by the music, addressing a silent prayer to Andrew and Harmony.

You're the two most important members of the crew now, even if you've never once set foot in space, never experienced the flashes of the paparazzi or hit the newspaper headlines. You are our anonymous heroes, our Survival Officers; as long as you can keep yourselves free of Serena's clutches, she won't dare press the button, and we'll stay alive!

ACT III

31. Genesis Channel

Sunday 10 December, 6:00pm

Static shot on outer space, filmed from the camera attached to the back of the *Cupido*.

There's no voiceover, no words, no drum-roll – nothing but the notes of a piece of orchestral music, its arpeggios sweeping slowly across the void. The *New World Symphony*.

We see the imposing body of the spaceship, with the planet Mars in the background.

In the foreground, the enormous rocket, now extinguished.

Then the rotor, now still.

And finally, the Visiting Room, now empty.

On either side of the glass bubble are the living quarters, sticking out like the raised arms of the Christ statue in Rio, which the media have compared the *Cupido* to so often.

The two capsules detach at the same moment, as though the giant were opening his hands to release two birds into Mars's red sky.

The capsules – minuscule metal cones that glow in the light of a sun far more distant than the one that shines on Earth – fly out, and allow themselves to be carried away by the music.

32. Off-screen

Interstate 80 West, State of Indiana
Sunday 10 December, 6:30pm

The symphony continues its crescendo.

It accompanies the ballet of the vehicles that have been slowed by the snowfall, which slide slowly along a highway plunged into winter darkness.

One vehicle is moving a little faster than the others: a black campervan with tinted windows.

Behind the windscreen, a young man with bags under his eyes is tightly gripping the steering wheel, like a sailor at the helm of a ship. The girl asleep beside him looks like a white mermaid washed up onto the shore.

The notes coming from the car radio envelop them both in a musical blanket that is silky, vibrant, alive.

'*The Genesis participants are giving us quite a gift with this magnificent music,*' says the announcer quietly, as if afraid to wake a sleeping child. '*My dear listeners, those of you without access to the images need only listen to the glorious* New World Symphony *to imagine the spectacle taking place above your heads. You need only . . . Oh, I'll be quiet and let the music do the talking!*'

33. Reverse Shot

Cape Canaveral Air Base
Sunday 10 December, 7:00pm

The symphony swells to its full scale.

Night-time on Cape Canaveral Air Base is as brightly lit as the day, pierced by countless projectors surrounding the platform from which five months earlier the Genesis rocket was launched. An ocean of journalists who have gathered to cover the landing and the weddings have circled around the gigantic aluminium floor, brandishing cameras and filming equipment and audio booms as though they were weapons. Dozens of soldiers in combat gear, machine-guns in hand, have been stationed all around the perimeter of the launch area. Behind them, the giant screens show the two capsules that are continuing to fall through the void, to the sound of the symphony that is coming out of the speakers.

A luminous message scrolls across the bottom of the screens: HEIGHTENED SECURITY PROCEDURES – THE ARMED FORCES ARE HERE TO PROTECT YOU – THANK YOU FOR NOTIFYING US OF ANY SUSPICIOUS INDIVIDUALS OR BEHAVIOR.

Suddenly a silhouette emerges from the secret innards of

the base via a hidden elevator, appearing behind the podium at the corner of the stage.

It's Serena McBee, her two arms raised in a V for Victory, here to show that she is still standing, that she's alive, that she's ready to rise up against the Genesis programme's real or supposed enemies.

The journalists start yelling as though they were meeting a rock star, a queen on her coronation day, a goddess incarnate.

Camera flashes start to crackle, in a flood of light that seeks to illuminate everything but which fails to show anything that really matters.

The soldiers kneel, holding the crowd at bay in the sights of their machine-guns, ready to open fire on the first 'suspicious individual' to threaten the *guard bee* of Mars herself.

34. Shot

D +160 days, 06 h 00 mins.
[23rd week]

The music numbs me and electrifies me; it jostles me and cradles me.

The music is the only thing that exists.

There is no fuel burning below my body, there are no vibrations shaking me from head to toe: none of the mad feelings that accompanied the launch of the capsules five months earlier.

I've lost track of time. I just let myself get carried away by the symphony that spins around and around, as we ourselves are spinning around Mars. On the black screen of my closed eyelids, I replay the film of our journey and – more than this – of my whole life. The strings shiver, the capsule spins, my memories rise up: it's a dizzying whirl.

I remember my first meeting with Marcus, in the bubble of the Visiting Room – simultaneously so intimate and so exhibitionistic; just the two of us, and yet the whole of Earth was there with us, too. I thought I was proving my courage by resisting him, but it was unspeakable cowardice letting him get away; I'd never felt so alive in my whole existence, but it took me five months and fifty-five million kilometres to admit it.

Earlier: I remember my throat constricting on the launch platform, when I didn't believe in love, and when I confirmed my commitment as though I were letting out a war cry: '*I accept, of course! I said I accept!*'

Earlier: I remember my first meeting with Kris when I arrived at the training camp in Death Valley, and also the first time we got the giggles together. I'd told her that with her crown of braids she reminded me of Princess Leia and that it was really appropriate as a hairstyle for someone going into space; she told me that I wasn't doing too badly myself, seeing as I had about as much hair on my head as Chewbacca the Wookiee warrior.

Earlier: I remember the day I won the 'worker of the month' medal at the Eden Food France dog-food factory; I had managed to fill three thousand *Classic Cassoulets* without a single mistake and I was so pleased – I thought, honestly, it was the best day of my life.

Earlier: I remember the orphanage, the humiliations and bullying, but above all the kindness of that nurse with the pink cheeks, who welcomed me every month into the hospital to carry out my skin grafts – each time, once the operation was done, she would give me a mint candy.

Earlier: I remember an old woollen blanket without which I couldn't get to sleep in the dormitory. Every evening I needed to feel my cheek touching it, rough as the tongue of a pet, letting its powerful smell fill my nostrils, a smell I'd forgotten, and which had buried itself into the deepest crannies of my memory, but which comes back to me now with the strength of a tsunami, at once repellent and intoxicating, dangerous and comforting – oh, if I could only put a name to it!

'*Atmospheric entry commenced!*' Kelly's voice announces into my helmet. '*Things are gonna hot up now!*'

The sense memory fades away at the exact moment I open my eyes, before I was able to identify it.

An explosion of red splashes across my field of vision, as if I'd taken a revolver bullet right to the middle of my forehead. Through the reinforced windscreen, the surface of Mars is bursting out at full speed – red mountains, red basins, red craters, and all so close!

The walls of the capsule start to tremble, gently at first, then stronger and stronger as the numbers on the altimeter drop.

200 km . . .

193 km . . .

186 km . . .

In the corner of the windscreen we suddenly see the vast gash of the Valles Marineris. It takes my breath away. It's nothing like the topographical models we studied at the training camp, nor the long-distance view we got of it from the Visiting Room, from out in the orbit of Phobos. It's grander, more majestic, more terrible than anything I could have imagined. And us, in our tiny metal bug, we're racing towards that mouth at seven kilometres per second – twenty-five thousand kilometres an hour!

86 km . . .

79 km . . .

72 km . . .

After about two hours floating almost weightless, my body

recovers its weight real Quick with a capital Q. Not just the forty per cent of gravity recreated by the rotation of the *Cupido*, nor even the one hundred per cent of Earth's gravity. We're exceeding 1G, going up to 2G, then 3G, I can feel it in my crushed flesh, in my compressed bones.

58 km . . .

51 km . . .

44 km . . .

The notes of the *New World Symphony* disappear behind the noise of the vibration. Sparks swarm across the windscreen, as though the entire planet were bursting into flame. Even though I know it's the heat from the friction with the Martian atmosphere, and that the ceramic cladding of the capsule is supposed to protect us, I can't help shuddering.

Fire!

Like my childhood nightmares!

All around me!

I want to shut my eyes again, but I can't do it. Because my muscles are paralysed by the acceleration. Because the sight of the blaze fascinates me, just as it terrifies me.

'*Hang on, girls!*' Kelly yells into my helmet, more excited than ever. '*We're about to enter the landing phase! You know what the NASA guys used to call this phase, back in the day when they were dropping all the equipment off on Mars from their control room, before it was all bought up by Genesis? They called it the* seven minutes of terror! *Isn't that a great name for a funfair roller-coaster? But they haven't got anything like this at Disneyworld! And we're going to be the first human beings ever to experience it live! Woohooo!*'

She bursts out laughing.

A part of me is thinking, *This girl has totally lost it!* But another part of me starts laughing along with Kelly, a crazy laugh, demented, that helps to exorcise my fear, and the winds of Mars laugh too. The capsule is thrown about in every direction like a car on a roller-coaster.

35 km . . .

28 km . . .

21 km . . .

All of a sudden, an enormous *BOOM* smashes into my eardrums, and I feel my stomach in my throat as we undergo a violent deceleration.

'*Hypersonic drag balloon inflated,*' announces Liz, her voice significantly less confident than Kelly's.

The tongues of fire stop licking at the reinforced windscreen, to reveal the gaping fault of the Valles Marineris, less than twenty kilometres beneath us. Even if the hypersonic balloon has broken our fall, we're still descending insanely fast. No way can we possibly survive something like this!

'*Am I dreaming, or are the boys taking the lead?*' Kelly's voice comes through suddenly. '*I'm still not going to get myself overtaken by a macho little nobody!*'

Huh?

What?

Fighting against the forces of acceleration that continue to crush me, I struggle to turn my head towards the left-hand corner of the windscreen.

There they are.

The boys.

Or rather, their capsule, which is hurtling through the air a few kilometres from our own, like a revolver bullet, barely slowed down by the hypersonic balloon. Marcus is in there, inside that metal meteor, made up of ceramic and flesh.

A scream tears me away from the sight.

I look straight ahead.

A translucent surface has just come between us and the Valles Marineris, like a huge glass plate.

'*What the hell is that thing?*' barks Kelly, gripping the joystick.

'*It's a . . . a cloud!*' cries Fangfang. '*A cloud of frozen carbon dioxide! Really rare in the summer! Just our luck. We'll be smashed to pieces on it!*'

'*Kelly,*' begs Liz, '*open the parachute! Quick!*'

But the Canadian girl is inflexible, her hands still clenched around the joystick.

'*No way we're going to be landing on that dumb cloud. I have no intention of freezing my butt off on a flying ice floe. I said I'd get you to New Eden, and that's what I'm going to do. Under thirty seconds to impact.*'

35. Reverse Shot

Control Room, Cape Canaveral Air Base
Sunday 10 December, 7:57pm

'This is completely unexpected, Ms McBee. It's absolutely contrary to all our models for meteorological prediction. There should *not* be a cloud above the Martian equator, especially not in this season!'

The grey-jacketed engineer is trembling like a leaf as he faces the programme's executive producer.

Behind him, ranks of men and women are busying themselves on their computers, eyes wide with terror. The digital wall at the back of the control room is showing the view from the girls' on-board camera: a wall of ice approaching at the speed of a lightning flash.

'How very unfortunate!' cries Serena McBee, wringing her hands. 'The seasons are all out of kilter, on Mars just like on Earth! My poor little things, victims of climate change, just like the polar bears and the Pacific atolls! What can we do? I'm begging you, tell me what we can do!'

'There's n-nothing we can d-do,' stammers the engineer, eyes shining. 'It's too late now: the images reaching us are coming to us three minutes late, so according to our calculations the impact has already taken place'

Serena gives a terrible cry – 'No!' – and falls into the arms of Arthur Montgomery, who is standing behind her.

She buries her face in the doctor's neck, so everyone believes she is in tears, except for the man into whose ear she whispers a few muffled words.

'This is so unexpected, Arthur. Six little spoilsports wiped out in one go, thanks to a little wandering cloud – that's already half the job done. If Léonor and the other girls disappear thanks to these heaven-sent conditions, I promise I'll never complain about bad weather again!'

36. Shot

Chest exploding.
   Skeleton shattering into a thousand glass shards.
   Skull splitting like a shell beneath a hammer.
   Blackout.

37. Off-screen

A million people hold their breath.

A million unknowns who have been here since last night.

A million fans who have followed the *Cupido* every step of the way and rejoiced to see it arrive safe into harbour, who have lived through the long anguish of the channel being suspended then the relief of the resumption of the broadcast, who have celebrated the forming of the Mars couples with great jubilation.

The huge square, currently invaded by night-time and snow, is silent as if deserted; the fans are as still as if they had been transformed into statues.

The only movement comes from the giant screens affixed to the buildings.

Split screen.

On the left, we see the surface of Mars, approaching at great speed, a glowing red geographical map whose reliefs are becoming clearer and clearer – the letters at the bottom of the screen indicate that this is BOYS' CAPSULE ON-BOARD CAMERA – 7:58:02pm

On the right, we see only a chaos of ice and fire, an abstract supernatural spectacle, like the pieces of glass turning in a kaleidoscope – the letters at the bottom of the screen indicate that this is GIRLS' CAPSULE ON-BOARD CAMERA – 7:58:02pm

7:58:05pm

A violent shaking takes hold of the image at the moment the parachute is deployed. The mountains and craters seem to be waltzing.

Then they stabilise.

7:58:05pm

A white flash fills the right half of the screens, illuminating Times Square as brightly as the Sun in daylight.

Then nothing.

7:58:25pm

The sides of the Valles Marineris canyon rise up like giant waves, several kilometres high, like a tidal wave of loose red rock, and the capsule is plunging into its heart.

7:58:25pm

Half-screen is black.

7:58:56pm

When the sandy ground of the Valles Marineris is only a few hundred metres away, it is suddenly lit up by flames: the retrorockets slow the capsule one final time, and it completes its descent gently until the image finally stills.

7:58:56pm

Half-screen is black.

38. Shot

'*Léo?*

'*Léo . . .*

'*Léo, can you hear me?'*

Kris?

Is that you?

'*Oh, Léo, for the love of God, don't tell me you're dead!'*

'*If I did tell you, though, I wouldn't really be, would I?'* I murmur, opening my eyes.

I can see Kris's face a few centimetres away, the visor of her helmet almost touching mine. She looks so startled that I can't help but burst out laughing. I regret it right away, as it feels like there's a mad musician playing the xylophone on my sides.

'*Aaargh!'* – my cry of pain comes back to me as an echo through the relay, with added feedback.

Kris hurries to release my safety belt.

'*Oh, thank God, you're alive!'* she cries, her voice distorted. '*Are you in pain?'*

'*I'm in perfect shape,'* I mutter, teeth clenched. '*And what about the others, Kris, how are the others?'*

209

'OK, I think. Safia fainted, too, but she's also come to, just a few seconds before you.'

I take a deep, slow breath, infinitely careful, alert to every feeling in my chest cavity. A vague smell of burning fills my nostrils. As for everything else, it seems to be OK, more or less. I might not have broken anything after all. All thanks to my made-to-measure seat, no doubt.

'Well, we're no longer being tossed around like in a salad spinner,' I say. 'So I guess we've landed. So my question is: have we reached our actual destination, or are we floating around adrift on a cloud of ice?'

There is a crackling in my helmet.

'Neither, my dear!' Kelly answers. 'I pulverised the cloud, just like Canada's curling team pulverised the Americans in the last Olympics! The problem is, the impact knocked us off course, and even with the parachute and the retrorockets, I couldn't recover our trajectory one hundred per cent'

Supporting myself on my arms, I raise myself off my seat, despite Kris's anxious protestations, as she'd rather I stay lying down. My five teammates are there, dazed but totally alive, and Louve is too. The capsule is a mess, with cables dangling out in every direction and warning lights blinking in a way that's not in the least bit reassuring.

'Couldn't recover our trajectory one hundred per cent – that means what exactly, in English?' I ask.

'Well, um . . .' says Kelly, 'it means I missed my target just a little . . .'

'It means we've landed more than a kilometre from New Eden!' explains Fangfang.

'You'd have rather we landed nicely on the cloud, ten kilometres *above the base?'* replies Kelly. *'Usual story, Madam doesn't do anything herself but allows herself an opinion on everything. Aargh, Fangfang! As the Planetology Officer, I'd suggest that you should have done something about it! You should have told us there was a risk of bad weather before we set off!'*

Fangfang is about to answer, but I sit up and take her arm.

'Listen to me, girls,' I say. *'We're alive. We've travelled fifty-five million kilometres to get here. So just one more isn't going to stop us, right?'*

They shake their heads.

We exchange glances, eyes misty with emotion, yet we're also close to collapsing into hysterical laughter. Yeah, no kidding: *fifty-five million kilometres!*

'Have the boys landed, Safia?' I ask at last.

The Indian girl turns a few dials on the busted dashboard, to no avail.

'The capsule's communications system is down,' she says. *'There's no way to contact the boys. Not even the control room. All we have is the relay between our six suits, just us girls. That's the only thing still working.'*

'You mean even Big Sister – a.k.a. Serena – can't see us any more?' Kelly asks feverishly, pointing a gloved finger at the on-board cameras.

'Yes, I'm positive. There's no one here but us.'

At these words, Kelly gives such a thundering roar it makes my helmet shake like a warning bell.

'What a megabitch! What a total cosmic cow! Her, a guard bee? If you ask me, Serena's nothing but a slobbery old cockroach, like those ones that croaked in the seventh habitat, and the day

the Earth finds out it'll be like a huge shoe that will crush her, and it's gonna make a really nasty noise!'

Kelly gives a big sigh of relief as she releases her safety belt.

'*Oh, that feels seriously good!*' she says. '*Nothing like being able to have a good rant off camera; it was worth having the crash! Whenever you're ready, girls. We ought to get a move on, while it's still light.*'

She points at the capsule's digital clock, which has converted automatically to the timeframe of our new world: MONTH 20 / SOL 551 / 17:07

'*How long before it gets dark?*'

'*We still have an hour, according to my calculations,*' replies Fangfang instantly, as if she had a computer for a brain. '*We're in Mars's equatorial zone where the Sun sets at nineteen hundred hours, but the sides of the canyon will plunge us into darkness well before that.*'

'*So we'd better get going, double-quick!*'

I just have time to stop Kelly before she deploys the lever opening the capsule.

'*Hey – not so fast! You've got to activate your unit for extra-vehicular survival and pressurise your suit. Because if you go out like that, it's not just you who'll be in a hurry to leave, but your organs too. Without the pressure from the capsule weighing on them and keeping them in place, they're going to hurtle off in every possible direction until you explode.*'

Kelly lets go of the opening lever, as if it were on fire, to slap herself on the forehead.

'*Argh, what am I like! Such a ditz. Activating the unit for extra-vehicular survival . . . Pressurising the suit . . . Got to make myself some kind of reminder . . .*'

She presses the button set in the sleeve of her spacesuit, and the other girls and I do the same.

There's a hissing sound in my ears as my suit fills with gas to recreate a pressure identical to that in the capsule, close to that on Earth. The vitals gauges in a corner of the visor of my helmet light up.

INTERNAL PRESSURE: 100%

OXYGEN RESERVES: 36 HRS

THERMAL REGULATOR: 20°C

PHYSICAL INTEGRITY: NOTHING TO REPORT

CLOCK: MONTH 20 / SOL 551 / 17:08

'*Everyone good?*' I ask, since it's still my role as Medical Officer to avoid accidents. '*All set? Well, then I think we can go.*'

This time Kelly presses the opening lever all the way down.

There's a whistling as the capsule depressurises automatically . . .

. . . the jingling of a complex bolt somewhere in its metal entrails . . .

. . . then the door opens slowly onto our new planet.

Kelly is just about to rush into the glowing red hole, when a white silhouette slips between her legs.

'*Louve!*' she cries, trying to catch the dog, who is wrapped in her own pressurised spacesuit, with her own mini-helmet.

Too late.

Louve is already outside.

'*Seriously?*' Kelly bursts out laughing. '*So the first man to walk on Mars wasn't a man at all – or a woman, for that matter!*'

Then she in turn steps outside, followed by Liz, Safia, Kris and Fangfang. I'm the last to leave the cocoon of our capsule.

I let my body glide towards the opening. I feel so light,

despite the spacesuit; the gravity of Mars, just a third that of Earth, reduces my weight by two thirds. My boots come down on something rubbery: the hypersonic balloon, which has deflated beneath the capsule.

I clear it in a few strides, and suddenly my soles find a quite different terrain, something supple and crunchy. I look down. That's when I see it for the first time – I mean, *really* see it, not just on a screen in pictures from a documentary, not from a great distance through the porthole of a spacecraft.

Mars.

There it is, all around me, as far as the eye can see: a giant expanse of red sand, rolling from dune to dune like the folds of a piece of fabric, like a thick velvet drape shimmering softly in the glow of the Martian day.

My head starts to spin.

I grab on to the wall of the capsule behind me, so as not to fall, until my vision is stabilised.

The movement of the dunes is only an illusion.

They are quite still.

Just like the purple rocks poking up here and there.

Just like the gigantic cliff that closes off the southern side of Ius Chasma, at the heart of the Valles Marineris – a rocky wall several kilometres high, without so much as a bush, a single blade of grass quivering on it. There's nothing alive here, nothing moving at all. There is only the sand, the rocks, and the minute sun that is perched all the way up there at the edge of the cliff, ready to slip out of sight.

'*It all looks so dry and dead.*' Liz's voice resounds in my helmet, as if echoing my own thoughts.

I turn towards the English girl, whose tall body manages to make even the spacesuit look elegant.

'*A real desert,*' she adds.

'*This desert isn't as dry as it looks,*' Fangfang's voice corrects her. '*We already know there's ice buried deep beneath our feet, which has been there for millions of years, and which the life-support station extracts to irrigate New Eden. But that's not all – look up there!*'

The Singaporean girl points up towards the top of the cliff. Not far below the edge we can see fine dark red streams, as if the rock were bleeding.

'*These flows are formed every year during the summer, only to disappear again in winter,*' explains Fangfang, her voice filled with wonder. '*Researchers believe the highly salty Martian rock is condensing what little humidity there is in the atmosphere, when the temperatures heat up. It's only been a hypothesis till now, but I'm going to be able to prove it! And I'll be able to penetrate all the secrets of Mars, in the name of science!*'

'*Don't get too excited yet,*' replies Kelly. '*You won't be doing any of that until we're safe. So where's this damn base, anyway?*'

'*There!*' cries Safia.

The Indian girl points towards a luminous shape, right up against the side of the canyon. It's a big dome made up of a thousand glass faces, shining like a thousand fires, surrounded by seven other domes, all darker and smaller.

'*New Eden,*' says Safia soberly. '*Inside that greenhouse are the plantations cultivated by the farming robots left behind on previous missions. Behind those glass ramparts stretches our new country, for today and the rest of our lives.*'

'*OK, fine –*' Kelly interrupts her – '*there'll be plenty of time*

215

later for big speeches and quotes to get us into the history books. For now, there's nobody listening to us, so no point wasting our breath. Even if we can in theory keep going for thirty-six hours in our suits, if you ask me the sooner we arrive at New Eden the better!'

'But . . . *we're leaving all our things in the capsule?*' asks Kris, kneeling down in the sand to attach a leash to Louve's suit.

'We'll come back for it all later in the rover. I don't think anybody's going to come by to steal your bits and pieces in the meantime, if that's what you're worried about. There's only one gangster on Mars, and he's over there.' Kelly points at the second capsule that is gleaming not far from New Eden, around which little bloated silhouettes in white suits are moving. *'I cannot believe that klutz Mozzie has managed to overtake me!'*

Kris looks imploringly at Kelly, then at the beached capsule, then back at Kelly.

'*OK, we'll abandon everything where it is,*' she concedes at last. '*But there's one thing, just one, that we really must take with us . . .*'

'*Kris is right!*' cries Fangfang. '*Our revision tablets! We can't go without our revision tablets!*'

'*I'm talking about our wedding dresses. Because today's the day we get married, or have you all forgotten?*'

On Earth, how long does it take to walk a kilometre? Ten minutes? Fifteen?

On Mars, it seems to take an eternity.

Is it because the grains of Martian sand move under my soles with each step?

Or because the reduced gravity makes it hard for me to find my balance, making me tip alternately forwards and backwards?

I have to say, the vacuum-packed garment bag I recovered in the hold of the capsule isn't helping. The wedding dress which has been in storage since the start of the journey isn't all that heavy itself, especially not here, but even in its compacted state it's so cumbersome! If I'd known, I'd have asked the Rosier guys not to give me such a long train.

What with all the falling over and getting back up again, my suit quickly becomes as hot as a steam room. I have to admit, for a moment I even worry about getting odd aftereffects following our shaky arrival, and no longer being able to control my legs.

The fact that I can see the others aren't managing much better than me, and they're getting tangled up with their own black garment bags, gives me a bit of reassurance. We may have trained on the *Cupido* treadmill, but the protected environment on the craft was nothing like this reality. Consequently, we go sprawling every few minutes, raising light clouds of red powder that sparkle prettily in the Martian day. The swearwords that come out of Kelly's mouth at machine-gun speed are distinctly less charming.

'*Stop swearing like a truck driver and look over here,*' says Fangfang. '*I think I've cracked it.*'

With her body leaning slightly forward, the Singaporean starts to jump from one foot to the other, hovering for a few seconds between each 'step'. The total effect is strange, dreamlike, a bit like those kung-fu movies where the fighters seem to be suspended by invisible wires, and oh, it does look pretty convincing, as Fangfang's travelled a good thirty metres in just a few strides, and without falling over once.

'*This world is nothing like the one we left behind,*' she explains through the relay. '*Now that we're here, everything needs*

217

reinventing, even the simplest things like how to move around. I've studied the conditions on Mars in books so much that my head is stuffed with figures, with data and statistics. But now we're moving into the practical phase, so my body's got to get used to it, and so do yours.'

Fangfang gives us another little demo, with a running commentary on her movements.

'The vertical forces keeping us on the ground are substantially reduced. As the length and duration of the strides increase, we spend twice as long in the air without any contact with the ground. If you try to fight against that, you're guaranteed to end up flat on the ground. Go on, your turn – have a go!'

We set about it, one after another, with more or less success.

Kris finds it hardest. She's always been a little clumsy, and even after five months on board the *Cupido* she's never been able to get totally used to the weightlessness.

'I don't understand,' she says, faltering in her boots. 'Are we supposed to run or kind of bounce?'

'Neither,' replies Fangfang. 'Or rather, yes, both at the same time. I don't know what you'd call it, I don't know how to describe it to you.'

'I do!' says Liz. 'You've got to . . . rounce!'

'Rou-what?'

'Rounce!'

The English girl has better control over her body than anyone, and she takes a few elegant strides.

'It's a new word I've just invented,' she says. 'You run and you bounce – you rounce! What could be cooler for a dancer than to name a new step?'

And so that's how we continue on our way towards New Eden – *rouncing* along, finding more and more ease as we go. The temperature in my suit becomes bearable again. I manage more or less to control my garment bag, wedging it into my armpit. Even Kris ends up coping not too badly, and at the end of her leash, Louve adopts a move not unlike ours, adapted for her four legs.

It becomes clear as we go that the boys are coming to meet us, moving laboriously in our direction.

'They have no technique!' scoffs Kelly. *'It's obvious they don't know how to rounce! Léo, d'you think your Marcus hasn't taught them? Was he snoozing during his planetology classes?'*

She may be joking, but I can sense the tension in her voice, and it isn't hard to understand why.

My own nerves are hypersensitive.

After five months of carefully timed meetings, of hopes and frustrations, we're finally going to meet the boys we have chosen.

And there they are, in their white suits that stand out palely against the red landscape of Mars, behind silent and impenetrable helmets that reflect the distant Sun. Who is who? Where's Marcus? Impossible to say. I can count one . . . two . . . three . . . four . . . five . . .

The sixth is missing. That must be Tao, who had to stay behind because of his disability.

I'd so love to hear their voices.

To hear them speak.

But the relay only works between us girls; between us and the boys, it's stone dead.

So all I can do is make great exaggerated gestures, like the other girls, and rounce higher, faster, further – towards them.

39. Genesis Channel

Sunday 10 December, 8:33pm

The picture jerks around as if from a handheld camera.

But there isn't a hand holding the camera, it's built into the helmet of one of the Genesis participants, as identified by the caption at the bottom of the screen:

SUBJECTIVE VIEW MALE PIONEER NO. 1 – KENJI

The red soil of Mars recedes further with each stride, then returns into frame, like the surface of a sea in the grip of a great swell. From time to time clouds of powder fill the screen (when Kenji stumbles), and on other occasions the sky is studded with a big burst of grains of sand that are as light as pollen grains (when he falls).

In the background it's possible to see the six spacesuits of the girls, as well as Louve's.

Kenji (off, his voice distorted by the relay): *'The girls don't seem to be having as much trouble getting around as we are; they're doing better than us.'*

In the foreground, the boy walking in front of Kenji turns

towards him: Mozart's face appears in the bubble of the helmet; his brown curls, damp from the exertion, stick to the glass, which has been tinted to protect against the UV rays.

Mozart: *'Doing better than us? But let me remind you your heroine deposited her teammates more than a kilometre away from New Eden, while I brought you down right at the door, like an ace.'*

Kenji, on the defensive: *'That's unfair – Kelly handled it very well. You couldn't have done better yourself with a cloud of ice right in front of you.'*

A third boy suddenly comes into frame: the steel-blue eyes of Alexei are sparkling behind the visor of his helmet.

Alexei: *'Are you all done? Have you finished telling us off? You want the girls to think we're whiny little kids? I'd rather they thought of us as heroes coming to their rescue – so make an effort, try to act like men – real men!'*

Mozart shrugs beneath his suit, muttering a few words in Portuguese: *'Ai, que idiota . . .'*

Alexei: *'What did you say?'*

Mozart: *'Me? Nothing, I just sneezed inside my suit.'*

A deep, slightly cracked voice, sounds from the speakers.

It's Marcus's. *'And how about we just let it all go for now, guys? During the entire journey, we talked non-stop, we were constantly building castles in the sky. But now we're here, maybe it'd be best if we just savoured the moment. We've all been waiting for it for such a long time. And you know, the best things in life happen once and once only – you've got to savour them when they do!'*

The boys keep walking.

The frame of the images keeps trembling.

The silhouettes of the girls keep getting bigger.

There's no sound but the boys breathing – and, if we listen carefully, the beating of their hearts, which are racing, picked up by the relay connecting their six spacesuits.

40. Shot

This is it . . .

I can almost make out their faces, through the visors of their helmets.

Kenji's elusive expression, and Alexei's determined one.

Mozart's caramel-coloured skin, and Samson's obsidian.

It's strange, it's as though Samson was making gestures with his gloved hands. He's drawing shapes in the void, like he did a few hours earlier when he was opposite Safia in the Visiting Room, just about to vote. I turn instinctively towards the Indian girl. She seems to be using this same sign language, which allows them to communicate in spite of the lack of audio connection between the girls and the boys. What might they be saying to each other?

I turn back to look at Samson, and this time I find Marcus's grey eyes, fifteen metres in front of me. All of a sudden, nothing else matters!

With each stride, my body flies up, but I can no longer feel my legs or my arms, nor even my dress in its garment bag. It's as if I've moved onto automatic pilot. Or rather, it's as though I were the spectator of a scene taking place before my eyes.

223

Yes.

That's it.

A viewer of the Genesis channel, one among billions.

All the same it can't be me, the little worker girl, who at this moment is treading upon the ground of Mars, fifty-five million kilometres away from the Eden Food factory; it's impossible that the girl who didn't believe in love should see herself reflected like this in the eyes of a boy like Marcus, and I can't even imagine how . . .

The clash when our two bodies meet brings me back to reality.

Not that it's a violent collision – on the contrary, because it's a very gentle collision, which is all the gravity can allow – I bump into Marcus as delicately as a butterfly landing on a flower, as a kiss being placed on a cheek.

His name escapes my mouth, as if to convince myself I really am touching him.

'*Marcus . . .*'

41. Genesis Channel

Sunday 10 December, 8:36pm

Full frame on Léonor's face, a magnificent explosion of freckles in the middle of which are two huge golden eyes.

Caption at the bottom of the screen:

SUBJECTIVE VIEW MALE PIONEER NO. 6 – MARCUS

Léonor's lips half-open, speaking a word that is inaudible. Her sumptuous red curls, which have escaped from their elastic band, twist around against the curved glass of her visor.

The camera seems to zoom in, but that's just an impression it gives – in reality, Marcus himself is moving forward, until his helmet knocks into Léonor's and he can't get a single millimetre closer.

Marcus, in a whisper: *'Léonor.'*

42. Shot

Month 20 / sol 551 / 17:36 Mars time

He can't hear me.

I can't hear him.

But I can read my name on his lips!

'*Léonor.*'

'*Léonor.*'

'*Léonor.*'

'*My red giant!*'

Giant? On the contrary, I feel so small, despite the spacesuit broadening my shoulders, when Marcus's arms close around me.

From the orphanage to the young workers' hostel, from the hostel to the Genesis training camp, I've never known what it felt like to be at home.

Today, held in these arms, I understand at last.

43. Genesis Channel

Sunday 10 December, 8:50pm

Wide shot on a large red valley, fringed on the left by a huge cliff over the top of which the Sun has already almost set.

Caption: WESTERN VIEW OF IUS CHASMA, EXT. CAMERA, NEW EDEN GARDEN / MARTIAN TIME – 17:50

In the foreground the New Eden Love Nests are twinkling, their shiny black solar panels reflecting the last fires of the day. Behind them, eleven white silhouettes are approaching, their shadows stretched infinitely long across the valley's blood-red powder. Five couples are hand in hand; the eleventh silhouette is ahead of them: it's Fangfang, who is dashing towards the base in great aerial strides, her black garment bag flying behind her like the wings of a crow.

The camera attached to the top of the main dome turns on its axis, sweeping across the glass cells that cover the building, to focus on the ground at the entrance to the base.

Tao is sitting there, unmoving, his light-coloured suit sunk into in the sands. He could be mistaken for an ancient marble statue that time has overturned. Warden is lying beside him like a sphinx, his little helmet turned towards the dusty horizon. Behind him is a metal cylinder, one end of which sticks into the glass – it's the access airlock to the Garden of New Eden.

Fangfang joins Tao and tries to help him up. Even though she's athletic, and even though Mars's diminished gravity has reduced the weight of things and people by two thirds, she still can't do it and collapses beside him.

The camera zooms in as the other astronauts arrive at the beached couple.

Then Tao pushes his gloves into the soil.

Using his arms, strengthened by years of performing in the circus, he drags his massive body onto the sands of Mars.

Like a colossus with broken legs, he transforms himself into a mythological creature – his arms like legs, his legs like wings.

And it's like this, walking on his hands, that he and Fangfang travel the final metres separating them from the entry airlock to New Eden.

Cut.

[COMMERCIAL BREAK]

Fade up on a stadium around which athletes in singlets are running at full speed, to a rock music soundtrack. The camera moves closer, making it possible to see their faces straining with effort.

A serious male voiceover: *'Performance isn't about racing the fastest . . .'*

Suddenly Tao appears in his sports wheelchair, the same

228

compact folding model he had with him on board the *Cupido*. The singlet he's wearing, in the colours of his platinum sponsor, the Huoma automotive company, is drenched in sweat. With his massive, powerful arms he pushes his chair unrelentingly, overtaking the runners who are still crawling around the track – until he crosses the finishing line, in first place. The music reaches its peak, rich with electric guitars.

Voiceover: '*Performance is about going the furthest.*'

The wheelchair morphs into a convertible car, with Tao at the wheel.

Voiceover: '*Tao's choice for going all the way to Mars: the new series Mars Crusader, with high-endurance electric engine, capable of a thousand kilometres between charges. Performance is HUOMA!*'

The logo appears on-screen.

HUOMA
Pure Performance

44. Shot

Month 20 / sol 551 / 17:58 Mars time

'It's unquestionably the day of the craziest firsts! The first man to walk on Mars is a female dog, and the first footprint in New Eden itself will be made by a hand! I daren't think what the first Martian kiss is going to look like.'

It's fine for Kelly to make jokes, since as long as we're wearing our helmets it's only us girls who can hear her.

Tao, walking on his hands, is swallowed into the airlock ahead of us: it's a metal corridor, two metres in diameter and five metres long, at the end of which stands a circular door closing off access to the Garden of New Eden.

Fangfang follows him, then each of the other couples, with the vacuum-packed garment bags and the dogs.

When Marcus's and my turn comes to make our way through the metal circle, I feel my heartrate rising. Only a few more moments before I detach my helmet and take off my suit. Only a few more seconds before I touch him *for real*.

Once all twelve of us are in the airlock, Alexei presses a big glowing red button attached to the cylindrical wall, on which the word EQUALISATION is written. Immediately, an identical circular door to the one in front closes behind us, sealing us in the metal tube. The purple light of the Martian dusk disappears, replaced by the white light of the LEDs that illuminate the module. A gauge in the wall above the equalisation button shows the change as the airlock fills up to become an environment that is breathable and pressurised, like that inside our suits and the glass structure of the Garden.

EQUALISATION 10%
EQUALISATION 20%
EQUALISATION 30%

'Never take your suits off before equalisation is complete, girls,' I say, fulfilling my responsibilities as Medical Officer (and also doing it to channel my nerves a little). *'Mainly because you'll risk a decompression incident, like a diver coming to the surface too quickly, but also because you'll get a nasty gust of wind in the face.'*

I point at the various air vents that punctuate the floor of the airlock. Red whirlwinds are forming, getting thicker and thicker, made up of all the sand and dust we've brought in with us.

'The suction system is designed to capture one hundred per cent of the Martian particles, which can be very corrosive and which tend to stick to our suits and the soles of our boots,' I say. *'Whoever leaves the airlock last needs to activate the evacuation procedures: the module will close up again behind them to eject the particles into the Martian atmosphere and so prevent them from polluting the garden.'*

EQUALISATION 70%
EQUALISATION 80%
EQUALISATION 90%

When the gauge reaches 100%, the equalisation button turns green.

There's a loud click that makes my boots quake, and the door opposite us slides open to reveal a scene of lush vegetation. A series of terraces rise in concentric circles from the edges of the dome; they climb gradually up to their highest point, which is hung with the powerful projectors whose brightness is making up for the evening twilight. Each level is ringed around with a railing, with mechanical arms attached to it. These headless farming robots are equipped with secateurs or watering pipes connected to the well in the life-support station, which is constantly thawing ice from the Martian underground; they are working on the plantations that were sown and which have grown in our absence, without a single human hand ever having played a part in this miracle. Right at the top, at the summit of this pyramid-shaped field, is a proud little cluster of bushes. The Garden is an oasis of life in the middle of the dead Martian desert. A haven peopled with cameras, whose black eyes can be seen behind each plantation, like animals crouching in the shadows.

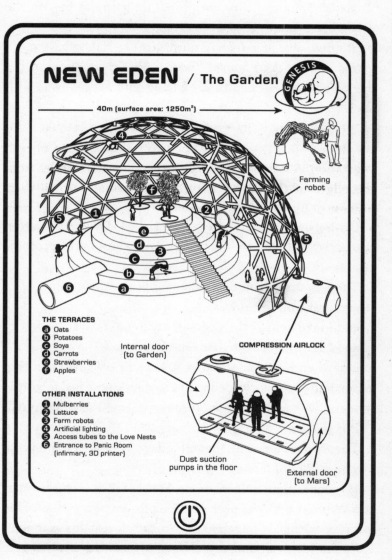

NEW EDEN / The Garden

GENESIS

40m (surface area: 1250m²)

Farming robot

THE TERRACES
- ⓐ Oats
- ⓑ Potatoes
- ⓒ Soya
- ⓓ Carrots
- ⓔ Strawberries
- ⓕ Apples

OTHER INSTALLATIONS
- ① Mulberries
- ② Lettuce
- ③ Farm robots
- ④ Artificial lighting
- ⑤ Access tubes to the Love Nests
- ⑥ Entrance to Panic Room
  (infirmary, 3D printer)

Internal door
(to Garden)

COMPRESSION AIRLOCK

Dust suction
pumps in the floor

External door
(to Mars)

'*Whoah!*' Safia exclaims, dropping her garment bag on the ground. '*It's fantastic!*'

'*It's like we're in a dream!*' murmurs Liz, flabbergasted.

'*Do you see that, Louve? Trees!*' says Kris, pulling on the dog's lead with one hand and clinging onto Alexei's arm with the other.

'*At last!*' begins Kelly. '*I was starting to suffocate in this . . .*' But her last words never reach me – she has already detached her helmet, simultaneously leaving the relay linking our spacesuits. She shakes her head, loosening her blonde mane, while the other girls free themselves in turn.

Having been the last to leave the airlock, I press the button that activates the waste evacuation procedure, as the protocol requires.

Then, in turn, I put down my bag,

and I take off my gloves,

and I take hold of the edges of my helmet,

and I breathe out one last time as I detach the collar . . .

and when I breathe in again, it's the air of New Eden that comes into my lungs, loaded with a smell my nose had forgotten in these five months of our journey, the smell of chlorophyll.

But that's not all.

There's another scent, that till today I've never experienced.

The scent of Marcus.

Here he is, right in front of me. He has taken off his helmet, too. Without the glass of the Visiting Room or the glass of his visor separating us, he seems even more . . . real. It's as though I were suddenly finding myself face to face with a movie star who has just emerged from the screen, incarnate in real life.

Before now I've had only image and sound – now I have all the rest.

I notice the velvety grain of his skin, pearled with drops of perspiration.

I feel the thickness of his hair, glossy with sweat, a deep brown.

I feel the caress of his warm breath against my forehead.

And I inhale his scent: he smells of tree bark heated in the sun, of tender ferns, of life awakening at springtime. So that's what Marcus smells like! This is the scent of his cracked voice, of his greyish eyes, of the forest of tattoos abounding on his skin – I never could have imagined it any different.

'It feels so good being able to breathe,' I say, 'and being able to hear the real sound of my voice. I was starting to feel like I'd been turned into Donald Duck inside this helmet!'

(Just something trivial to relieve the tension, so as not to say how good it feels being able to breathe *him*, and only him.)

A half-smile appears on Marcus's lips – like at our first session in the Visiting Room, when I thought it a smirk that really irritated me. I know now it's a really genuine smile, like a flower about to open, like a bird readying its wings to fly. And that makes me go totally nuts.

'Sorry,' he says. 'What with the landing, the improvised hike, and this suit that's about as hot as a sauna, I must smell like a wild animal.'

'You're not wrong there.'

'Ouch! But coming from a leopard, maybe that isn't necessarily a criticism?'

'You're not wrong there, either.'

His smile widens. He opens his mouth to say something else.

But instead the voice I hear is the one I hate most in the world, and it brings the whirlwind of my senses to a brutal halt.

'My darling little friends! Safe and sound!'

Marcus and I look up at the same time.

And we see the nightmare.

It's Serena McBee's face, dozens of metres high, projected onto the inside of the glass plates that make up the dome of the Garden. Her eyes are as big as ponds of blue-green water; her silver hair stretches towards the sky like metallic mist; her made-up mouth is so big she could swallow all twelve of us up in a single gulp.

'I was so afraid!' she cries, her voice coming from everywhere at once, as if we were in a surround-sound cinema watching some kind of horror movie. 'We were all so afraid! When we saw that ice cloud appearing in front of the girls' capsule, the hearts of three billion viewers stopped beating. Not to mention mine! Oof – just thinking about it gives me chills!'

Serena bats her long eyelashes, like ropes clumped with mascara as thick as knots.

'But apparently space angels have their own god watching over them,' she continues. 'And there you are, all arrived safely into harbour. What a wondrous sight, seeing you all there, six new Adams and six new Eves, in this new Garden of Eden! It's the realisation of everything I've worked for since the start of the programme – what am I saying, of everything I've hoped for my whole life.'

Suddenly a yell cuts Serena's sickly declarations short.

'Louve – no!'

It's Kris.

She's crouched down on the aluminium floor, and Louve's spacesuit hangs limply from her hands like a dead skin. Not far from her, Samson is holding Warden back, while the dog barks his head off. In a flash, I understand what's happening: ever since Louve was let off the leash she's been afraid of the boys' dog, and she's escaped. She's currently running flat out towards me and Marcus.

Reflexively I lean over to try to catch hold of her, but my spacesuit slows my movements. Louve slips through my fingers and into the airlock, whose internal door has just started to close for the evacuation procedure. Above the metal girder a countdown is ticking away in luminous numbers:

29 seconds . . .

28 seconds . . .

'Louve!'

Without stopping to reattach my helmet, I hurl myself into the half-open airlock in pursuit of the dog, the others' shouts and Warden's barks exploding behind me.

'Louve! Come here!'

Paralysed by panic, she curls up into a ball at the end of the airlock against the second door, the one which will open as soon as the first is closed, to evacuate the sand and dust it's sucked up into the Martian atmosphere – and to expel the two of us, too, along with it! My fingers sink into her curly coat. I drag her along the floor and turn around, breathless, to get back to the Garden, the door to which is already three-quarters closed.

But at that moment I feel a violent pain pierce my hand.

I look down: Louve's jaw has closed on my palm – my blood tints her white muzzle, beneath her terrified black eyes.

I drop her.

She lodges herself between my legs, I falter a moment and try to regain my balance, but the one-third gravity makes my movements clumsy: I collapse and sprawl on the metal floor.

When I look back up, the internal opening of the airlock, two metres away, is no more than a crack through which I can see the alarmed expressions of my friends, and, behind them, on the dome's giant screen, the impenetrable face of Serena McBee.

45. Reverse Shot

Fallout Bunker, Cape Canaveral Air Base
Sunday 10 December, 9:04pm

'Oh, that's just too horrible! In only a few seconds, when the internal door closes completely and the external one opens, Léonor and Louve will be ejected into the desert of Mars like bits of common debris!'

Sitting tense in her padded leather armchair, her face turned towards the bunker cameras, Serena McBee's eyes are shining.

Opposite her, the digital wall is showing the view from the airlock camera.

Léonor is lying on the metallic floor, her hand bleeding. In front of her, the opening to the Garden is practically shut.

'Exposed to the Martian atmosphere without the protection of their helmets, their eyeballs will pop out of their heads!' moans Serena.

Under the round table she is holding Arthur Montgomery's hand, as he sits beside her out of shot.

'Their organs are going to explode! Their skin is going to

tear! Not to mention the fact that they're going to freeze and suffocate simultaneously! And there's nothing we can do to stop it, not even me, not even the engineers in the control room, not even the boys and girls who don't . . .'

Serena stops dead.

Marcus has leaped forward from the Garden and wedged himself into the opening of the internal door. It's possible to see the half of his body that has come through, his cheek squashed against the jamb, hand reaching out towards Léonor. The edge of the metal door is squeezing his torso, which is only just protected by the partial rigidity of his thick spacesuit.

'What an idio . . . what a hero!' murmurs Serena half-heartedly.

Under the table, her nails stick into Arthur Montgomery's hands.

'Risking his life to save the girl he loves! But I fear courage won't be enough to protect him from that implacable mechanism, which is programmed to close at all costs in order to protect the Garden at the moment of the evacuation of the debris.'

On the digital wall, the door continues to slide shut.

Marcus's spacesuit is being deformed from second to second like an empty tin can being squashed beneath a heel.

'What can the weak shell of a spacesuit do against the cylinders that activate the doors of the base, moulded from an impossibly sturdy aluminium-lithium alloy?'

Her face twisted in horror, Léonor manages to get up.

She hurls herself towards Marcus, but instead of taking his stretched-out hand she pushes against his body with all her strength, trying to slide him out into the Garden – to the side of life.

'Marcus!' she screams. 'Marcus!'

She can't move him a single centimetre.

The breast of the suit tears.

Polymer splinters fly apart.

The different protective layers of the suit appear as if on a cut-away diagram – Nylon white as ligaments, Spandex blue as nerves, Lycra red as arteries.

'Marcus!'

'Up there . . . you can still . . . make it . . .'

Marcus is paralysed by the pressure of the door that's crushing him, unable to make even the smallest gesture. Only his eyes move in their sockets. They roll towards his forehead, towards the gap that exists above his head between the door and the doorframe – barely forty centimetres, the thickness of his squeezed body and the extra-vehicular survival unit he's carrying on his back.

'C-climb over me . . .' he stammers. 'Climb over the top of me and get back into the Garden . . . Go on, do it now . . .'

'But what about you, I can't let you get crushed!' screams Léonor. 'Try to get loose!'

Marcus's breathing starts to wheeze. His face is getting visibly paler. He gives a faint smile.

'Sorry . . . I'm trapped . . . I can't follow you . . . Looks like my date with death has come today . . . and she doesn't like it when you stand her up . . .'

46. Shot

Month 20 / sol 551 / 18:04 Mars time

'Marcus, I'm warning you! You have no right to die! If I'm the one who gets stood up by you, I swear I'll kill you!'

The shouts come out of my mouth like a hail of bullets.

My fists pummel Marcus's shoulder like a punch-bag.

But however much I shout, however hard I hit him, my efforts are in vain.

I see his pupils dilate.

I hear the purring of the jacks crushing him.

He's in his death throes right here, before my eyes, and there's nothing I can do,

nothing,

nothing,

NOTHING!

Suddenly there's a shrill whistle.

At the time, I think it's the noise of the external door of the airlock which has just opened, and I feel my whole body clench, ready to be sucked into the gaping mouth of Mars.

But I'm not.

There's no suction.

No asphyxiation, no depressurisation, no exploding organs.

Even the humming of the jacks stops, replaced by an automated voice out of nowhere.

'*Warning! Fire detected! All operations on the base have been interrupted. I repeat. Warning! Fire detected!*'

That's when I notice it, in the gap above Marcus's head: *Mozart.*

He's brandishing a cigarette lighter in his fist, like a Statue of Liberty, expression frozen. The little flame is dancing wildly, consuming the oxygen in the Garden, driving the automated voice wild, as it keeps repeating: '*Warning! Fire detected! Fire defence procedure engaged!*'

While the boys pounce on the internal door, the one that is squeezing Marcus's body, and grab hold of it to make it slide back, the space is filled with a hiss. The Garden is veiled in a fine shower: the countless sprinklers carpeting the dome are all set off at once, making an artificial rain fall on the stalks of oats.

The internal door, no longer being pushed by the jacks, can finally be retracted, freeing Marcus and allowing me access to the Garden.

My fiancé's body collapses on the floor, amid the tattered remains of his suit.

'Keep back!' I order the others. 'Let him breathe!'

I kneel down on the damp floor, and start to administer first aid. It's totally unlike the start of the journey, when I felt so helpless when faced with Kris's accident – at the time, her bump had totally traumatised me, and since then I've swotted up on my handbooks very thoroughly. Right now, it's as though the demon of medicine has taken hold of me.

I put three fingers on Marcus's carotid artery, above the collar of his deformed suit, the exact spot where the stem of his rose-shaped tattoo is born – the one that explodes onto his chest in petals that say '*Seize the day*'. I press down hard. There's still a pulse. Weak, intermittent, but there.

But his chest isn't rising.

I can no longer hear his breathing as I lean over him, letting the heavy curtain of my hair fall around us.

I put a hand on his forehead – he's cold – and block his nose, pinching it between my thumb and index finger.

With my other hand, I raise his chin.

I press my mouth to his – pressing firmly, hard like the airlock of a capsule attaching to a spacecraft – and I blow out the air from my lungs so it will go into Marcus's.

His chest swells, parting the bits of torn fabric; then it hollows out again, slowly, while I recover my breath before diving back down onto his mouth.

I blow.

I breathe in.

I blow.

I breathe in.

Each time I sit back, my hair flows up the sides of Marcus's face like an incoming tide; each time I lean towards him, it breaks like crashing waves on the ever more waterlogged ground.

Nothing matters except this rolling back and forth, like a tide, drowning out the hiss of the sprinklers, the panic-stricken murmuring of my friends, Serena's voice and all my thoughts.

And then all of a sudden, just as I'm about to blow for what must be the twentieth time, Marcus takes his own breath.

His mouth takes in a great gasp of air, and some loose strands of my hair. His eyelids open over his shining grey eyes.

I move away to let him breathe.

But a gentle pressure on the back of my neck stops me moving too far away. By the time I've realised it's Marcus's hand, he has already brought me back towards him. I feel his pulse regaining its strength beneath my fingers – is it his heart that's beating so hard, or mine? Our lips meet once again. This time, they don't press into one another like an airlock, they slot together like two feathers.

I shiver.

Now it's my turn to close my eyes.

47. Genesis Channel

Sunday 10 December, 9:10pm

Wide shot of the Garden of New Eden.

The other ten boys and girls are standing around Marcus, who is lying on the floor, and Léonor, who is kneeling over him, both of them masked by the canopy of red hair. All around them, in the light of the projectors, the sprinkler-shower sparkles in a thousand colours and draws a rainbow that spans the entire dome.

Kirsten: 'Léonor's stopped doing mouth-to-mouth. Is Marcus . . . dead?'

Semi-close-up on the German girl. In her arms, she's holding a trembling Louve. Below her crown of waterlogged braids, her face is a mask of anguish, raindrops mixing with her tears.

Alexei puts his arm over her shoulders: 'I don't think so, my angel. Look: Marcus's chest is rising. He's breathing. He's alive.'

Kirsten gulps back her sobs: 'Yes, you're right. But then why do they just stay there like that, why aren't they moving?'

The sound of a whistle.

Cut.

Close-up on Kelly's face – she's the one who whistled.

'Hey, Léo and Marcus, you will tell us if we're bothering you, right? Want to get a room?'

Finally Léonor does look up and pushes her thick hair behind her, a gesture that's both graceful and a little clumsy. The camera zooms in: there's a touch of red colouring her cheeks. Below her, Marcus half sits up and rests on his forearm – his other hand is still resting delicately on the back of Léonor's neck.

Léonor murmurs shyly: 'Everything's fine.'

Reverse shot on Kelly, who is positively beaming: 'Yeah, it looks like it! When I predicted that it was going to be quite something, the first kiss on Mars . . .' She turns towards the camera that's filming from the edge of the dome: 'Well, everyone, did you see that? Even better than at the movies, isn't it? An Oscar-winning best kiss, coming to you live, a lot of bang for your buck! Maybe Léo and Marcus can let us have an action replay of that, but the uncensored version this time, without all that hair blocking our view?'

Reverse shot on Léo, who is terribly embarrassed: 'Oh, stop that, please don't talk garbage. It hardly deserved an Oscar.'

Marcus: 'Well, I think it did.'

The frame pulls out gradually to show the whole little group, torn between tears and laughter. It's the relief after the tension. Marcus isn't the only one breathing easier now.

Fangfang picks up her glasses which fell during the confusion – the frame is broken in two, at the nose – while Mozart puts his lighter away.

He says suddenly: 'When I thought about bringing a lighter with me just to have a little smoke once in a while . . . If I'd known I'd be using it to save an old rival!'

Fangfang blinks short-sightedly: '*A little smoke?* Here? At New Eden? But drugs are strictly prohibited by the regulations – and by law, for that matter!'

The Brazilian smiles: 'Don't panic, I'm only talking about cigarettes.'

But Fangfang doesn't let go. 'They're banned by the regulations, too! Smoking kills!'

Eventually Marcus just shrugs: 'Maybe you couldn't tell without your glasses, but in this case, smoking happens to have saved a life. Just goes to show . . .'

As Fangfang is just about to answer, the huge image of Serena McBee, projected onto one side of the dome, joins the conversation with a six-minute delay.

'He's alive? Marcus is alive? Can you confirm this is correct? Oh, I'm begging you, the anxiety is killing me, and our viewers, too! What a terribly stressful moment for all those families gathered around their screens, waiting so impatiently to see the marriage ceremony, not to mention all those people who've travelled to Cape Canaveral to witness the spectacle! But now that everything is back in order, I trust we're going to be able to make up for lost time and resume the schedule, as planned.'

The sprinklers stop.

The shower dries up.

The base resumes its usual functioning: somewhere deep inside, the jacks go back to their humming, activating the internal door which closes – shutting off the airlock, which is empty now.

Léonor turns her face to the camera. Her long rain-drenched

hair hangs on either side of her face like the cloth of a crimson robe. 'You needn't worry, Serena. The viewers needn't worry. Marcus is alive. We are both alive. I'm sure this news must fill you with utter joy, and will allow you to hang on till tomorrow for the continuation of the broadcast. The marriage ceremony can wait. It's late. We're worn out. We need to sleep. And you ought to get some sleep too. Where's the use in rushing things? We have all the time in the world ahead of us. Remember this programme's slogan, which you wrote yourself: we have *an eternity to love*.'

48. Off-screen

Interstate 80 West, State of Illinois
Monday 11 December, 6:00am

Andrew grips the handbrake tight.

The campervan stops on a small patch of deserted highway. When the headlamps go out, the only light remaining comes from an almost full Moon, and from the small digital clock on the dashboard, which shows 6:00 precisely.

Andrew catches sight of his reflection in the rear-view mirror. His eyes are so tired that his glasses can no longer hide their bags; he's been going for much of the night, and can't manage any more. He needs to sleep.

He sets his alarm for 8am, then turns to the girl stretched out in the seat beside him.

'A quick couple of hours' sleep should be enough,' he murmurs half-heartedly. 'Then I promise we'll be straight back on the road, Harmony, so you needn't worry.'

Harmony doesn't answer, of course. She's already plunged into a deep sleep herself. The blanket she was wrapped in has slipped down during the trip, revealing her shoulders covered only in fine lace. Andrew starts to pull it back up again, the better to protect her from the cold.

There's a glint of light in the darkness – it's Harmony's locket, shifting on the woollen blanket.

Andrew stops what he's doing.

For a moment, he is as still as his strange passenger.

Then, with infinite care, he lifts the locket at the end of its chain to examine it more closely. It's a massive gold oval, made in the traditional manner, delicately worked – the kind of jewel in which one hides distant memories or precious secrets. There's a button allowing access to the inside.

Andrew presses it with his index finger.

Inside the locket, there is a portrait.

But this is no secret, it's one of the best-known faces in the world.

It's no memory, it's one of the smiles that lights up millions of TV screens around the globe every day.

For this face, this smile, belongs to one of the six male contestants from the Genesis programme.

They belong to the Brazilian boy: Mozart.

49. Shot

I open my eyes to see the dome in near darkness.

Way up there at the top, the projectors are off.

On the terraces, the long arms of the farming robots are totally still.

There's silence, disturbed only by the breathing of the boy who is lying beside me on the aluminium ground of the Garden. The Mars night is dimmer than that on Earth, as there is no moon to light it, Phobos being too small to fill that role. But the glow from the small opalescent nightlights scattered across the dome are enough for me to make out Marcus's regular profile, his straight nose, his untroubled broad forehead, his thick hair. When he has his eyes open, the magnetic grey of his irises fascinates me like a mystery, but when they are closed, he looks simply like a boy who is sleeping and who I'll do anything to protect. Yesterday, before we went to sleep, I helped him take off his torn spacesuit. I also listened to his chest through his undersuit, not really knowing what I was looking for, what signs or sounds ought to have worried me – I have so little experience. Finally, it was Dr Montgomery who helped me to carry out the consultation remotely, as the programme's Medical instructor. It was such a bitter feeling, having to leave it all up to this man who I'd always trusted completely, who trained me for a year before betraying me with a dagger in the back! What torture to trust the fate of the man I love to one of those I despise most in the whole world! But Arthur Montgomery must have been saying the same things to himself. He too was forced to play the game for the cameras. The medical doctor and his grateful student: a lovely image for the viewers, however false it might be! Ultimately, I don't really care, the only thing that matters is Marcus's health. He's weak, but there's nothing broken, no bones fractured. With Arthur Montgomery's agreement, I gave him various medicines from my first-aid kit – mostly painkillers (but not aspirin, in case the pressure of the door had caused any internal bleeding). Now he's asleep. That's good. He needs his rest.

But I'm not sleepy at all.

So I get up gently, making no sound.

My friends' bodies are stretched out, scattered across the ground, curled up against one another in their black undersuits – with the exception of Kenji, who absolutely insisted on sleeping in his full spacesuit, helmet included. This isn't quite how we'd imagined our first night on Mars. I feel suddenly dizzy – it looks as though my teammates are already dead, like in a documentary I saw ages ago about the victims of the eruption of Vesuvius at Pompeii. Bodies all shrivelled up, charred, overcome by the volcano's toxic vapours.

And what if Serena McBee has depressurised the Garden, despite the images being broadcast live on the channel?

What if she's cracked under the stress and spread a deadly gas while we were asleep?

I take a deep breath to convince myself that there's no suspicious odour in the air, to drive these absurd thoughts away, since I am obviously perfectly alive.

'Already awake?' whispers a voice behind me.

I turn around, startled.

It's Alexei, his blond hair glowing beneath the stars, his too-blue eyes shining in the shadows of his face.

'Yes,' I say, a little defensive. 'I couldn't get to sleep.'

'Same here. Everything that's happened the last few hours, I couldn't stop turning it over and over in my head.'

Instinctively I glance all around us, taking in the multiple cameras ringing the Garden. Alexei's well aware that this place is filmed and mic'd twenty-four hours a day – one wrong word and it's all over.

But he just smiles, that sparkling smile that made more than one of us fall for him over the course of the journey.

'I got up a little while ago,' he says. 'I took a bit of a walk. And I found this really nice spot. Want me to show you?'

Should I follow him? Why not? Officially we're reconciled now.

I nod, then I follow him.

He leads me towards the aluminium steps to the first terrace, covered in tall stalks of oat. We start to climb, level by level. In the gloom, the unmoving mechanical arms of the robots on their rails look like the legs of giant insects. Here and there I can make out the lenses of the cameras that are fixed all around the dome and in the plantations. Finally, we reach the top of the pyramid. From up there, fifteen metres or so above the ground, we can barely make out the sleeping bodies, whose black undersuits melt into the darkness; only Kenji stands out, in his white suit. I tell myself he's right, this so-called phobic, and that it's actually the rest of us who are unaware of the dangers of falling asleep so totally unprotected, on the basis that the Garden is supposed to remain permanently on air. In future, we should at least organise for people to do guard patrols, for some of us to warn the others in the event there's even a small anomaly in New Eden while we're asleep.

'Can you smell that?' Alexei asks, yanking me out of my contemplation of the sleepers.

I inhale, and a wisp of something sugary tickles my nostrils.

'That scent, something fruity . . . like . . .'

'Yes,' says Alexei gently. 'The smell of apples. The farming robots have actually managed to make apple trees grow here.'

He points at the thick clump of trees that sits at the top of the pyramid, just a few steps away. From this close, the bushes seem bigger, denser than they did from the ground. Their branches stretch out disproportionately wide, covered in an infinity of strangely elongated leaves.

'Apple trees, like in the first Garden of Eden, the one in the Bible,' Alexei continues. 'Except that here, the reduced gravity seems to have had unexpected effects.'

He takes a few steps forward then sticks his hand into the rustling foliage, as dense as a hedge.

He extracts a round shape, which looks as fat as a grapefruit in the pale glow of the nightlights.

I move closer to get a better look.

'A . . . an apple?'

'An apple from Mars. The first one ever picked. Want to taste it?'

For a moment, I consider the red fruit he's holding out to me, so different from any apple I ever saw on Earth. This apple is so huge because during the whole period of its growth it only experienced a third of terrestrial gravity. Yes, that's the logical explanation, the scientific reason, and yet I can't help shivering.

'I'm not hungry,' I say at last. 'And anyway, in the Bible, it's Eve who offers the apple to Adam and not the other way around, if I'm not mistaken.'

Alexei smiles a bit more. Those adorable dimples appear on his cheeks.

'You're right,' he says. 'But we aren't in the Bible. And I'm not your Adam. Remember, it was Marcus you chose.'

He crunches his teeth right into the enormous apple, never taking his eyes off me.

A thread of juice runs down his perfectly shaped jaw.

He wipes it away with the back of his hand.

'Come,' he says.

He plunges into the apple orchard, and the branches close up behind him like an impenetrable curtain. It's as if he's disappeared, and from one moment to the next I seem to find myself alone on the upper terrace. A moment later, I disappear into the leaves in turn. They're so dense that at first I can't see a thing – not the lights, not the distant stars beyond the dome. Then someone takes hold of my arm, and I jump.

'You didn't see me coming? I told you, it's really dark in here.'

Alexei is here, so close; I can feel his breath on my ear, its apple scent, as he continues to speak quietly.

'I'm certain the cameras can't film us, not even with infrared, and the sound is muffled by the boughs of the trees. I've been up for three hours and I've had plenty of time to feel my way around them properly, and they don't contain any mics. So long as we keep our voices down, no one will be able to hear us. By the way, is your hand doing better?'

'It's OK,' I reply, pulling my arm free. 'I put a bandage on it. Louve's bite didn't go too deep. But why have you brought me here? What do you have to say to me?'

My eyes are getting used to the near-total darkness now, and I can make out Alexei's silhouette a few centimetres away.

'I just wanted to make peace,' he says.

'We've already made peace, don't forget. In the spacecraft. You apologised for what you said to me, that I was *disgusting* and all that.'

'That wasn't what I believed. Those words damage me as much as you. They aren't what I want to be . . . They're so unlike my knightly ideals.'

'You said those things in anger. It can happen to anyone.'

'Any man worthy of the name should never insult a woman. Especially a woman like you. You're the total opposite of *disgusting*. You're very beautiful. Really.'

All at once I have no idea what I'm doing in this invisible orchard, with this boy murmuring sweet nothings into my ear. Is Alexei trying to chat me up? No, it's not possible! He's been totally crazy about Kris since the start!

My head is spinning, my breath catches in my throat, and I grab hold of the nearest branch.

'I kind of think Kris is the one who should be here with you, not me.'

'That's the plan. The marriage ceremony will be happening right beside the apple orchard, remember. This is where I'll be offering Kris the ring I promised her on our speed-dates, and which I've worn on a chain around my neck the whole journey. I've been dreaming of that moment since I first set eyes on her! The diamond, I told her, is the symbol of our indestructible love. Kris is so pure, so graceful, so perfect. She will be my queen; I will be the knight in her service. You know her so well – do you think she's going to find it too old-fashioned if I kneel down to put the ring on her finger?'

Ha, so I was just imagining things!

'Not at all, I think she'd love it,' I say, relieved. 'She's such a romantic.'

As I recompose myself, getting my breath back, my fingers feel the surface of the branch I grabbed hold of. The bark is different from trees on Earth, smoother, without ridges, almost like a human skin. I pull my hand back sharply. The apples all around me sway heavily, their plump silhouettes bumping together.

All at once they seem as monstrous as the Genesis logo itself, that vast womb-planet containing a foetus. Nature makes the strangest things here. And what about us, are we supposed just to carry on regardless? Give birth to babies that are as strange as these deformed apples?

'Have you seen what the conditions on Mars have done to these trees?' I murmur. 'The fruits, even the branches, are totally different.'

258

'Yes, it's fascinating.'

'It's terrifying.'

'Those two things sometimes go together. Whatever is new fascinates us and makes us afraid at the same time, doesn't it?'

'Nobody expected the plants to develop like this, or at least if they did, nobody told us. It wasn't part of the programme for our training year. Nor did they tell us anything about how the reduced gravity might affect any future children. Everyone's been acting like giving birth on Mars would be just like doing it on Earth. But if you look at these apple trees, I've real doubts.'

I lean in towards Alexei once again, to be absolutely sure nobody but him can hear my words.

'Listen, you're the Medical Officer, like me. There's something bothering me, but I can talk to you about it: pregnancies. We absolutely have to avoid them. Not only because of the potential risk linked to gravity, which I think is very real. But also and especially because we don't know if we'll be surviving beyond twenty-two months. If all twelve of us die when the Great Storm comes, it will be a tragedy and we'll be the victims. But if along with us we also condemn innocent babies, that would be a crime for which we alone would be responsible. You understand?'

My lips are so close to Alexei, I can feel the heat coming off him.

'Yes, I understand,' he whispers. 'We have to avoid any pregnancies. It would be a crime.'

A wave of gratitude fills my chest. It isn't so easy to talk about this, and the fact Alexei understands me so well helps things a bit. Behind his outbursts and that intense side which

259

unsettles me a bit, he's a boy with his head firmly screwed on, and someone who takes his responsibilities seriously. His stories of chivalry aren't just passing fancies, he has real moral values. If he idealises Kris like that, he must really love her very much. I'm glad they chose each other, after all.

'I haven't got any contraceptives in the girls' first-aid kit,' I say. 'No pills, no coils, nothing. The organisers were very careful about that, since the principal aim of the Genesis programme is to populate this planet as quickly as possible. Down there, on Earth, our viewers and sponsors are waiting impatiently for the first Mars babies. Have your side been given any . . . um . . .'

'Condoms? No.'

'You know what that means, then.'

'A is for Abstinence?'

'Exactly,' I say, a lump in my throat. 'We all need to take a vow of abstinence. A secret vow, of course, since officially for the Genesis channel we have to be trying to make babies. But in fact we'll be remaining chaste.'

'Agreed. It's a big sacrifice, but we have no choice, at least not until we've identified and repaired whatever it was that made the habitats fail. That's the job we have to do. In the olden days, valiant knights knew how to wait – sometimes for years – for the favours of their lady. And tomorrow, if the viewers start getting impatient, we'll let the scientists come up with some explanation – I don't know, something about how conditions on Mars reduce human fertility. Talk to the girls about it. I'll talk to the boys. You can count on me.'

50. Genesis Channel

Monday 11 December, 11:15am

Wide shot of the Garden dome.

Beyond the panes of glass, the night is growing visibly paler.

A small clock superimposed on the bottom of the screen is showing Martian time: 07:55.

Suddenly, at 07:56, beams of sunlight burst through the glass walls, illuminating the levels of oats and soya, making the chrome arms of the farming robots gleam; up at the top of the Ius Chasma cliff, the Sun has just appeared, giving birth to a new morning.

The camera pans across the floor of the Garden.

The boys and girls wake up, one by one. Some are immediately ready to begin their day, like Elizabeth, who stretches her long body, doing a graceful series of limbering exercises, or Marcus, who practises 'rouncing', doing laps of the plantations. Others struggle to get up, like Mozart, who buries his face in the suit he has been using as a pillow, to shield himself from the light. But it's a waste of effort; Louve starts to bark frantically, and this barking is taken up by Warden who echoes her, pulling on his leash and baring his teeth.

Kelly groans like a grumpy bear.

'Those two again!' she grumbles, her blonde mane dishevelled and her eyes mere slits. 'The engaged couple from the animal kingdom can't stand one another, it's ridiculous!'

Clinging to the other end of the Doberman cross's leash, Samson tries to protest: 'We need to give them some time. They're just on edge, it's understandable in this new world where they've got no points of reference. We at least know why we're here, we signed up for this. But they've just found themselves on Mars without ever having asked for it – try to imagine how upsetting that must be!' He crouches down in front of Warden, who finally stops barking to come and nestle his muzzle in the boy's hands. 'The organisers could at least have let us have some toys to calm them down – I don't know, a ball, a frisbee, whatever. I did ask them.'

Still buried in his spacesuit-pillow, Mozart gives a faint groan: 'Me too. I wasn't allowed to bring my guitar. Too expensive, apparently, as every kilo sent into space costs millions in fuel. I only managed to bring the strings, hoping I might be able to cobble an instrument together here, but it's a long shot.'

The camera pulls away from the grumblers, to take an interest in Alexei and Léonor. The two of them are flitting between the various inhabitants of New Eden – him from boy to boy, her from girl to girl – to whisper a few words into their ears.

The camera is curious, and zooms in on Samson at the moment Alexei brings his hand to his friend's cheek. The Nigerian boy's magnificent emerald eyes widen as he learns the secret message, which the Genesis channel's sound system is unable to pick up. The surprise is evident on his face. But the expression he is left with, when Alexei finally pulls his hand away, is one of determination.

Samson looks his interlocutor straight in the eye: 'I

understand. But no, don't worry. I'll make sure.'

The Russian pats him on the shoulder, a manly gesture of gratitude. 'That's great, pal – I knew you'd be the kind of guy to take this seriously.'

Then he walks over to Tao, who has just hauled himself with his strong arms into his wheelchair: 'Hey, acrobat, can I say something in private?'

Tao: 'Of course . . .' A shadow of a doubt passes over the big Chinese boy's face. '. . . but are we really allowed to speak in private? Isn't there a chance we'll get into trouble with the channel?'

Alexei: 'Don't worry. I'm the Medical Officer and what I've got to tell you is something to do with doctor-patient confidentiality. Nothing serious, you needn't worry, but it's totally private.'

At this, he leans over to Tao's ear and delivers his *doctor-patient confidentiality* message.

Annoyed at not being able to take part in these secret conversations, the camera tries its luck with the girls. It moves over to Léonor, who is busily murmuring something in Kelly's ear.

All at once, the Canadian's sleep-heavy eyelids open wide, and her thickly glossed mouth turns into a round O of astonishment.

Kelly: 'No, you're kidding!' Then she continues, almost at once: 'But, yeah, you're obviously right.'

Léonor sinks her golden gaze into Kelly's, as if to intimate that she should say no more, as well as to ask her to make the same commitment as the others.

Finally, Kelly gives a long sigh: 'Pah, better to be warned, at least. Thanks for letting me know, Léo. You can count on me.'

51. Shot

'Well, then, what's with all these secret consultations?'

I pull my hand away from Kris's cheek – she's the last girl I asked to take the vow of abstinence – and look up towards the dome.

Serena McBee has just appeared there. She's more stunning than ever, her silver bob now transformed into a bun worthy of a catwalk, specks of gold illuminating her lips and eyelids. She's wearing a dress in pearl-grey taffeta, with a matching lace bolero on top: a real mother-of-the-bride outfit, offset by a little final touch, the black ribbon on her lapel that's supposed to be in remembrance of the fake attack she invented herself.

'Alexei, Léonor – would you like to share your secrets with the viewers – and with me?' she asks, batting her eyelids.

'It's nothing, Serena,' I say. 'It's just a bit of stress before the weddings . . . and the wedding nights. Because some of us have never . . . It's important that nobody feels bad or uncomfortable. Anyway, as Medical Officers, Alexei and I should be responsible for giving . . . um . . . *technical advice* to the girls and boys, if you know what I mean. It's not the kind of thing we can easily talk about on the air.'

I can feel myself blushing all the way to the tips of my ears. Not because it's a lie.

Not because instead of *technical advice* I was preaching abstinence to the girls.

But because, like I said, I'm very conscious that we're on the air at the moment. I know all too well that there are billions of people listening to me and watching me. And claiming to be giving a sex-ed class to your friends when you've never even let a boy touch you is more than a little awkward.

It's horrifically embarrassing.

It's an opportunity Serena McBee hurries to exploit to crush me, with all her usual haughtiness.

'*Technical advice*, I see . . .' she repeats, after a six-minute pause, a falsely indulgent smile on her lips. 'How considerate! And how brave of you to tackle this subject which, I grant you, is not all that easy. I can't help wondering which bits of first-hand *technical advice* you could have given your friends that would leave them with such shocked expressions! The viewers will never know, of course, since I might remind you that the intimate moments shared by our couples will not be filmed. The cameras in the Love Nests will stop rolling at midnight, to resume at 8am: that is, eight hours and forty minutes of respite for our lovebirds – the Martian sols comprising forty minutes more than Earth days. The boys and girls will undoubtedly be able to put this time to good use and make us some gorgeous babies, thanks to the enlightened advice of Dr Léonor. If she weren't on Mars, I'd invite her to host my famous talk show, *The Professor Serena McBee Consultation!*'

I doubt the viewers will get what's behind Serena's words, I'm sure I'm the only one who can spot all her humiliating insinuations. That little speech leaves me wanting to disappear six feet underground. But that would make her too happy. So I hold firm, standing up straight in my boots, looking right at the giantess taunting me.

And I share the second resolution Alexei and I took with the others.

'I'll also take this opportunity to tell you – you and the viewers – that every night two of us are going to be on guard duty in the Garden, in their spacesuits. It just feels more reassuring, just to be sure the base is functioning correctly while the others are asleep, and to be able to react in case there's any incident. I'm certain you'll approve of our caution, Serena.'

If she thought we were going to leave ourselves at her mercy every night for nearly nine hours, she had another think coming. At the slightest sign of something suspicious, if she tries to depressurise the habitats of the other five couples, the two night watches will intervene. I doubt they'd be able to save us in a scenario like that, but they should at least survive long enough in their suits to get rid of Serena, live. Because the Garden, unlike the Love Nests, will remain on the air every minute of the day and night. If we fall, Serena falls too: simple as that.

Six minutes after I've finished speaking these words, I have the pleasure of watching America's best-known smile fade for a few moments.

'Oh?' says Serena, feigning indifference. 'Cute idea, that night-watching thing. In your uncomfortable suits, too! It's a totally needless precaution, though, if you ask me. But

whatever, Mars is your home now; you do as you think best.'
She recomposes her pleasant expression. 'For now, the time
has come for you to make yourselves look beautiful. I can see
that everyone's in good shape, and your own dear Marcus
seems to have recovered from his heroics yesterday. We will be
able to proceed with the ceremony. It wasn't easy to postpone
it from yesterday evening to today – but all the same, it's still
the biggest, most beautiful, most marvellous party ever held
to commemorate some nuptials. Yes, I'll admit it you've caused
me the prickliest headache in my whole career. And yet what
would I not do for you, my beloved children? After all, you're
unique, and getting married on a Monday isn't just unusual,
it's also the latest fashion! My dear Genesis participants, and
you, dear viewers – prepare yourselves: the weddings of the
century will take place at noon on the dot, Mars time!'

The image of Serena disappears from the surface of the dome,
giving way once again to the desert landscape of Ius Chasma.

I look away from the glass.

My eyes meet Marcus's.

He is looking at me with his famously charming half-smile
on his lips, the total opposite of Serena's contemptuous smile,
teeth bared.

I become aware that my face is still hot from shame.

'I must be as red as a tomato,' I say, lowering my eyes.

'You're ravishing.'

'Don't talk nonsense.'

'Serena's right.'

'What?'

'You'd make the ratings of her programme go through the

roof, if you took part. But I've got you all to myself. I'm the lucky one, I'll be able to enjoy your red-hot *technical advice* in private!'

He gives me a wink that really makes me want to shut him up, and at the same time makes me want to kiss him even more.

'You won't be disappointed,' I retort, trying to make myself sound more confident than I am.

'I'm sure I won't,' he replies, holding my gaze.

If I was thinking of sending him packing with a contest of nerves, I've failed.

He gazes at me with his light eyes that unsettle my feelings in a way that's totally contradictory, as though I were both naked and dressed in the world's most sumptuous gown all at once.

I feel my doubts overwhelming me. What regions has Marcus already explored in that continent about which I know nothing: love? He, who is so seductive, how many girls has he been out with already? How many of them has he made love to? What will he expect, in our situation, and will I be able to live up to those expectations? When he learns I'm a virgin, will he tell himself that I've saved myself for him, or that because of my scar there's never been another boy who's wanted me?

Like the other guys, I saw him take his vow of abstinence when Alexei asked him to. But this thought doesn't reassure me as much as it should. Because now I'm not so sure what this vow really means. Because once again the Salamander is pouring its poison into my ear.

(*So why have you really imposed this abstinence idea, Léonor? To protect the babies of Mars, as you claim? Or to protect yourself, from something that both attracts and terrifies you?*)

52. Off-screen

'Hello? Mr Bill? I'm just calling for a quick *yoo-hoo*! Yeah, yeah, I'm still at Cape Canaveral – I spent the night here! Under the stars, with all the other fans, just imagine! We're keeping ourselves warm, and anyway the climate really is tropical here. You can imagine, nobody went home when they decided to postpone the ceremony from Sunday to Monday at the last minute. There's even more folks here today than yesterday, it's wild!'

'Make sure you don't get people treading on your feet, OK, hon? I'm counting on getting my waitress back in working order.'

'Don't worry, I'll be careful. And Mr Bill?'

'Yeah?'

'Thanks again for giving me these three days off.'

'Oh, there's no call to thank me. And take another day or two if you need it. I can easily keep the old place going a few days on my own, for the handful of nobodies who pass through. I know how much the Genesis programme means to you. To me too, I guess, but long-distance travelling is too much for me at my age. You'll tell me all about it.'

'Oh, I sure will, Mr Bill! You can count on me!'

Cindy turns off her cellphone, sticks it in her handbag and glances around her. The crowd that has come onto the peninsula is huge, even denser than for the launch ceremony. To manage the record numbers, all vehicles have had to park on the mainland; their roofs, in their hundreds of thousands, make up a metallic horizon reflecting the Florida sun. The visitors have done the rest of the journey on foot, entering the peninsula towards the east, passing through the various checkpoints that have been set up since the riots of the night before. The people gathered around the barriers that circle the base are so numerous that it's no longer possible even to see the ground or the heather; the only things breaking through are the loudspeakers mounted on metallic pylons, the same ones used for the commentary for the *Cupido*'s launch ceremony five months earlier. Most of the people are dressed up to the nines, in their Sunday best as though attending the wedding of a member of their own family; some of them are even wearing morning coats or big white dresses as if they were to be married today themselves. Whatever their attire, all of them, Cindy included, are wearing a black ribbon pinned to their lapel.

'It's Woodstock all over again!' gushes a reporter being filmed by a cameraman, as the two of them walk close to where Cindy is standing. 'It's a new universal festival of peace and love! Two million people have come from all over the world to gather here at Cape Canaveral, to witness the weddings of the century!'

The reporter turns abruptly towards Cindy, sticking his microphone under her nose.

'Young lady, can you tell us why you've come here today?' he asks out of the blue.

'Umm . . .' stammers Cindy, caught off guard.

She tugs on the sleeve of the mauve dress that shapes her generous curves, then brings her hand to her carrot-coloured hair, which has been carefully smoothed with straighteners.

'Could I just powder my nose first if I'm gonna be on TV?' she asks shyly.

'What's a young woman like you doing here on her own?' the journalist fires back, instead of answering her question. 'Isn't that a *Heart Available* badge you're wearing on your dress? Are you one of those thousands of single people hoping to find love here today, while celebrating the weddings of the century with all these other Genesis fans?'

Cindy looks down at the heart-shaped badge that's shining on her dress, next to the black ribbon. She goes as red as a beetroot, which makes her look rather charming.

'Oh, I'm not all that young, you know,' she just about manages to say. 'I've recently turned forty. And yeah, I'm single – back where I live there aren't many people passing through, not a lot of chances to meet someone amazing. I'm too old to sign up for the second season of Genesis, but I reckoned here at Cape Canaveral I might maybe meet somebody.'

'Forty years old, and as romantic as an eighteen-year-old!' the reporter interrupts her, spinning back towards the camera. 'Well, isn't that just the magic of the Genesis programme? Let's hear from some of the other fans here today.'

The reporter is already moving away, cutting through the crowd with his technical crew, like sharks in a fish-filled sea.

Cindy takes advantage of his departure to catch her breath, then finally pulls out her powder compact. She spends the next few minutes dabbing at her skin which has turned shiny from the bursts of excitement due to the density of the crowd that's so new to her, accustomed as she is to the vast open deserted spaces of Death Valley.

The moment she closes the case, the loudspeakers begin to broadcast the first chords of the Genesis theme music across almost the whole peninsula. Immediately, two million people – as one – fire up their cellphones, their laptops or tablets to follow the show that will soon be starting beyond the fences of the base, where only the lucky few with their press passes have been invited.

53. Genesis Channel

Monday 11 December, 3:20pm

THE GARDEN OF NEW EDEN, 12:00 (MARS TIME)
This is the caption that appears at the bottom of the picture, a wide shot of the apple orchard bathed in the glowing red daylight of Mars.

The dozen boys and girls are gathered, two by two, in front of the bushes that are covered in fleshy red berries. The boys are in suits, with waistcoats and black bow ties, creating quite a striking group impression, which the girls are livening up with their various white dresses. Only one couple is apart, and they are not human: Louve and Warden are attached to a pair of apple trees slightly removed from the rest, on their respective leashes; they eye one another suspiciously.

Opposite this small group, projected onto the internal surface of the dome, is an image of the launch platform at Cape Canaveral, which has been decorated in a nuptial white for the occasion.

Cut.

CAPE CANAVERAL AIR BASE, 3:20PM EST
Bird's-eye view of the platform, filmed by an airborne camera.

Giant white satin drapes have been hung from the tall pillars, and big vases filled with white lilies have been positioned all around. Rows of journalists in tuxedos and cocktail dresses are gathered at the foot of the metal structure. The camera moves in for a closer look; many of them have been here since the previous night, judging by the bags under their eyes, but the delight at being among the chosen few, selected to cover the "Weddings of the Century", is enough to make them forget their tiredness.

The image switches to a static shot that takes in the entire platform, at the moment when Serena McBee makes her entrance. She is followed by the long train of her pearl-grey taffeta dress, but that isn't all. Representatives from many religions follow behind her, too: a cardinal in a red cassock, an Orthodox priest sporting a long white beard, a minister dressed all in black, a monk in a saffron-coloured robe, a Brahman with coloured symbols adorning his forehead. They take their places in front of one of the immense satin curtains, while Serena climbs the steps to the lectern.

'My dears!' she says into the microphone attached to the podium, turning to the four giant screens that are transmitting a picture of all the betrothed couples. 'How lovely you look! I'm so moved to see you gathered there today, before me and before the men of God who are here with me. Eighteen months have gone past since I first selected you for this programme, and yet it feels more like eighteen years. I do feel like you're my own children, fed and raised at my breast. They say that watching your daughter being led down the aisle is the happiest and most poignant day in a mother's life. Well, for me today, the emotion is multiplied twelve-fold.' Serena pauses a moment, the time it takes to pull out a grey silk handkerchief and delicately dab the corners of her eyes; then she continues, cheerfully: 'I promise I'll do my best not to cry. I don't want my tears to tarnish this day of joy and everything it represents. As you know, in order to respect the beliefs of each one of you, we have planned an ecumenical ceremony.'

The camera pans along the line of religious figures, while Serena's commentary continues in voiceover.

'Such a beautiful vision of fraternity between peoples, made possible thanks to our twelve heroes. That's what the noble spirit of the Genesis programme is about. It's human diversity in all its splendour, in images . . . and in music!'

At these words, the curtain behind the religious men parts to reveal a tiered stage on which dozens of singers of all skin colours are standing, blended into a single group by the identical, immaculate gospel robes each of them are wearing.

The camera zooms in on the centre of the tiers, where a podium stands that looks like ancient column, lined with grooves, in the Doric style. There is a couple standing there at the top of the column, like two Greek statues dominating the world from the pediment of a temple. They are Jimmy Giant and Stella Magnifica, the official pop stars of the Genesis programme. They too are wearing white – him in a perfectly tailored suit, her in an evening gown with a plunging neckline, studded with glimmering crystals – and each is wearing a huge pair of white-feathered wings.

Serena (off): *'Jimmy and Stella will be our masters of ceremonies today. What could be more perfect than these two angels, to marry our other twelve angels?'*

From his perch high above the podium, Jimmy Giant gives a deep bow, his white wings rising up behind him: 'Ladies and gentlemen, this is such an exciting occasion. Stella and I just hope we're up to it.'

Stella Magnifica pretends to look over the edge of the column. She looks down into the void, her eyes as blue as the southern seas, then exclaims: 'Oh, I really do think we're up to it, Jimmy – ooh, this is *very* high!'

The other singer replies – tit for tat – reciting what is obviously a pre-scripted exchange: 'Don't tell me you're afraid of heights, Stella? You've got to be used to them, with those stratospherically tall stilettos you wear!'

Stella Magnifica gives a little laugh that's as natural as a singing exercise, while blinking her eyes which have now become aniseed green (she's wearing evolving lenses, the latest trend on the catwalk): 'Oh my gosh, Jimmy, you're so funny! Stop making me laugh like that, you're going to make me fall!'

She feigns a little falter, but Jimmy Giant catches her by the waist and suggests, charmingly: 'Fall in love?'

Stella Magnifica bats her long fake eyelashes, which are adorned with tiny white down feathers, contrasting with her stunning violet irises: 'Keep talking like that and I'll fall for you, Jimmy, you rogue! But how about you deal with the programme participants for a bit instead of teasing me?'

The man the press has baptised *the new James Dean* throws back his hair with a gesture of practised nonchalance: 'You're right, Stella. Today belongs to the guys and girls of Genesis. To the first couple to be married, who will be Kris and Alexei. And talking about falling for a rogue . . . Just as well he's on

Mars and not on Earth, or I'd have some serious competition!'

Laughter from Stella Magnifica on the podium, and from the crowd all around them. 'I'm kidding. The big Russian guy has settled down with the ravishing German girl, and I think I can say everything between them is unbreakable as steel – isn't that right, Alex?'

Stella gives her on-stage partner the evil eye, which is even more impressive now that the eyes in question are a fluorescent orange: 'Come on, Jimmy – you're a modern-day rebel, as we know from the title of your recent album *Rebel Without a Cause* – an excellent album, by the way, which everyone should rush out and buy. But how about the rebel acting a bit more civilised today and bowing to tradition? These are the weddings of the century, after all. What say you ask Alexei his consent a bit more formally?'

Jimmy Giant agrees: 'You're right, Stella. And while I remember, I should mention how much I liked your recent single, "Diva Divina", it's the bomb!'

The promos completed, he turns to look straight into the camera and asks: 'Alexei, do you take Kirsten as your wife, to love faithfully in good times and bad, till death do you part?'

The choirs sing a piece of Russian religious music, for the time it takes for the solemn question to cover the fifty-five million kilometres separating the huge temporary chapel at Cape Canaveral from the Garden of New Eden.

GARDEN OF NEW EDEN, 12:14 (MARS TIME)
Close-up on the first couple: Alexei and Kirsten.

He is standing proudly bolt upright – high forehead, blue eyes. She is on his arm, a wonder of beauty and coolness. She is wearing a delicate white linen dress with an Empire waist, her chest adorned with a romantic lace trim. Into her crown of blonde braids, crafted especially for the occasion, she has artistically slipped long leaves from a Martian apple tree. She looks like a heroine out of the pages of a novel, a young girl in flower, timeless.

Opposite them, on the screen of the dome, Jimmy Giant has never deserved his stage name more. In a close-up several metres tall, his face really is a giant's.

A stentorian voice comes from his lips, amplified by the dome's acoustics: 'Alexei, do you take Kirsten as your wife, to love faithfully in good times and bad, till death do you part?'

Alexei puffs out his chest as if he wants to make himself as huge as the colossus addressing him.

'Yes!'

Cape Canaveral Air Base, 3:37pm est

'Yes!' – the word echoes from the speakers positioned around the base, below each of the four screens broadcasting Alexei's face.

The Russian singing is drowned out by the roar of the crowds, so powerful and seemingly endless that Stella Magnifica is forced to raise her hand to call for silence so she can take her turn to speak: 'And you, Kirsten,' she asks, 'do you take Alexei as your husband, to love faithfully in good times and bad, till death do you part?'

The choristers begin a new piece of music, this time inspired by Gregorian chanting. At the end of the chant, the view switches back to Mars.

Close-up on Kris's radiant face, as the question spoken by Stella Magnifica three minutes earlier is heard here.

The girl explodes with delight: 'Oh – yes!'

No sooner has she given her consent than Alexei drops to his knees beside her. He undoes his bow tie and pulls a chain out of the collar of his shirt, at the end of which hangs a ring that is set with a diamond. He removes the ring from the chain, then places it delicately onto Kirsten's finger, as her eyes mist up with emotion.

As Alexei gets back to his feet, Jimmy Giant and Stella Magnifica on the screen of the dome speak in a single voice the words they have been rehearsing for days: 'Alexei and Kirsten: you are now united in matrimony. We pronounce you husband and wife!'

The image of two of the religious men appears briefly on the screen: the Orthodox priest and the cardinal, each of them making a brief gesture of blessing.

Then the camera turns to the second couple, Kenji and Kelly.

The mysterious Japanese boy has sculpted his thick black hair into what looks like a spiky warrior helmet. For the first time, Kelly is wearing her hair in a ponytail, which emphasises the perfect structure of her high-cheekboned face. In her long crinoline dress, she is undeniably stylish.

Jimmy Giant gives an admiring whistle: 'Whoah – that's pretty classy, Kelly! And I'm not just saying that because we're compatriots. Or because you're one of my biggest fans. You've

279

already shown us that you know how to be wickedly sexy, but today you've proved you can be as refined as a princess too. You've got everything, a bit like our beautiful country: back home, we've got both lumberjacks and the queens of England! The ideal woman is Canadian!'

Stella scolds her co-presenter: 'Hey there, you do know it's not you who's going to be marrying Kelly today, right?'

Jimmy Giant pretends to be put out: 'Oh, that's true . . . It's that lucky kid named Kenji.' He turns towards the giant screens. 'Kenji, do you take Kelly as your wife, to love faithfully in good times and bad, till death do you part?'

On the four giant screens, Kenji remains still, while a deep murmuring rises up from the choir – it's a Zen Buddhist chant. As time seems to stand still, the young Japanese man looks almost feline. His black pupils seem liquid, like two flickering pools of ink. This tremulous uncertainty usually gives him a lost expression the viewers know well, but in such close-up, it isn't so much distraction that is reflected in Kenji's eyes, but concentration – like a great wildcat, he seems to be contemplating a horizon other people cannot see.

All of a sudden, as the six minutes come to an end, he opens his lips slightly: 'Yes,' he murmurs.

This time the crowd does not yell.

There's something in the Japanese candidate that both impresses and intimidates them.

A single burst of applause breaks through the silence; it's Stella Magnifica clapping from the top of her podium. 'A yes! It's a yes!' she exclaims with exaggerated enthusiasm, in an attempt to wake the audience. 'All together now, a big hooray for Kenji!'

She raises her arms up towards the sky to try to create a Mexican wave, like when a player scores at the Super Bowl, but nobody imitates her, so she hurries on: 'Hmm, well . . . I still have to ask you, Kelly – do you take Kenji as your husband, to love faithfully in good times and bad, till death do you part?'

The choir begin the piece dedicated to Kelly – a real bit of gospel music, that drags the crowd out of their torpor. The thousands of people start clapping along with the singers, while the screens frame the Canadian girl's face. Usually so sure of herself, she seems overwhelmed by emotion, by the magnitude of the moment.

Six minutes later, she replies in a clear voice: 'Yes, I accept.' Then she adds immediately: 'Hi Mom, hi Bros! It's me, your little Kelly, getting married. I so wish you were here standing next to me today. I love you!'

The screens show no more than this, for the ceremony being conducted via a link-up with Mars is planned as tightly as clockwork. The gestures of blessing from the monk and the minister follow quickly, then the next couple appear. Tao in his wheelchair and Fangfang standing beside him, her hand on his shoulder. With her figure hugged by a white sheath dress with a Mao collar, embroidered with a design showing a subtle tracery of flowers and dragons, she represents all the refinement and sophistication of Singapore – with the possible exception of her broken glasses frame, which she has patched up as best she could, with a piece of sticky tape.

54. Reverse Shot

Launch platform, Cape Canaveral Air Base
Monday 11 December, 3:52pm

Tap!

Serena McBee looks down from the launch platform, like a huge statue turning its back on us. She is standing alone at the lectern which back in July she shared with Director Lock on the occasion of the launch ceremony.

Tap!

Five months on, the programme's participants are no longer on the platform, but on the screens surrounding her. It's now Samson's and Safia's turn to speak their vows. The Indian girl is dazzling in a white silk sari with a matching long, embroidered scarf, which she wears elegantly over her shoulder. Her beautiful black hair is tied in a thick braid threaded with gold, and the jewels decorating her face are gold, too: a ring in her right nostril, linked by a fine chain to an earring. The bindi adorning her forehead, though, is emerald green, in perfect harmony with Samson's incredible eyes.

The choir begins a song from Africa.

Tap!

From Serena McBee's perspective at the lectern, the singers arranged in tiers look like smart rows of little toy soldiers. Jimmy Giant no longer has anything giant-like about him. He and Stella Magnifica, so impressive when the cameras are filming them in close-up, seem insignificant: two little white figurines moving about on their pedestal. Even the religious men look like pawns. As for the human tide swelling up against the platform, they are merely an undistinguishable mass.

Serena's hands seem outsized, the hands of a colossus, faced with this miniature universe spreading below her – this puppet show she has staged entirely herself. One metallic grey nail, varnished the shade of steel, taps rhythmically against the wood, like a guillotine blade on its block.

Tap!

Tap!

Tap!

55. Shot

Month 20 / sol 552 / 13:04 Mars time
[2nd sol since landing]

'I don't know if God exists,' I whisper, lifting myself up on tiptoes – even with my Rosier heels, I need to do this to reach Marcus's ears as he stands beside me.

Might as well raise the subject now, I tell myself, while the Brahman and the minister bless Safia and Samson's union. I must have been baptised as a baby, since they discovered a baptism medallion in the trashcan where they found me. And so I ticked the box marked *Catholic* in my application form for the Genesis programme – it was a way of giving myself some kind of identity, at least. But I can count the number of times I've been into a church on the fingers of one hand. No, when my friends nicknamed me the Determinator, they thought I was always so sure of myself, but this is just one more area where I'm not certain at all – about heaven, which has always seemed so far away. Not like Kris, who's a real believer – for her the sacrament of marriage is really important. And not like Fangfang, who didn't hesitate to tick the *No Religion* box on her form.

I don't know what I think.

And I don't know what Marcus thinks either; we've never talked about religion, him and me; in our Visiting Room sessions, there was always so little time.

'Me neither, I have no idea,' he murmurs in reply, still standing very straight in his black suit, facing the screen on the dome, in a voice that rings harsh to my ears. 'But if God exists and he's created a world like ours, with all its injustices, he's someone I hope I'll never meet. I prefer to think that a wedding ceremony is just words, no more than that.'

I look up at him discreetly.

From where I stand, my shoulder touching his, I can see the shape of his jaw clenched over his bow tie.

Once again, his hand closes over mine in its white silk glove.

'I believe in you, because you are here, standing beside me at this moment, and you're the most beautiful of all the brides,' he adds, his voice sweeter now. 'That's enough for me. You're everything I'll ever need.'

Believe in me?

I look down at the white satin top dotted with pearls that cinches my waist and covers my shoulders – just enough to hide the Salamander – and then at the train of holographic fabric that ruffles at my feet. It looks like a sea that is at once moving and still, capturing a rainbow in its white foam. I'll bet Stella Magnifica herself has never worn a finer creation.

Contrary to what Marcus may suggest, there's nothing divine about me, even if the Rosier guys have used all their talent to dress me like a goddess emerging from the waters. I'm nothing but a regular girl, and the faith that my husband-to-be places in me is intimidating. I look away from the dress, letting my eyes wander across the Garden; they finally come to rest on the couple of the moment: Mozart and Elizabeth.

His eyes set on the dome's giant concave screen, Mozart looks so unlike the hoodlum I met five months ago, a T-shirt shaping his pecs, boxers visible on his hips and a rebellious lock of hair in his eyes. Today his hair is smoothed back, leaving his forehead clear, making him look classy, a bit solemn. Beside him Liz is dazzling in a mermaid dress of white organza. They make a beautiful couple, they really do.

'Mozart, do you take Liz as your wife, t . . .'

The moment Jimmy Giant says that word – wife – Mozart turns towards me. It's, oh, just the smallest movement, barely turning his neck a few degrees, which will have passed unnoticed by the cameras, but it's enough for me to come into his field of vision, and for just a moment, for our eyes to meet.

I look down again at once, and I keep my eyes riveted to the floor for the rest of the time it takes for Mozart and Liz's exchange of vows. Why did he look at me? I'd be lying to myself if I said I believed it was just chance. There was absolutely no hesitation in the way his eyes fixed on mine. It's as if I can still see them now, by persistence of vision: two black pupils, shining, burning, fixed on mine. We shouldn't trust appearances – despite his elegant suit and his carefully tended hair, Mozart is still the hot-headed boy I first met. And all the evidence would suggest that at that moment – just when he should have been thinking about no one but Liz – he still has feelings for me.

I do have to look up again when it's Marcus's and my go, but

I'm careful not to look in Mozart's direction. Jimmy Giant is already turning to us on his enormous screen in the glass dome.

'Marcus,' he says, 'do you take Léonor as your wife, to love faithfully in good times and bad, till death do you part?'

'Yes,' says Marcus simply.

Six minutes pass.

While another piece of gospel music is coming out of the speakers, I think back to that other ceremony, the launch, when I had those hesitations about leaving, when I knew nothing about the boys who were standing behind that curtain. And now I'm just about to marry one of them – it's totally crazy!

Stella Magnifica's face appears before me – it's strange, her eyes changing colour so often now it's like looking at a chameleon.

'Lovely dress, Léonor,' she says, a touch of envy in her voice. 'Shame you only get to use it once . . . But I'm getting distracted. So tell me, do you take Marcus as your husband, to love faithfully in good times and bad, till death do you part?'

Are they just words, as Marcus claims? Perhaps. But even if today they're just part of a performance, these words have been full of meaning for the generations who have heard them. As for the last bit, '*till death do you part . . .*' my heart skips a beat each time the masters of ceremonies say it.

'Yes!' I cry, echoing the millions of girls who have answered that question before me. 'A thousand times yes!' I say again, a challenge to death itself, which will not part us for a long time – I swear it.

I notice Kris smiling at me from down at the other end of the orchard. She took particular trouble working on my hair today, recreating the magnificent bridal bun she made on the *Cupido* that one time. And I took charge of her make-up, though it doesn't take much to make her look pretty. Right now, she's glowing with happiness, to the sound of the choirs who have stood to sing a hymn in French; Alexei was right, she really does look like an angel.

'Marcus and Léonor, you are now united in matrimony. We pronounce you husband and wife!' cry the two stars six minutes later, while at the bottom of the podium the cardinal gives us a smile filled with kindness and a gesture of blessing.

'All twelve of you are now married!' concludes the prelate. 'And, um, as is the custom – and I'm speaking with the authorisation of my brothers from the other denominations, you understand – well, I believe the husbands may kiss their young brides!'

I feel dizzy all of a sudden; for a brief moment, I think it's just the reduced gravity playing tricks on me, though I'd have expected to be used to it by now. But I quickly realise gravity has nothing to do with it. A powerful hand slides onto my back to hold me up, the other takes my chin delicately, the way I took Marcus's chin to revive him yesterday evening.

'Marcus, I . . .'

'Tell me if I'm a good student, and if I've remembered all the *technical advice* you gave me yesterday.'

His lips press up to mine, muffling my words and any desire I might have had to protest.

56. Genesis Channel

Wide shot on the apple orchard at the top of the Garden of New Eden.

The six couples of Genesis participants are embracing in front of the fruit-laden bushes.

On the giant screen of the dome, the choirs get to their feet again – for the grand finale, they're bound to be performing *Cosmic Love*. But this time, the tackiness of the Genesis programme's anthem is transcended by the fervour of the singers. These hundreds of human voices, all united, along with the crackling of the magnificent fireworks, launched in broad daylight using brightly coloured smoke, manage to cover up the over-extravagant violins and synthesisers; even the sound of Jimmy Giant and Stella Magnifica's voices are lost in the throng.

As the song swells louder, as the sky takes on new colours, the dome is covered with images beamed in from every corner of the world. Couples of all ages and nationalities have gathered in squares and stadia, till everywhere is filled nearly to bursting.

And these couples are kissing.

Thousands of men and women,
of boys and girls,
of boys and boys,
of girls and girls.
At the bottom of the screen, a counter is speeding upwards:

THE GREAT GENESIS KISS

MONITORED BY

THE GUINNESS WORLD RECORDS ADJUDICATION COMMITTEE

KISSES RECORDED:

[963,254,783]

. . .

[982,567,001]

. . .

[999,893,123]

. . .

[1,015,299,237]

. . .

57. Shot

Month 20 / sol 552 / 13:30 Mars time
[2nd sol since landing]

'More than a billion kisses!'

The voice of Serena McBee brings me back.

My body tips slowly back to the vertical, and I'm back in Mars gravity after the most staggering weightlessness experience of my life.

'*You've all unleashed some real passion!*' says Serena in voiceover, while all around the dome a kissing multitude are spinning. '*You've beaten all the records! I repeat – more than a billion kisses – the number seems so unbelievable, and yet I'm told it's been formally ratified by independent adjudicators!*'

I leave Serena laying it on with a trowel as usual, because for me, amid all those billion kisses, there was only one that mattered.

'I must admit, my first-aid student didn't do too badly,' I say to Marcus, who is still holding me in his arms. 'Congratulations from the judges.'

'He's eager to learn more,' he replies, with a smile somewhere between mischievous and challenging. 'He really wants to get good grades. He promises he's going to study real hard.'

'Wow, sucking up to teacher pretty nicely!'

I straighten myself up completely, while the Earth couples fade from the dome to be replaced by Serena McBee, who's back on the screen now – all good things must come to an end.

'Hot stuff!' she says, miming a fan in her hand. 'Such excitement, my young friends. Such gladness, such joy!'

Then she is suddenly serious again, and announces: 'At this moment of universal happiness, let me spare a thought for your deceased instructors. And let me invite onto the stage those who have been the guides and inspirations at the heart of the Genesis programme, for three minutes of contemplation.'

The image reflected on the inside of the dome expands to cover the entire launch platform, while the poignant notes of a well-known song rise into space: it's Queen's *The Show Must Go On*. The giant screens start to show portraits of our instructors – images posthumously Photoshopped, in which Geronimo Blackbull's wrinkles appear to have been ironed out, and Odette Stuart-Smith's tense smile seems almost to have some warmth to it. A chilling spectacle, to be honest, which instantly sobers me up after the excitement of the ceremony. While the images of these murderers who are being presented as martyrs scroll past, the entire Genesis team walks up onto the stage, joining the religious figures and the singers. The men and women who made the mission possible have been allowed to take off their grey uniforms and are wearing their finest suits and most beautiful dresses. Just to look at them you can tell they're really moved to have been invited to the weddings of the century. You can tell they're shattered by the memory of those who left them – only Arthur Montgomery remains now, stiff as a broomstick in his tux. Their totally genuine emotion tears at my heart, because it's built on a lie. They think they're witnessing a dream come true, never suspecting the nightmare that lies behind it; they think they're crying for colleagues who have gone, while really they're been manipulated by just about the worst gang of bastards you can imagine. The day they learn the truth, that without realising it they've been accomplices to a venture that's sent us to our deaths, their disappointment will be so terrible.

When the melody comes to an end, and all the screens turn black except for an inscription 'WE WILL NEVER FORGET', I feel so bad for them, and for the religious men Serena has used to give her credibility, for the choristers who have given us their all, for the countless viewers of the Genesis channel.

'Right, the three minutes are up!' – an abrupt interruption from the woman who's pulling the strings of this grotesque extravaganza.

The camera is framed on her again, and she has recovered her smile as quickly as she lost it.

'The proceedings of this historic day can continue!' she declares. 'Now that you are married, my handsome young men and beautiful young women, you are no longer merely participants in our programme, you are now officially the *pioneers* of Mars! That is what we will be calling you from now on, as you find yourselves at the forefront of our species' progress, opening up a new territory, a radiant future, on behalf of all humanity.'

Serena's smile widens a few millimetres, a change that is too tiny to be noticed on our viewers' TV screens and tablets, but totally visible on our giant dome screen.

'It is now time to move on to the second great event of this historic day: the auction!' she goes on. 'All the money the donors have generously sent you over the months will be of some use to you at last! Pioneers – we'll be back with you in a few moments, after this commercial break.'

58. Genesis Channel

Monday 11 December, 4:57pm

Open onto a huge opera stage.

Suddenly the sound of a chord, from Prokofiev's famous ballet of *Cinderella*.

Dozens of barefoot dancers in colorful tutus take it in turns to pass the dancer who plays the Prince – a young man in a leotard, down on one knee, holding a glass slipper that sparkles like a diamond.

Close-up on the naked feet that try, one after another, to slip it on, but none of them fit.

A caption appears on the screen, handwritten with elegant upstrokes and downstrokes:

Life often brings us little disappointments.

Wide shot: a new dancer in a grey tutu appears upstage. It's Elizabeth, in the ballet's title role, Cinderella. She gives a magnificent grand jeté, as though she were actually flying to the Prince.

Close-up in slow motion, as her foot begins to enter the

glass slipper – but the impact is too powerful, and the glass shatters into a thousand shards.

Semi close-up on the stunned Prince, while another caption appears:

Sometimes life forces us to deal with serious accidents.

The prince gets back up: 'Mademoiselle, you have shattered the glass slipper!'

Elizabeth answers with a broad smile: 'Don't worry about it, Your Highness: I'm insured by Walter & Seel.'

The Prince's expression brightens and he kisses Elizabeth. Freeze.

One last caption appears, as the final chord of the ballet sounds:

Walter & Seel

Comprehensive Insurance,
Flexible Policies
You'll find your perfect fit with us!

Cut.

59. Shot

Month 20 / sol 552 / 13:39 Mars time
[2nd sol since landing]

'Which commercial do you think they're running now?' asks Kris.

The surface of the dome we're looking at is transparent again, allowing us to see the unchanging red landscape of Ius Chasma. There's something staggering about the stillness after that procession of choristers, priests and pop stars, and the billion kissing couples all over the world.

'No way of knowing, my angel,' replies Alexei, with a kiss on Kris's forehead, 'as long as we don't have access to the pictures from the Genesis channel. Though I'd have loved to see you perform. I'm sure you have awesome screen presence.'

'Oh, far from it!' my friend protests. 'When the Apotech labs made me do my shoot, I had to do about twenty takes I was so terrible!'

The memories of my own shoot come back to me now. At the end of our year's training in Death Valley, each platinum sponsor had the right to one week with their participant – whom they'd bought at the price of gold – for photoshoots, filming commercials, interviews – in short, the production of all the marketing material for use once the mission had begun. And the team at Rosier & Merceaugnac were lovely to me, I have to confess. They brought me delicious little fondant macaroons, they never stopped asking me if maybe I was a bit tired, they accepted my clothing demands without any argument – nothing with a bare back or uncovered shoulders (well, they did manage to slip a tiny sleeveless satin nightie into my suitcase, but I'm sure they meant well). A physio gave me a neck massage between each take (and here again I didn't let her massage my back, to be sure that the touch of her fingers wouldn't discover the Salamander beneath my dress). Everyone took care of me like I was a movie star – I was totally embarrassed by the whole thing! Those seven crazy days left me on my knees with exhaustion, but grateful, intoxicated by the feeling of being appreciated – because that's how it felt, that all those people weren't only there to make money but because they loved their job, and that they loved me a little bit too, not just as their mannequin or mascot, but for me, Léonor, for who I was.

'And now we're back – for the auction!' Serena McBee's voice returns suddenly, yanking me brutally back to the present.

She's on the dome again, blocking our view of the Martian landscape. She's somebody else I thought loved me once. And I was so totally wrong. The truth is, I'll never know what the Rosier & Merceaugnac guys really thought of me; they belong to another world, and it's gone for ever now.

I press myself tighter against Marcus's body, while Serena does her thing.

'Take a good look at what we're going to project on the dome, my dear pioneers – and on your screens, dear viewers.'

A chart appears beside her: the list of all the things we're able to buy with the dollars in our Dowries.

'The lots are listed by category, with the number of available units of each and their price,' says Serena, slipping with disconcerting ease into the role of a Shopping Channel presenter.

'In the *Living Spaces* category, we have six superb Love Nests – the seventh, you'll recall, was originally planned for use in case of an accident.'

I can't help stiffening when I hear this millionth lie. The reality, which the viewers don't know, and nor do the engineers at Cape Canaveral, is that the accident has happened already. At the heart of the penultimate Great Storm, on sol 511, month eighteen, when contact between Mars and Earth was lost for an hour, the animals sent up in secret all died at once, and nobody knows why.

Serena continues regardless.

'This final habitat will also function as the Rest House for the private consultations I will be granting the pioneers, in order to help heal any huge wounds to the soul, and any little booboos to the heart!'

NEW EDEN /
Auction lots

LIVING SPACES

Large Love Nests x2
$250,000,000 ea.

Small Love Nests x4
$150,000,000 ea.

MOBILITY

All-terrain mini-rover x4
$72,000,000 ea.

COMFORT

Robot butler x2
$95,000,000 ea.

3D printer x1
$100,000,000

Hot water: 375 liters /day
$100,000 / liter

FOOD

Apple trees x12
$8,000,000

Carrot plants x6
$10,000,000

Strawberry plants x6
$10,000,000

The Rest House . . .

I think I'm going to have trouble getting used to this latest hypocrisy. Of course, she couldn't have called it the Death House while on the air, even if that's the reality. Still, this way, whenever one of us is going to see her, we can say, '*Serena's calling me – I'm going to the Rest Room!*' – it would be totally appropriate.

'In the *Mobility* category, just look at these four all-terrain, super-strong Mars rovers – they have three seats and are exclusively for private use, unlike the common twelve-seater maxi-rover, which is available to everyone for exploratory missions.

'In the *Comfort* category, we're offering two superb robot butlers, a really useful 3D printer, and hot water produced by the nuclear micro-plant installed in the New Eden support station, at a rate of 375 litres per day.

'And last but not least, in the *Food* category, in addition to your daily rations of oats, potatoes, soya and vitamins, we're putting the apple trees, the strawberry plants and the carrots up for sale – they have been selected for the nutritional benefits they provide in vitamins, and genetically modified to produce crops all year round.'

Serena rubs her ring-decked hands.

'So, there you have it, my friends – I think we can begin! Samantha: the gavel, please.'

A young woman with hair pulled back and an earpiece in her ear comes into shot to hand her an elegant wooden hammer resting on a velvet cushion.

'Here you go, Ms McBee. In cherry wood, as you requested.'

301

Serena takes the object, giving one of those little crystalline laughs that manage to make every hair on my body stand on end.

'A real auctioneer!' she says, delighted. 'How thrilling! I've always wanted to do this, to say those words – *going once, twice, three times – sold!*

She hits the lectern with the gavel three times sharply, as if to test its sound: *bam! Bam! Bam!*

Apparently satisfied, she continues at once: 'We'll start with the *pièces de resistance*, as the French would say, the Love Nests! You can see them appearing on the screen – two magnificent three-bedrooms, at 132 square metres, and four cute little two-beds at sixty-three square metres. Bids are open! Opening price for the first Love Nest: two hundred and fifty million dollars! Who would like to bid? Come on, come on, let battle commence!'

Beneath the Garden dome, looking up at the floor plans of the Love Nests, we meet her question with silence.

We stare at one another – all done up to the nines as we are – with no clue how we're supposed to respond. In other circumstances, we might find the whole circus kind of funny, even exciting. But right now, nobody wants to be a part of the game.

'Well, don't look at us!' Kelly exclaims all of a sudden, her arm draped casually around Kenji's neck, as he watches us in silence.

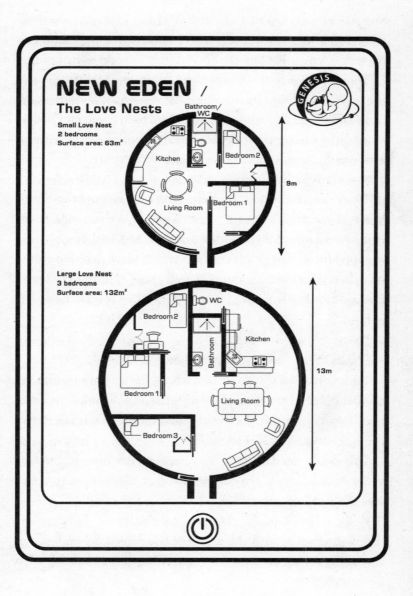

NEW EDEN /

The Love Nests

Small Love Nest
2 bedrooms
Surface area: 63m²

Bathroom/
WC

Kitchen

Bedroom 2

Living Room

Bedroom 1

9m

GENESIS

Large Love Nest
3 bedrooms
Surface area: 132m²

Bedroom 2

WC

Kitchen

Bathroom

Bedroom 1

Living Room

Bedroom 3

13m

She has already hiked the bottom of her crinoline dress up above her knees, because she was too hot; he has pulled his hair back down over his bag-shadowed eyes as soon as he could.

They make a funny couple, the platinum-blonde girl and the mysterious brunette boy, the most demonstrative girl on the team and the most withdrawn boy. Hard to imagine two people more different. Opposite poles. But they both said yes without a moment's hesitation, and I can really sense something electric between them, both rebels in their way.

'Don't expect us to bid,' Kelly goes on. 'The opening price is already more than our whole Dowry. We're going to be completely slaughtered in the auction, and find ourselves in a crappy little hovel with cold water, with one pathetic rotten strawberry for dessert, and that's all there is to it. Like I said, I'm used to being skint. My whole life I've always been left behind.'

'We don't need to bid.'

'What? What are you saying, Léo?'

As so often in the past, the words have come out of my mouth before I've even realised what I'm saying – just like that, totally impulsively. But it really does make sense, now I think about it. Yes, it really does!

'We don't need to bid,' I say again. 'Because an auction assumes the buyers are competing. But we're a team, aren't we? We're all together, right? Let's share the loot!'

Kelly is ferociously chewing on the piece of gum she threw into her mouth the moment the ceremony ended, and frowning; she seems to be having trouble understanding what I'm suggesting.

'Wow,' she says finally, after popping a lemon-yellow bubble. 'Looks like Marcus might have been making out with Léo a bit too long – she's obviously been a bit oxygen-deprived and she's totally lost her mind. Did you hear that? Share the loot? She's talking like a pirate! She thinks she's Léo the Red!'

Ouch – that's a low blow, talking about the character I invented for myself when I was feeling lonely on board the *Cupido*, and who I drew in such detail at length on my sketching tablet. Seen from the outside the whole thing must have looked pretty nuts.

But Marcus comes to my rescue.

'Listen to Léo,' he says. 'Life's too short to be worrying about material things. There's only one way to be rid of the burden: we've got to share.'

'Well said, Marcus!' says Samson, holding Safia in his arms. 'Léo's right!'

'I always knew you were a genius, my darling Léo,' gushes Kris, always ready to bestow labels on me I don't deserve.

'And one more thing,' Marcus continues. 'About us making out. Just to silence the unfounded rumours that seem to be starting up, I must point out that Léo was perfectly capable of breathing while I was kissing her. That was the whole aim of the manoeuvre; for your information, she has awarded me my first-aid certificate, with congratulations from the judges!'

And now I'm blushing again!

Oh, but what a silly little thing I've turned out to be after all these years!

Léo the Red – yes, blushing red in embarrassment!

'What's this I'm hearing? No bidding? Sharing?'

Serena McBee isn't red at all, she's pale. The gavel she was so excited to be trying out is resting uselessly in her hand like a broken toy.

'But you have no right!' she says. 'The regulations are very strict! The donations were allocated to you *as individuals*! You can't transfer them from one couple to another, it's utterly impossible. Remember, you must adhere to the rules of the game, not least out of respect for those people out there who've filled your Dowries and who are watching you at this very moment!'

What we can hear in Serena's voice isn't only disappointment – it's also a threat. The way she's pointing her index finger at us, it's to remind us that we're still under her control and that we need to honour our part of the bargain. We have to keep entertaining the public as if our lives weren't an inch away from death – the inch between her fingertip and the depressurisation button.

'Don't worry, Serena – nor you, ladies and gentlemen who are watching this,' I say, as calmly as I can. 'We'll stick to the rules of the game. They stipulate that the money can't be transferred between the Dowries? Fine. But there's nothing that forces us to bid against one another, right? Nothing to make us go any higher than the opening bids?'

'That's so awesome!' says Kelly, who's finally worked it out. 'The solution is that we all agree on who's going to buy what, without raising the prices that are already crazy enough as it is!' She turns to the cameras. 'Understood, ladies and gentlemen? The money you've sent us is going to be used to bind us even closer together, instead of dividing us. Kris is right – Léo's a mega-genius! Down with the brutality of capitalism! Down with Ultra-libertarianism! Up with sharing!'

The Canadian girl falls into my arms.

'Come here, my heroine – it seems Marcus didn't kiss you enough after all!'

I fight it as best I can, but soon all the girls are at it, encouraged by the boys, and the whole thing ends up in a big joke – the first real laugh we've all had on Mars, at Serena McBee's expense, and it feels *so* great!

60. Off-screen

Harmony opens her eyes slowly.

'Where am I?' she murmurs. 'What time is it?'

As her eyelids open, she becomes aware of the road unspooling before her, hypnotic and monotonous, licked here and there by tongues of fog pierced by the fading daylight.

Her body instinctively stiffens, her fingers grip the stuffing of her seat.

'It's just after five in the afternoon, and you're safe.'

She turns her head left, towards the voice that made her jump. Andrew is there, hunched over the wheel, his face crumpled like a ball of papier-mâché.

'But I really did think you were never going to wake up. You were out for nearly twenty-four hours. What was in that sleeping pill you swallowed?'

Harmony lowers her eyes.

'Thing is, it wasn't really a sleeping pill,' she admits. 'It was a powerful painkiller with codeine, prescribed by Dr Montgomery for my migraines and my nosebleeds. I've learned

308

from experience that it's good for my Zero-G withdrawal – at least, for the first few days.'

'Codeine!' says Andrew. 'But that's basically like morphine . . . No wonder it knocked you out so fast! And this whole time I was worried sick.'

'I'm sorry, Andrew,' she says, quietly. 'I've been acting like an irresponsible little girl since the beginning. I was speaking out of frustration when I said I didn't want your help, even though you've saved my life. I've behaved selfishly, even though there are twelve lives up there that depend on us – not to mention your family, Andrew, apparently under the protection of the police but really at the mercy of my mother! You have a lot more reasons to worry than I do. And I should have told you I was taking codeine before I went to sleep.'

'Yes, you should have told me,' says Andrew, firmly. 'About the codeine . . . and all the rest of it.'

There are a few moments of silence between them, intensified by the humming of the engine.

'The rest of it?' asks Harmony at last.

'You claimed you'd told me everything about you and your life. But that's not true. You lied to me. You haven't told me everything. And I can't help you clear things up about your past if you deliberately keep certain parts of it hidden from me.'

'I don't know what . . .'

'I opened your locket while you were sleeping. I shouldn't have done it, but I did.'

Harmony's face freezes.

'So you saw . . .'

'The photo of Mozart, the Brazilian candidate? Yes. I didn't know you were such a groupie of the Genesis programme that you cut out a photo of your favourite star from a magazine and wore it close to your heart.' Andrew gives a jerky laugh, hoarse from his lack of sleep. 'Oh, but wait – no, it's not a photo cut out of a magazine. It's a real passport photo, and beneath it there was a lock of curly brown hair – Mozart's own, no doubt!'

Harmony grabs feverishly at her pendant. She opens it with trembling fingers, to make sure that the photo is still there, and the lock of hair too.

'If you could see yourself now!' shouts Andrew, pitilessly. 'Like Frodo checking he's still got the One Ring round his neck! You needn't worry, I didn't steal anything.'

Harmony closes the locket gently, but can't quite bring herself to let go of it.

'The One Ring,' she murmurs. 'You're so cruel, Andrew. But you're right. And actually, your comparison is too kind, as I feel more like Gollum than Frodo. A wretched, scrawny creature, a pathetic weakling eaten up by neuroses.'

When he sees the girl's distress, Andrew is quickly himself again.

'Don't talk crap,' he says, more gently now. 'You're nothing like Gollum – nor a hobbit, for that matter. If we're staying in Middle-earth, you remind me more of an elf, with your almost translucent complexion and your light eyes. But even elves, however pure they may be, can still be haunted by a dark side. Like Galadriel. Like you, Harmony. I think it's time you told me the *whole* truth.'

Harmony nods.

She lets the locket slip from her fingers.

'It all started a year and a half ago,' she begins. 'You remember when I met the six Genesis programme girls, like I told you yesterday? Well, the following day the boys also came to the Villa McBee at my mother's invitation. That was when I saw him for the first time: Mozart.'

Harmony's voice seems to stop mid-phrase. A whirlwind of emotions passes across her delicate face – yes, translucent as an elf's, or as a piece of porcelain that the tiniest thing might shatter.

'He was everything I'd ever dreamed of, the perfect man I'd been chasing after my whole life in books, page after page,' she murmurs. 'He was Darcy and Rochester, Heathcliff and Romeo. He was strength, confidence, light. He had all the energy of the girls I'd met the day before, but also something else, a radiant sensuality, which glowed from his skin, tanned beneath the skies of some unknown land – and which blinded me at once – me, the too-white little creature who runs for the shadows at the sight of the first nice day so as to be sure not to catch any sun.'

Harmony sighs sadly.

'From the first moment he smiled at me, I felt myself melt,' she said. 'When I heard his voice, I knew that a whole new chapter of my life was beginning. Because he did speak to me, at length. While the other participants just addressed a few cool polite words to me, he took the time to comfort me, in that warm voice of his. We went under the arbour, at the bottom of the garden, while his friends chatted with my mom, or went to enjoy the pool or the tennis court. I dismissed my dear Balthazar with a few words and a smile, promising him everything would be fine, that I'd call if I needed anything.

'Mozart asked me lots of questions about myself, about who I was, about my dreams, my fears. Nobody had ever asked me questions like that before, and nobody had ever listened to my answers with eyes that shone the way his eyes shone. He told me he understood my loneliness, that he sometimes felt lonely too. He'd not read many books, but he'd heard a lot of stories being told, since that was how people brought stories to life back in his country. He also knew so many songs. He hummed me a few, down in the ivy-covered arbour, and for the first time in my life I felt transported far away from the Villa McBee.

'All too soon it was time for him to leave. The Sun was sinking in the sky, the shadow of the wisteria stretching out on the lawn. Mom had them ring the bell to call the boys back to the courtyard to get in the limo that was taking them back towards New York, towards the airport, towards Death Valley. When I saw Mozart stand up, I felt my heart tearing as though someone was ripping open my chest. I heard a refrain echoing over and over in my head: *You're never going to see him again – never – never – never!* But then he pulled me to him – he held me against his crisp shirt that smelled so nicely of lavender – and said to me: "I'm leaving, but I'll always be here." I felt his fingers slip something into my hand. His body moved apart from mine. He smiled, sadly and happily together. Then he set off for the courtyard, and the light flooding out of the setting Sun behind him swallowed him up. Only then did I look down, and saw in my palm a small plastic sachet filled with sparkling powder, like a crushed diamond.'

The protracted complaint of a horn interrupted Harmony's tale, like a foghorn crying in the mist.

'That powder – it was Zero-G,' murmurs Andrew.

'Yes. My first hit. The others followed by carrier pigeon, landing directly on the windowsill of my bedroom. At first the bird also brought little notes from Mozart tied to its leg. That's how I got this photo and the lock of hair. And that's also how I learned the price I needed to pay to keep receiving my hits; with each delivery, I had to attach one of the jewels I'd been given by my mom to the pigeon's leg. She's always been too busy to notice they were missing.'

'What a piece of shit!' growls Andrew. 'He really does deserve to die on the far side of space!'

'Don't say that. Zero-G is the best gift anyone's ever given me.'

Andrew stares at Harmony in the rear-view mirror, his eyes wide despite the bags that seem to weigh them down.

'Don't you understand?' says Harmony gently. 'Mozart offered me a window to elsewhere. The first person to open the door of my prison, before you came along.'

'What?' cries Andrew. 'I'm the one who freed you, not him!'

'Is it really so different, opening a door in the wall or opening a door in someone's head?'

'He didn't open anything for you! Just the opposite! He's a nasty little drug dealer who's just trapped you even more – in an addiction!'

Andrew's rage doesn't seem to get through to Harmony. Her memories seem to be taking shape around her, like a whirlwind, an unbreachable bastion.

'There's no way to describe what Zero-G feels like when it takes over your body,' she says, dreamily. 'It's as though each one of your hairs, every pore in your skin, every cell in your being is electrified. And all of a sudden you are weightless. You take flight. All those doctors in their white coats, in those public health warnings they show on TV, they all claim that Zero-G deceives you into thinking you no longer have a body, but that's not true – you do still have a body, but freed of any weight, any constraint. You'd never understand what it's like without trying it. You know what they say: taking Zero-G is like making love with the stars. Well, that's where Mozart is now, with the stars . . .'

61. Shot

'And that's that! All our purchases optimised according to the Dowries and each person's needs, without any bidding and with a minimum of wastage!'

Fangfang proudly holds up the chart that she has compiled on Tao's tablet – hers is still in our capsule, a kilometre from New Eden, like all the rest of our belongings apart from the wedding dresses. The doctor of pure mathematics has put her brain to work to devise the best possible allocation of the riches of New Eden, without anyone getting taken for a ride.

And now she is sharing her conclusions with us – with us and the billions of viewers watching us; there's no need to hide what we're doing, there's nothing illegal about our agreement and it doesn't contravene any regulations – that's the beauty of it.

'Let me summarise, just to be sure we're all in agreement, before we send our shopping list up to the production team,' says Fangfang. 'On the Love Nests – Krisalex get one of the big ones, since they've got the money and it makes sense for them to invest their savings somewhere.'

Couple's Dowry	Krisalex $580,999,878		Léorcus $404,918,419		Mozabeth $403,356,163		Samsafia $325,024,983		Fangtao $323,135,790		Kenkelly $234,776,664	
Large Love Nest x2 $250,000,000	1	$250,000,000		$0	1	$250,000,000		$0		$0		$0
Small Love Nest x4 $150,000,000		$0	1	$150,000,000		$0	1	$150,000,000	1	$150,000,000	1	$150,000,000
All-terrain mini-rover x4 $72,000,000	1	$72,000,000	1	$72,000,000	1	$72,000,000	1	$72,000,000		$0		$0
Robot butler x2 $95,000,000	1	$95,000,000		$0		$0		$0	1	$95,000,000		$0
3D printer x1 $100,000,000		$0	1	$100,000,000		$0		$0		$0		$0
Hot water 375 liters / day $1,000,000	103	$103,000,000	54	$54,000,000	53	$53,000,000	59	$59,000,000	50	$50,000,000	56	$56,000,000
Carrot plants x6 $10,000,000	1	$10,000,000	1	$10,000,000	1	$10,000,000	1	$10,000,000	1	$10,000,000	1	$10,000,000
Strawberry plants x6 $10,000,000	1	$10,000,000	1	$10,000,000	1	$10,000,000	1	$10,000,000	1	$10,000,000	1	$10,000,000
Apple trees x12 $8,000,000	5	$40,000,000	1	$8,000,000	1	$8,000,000	3	$24,000,000	1	$8,000,000	1	$8,000,000
Balance		$999,878		$918,419		$356,163		$24,983		$135,790		$776,664

Krisalex is the abbreviation Kelly came up with to combine the couple made up of Kris and Alexei in three syllables. She's attached that kind of nickname to each of us, like a Hollywood star couple – and why not? As long as we have the cameras on us . . .

'The second large Love Nest will go to Mozabeth,' Fangfang continues. 'We think our dancer will make good use of the space to practice, and to prepare the choreography for her *New World Symphony*.

'As for the four mini-rovers, they will go to Krisalex, Mozabeth, Samsafia and Léorcus.'

Léorcus – true, it really does sound pretty weird, but I guess it's not as bad as *Marconor*, *Marléo* or *Cusonor*, right?

'One of the robot butlers will come to us, Fangtao, who have priority – it's a mobility issue.' She rests her hand tenderly on Tao's shoulder, as he sits in his wheelchair beside her. 'The other will go to Mars's very own Rothschild couple, Krisalex.

'By popular opinion, it'll be our national artist – by which I mean Léo – who will make best use of the 3D printer.

'As for the hot water, we've established a general rule for the whole base: at least one hot shower per person per day. Calculating for twenty-five litres per shower – turning off the tap while you're soaping yourself down – that means a minimum of fifty litres per couple. So it's only Krisalex who are allowed showers morning *and* night.'

Kelly bursts a bubble of gum enthusiastically.

'A hot shower every day, that's already a total dream!' she says. 'I didn't always get one back in our caravan in Toronto, especially when my bros were ahead of me in the line. It was

317

that or their smelly feet – they claimed I smelled OK anyway because I was a girl.'

'They were right,' Kenji says suddenly, emerging from the silence in which he has been shut away since the start of the conversation.

'What was that, Tiger?'

'Your brothers. They were right. You smell nice, even without having had a shower in twenty-four hours.'

'Uh . . . It's probably the smell of the gum . . .'

'No, I tasted that when we kissed – lemon, isn't it? But no, the smell of your hair, it's more kind of *yuzu*.'

'Yu-what?'

'*Yuzu*. A citrus fruit that comes from back home, in Japan. Somewhere between lemon, grapefruit and mandarin. Tradition says you should take a *yuzu* bath on the day of the winter solstice; that way you won't catch a cold all year round. There are no *yuzus* here, and no baths.' He suddenly raises his eyes ringed with shadow and meets Kelly's, with that sharp frankness that even the shyest are sometimes capable of. 'But there's you and there's fifty litres of hot water per day. If you want, we could take our shower together, and that way we could also have one both morning and night.'

Mozart whistles: 'Well! It's not just the shower that's boiling hot! This kid's been hiding his game well!'

I wasn't wrong – whatever's between Kenji and Kelly is electric.

Is it just me, or is she blushing slightly?

It's reassuring to know that I'm not the only one, that even a girl who's so sure of herself blushes too!

'Hmm . . . right, well, let's go on,' says Fangfang, straightening the collar of her beautiful Chinese dress, a little embarrassed. 'No *yuzus* on Mars, that's true, but we do have carrots and strawberries. We've done the calculations in such a way that each couple can enjoy one plant of each. Same thing for the apple trees; there too we have a simple rule: each couple will receive at least one of them. And with five trees to Krisalex, our top chef will be able to make us plenty of delicious apple strudels, like she promised!'

Fangfang holds up the screen as though it were a Tablet of Law.

'So – everyone agreed? Can I send this up to the team?'

Everyone nods.

From his place in the wheelchair, Tao looks up at his new wife with tenderness and admiration – you can tell he's so proud of her. It's really cute and touching.

She presses the *Send* button.

At that moment, Marcus collapses beside me on to the soil of the apple orchard, unconscious.

ACT IV

62. Shot

Month 20 / sol 552 / 18:30 Mars time
[2nd sol since landing]

'How's he doing?'

Kris stands, shivering, beside the bed where Marcus is lying – it's a metal structure bolted to the floor like the ones on the *Cupido*. She has taken off her wedding dress and changed into one of her blue outfits. Her long hair, freshly washed, cascades down onto her shoulders. The diamond solitaire shimmers on her finger. Alexei is beside her. He's slipped off his jacket, and he has his arms protectively around his new wife's waist. Louve is sitting at their feet; she's looking at me with her clever, shining black eyes, as if asking my forgiveness for having bitten me yesterday.

'He's doing better,' I say. 'He's asleep now.'

I stroke Louve's head, then reach over to the bedside table to take a sip from my glass. But it's empty, and my throat is so dry. I can't help sighing painfully as I get up out of my chair – the folds of my holographic dress rustle, and my joints crack after so many hours sitting still watching over Marcus. I didn't waste any time bothering to shower, or even change. My satin top is clinging to my skin.

Just as I'm about to head over to the kitchenette to fill my glass, a shape appears from behind Kris and rolls over towards me with a soft humming – yes, it *rolls*, as it's one of the two robot butlers: a vaguely humanoid sort of thing, nearly four feet tall, with two pairs of all-terrain wheels in place of legs, two long appendages ending in pincers in the place of arms, and one big camera eye instead of a face. An incongruous detail: Kris has decked him out in a bow tie, probably the one Alexei was wearing for the marriage ceremony.

'Don't tire yourself out, you can sit back down,' she says, proudly pointing to the robot that Krisalex acquired during the allocation of the auction lots. 'Günter can go fill your glass for you. He's very well brought up, you know.'

Taken aback, I see the robot raise his arm towards me and delicately take the glass in his pincers. This grotesque machine was devised to construct and maintain the New Eden base before the arrival of the humans, not to win design competitions, no doubt about that. It took a bit of Genesis marketing genius to recycle the multitasking worker into a butler.

'*Günter?*' I repeat, kind of curious.

'I've always said that would be the name I'd give my first son,' says Kris. 'I think it suits him, don't you?'

There's something poignant about the way Kris talks about her first son. Because she knows just as well as I do there's a risk that son will never come. So she bestows her affection on this automaton, in anticipation of that day.

'That son of yours definitely isn't my child!' smiles Alexei. 'A scrawny little runt, without legs, with just one eye, and mute as well; he definitely doesn't look like he's got my genes. Nor yours either, for that matter.'

He squeezes her a little tighter in his arms, while Günter comes rolling back towards me with a now full glass, oblivious to the sarcastic comments from his adoptive father.

'If you like, we can lend you Günter to watch over Marcus, while you relax,' says Kris.

'That's nice of you, but I don't feel I can abandon him, not even for a minute. I blame myself so much for not having noticed that he wasn't completely recovered from his accident yesterday! I forced him to stand through the whole of that endless ceremony. I really am totally useless.'

'You didn't force me to do anything.'

All three of us look over towards Marcus, who has opened his eyes. He hasn't been able to change his clothes or shower either, after briefly losing consciousness in the orchard. The boys helped me to stretch his body out in one of the bedrooms in our Love Nest. I unbuttoned his shirt and, as delicately as I could, freed his shoulders and torso. His forest of tattoos appeared suddenly beneath my fingers. In the middle of his chest, on his breastbone, there was a huge blue bruise, like a puddle made by a rainstorm in the undergrowth. The door to the airlock had created this impressive contusion when it closed, but Marcus was careful not to tell me about it at the time. He'd sworn to me that he was OK, that he couldn't feel a thing, and I took him at his word.

'You're a liar,' I say, my voice swelling with reproaches which are really just aimed at myself, pathetic doctor that I am.

'I didn't want to worry you before the wedding.'

'I don't care *why*. A lie is a lie, that's all there is to it. You told me you were doing better. It wasn't true. How do you expect me to trust you now?'

A shadow crosses Marcus's face, which is still resting against the pillow, and I'm immediately sorry for being so tough on him.

'I'm only saying this because I care about you,' I add, taking his hand. 'It's like you said yourself: a wedding ceremony is only words. There was no need to put yourself in any danger because of that.'

Marcus gives me a smile, a strange and sad smile I've not seen on him before.

'We're all in danger . . .' he murmurs.

Within a moment, I can feel Kris and Alexei stiffening behind me, and my own eyes dart across the room towards the camera domes attached to the walls.

We're all in danger . . . – if Marcus finishes that sentence, if he mentions the Noah Report and spills the beans, it might be the end of everything.

'. . . you, and me, and all the viewers watching us,' he goes on. 'We're all in danger, from the very first day of our lives, from the first breath we take, our first cry. You know why I love roses so much? Not because they're romantic flowers or because they allow me to play the ladies' man, which you accused me of when we first met. There's nothing soppy or nice about roses, they're just *true*. Cruelly true. If their petals show us that life is breathtakingly beautiful, their thorns remind us it's deadly dangerous, too.'

I look down at the tattoo on Marcus's right pec: the black rose that forms the words '*Seize the day*.' He didn't choose the motto only for its petals, but also for its thorns. I suddenly get a dizzy feeling that the two of us are strangers. In a flash of lucidity, I realise that, whatever the Genesis programme would have us believe, a handful of minutes in the Visiting Room count for nothing in the hourglass of a life. I don't know a thing about Marcus. And he doesn't know a thing about the girl he's just risked his life for. And yet does this distance pull us apart? No, the opposite. There's only one thing I want: to spend every minute I have left at this boy's side, emptying the sand of my hourglass into his arms.

Alexei's resonant laugh tears me away from my thoughts.

'Hey Marco, you're really sure you're OK?' he says. 'You didn't hit your head on something when you fell? It's obvious your thing with the roses is just for seducing girls, and you're never going to be able to persuade us any different!'

Marcus smiles again, but this time it's that half-smile of his that's full of life, the one that doesn't contain any shadows, it just sparkles.

'OK, yeah, I confess it can be a bit useful for that too,' he says.

'Aha, finally you're talking some sense!'

Alexei punches Marcus's bicep – the right one, the one with the tattoo in thorny letters: '*Dream as if you'll live for ever, Live as if you'll die today . . .*'

'Alex – careful!' says Kris, panicking.

'It's fine, he's not made of glass! Isn't that right?'

'Just wait till I'm back on my feet, then you'll see!' replies Marcus, smiling.

He sits up in bed and tries to punch Alexei's leg, but his friend jumps aside, over the train of my dress, while Louve bursts into a startled yapping and Günter recoils on his four motorised wheels.

'Missed!' says Alexei. 'I reckon you've been spending too much time playing with those pretty little flowers of yours instead of working on your right hook. That's why we nearly saw the end of you yesterday, in the door to the airlock: dulled reflexes. Not great for surviving on Mars, that. Don't forget the girls need strong men to protect them: warriors, not poets.'

'Hey, Sir Lancelot, seeing as you think so poorly of *pretty little flowers*, want to tell us what you've got in your pockets?'

'In my what . . . ?' says Alexei.

Instinctively he shoves his hands into the two pockets of his white trousers.

'What the . . . whoah!'

The expression that passes across his face is one of surprise more than pain.

When he takes his fists from his pockets, each is holding a crushed rose, their thorns sticking into his palms.

'How'd you do that? These trousers didn't have anything in the pockets when I put them on earlier. You slipped these things in just now, under our very noses, without any of us noticing!'

'So maybe my reflexes aren't as dull as all that?' replies Marcus. 'And maybe my pretty little flowers aren't quite as harmless as you say.'

Alexei lets go of the roses, which fall to the ground.

Louve immediately wanders over to sniff at them curiously.

'Well played. You got me that time,' Alexei admits. 'I already screwed my hands up yesterday, trying to open the airlock door!'

'Aw, did our poor brave warrior forget to work on his paws in the *Cupido* gym?' says Marcus, smiling.

'No, it's just that they forgot to supply us with the right equipment. They thought of everything, except a pair of power grips. But they're an indispensable bit of gear!'

Kris takes Alexei's hands in hers to examine them.

'Oh, but you've scratched yourself!' she cries. 'You boys, always trying to compete, showing off like peacocks!'

'Don't worry, it's nothing,' he replies tenderly, placing a kiss on her forehead. 'And anyway, it's only because we're as proud as peacocks too, ready to fight for you, that you love us – isn't that right, girls?'

'We'll have to disinfect that and give you a bandage. Léo, do you have your first-aid kit?' Kris corrects herself at once – 'Oh, no, I'd forgotten, we left all our things in the capsule!'

'I do have my kit, in our bedroom,' Alexei reminds her. 'But you're right, my angel, we should go and fetch your things. We'll arrange an outing tomorrow, on the shared maxi-rover, it's got a big enough trunk to load everything in. I'll go with the two Navigation Officers, Kelly and Mozart, plus Fangfang as Planetology Officer. The rest of you, the Engineering, Biology and Communications Officers, will stay here to carry out the checks necessary for assuming control of the base, as planned. What about you, Léo, will you come along with us?'

I shake my head.

'I'd rather stay here too, at least till Marcus is better. Alexei, you can fetch my first-aid kit and all the rest of the medical gear I brought with me on the *Cupido*.'

'I see . . .' he says, his voice loaded with innuendo. 'You're not to take advantage and try to play doctors and nurses.'

'What do you mean, "play"?' I reply, smiling. 'Here on Mars, I'm a real doctor, just like you. I have the right to do anything I like to Marcus, in the name of science!'

63. Reverse Shot

Fallout Bunker, Cape Canaveral Air Base
Tuesday 12 December, 11:51am

'It's the big day, Ms McBee! In just a few minutes, at noon, the electoral college vote will be a done deal!'

Samantha's face appears on the digital wall, in the window hooked up live to the editing suite. She looks as proud and devoted as a hunting dog laying a partridge at her mistress's feet.

'Very good, Samantha,' Serena McBee replies from her black padded leather armchair – today her taffeta dress has been replaced by an elegant mauve suit. 'The voting papers are in the ballot boxes, and as Caesar would say: *Alea jacta est.*'

On the digital wall, Samantha smiles innocently.

'You really are going to be vice-president of our great country, Ms McBee! I'm so thrilled!'

Serena gives an embarrassed little cough.

'As you know, Samantha, I'm only doing my duty as a citizen. I can't help it if the American people see themselves in me. Right now, what I've got to do is face up bravely to my responsibilities and sacrifice myself for the common good – but if it were just up to me, you know, I'd be spending my days in the garden of my villa, growing my flowers and collecting the honey from my bees.'

'You're too modest, Ms McBee,' ventures Samantha. 'I can tell you that the whole household back at the villa is behind you too – our benefactress. Even Balthazar, who regained consciousness yesterday.'

Serena raises a finely plucked eyebrow.

'Really, he's regained consciousness?' she repeats, a slight touch of distress in her voice. 'Does he remember anything about the burglars who attacked him?'

'No, nothing at all. He doesn't remember anything about what happened in your study. The broken window . . . it's a mystery. Brandon and Dawson, your valets, have confirmed it: it looks as though nothing was stolen.'

'Well, I suppose that's the important thing. I'm glad to hear our good old Balthazar is doing better.'

'He just asked when Harmony would be coming back to the villa. You know how attached he is to your dear daughter.'

'Tell him it's too early to answer that question just now. As you know, with all the pressure surrounding me, the attack on the Atlas jet, all those threats . . . I thought it wisest to send Harmony to Scotland, to stay with my sister Gladys, at the castle of the McBee clan. Do we have anything else to deal with, Samantha?'

The personal assistant consults her tablet.

'We have a request from two of the platinum sponsors, Rosier & Merceaugnac and Eden Food,' she reads. 'They've decided to form an alliance, matching the alliance between their respective protégés Léonor and Marcus, to produce a range of co-branded deluxe frozen meals. The idea being to capitalise on the image of one of the programme's most popular couples, by marrying their two areas of expertise: Merceaugnac's gastronomic refinement and Eden Food's industrial know-how. The people at the communications company brought on board to launch the new product are asking us if they can use some images from the Genesis channel archive, to create a commercial tracing Léonor and Marcus's love story.'

'What a delightful idea!' says Serena McBee. 'I'm sure the new product range will be a smash, and will bring its creators a great deal of money. And so we can charge them top dollar for the use of the archive. A million dollars per second as a fixed rate – in addition, of course, to the royalties that will mount up with each broadcast – I'll let you sort all that out with our finance team.'

'Very well, Ms McBee. Oh, and there is one other thing: there are two people who've been asking to speak to you. One is a Professor Barry Mirwood, who says he met you at President Green's garden party in September. He won't stop calling for an appointment, and he says he's sent you many emails about some sensational new idea.'

'I've blocked his messages,' Serena interrupts her. 'I'm not interested. And the other person?'

'A gentleman from the police, who would like to meet you in private whenever you have a moment.'

This time the executive producer manages to raise both eyebrows, despite the botox freezing her forehead.

'You're talking about Inspector Garcia from the F.B.I., I presume?' she asks. 'He's already questioned Dr Montgomery about the plane being diverted, and regrettably I have nothing to add. Unless he's looking for an autograph, as a long-time fan of my talk show, *The Professor Serena McBee Consultation*.'

'It's not Inspector Garcia, Ms McBee. I'm talking about Agent Seamus from the C.I.A. When and where would you like to receive him?'

Serena takes a moment of silence before answering.

'In private, you say? Well, in that case you can tell him to join me now, here in the bunker – and we're not to be disturbed.'

64. Shot

My skin is on fire.

My sweat is crackling on my skin like oil thrown into a frying pan.

My lungs fill with black smoke, carbonising them from the inside.

I can draw just enough breath to scream.

'No! The habitats have been depr—'

A gag comes down on my face, crushing my lips, muffling my final words.

I open my eyes onto a darkness studded with little white nightlights.

I realise the air I've been inhaling is not poisoned. On the contrary, it smells good – dry wood and fern.

I feel the warmth of the gag, which is made not of fabric but of flesh. It's a hand covering my mouth and chin, the hand of Marcus who is stretched out beside me in the bed of our dark habitat.

'You had a nightmare, Léonor,' he murmurs into my ear,

with that hoarse voice that feels like a balm. 'It's over now. It's over. Can I take my hand away? You won't scream any more?'

My eyes answer *yes*.

It was a close shave.

My dream was so real, I truly thought I was there – the nightmare of flames that has been pursuing me since my earliest childhood, now combining with the internalised anxiety about the depressurisation of the habitats. Utter horror! If Marcus hadn't had the reflex to silence me, I would have blurted out something about the depressurising of the base, I'm sure of it. I might even have mentioned Serena by name . . . and, um, I didn't do that, did I?

'When I shouted . . .' I stammer quietly, consumed by a terrible doubt. 'I hope I didn't . . . The viewers . . .'

Through the dim light of the room I'm looking instinctively for the dull green reflection of the camera domes.

'No, you didn't scream the name of an ex I'm not supposed to know about . . .' says Marcus.

Despite the dimness of the light, I can sense the half-smile forming on his face.

'. . . and as for the viewers, you've forgotten the cameras stop rolling at night.'

Such a relief: I'd forgotten the night-time break!

And Marcus took advantage to wind me up, lying bastard!

He takes me in his arms, and holds me against his bare torso – that's how he fell asleep, still wearing the trousers from his suit. As for me, I spent the night in one of my shapeless XXL T-shirts. Less sexy than the tiny backless satin nightie that the Rosier guys snuck into my wardrobe on the quiet, which I'd never wear. But anyway. Even with the T-shirt completely covering my shoulders, I feel more fragile than ever. The cotton between Marcus's skin and mine feels unbelievably thin.

'Careful,' I say, quietly. 'Your bruise . . .'

'I promise it's getting better, and this time I'm not just pretending.'

'Good thing I didn't accidentally spill the name of one of my exes, as there are so many of them I might have talked about!' I say, to try to make myself feel more confident.

'A lot of lucky guys,' says Marcus.

Does he suspect that I'm lying, and that the list of my exes runs to a grand total of zero?

Does he guess that the girl hiding under the XXL T-shirt is a total novice?

Should I admit it to him now?

'But for now I've got you all to myself, and that's all that matters,' he concludes, cutting short my thoughts of honesty – the truth can wait.

I manage to extract one of my arms from Marcus's, to slip my hand beneath the mattress and check for Ruben Rodriguez's phone. I slipped it down there the night before, just as I'd done on board the *Cupido* – but I won't forget about it this time, I'll take it out at the first sign of betrayal by Serena, to show it to the viewers!

Reassured by the touch of the telephone against my fingers, I let Marcus hold me again.

'I hope I didn't wake you up,' I murmur.

'Don't worry about it. I've only been awake for a moment. Whereas you, my red vixen, you've been sleeping like an old groundhog.'

'A vixen, a groundhog or a leopard? Are there any other animals to complete the zoo?'

'Well, I had a white dove called Ghost for my magic tricks back on Earth,' Marcus says with a smile. 'But the organisers decided it had to stay behind in the animal store on Cape Canaveral . . . We have all left something behind, haven't we?'

Unable to answer this question, I look down at Marcus's flanks, the big indented muscles, where verbs flourish in the shape of laurel leaves: *Run . . . Believe . . . Change . . . Give . . . Desire . . . Dance . . . Love . . .*

I have a desperate urge to draw him.

But more than that, I want to touch him.

I run my finger shyly across his perfectly defined abs. A strange anthology of leafy phrases branches off at angles around his flat navel, just beneath his six-pack:

1 teaspoon white Karo
1 big can evaporated milk
equal part boiled water or distilled water
1 egg yoke
mix and chill
Don't feed him meat or formula cold
1 drop vitamin solution per day.

'What's this?' I ask, intrigued. 'Looks like a recipe.'

'Exactly.'

I can't help laughing. Just a common recipe, in the middle of all these inspirational quotes!

'Very practical, as a reminder, so you don't forget to pick up all the ingredients you need when you go shopping,' I say. 'Only problem is it's a bit hard to rub out – you've got to be sure you want to keep swallowing this same cocktail till the day you die! Go on, seriously, what is it? A protein shake to feed your body after the gym?'

Now it's Marcus's turn to laugh, and I feel his waist tensing beneath my fingers.

'Don't worry, I've never even tried this cocktail,' he says. 'And the recipe isn't something I invented myself.'

'Well, then? So who was it if not you?

Marcus points at his right bicep, which is circled by the quote from James Dean.

'Him,' he says. 'James. It's the last thing he wrote, the night before September thirtieth, 1955, when he took his Porsche 550 Spyder off to race at Salinas in California. A recipe to prepare for his cat, who he'd entrusted to an actress friend in his absence. What he didn't know was that the absence would last for ever: he died in an accident on the road from L.A. to Salinas, and he never came home. He'd only just gotten started in his career, in his life, he was already such a great actor, and he disappeared. Just like that, aged twenty-four, snuffed out like a candle.

'So – yes – I do look at this list often, though not when I'm shopping. I look at it when I get up in the morning, to remind myself that I don't know what will come down the track tomorrow and I should live today as though it's my last.'

Through the gloom, I can see the metallic reflections of the nightlights in Marcus's eyes. They're like two silver stars, watching me.

338

'That's a terrible, sad story,' I murmur. 'But you've learned a good life lesson from it. What happened to the cat?'

'I don't know. But it's a question I ask myself all the time.' He seems to hesitate for a moment, then goes on: 'And what about you, if I just disappeared tomorrow – say, from the aftereffects of the accident – what would happen to you?'

The question is so unexpected it makes me laugh again.

'That doesn't make any sense, Marcus! I know the accident with the airlock has worn you out, but your life isn't at risk! You don't need to worry!'

But Marcus doesn't drop the idea.

'Yeah, I know it's not likely, but still, if I did die from the effects of the accident, would you wish you'd not married me?'

'What are you talking about? This is getting more and more ridiculous!'

'Just answer me, would you regret having chosen me, the dead guy, rather than some other guy who was still alive – Mozart, for example?'

'Of course not, idiot – of course I wouldn't regret it!' I cry, half-exasperated, half-amused. 'Even if you just disappeared, just like that, this very moment, I wouldn't regret a thing!'

Marcus's arms close around me once more, wrapping me in a cocoon of skin and ink. I feel a shiver run through my body, the moment his husky voice whispers in my ear: 'I love you.'

That exact moment, the halogen spotlights dotted around the bedroom all come on at once, spreading a light that gets brighter with every second, eclipsing the gentle glow of the nightlights.

'What's going on?' I say, alarmed. 'Did you turn those on? Or have I pressed a button without realising it?'

'It wasn't either of us,' says Marcus. 'It's 8am on the dot, and the show is starting up again. The lights are coming back on and the cameras are rolling again, so the viewers won't miss a single crumb of our thrilling lives.'

The reality of the programme hits me sharply: the Genesis channel, the eight hours and forty minutes of privacy, the Fangtao duo keeping watch all night in the Garden so that we can sleep peacefully. I can feel my modesty overcoming me, burning as bright as the spotlights which are now reaching their maximum intensity, as strong as daylight.

I push myself away from Marcus's body; even if it pains me to tear myself away from him, I don't want the spectators to interrupt this moment of intimacy that belongs only to us.

'Just think, this whole bedroom was assembled just by machines,' I say, changing the subject to hide my frustration.

My eyes take in the room: the metal bed bolted to the ground; the aluminium floor; the curved white plastic walls. The whole thing looks like the cabin of a plane, except there's no porthole. The whole habitat is a kind of big balloon kept inflated by the internal pressure. Everything else – furniture, finishes, electrical circuits – was installed by the two multitasking robots, which the Genesis programme has now transformed into butlers in service of the show. The same 3D printer I've inherited was used to produce a whole load of items that were essential for the construction of the base. So crazy to think that New Eden, the first human town not on Earth, was constructed remotely, by machines steered from the NASA control rooms.

Does the seventh habitat look the same as this one? What condition would the dead animals be in, after all these months? Are there any clues we might pick up? Some way of understanding what happened when contact was lost last summer, during that mysterious hour that saw the trial animals' death sentence? I'm burning to go see for myself, but not just yet. We've agreed with the others: I'm going this evening.

The exploration will happen then.

Once Alexei has retrieved all the equipment from the girls' capsule.

When everyone is back at the base.

When Kris relieves me at the bedside of my beloved patient.

Then I'll be the first to go into the seventh habitat, to try to understand what happened last year, on sol 511, month eighteen, during the silent hour between 22:27 and 23:29.

I haven't told Marcus, so as not to unsettle him. He doesn't need to know, as I'll be away from him for just a moment. No point him worrying over nothing, right? For now, I'm all his.

'I don't know about you, but I'm starving!' he says, springing up to a sitting position, leaning against his pillow, never suspecting the thoughts that are running through my head.

'Stop that! Don't move another muscle, or I'll have to sedate you!' I say, smiling. 'You really need to rest. What would you say to a bowl of oatmeal with pieces of fresh strawberry and apple? The first muesli on Mars, for breakfast in bed – man, you're a lucky guy!'

65. Reverse Shot

Fallout Bunker, Cape Canaveral Air Base
Tuesday 12 December, 1:32pm

'Thank you for taking the time to see me, Ms McBee,' says
Agent Seamus, stepping inside the bunker.

He's wearing his black suit, which matches his hair and
the patch over his right eye; his left eye shines in the gloom,
catching the light from the digital wall that shows views from
the various cameras on the New Eden base.

'So this is the place where you control the editing for the
biggest broadcast of all time,' he murmurs.

She gestures to a seat facing away from the digital wall,
opposite her padded leather armchair.

'Please, take a seat.'

'Thank you . . . and I should take advantage of this opportunity
to congratulate you on the election.'

'What do you mean? The results aren't official yet, as far
as I know.'

'They might as well be. You know that a country as important
as the U.S.A., in the midst of a time as unsettled as this one is,
where the terrorist threat is so high, can't let itself be surprised

by events. We need to plan in advance. Anticipate the future. Get the insider info. Listen to the silence. That's the C.I.A.'s mission – it's my mission, Ms McBee.'

Agent Seamus pauses a moment. His face is unreadable, seemingly cut in half, his right side swallowed by the shadow of the bunker and the black of the eyepatch.

'*Listen to the silence,*' repeats Serena in a voice that is perfectly toneless, perfectly controlled. 'I'm not sure I understand . . . You mean that . . .'

'I mean we have a very clear idea of the electoral college votes, yes. Even if we can't announce them to the public till January sixth, the official date of the counting of the votes according to the Constitution, I can tell them to you, Ms McBee, with the authorisation of President Green. The intelligence we're receiving is very clear: there aren't going to be any surprises – you will be elected to the vice-presidency of the United States of America. So my congratulations once again.'

Serena's smile widens barely perceptibly. She seems, through her fitted suit, to be breathing more easily all of a sudden.

'Thank you, Agent Seamus,' she says. 'So that's why you wanted to talk to me, to tell me that?'

'Yes, that's why. And also to tell you that your security – which was a high priority already – is now a state matter. So I will have to remain at your side from now on. I promise to make myself as discreet as I can.'

'I understand,' says Serena. 'Security is the most important thing of all, that's quite normal. On that matter, Agent Seamus, I do worry about the families of those who disappeared.'

'They have been placed under police protection, as you

know. Highly experienced agents are guarding their houses round the clock, in addition to the drones programmed to keep watch over the surrounding areas.'

'Yes, I know about that. Still, I can't help but worry. If something were to happen to them, in the middle of the terrible ordeal they're already going through now . . . Would it be possible to provide me with a detailed daily record of the comings and goings of these families? And also a list of all those who visit them?'

Agent Seamus gives a nod, a lock of black hair falling over his eyepatch.

'Of course that would be possible, as it's the American vice-president who is asking for it,' he says. 'All this concern of yours does you credit, Ms McBee. Is there anything else I can do for you?'

This time, Serena's smile widens, revealing the two rows of sparkling teeth that so often illuminate the screens of the Genesis channel.

'Yes, there is one last thing,' she says. 'Talking about the victims' families. Andrew Fisher, the son of the former Communications instructor, has been wanting to talk to me for some time – to share some memories of his dear old dad, no doubt. My domestic staff told me he'd been camping outside my villa, up in the Hamptons, but I wasn't able to see him then, I just didn't get the time. The programme was so demanding in the last days before the *Cupido*'s arrival! I feel bad for having neglected that young man. I'd like to make amends to him, do the honourable thing. Except that I don't know where he is just now, and that troubles me. The C.I.A. would be doing me a great favour if they could bring him to me.'

66. Shot

'So that's that, we've recovered all the gear from our capsule,' Kelly announces proudly, still sweating from her Martian excursion. 'Just as well everything weighs a third as much as it does on Earth! The maxi-rover, on the other hand, drives like a tank. There's no power steering. I've got to be careful or I'm going to end up with muscles like a trucker and I'm not sure my Tiger will like that.'

The girls have all gathered around her in the Garden to retrieve their possessions, which have first had the dust removed from them by the suction pumps in the airlock. The boys are there, too – except for Marcus, who is recuperating calmly in our habitat.

'If you were so afraid of getting muscles like that, you could have let me do a bit more of the driving,' says Mozart.

Nervously, he smooths back his black hair, damp with sweat; I've noticed he does this whenever he takes off his helmet, as if to reassure himself that the little metal marble in the back of his neck is well hidden. Each of us has their complex: for me, the Salamander; for him, the Death's Egg . . .

'It's normal that I should be driving the rover,' answers Kelly. 'We were going to fetch the things from *our* capsule.'

'The capsule you sent crashing into the scenery, more than a kilometre from the base, remember? Women drivers!'

'Chauvinist pig!'

As our Navigation Officers, these two were forced into each other's company, along with Alexei and Fangfang, to take charge of the outdoor manoeuvres. The others carried out tasks according to their respective roles, as planned in the protocol for taking over control of the base, which we were taught during our training period in Death Valley.

'Don't you two start again!' Alexei intervenes just as Mozart is about to answer. 'My head is throbbing after four hours of the two of you in stereo in my helmet! Nobody else gives a damn about your squabbling. So, how about they tell us about their day instead? Wouldn't you like to know whether New Eden is running nice and smoothly? Safia, Kenji, your report!'

I'm not completely happy with Alexei as team leader, though he seems to have no problem at all with taking on the role. His voice sounds like a captain's, and the two youngest in the team practically stand to attention.

'We've inspected all the base's laser and radio systems,' says the Indian girl. 'As far as we can tell, there's nothing to report; everything is working well.'

'Everything is working *for now*,' Kenji corrects her, true to his usual pessimism.

His eyes have even deeper bags under them today than they did yesterday, suggesting he's been sleeping really badly since we arrived at New Eden.

346

'We are still very close to Earth,' he warns us. 'Sixty million kilometres – it's really not that far. But the distance is increasing! As the orbit of Mars drags us around the solar system, the latency period will increase too. When the two planets are at their furthest point from each other, there will be four hundred million kilometres separating them. At that point, the gap between a question and its answer will be forty-four minutes – assuming the communications system is even still working then.'

His words cast a chill over us all.

The six minutes of communication latency are already torture, a moment of unbearable uncertainty in which a thousand things might happen. I can't even imagine what three-quarters of an hour will be like.

'The maximum distance won't be reached till more than a terrestrial year from now,' Fangfang explains, in an attempt to reassure us, but her voice wavers. 'And anyway, I'm sure the communications system will hold out, that's what it was designed for. Just like the rest of the equipment – isn't that right, *baobei*?'

Baobei means *my darling* in Chinese – in other words: Tao.

Fangfang turns towards her husband, who as Engineering Officer has been spending his day criss-crossing the base in his wheelchair to check over the life-support systems.

'Nothing to report from our side either, *tian xin*,' he says. (Translation: *sweetheart*.) 'The lighting from the nuclear mini-generator, the running water thawed from the ice under the Martian ground, oxygenation via electrolysis; we've checked everything, Liz and I. Even the panic room. The isolation system is working perfectly.'

He turns round to face the farming pyramid, and points at the reinforced door in the side of the first terrace – the one where the crop of oats is growing. Behind that door is the panic room, buried away beneath the plantations, which is supposed to be the best-protected location on the whole site. It was designed as a place of retreat in case of a quake or any other major crisis: it has walls more than two metres thick, and a separate oxygen supply that allows it to maintain air pressure and breathability for twenty-four hours. This is also where the infirmary and the precious 3D printer have been set up.

'We've even dug out the master key that allows us to unlock all the doors on the base in the event of some problem,' he concludes, holding up a kind of long metal key that was hanging from the armrest of his chair. 'If there's another accident like the one that happened to Marcus with the airlock, we'll know what to do!'

Reassured that the base is functioning well, Fangfang seems to breathe a little easier.

She takes Tao's hands in hers.

'If you knew how proud I am of you!' she says, her glasses patched up with sticky tape, softening her slightly cold perfection, giving her a fragile, touching look.

Tao's big hands stay open, as if he's afraid of closing them on his young wife's.

'Careful, you'll hurt yourself,' he says. 'You have such delicate skin – and I was born to have calluses instead of palms, like my whole peasant family. Except it wasn't the handle of a sickle I got my calluses from, it was the trapeze at the circus, then after that the wheels of my chair.'

Ignoring his warning, Fangfang squeezes Tao's hands even tighter.

'Which makes you all the worthier of having become our Engineering Officer, *xiao zhu gong*!'

While Fangtao gush over one another very sweetly, without subtitles, the Biology Officers give their report in turn.

'Kris and I have inspected the plantations,' says Samson.

'One half for each of you, right?' asks Alexei out of the blue.

'Um . . . meaning what?'

'I mean this is a pretty big space, with so many plants, you must have divided the task up. You didn't just stick together the whole day. That wouldn't be . . . productive.'

Aha. It would seem the Russian knight is a teeny bit jealous. Samson throws Kris a baffled glance, and she hurries to answer her husband.

'Yes, Alexei, of course we divided up the task. Samson focused on the cereals and tubers, I checked the fruit and vegetables. He looked at the oats, the potatoes and carrots, while I checked the soya, the strawberries, mulberries and apples. Talking of which, our five apple trees have produced a nice big crop – I think I'm going to make some juice, it's easier to store. And what about you? Tell me, did you bring the refrigerated silkworm eggs that were in our capsule?'

'I did, my angel,' replies Alexei, distracted.

'I also used the day to investigate the kitchen in our habitat; it's reasonably well equipped, but it's still missing some basic accessories. There's no potato masher, for example. Given how many potatoes we're going to be eating it's a shame, though! You don't think that should have occurred to them?'

But Alexei doesn't seem in the mood to talk kitchen utensils; another idea pops into his head. And sticks there.

'I've got to trust you, Kris, when you say you haven't spent the day with Samson,' he says. 'Because there were no witnesses, were there?'

It's hard to know if he's kidding or being serious.

Samson gestures discreetly to Safia, who smiles back.

Which was all that was needed to make the powder keg explode.

'What are you saying to each other, Samsafia?' shouts Alexei. 'You don't think we've noticed your little arrangement, ever since we were up in the Visiting Room? You have some kind of secret language, right? Like schoolkids messing around behind teacher's back?'

'Alex, please!' says Kris.

Samson has stopped smiling.

'Hey, you just calm down, and change that tone if you're going to speak to us. We aren't kids and you aren't our teacher. We're all equal here, we're all just as much in charge. If Kris told you she and I weren't flirting, that's the truth. As for our language, me and Safia, it's the signing code that Sherman Fisher taught her for using on spacewalks or any other occasions when we need to communicate without sound.'

'Sherman Fisher?' asks Alexei, suspicious. 'He was the Comms instructor, so I can see how Safia might have learned that code. But you . . .'

'Well, try to imagine other people were doing interesting things while you spent your days working up a sweat in the *Cupido* gym to maintain your Mr Universe physique,' says

350

Samson. 'Learning stuff, for example. I asked Kenji to teach me the code; I figured it might come in useful to me some time.' Samson lowers his voice, and smiles with his white teeth. 'Want me to give you a little lesson?'

Alexei gives a little grunt, then declines his offer.

'No. Thanks. No time to waste on that.'

He pats Samson on the shoulder (this clearly being a mode of communication approved between males), a way of saying that everything's fine now and his little moment of freaking out is over.

'So, our cereal expert – everything good on your side?'

The farming robots really have done a good job getting it running. As of tomorrow, I'm going to lend them hand, to try to improve the yield so all twelve of us can live off the crop.'

'Well, I hope it won't just be a hand, but also some green fingers!' says Kelly. 'Though for now, I don't know about you, but I'm more thirsty than hungry. What with Marcus getting ill yesterday, we forgot to drink to our weddings – time we made up for it. Problem is, it's not just the silkworm eggs that are very refrigerated, our bottles of champagne also froze a bit during the twenty-four hours they spent outside. Boys, will you invite us for drinks today? Then of course it'll be our turn as soon as our booze has defrosted.'

'Works for me,' says Alexei. 'Meet back here in the Garden, eighteen-hundred hours, to give us time to shower.'

That was the signal, the moment I was waiting for.

Everyone has returned to the fold, we've recovered our things and checked the base is working properly, and Marcus is doing better. Not a bad result after three sols, given the way our lives on Mars started! But now it's time to move into the next phase if we want those lives to last as long as possible.

'I've already had my shower,' I say. 'I have to confess, everything that's happened the last few hours has really turned me upside down: the disastrous landing, the bite from Louve, Marcus's accident then his illness. I think I need a turn in the Rest House to have Serena cheer me up. So she can get me practising some breathing exercises, something like that. It'd do me good.'

Alexei nods seriously. He's just making sure that everyone has understood my meaning, that I'm going to be the first to explore the seventh habitat. As the Medical Officer, it makes sense for me to go first, since it's about all our health.

'OK, Léo,' says Alexei. 'We'll keep a glass cool for you, and we'll . . .'

'You sure you don't want me to go with you?' says Mozart abruptly, interrupting him.

He looks at me intensely, his black eyes shining. Does Liz see it too? But she's standing behind him, eyes fixed on the floor, snuggled up in her wrap that she's just retrieved.

'You know the sessions in the Visiting Room are supposed to be one-on-one, Mozart,' I say, uncomfortable. 'I should go on my own.'

'Oh, Léo, do be very careful!' says Kris – then at once she bites her lip, realising that yet again her tongue almost slipped.

I make an effort to smile at her.

'Don't worry. Serena isn't going to eat me! On the contrary, she's going to help me relax!'

67. Genesis Channel

Tuesday 12 December, 9:17pm

Wide shot of the eleven pioneers, gathered in a circle around the pile of things recently retrieved from the girls' capsule.

Léonor lifts her freckled face towards the glass vault, behind which the Martian night has already fallen.

'Did you hear me, Serena?' she asks. 'I'd be grateful for a consultation with you in the Rest House . . . please.'

For a long moment, the pioneers remain still, in the silence. Despite the sweat some of them are soaked in, despite the aches of a strenuous day, nobody is rushing off to the showers.

They wait, their eyes turned towards space, for a word from the heavens.

It arrives, at last, six minutes later.

Serena (off): *'But of course, Léonor! It's quite normal to need to talk, after the bumpy landing you experienced . . . not to mention your first night of love! I'll be waiting for you.'*

Cut.

[COMMERCIAL BREAK]

Open from black onto a man wearing a suit, very serious-looking, seated at his desk behind a heap of files. The phone rings and he picks up.

The serious man: 'Yes, Smith & Co., import-export, how can I help you?'

An incomprehensible voice answers, off: '*Gloobgloobgloob!*'

The serious man's expression turns irritated behind his glasses. 'I'm sorry, sir, I can't take your order – that's Chinese, I don't understand.'

New scene.

A family is sitting together in their living room – a dad, a mum and their young lad – when the telephone rings.

Mum: 'That must be the new foreign pen-pal they assigned you at school, Tommy! Quick, answer it!'

The boy picks up the receiver: 'Hello? My name is Thomas, I'm ten years old, I like soccer and peanut butter. What about you?'

Once again, the incomprehensible voice can he heard from the other end of the line: '*Gloobgloobgloob!*'

New scene.

A crowd has gathered in an enormous square, in front of a giant screen featuring planet Mars and the title *First contact*. But the only sound coming from the loudspeakers is the now famous incomprehensible voice: '*Gloobgloobgloob!*'

Suddenly, a girl detaches from the crowd and addresses the camera. It's Safia.

'Chinese, gobbledygook or Martian, do you have trouble

understanding?' she asks. 'That's because you aren't using the new Karmafone Babel with integrated translator: a hundred and ten languages, in simultaneous translation!'

She pulls a cellphone from the folds of her sari and puts it to her ear. 'Hello? This is Safia speaking, who's that?'

The planet Mars disappears from the screen, giving way to a little green man with antennae on his forehead, who is likewise holding a Karmafone in his three-fingered hand.

The little green man: 'Oh, finally! We were seriously starting to think you Earthlings were all hard of hearing! Yes, we'd like to place an order – five million Karmafone Babels, please!'

Closing shot on the crowd as it raises its arms in the air and starts a dance performance in the ultimate Bollywood style, everyone singing at the tops of their lungs: 'Wondering what the world has to say? Buy your Karmafone Babel today! Kar-ma-fone!'

The sign-off appears on the screen:

KARMAFONE
Buy your Karmafone Babel today!

Cut.

68. Off-screen

Interstate 80 West, State of Wyoming
Tuesday 12 December, 7:25pm

Beep!

The cellphone resting on the dashboard – a Karmafone model – vibrates briefly. Andrew lets go of the steering wheel and grabs it.

The look he gives the little screen is weighed down with weariness and the thousands of kilometres he has travelled from the East Coast.

New Message
From: Lucy
To: Drew

Hey slacker.
   I guess no news is good news?
   Ever since the attacks on Genesis the house has been under police protection. I've got armed men with me, even when I just go out to walk Yin and Yang. They've been asking us where you got to, but since we have no idea we can't tell them anything.

Answer this message.

This is the I-don't-know-how-manyth time I've written.

When you stay away without any sign of life for this long I get scared . . . that you'll just disappear all of a sudden, like Scarlett.

Answer.

Pls.

XOXO – your forgotten sister

'Your little sister again?' asks Harmony weakly.

Snuggled up in her blanket, she is as white as a sheet, and looks even more exhausted than the driver himself.

'Yeah,' replies Andrew, putting the phone back down on the dashboard.

'You really aren't going to answer?'

'It's too dangerous. They could easily geo-locate me even from one call. I have no choice but to keep quiet and pray nothing bad happens to Lucy and my mom.'

He clenches his jaw, then adds: 'I swear, if Serena McBee touches one hair on their heads, I'll make her pay!'

Harmony takes a trembling hand from under the blanket to pick up the telephone, and reads the message in turn.

'*I get scared that you'll disappear all of a sudden, like Scarlett . . .*' she reads. 'What does she mean by that? Who's Scarlett?'

His eyes fixed on the road ahead, Andrew is silent at first, as if tiredness has poured stoppers of wax into his ears and he hasn't heard Harmony's question.

But at last he answers, the tiredness slowing his voice.

'Scarlett was my cousin, the only child of my father's brother, my uncle Patrick. She was also my little sister's best friend, and Lucy's never gotten over her death four years back.'

'Oh! And how did your little cousin die?'

'That's mostly still a medical mystery. It all started with the first attack, which happened at our place, at our home in Beverly Hills. Scarlett was playing in the house with Lucy. They were both seven years old, I was thirteen. My parents had gone out for dinner with my uncle and aunt, and I was in charge of babysitting in exchange for a bit of pocket money to help me buy a new spaceflight simulator. I was rereading Bradbury's *Martian Chronicles* for the tenth time when I heard Lucy screaming. I rushed to her room. Scarlett was lying there, on the carpet, surrounded by a pile of dolls. In horror movies, there's a whole load of sound effects and shrieking music to make the audience's hair stand on end, but I can tell you, the really horrific thing was the silence, when you put your ear to the chest of a little girl who's not moving and you don't hear anything, nothing at all.'

Andrew swallows, as though the taste of the memories was too bitter in his mouth. But he overcomes his revulsion and his fatigue, continuing the story he has begun.

'My cousin Scarlett died for a moment. Then she came back to life. By the time help had arrived, her heart was beating, and she was breathing again. They kept her under observation in hospital for several days. She had no aftereffects, no neurological lesions, which you'd worry could happen when the flow of fresh blood to the brain is temporarily interrupted. She was unharmed – a miracle. The doctors took the opportunity to carry out complicated tests, to try to understand what had caused her to fall ill. They couldn't find a malformation of the heart, or an aneurism.'

Andrew exhales slowly.

The headlights of the car behind the campervan are reflected in the rear-view mirror and, playing off the mirror, in his glasses. With a movement of his hand he tips the rear-view mirror to the 'night-time' position so as not to be dazzled.

'But Scarlett's remission was only a trick,' he continues. 'Almost a year to the day after her first attack, she was struck down by a second attack, and she never recovered from this one. At the time of the autopsy, the doctors discovered that she was carrying a gene that . . .'

Andrew stops suddenly, his eyes on the rear-view mirror, in which the car behind them is closer than ever.

He stiffens.

'They're following us!'

'What?'

'Behind us. I'm sure of it.'

The girl turns around in her seat, but she blinks. The headlights are dazzling her through the rear window.

'Is it the police?' she says. 'I can't see anything.'

The lights of the unknown car are all the more blinding because there is nothing to offset them: all around, it's the pitch-black night. On this stretch of highway lost in the middle of Wyoming, at this late hour of the darkest month of the year, there's neither traffic nor public lighting. There's only the vast, snowy plain, beneath an indifferent floating moon.

Suddenly the red splash of a revolving light mixes with the yellow glare of the headlights.

'The police!' says Andrew.

A voice rises through a loudspeaker over the sound of the engines.

'*In the name of the law, stop your vehicle and pull over to the side of the road. I repeat: pull over to the side of the road.*'

Harmony starts fiddling with her locket, as she does whenever she's overtaken by panic.

'What are we going to do?' she cries.

'We've got to stop,' says Andrew, blankly. 'We have no choice.'

He presses down on the brake. Then, as the campervan slows down, he turns his head towards Harmony for a moment, and sees her clutching her pendant.

'That little thug again.' He whistles. 'He can't do anything for you now, no more today than he could before. Promise me just one thing: you haven't got a single gram of Zero-G on you, right?'

'If I had, I wouldn't have needed to go for the codeine.'

The humming of the engine stops.

The campervan comes to a halt, and the police car does too, a few metres behind it.

The great silence of the Wild West crashes down onto Interstate 80. The red revolving light, which is still spinning noiselessly, turns the snowy banks beside the road blood-red.

'*Remain in your vehicle,*' commands the voice through the loudspeaker. '*Keep your hands on the wheel.*'

The slam of a door pierces the night.

It's followed by the echo of the officer's boots against the tarmac.

Andrew frantically shoves his hand into his backpack and pulls out a second cellphone.

'Who are you going to call?' asks Harmony.

'No one,' he whispers, quickly. 'This thing isn't a phone, it's a camouflaged device that zaps out electrical impulses. A bit of self-defence to paralyse an attacker. Basically a Taser. Couldn't use it against Balthazar the other day. You've got to be in direct contact.'

Andrew puts the Taser down on the seat beside his thigh and hurriedly replaces both hands on the steering wheel, just seconds before the police officer reaches his door.

Using the end of his flashlight, he taps three times on the window, to ask the driver to lower it. Andrew does so, exposing the campervan to the night-time cold. The officer's black anorak is barely visible in the darkness, just like his short-brim cap on which gleams the star insignia of the State of Wyoming patrol. The butt of a revolver and the rings of a pair of handcuffs are shining at his waist.

'Do you know why I pulled you over tonight?' the police officer asks, in accordance with protocol.

'I don't, officer,' says Andrew, his hands still on the wheel.

The officer shines the flashlight inside the cab of the vehicle, the better to see the faces of the driver and his passenger.

'You look pretty zonked, both of you!' he says. 'No wonder you were driving right in the middle of the highway!'

Andrew gives a sigh of relief.

'I'm sorry, officer,' he says. 'There was no one else on the road, so I thought . . .'

'Whether there's anyone else or not, that doesn't change anything,' the police officer cuts him off. 'The traffic code is there to be respected. And no one should be behind the wheel in the kinda state you look like you're in. Have you been drinking?'

'No, officer.'

'Let's have a look at your papers.'

Andrew remains still for a moment.

'Didn't you hear me, young man? You can take your hands off the wheel now, I'm allowing you. And I'm asking to see your papers. If you don't have them, we're going straight down the station.'

Moving slowly, Andrew takes his wallet from his pocket and holds his licence out to the police officer, who takes it from him.

The man reads the details out loud into his walkie-talkie.

'Hello? Derek here. I want an ID check, please. Name: Andrew Fisher. Age: eighteen. Licence number: 1938-65-7098.'

While the guys at the station are checking this information, the officer uses the time to breathalyse the two teenagers.

'Blow in here,' he says. 'You and the young lady too.'

After a few moments, a woman's voice crackles through the walkie-talkie.

'*ID confirmed, Derek. All in order.*'

The officer takes back the two breathalysers, glancing at them briefly.

'This seems in order too, kinda unexpectedly.' He hands Andrew back his driver's licence. 'You can get back on the road. But take it slow, the highway's often frozen over, and keep well to the right. I'd also suggest you stop for some sleep at the next motel, it's fifteen miles from here. You look like death, if you don't mind me saying, and I don't want to find your campervan upside down in a ditch tomorrow morning.'

'Yes, officer,' says Andrew, putting away his licence. 'I'll do like you suggest.'

He's already got his hands on the ignition key, ready to start the engine.

And the police officer has already turned to walk away.

When – at that moment – the walkie-talkie crackles back into life.

'Hey, Derek – you still with that guy, Andrew Fisher? I hadn't seen it at first, but his name's on a list – seems the C.I.A. are looking for him.'

The police officer turns back to the still-open window of the campervan.

Andrew turns around even faster in his seat – quick as a flash, he thrusts the Taser through the opening and presses it against the police officer's neck. The man is taken by surprise – he is shaken by violent spasms, then collapses heavily onto the icy tarmac of the road.

69. Shot

I can hear the noise of my own breathing in my helmet's audio relay.

There it is, the seventh habitat, just a few metres ahead of me.

The access tube where I'm standing is identical to the other six, which lead to the other Love Nests, all arranged in a star formation around the Garden. There are two doors, one at either end, like the airlock through which we enter the main glasshouse. That way, if there's a problem with one of the habitats, it can be isolated from the rest of the base by blocking off the corridor.

The seventh corridor has not been blocked off.

The door from the Garden opened and then closed behind me, without any problem.

The door facing me now looks like the one at the entrance to my own habitat, where right at this moment Marcus is resting: a simple aluminium disc, marked only with a large number 7.

And yet, behind this number is the unknown threat that

might kill all twelve of us. Behind this door, just over one Martian year ago, during the course of an hour where the last-but-one Great Storm prevented any data from travelling from Mars up to the Earth, death mowed down every living thing.

What will I find in the seventh habitat?

A mass grave of cockroaches, lizards and rats?

Or have the bodies of those poor creatures decomposed, given that their sudden death dates back two Earth years?

At least with my helmet on I won't smell the stench. I'll be protected from toxic vapours, harmful rays or any other threat that might linger in these places – even if the reports say everything's gone back to normal, I don't want to run any risk.

The viewers must suppose I'm really not thinking clearly, getting myself all kitted out like this just to go see the shrink, as we're supposedly in a base that's totally pressurised. I claimed out loud that I had a migraine and that the pure oxygen from the canisters did my head good. I wonder if anyone really would have believed that nonsense. At worst, they'll think I'm totally nuts, and they'll be even surer I do need a consultation – *poor Léonor, we've always known she was fragile, but she's really lost it now.*

I put my gloved hand on the access lever fixed to the middle of the door.

I press firmly.

There's a click.

I feel my belly clenching, my body weighing heavily down to the bottom of my boots as though in a reflex to withstand some decompression, an explosion, who knows what . . .

. . . but the door just slides open, without a sound.

For the first few moments, I can see only darkness.

Then the halogen spotlights come on, getting gradually brighter, pushing back the shadows.

There's nothing.

No corpses.

No cages.

No trace of the animals that, according to the demographic data in the Noah Report, were swarming in their hundreds at the moment when death surprised them.

Instead of a slaughterhouse, what I have before me is a Love Nest, empty and clean.

I step uncertainly onto the parquet floor, which hasn't a single speck of dust between the immaculate white walls. I wonder whether the dead bodies might be in the first bedroom, and I open the door that leads there.

No.

There's only a metal bed, made with perfectly smooth sheets like in a newly prepared hotel room.

Same thing in the second bedroom and the bathroom: a dizzying normality!

'*Hello, Léonor – and welcome to the Rest House!*'

Serena's voice makes me jump – she seems so close, as if she were murmuring right behind me. But that's just an illusion, the effect of the speakers integrated into my helmet.

I mustn't let myself get knocked off balance.

Now more than ever.

'*Rest House?*' I say into my microphone. '*No need to use those terms here, since it's just the two of us, isn't it? What does this deserted habitat mean? Where are the dead animals? What's this new trick you're playing at now?'*

For several long minutes, I hear nothing but the beating of my heart in my temples, and the sound of my own breathing in the audio relay in my helmet. I do try to calm my breaths, but it doesn't work.

I go into the living room.

The wall screen set opposite the sofa is lit up to show the face of the executive producer, half consumed by the shadows of her bunker.

'Yes, it's just the two of us,' she answers finally through my earphones once the communication latency is done. *'As I said in my announcement, the Rest House is a private space, from where the images come to me alone. Why are you so suspicious, Léonor? Why the helmet and the suit? I wouldn't have made you come someplace dangerous, after all – our destinies are linked, don't forget, and my future depends on your survival. I can see your nerves are raw, I can hear the sound of your constricted breathing, and it pains me. I would suggest you do a few relaxation exercises, before we start our conversation, but I doubt you'd agree.'*

My nerves are raw? That's putting it mildly! It's like I can feel every nerve-ending in my body, right down to the movement of my eyeballs in their sockets. They swivel like marbles, examining the motionless room, looking for a sign they don't find.

'So let me answer your questions. Yes, the seventh habitat is empty, but that's quite normal. You see, the New Eden base is regulated like a perfect little world, closed up in itself. There's no question of leaving organic waste to accumulate, at the risk of breeding germs and illnesses, polluting the air; they must be

367

eliminated as you go along, in order to preserve the balance of the whole ecosystem. One Martian year ago, the multitasking robots incinerated the bodies of the trial animals, disinfected the habitat, and wiped away any trace of that sad event.'

And there it is. Serena has managed to make me overcome my anxiety, but not with her relaxation exercises: by making me mad, which she has quite a gift for!

'Why didn't you tell us any of that?' I shout, creating a loop of feedback. *'We thought we'd find some clues in this habitat, something that would allow us to understand what happened during that hour when contact between New Eden and the Earth was lost! Some sign that might have told us what the animals died of! You haven't respected our commitment of Transparency, you deserve to have us burn you and reveal everything, just like the robots burned the dead bodies!'*

I start pacing around the room, covering every inch, paying no attention to the face on the screen.

I tear the sheets off the beds.

I turn the mattresses upside down, so light to lift in this reduced gravity.

I send the sofa cushions flying, searching for something, anything! But the multitask robots have done their job well. There's nothing left to find here.

'Yes, yes, I can assure you, I have complied with my Transparency commitment!' Serena protests on the screen, after a six-minute lag.

There's panic in her voice, which offsets my own a little.

'The robots did their cleaning work long before we concluded our deal, you and I, before you'd even set off for Mars!' she

continues. '*There's nothing I can do about it if the creatures have disappeared! There's nothing I can do if the signatories to the Noah Report weren't able to ascertain remotely why it is they died! Archibald Dragovic was a peerless biologist, but he wasn't a psychic! And I'm not a magician. I swore I'd do everything in my power to help you – you know it's in my interest for you to live as long as possible, I'll say it again, because when you die, my own daughter will reveal the Noah Report to the public! But I can only take action in the present, not the past!*'

For a moment, I stand panting in the middle of the habitat I have just torn apart, sweat making the undersuit cling to my back, mist obscuring my vision. How could Serena help us? Apart from Ruben Rodriguez's cellphone which I'm keeping under my mattress, and the few screen caps that are in the hands of Andrew and Harmony, there's nothing left of the Noah experiment now.

I feel like I'm in a dead end, a tunnel with no way out, that's how unclear my visor is. But bit by bit the helmet regulator clears the mist to optimise my vision. That's when I see it, almost at ground level, just a few centimetres above the living-room floor.

I hadn't noticed it before now, being too busy turning the whole habitat upside down.

But there it is.

A plastic weld, a few centimetres in diameter.

A rough circle, like a blister, in the smooth white skin of the wall.

There was a hole here, and it's been stopped up.

70. Reverse Shot

East coast of Florida, the entrance to Cape Canaveral
Wednesday 13 December, 4:29pm

The wind blowing on the coast ruffles Serena McBee's hair, messing up her silver bob.

Behind her stretches the peninsula of Cape Canaveral. Bits of paper, plastic bags and other pieces of packaging float about with the wind, between the pylons carrying the silent loudspeakers; no other trace remains of the vast crowd that gathered here two days ago, to attend the weddings of the century. All the way down there, beyond a dozen checkpoints with barriers topped with barbed wire, it's possible to make out the fence around the launch base, surrounded by heather that trembles in the breeze.

The android Oraculon does not tremble.

He stands ramrod straight in his dark suit, his two leather-gloved hands perfectly still, perfectly symmetrical on either side of his torso which does not rise and fall with the signs of any breathing. The helmet that serves as his head reflects back the image of the changing sky on its smooth, opaque, reflective surface. The Mercedes in which he arrived at the entrance to the base is parked behind him.

'Delighted to see you again, my dear Oraculon,' says Serena, straightening the jacket of her suit. 'But I ought to warn you, I haven't got the whole day free. The Genesis programme never stops; it needs a producer at the controls. The jeep that brought me here onto the mainland will be back to fetch me in a quarter of an hour to take me back to my bunker.'

'If it were only me, I could have come to see you in your bunker, Ms McBee,' answers the android in his strange synthesised voice. *'But it's not me – the machine programmed to sustain a human conversation of average complexity – who needs to speak to you today. It is my masters, the board members of Atlas Capital. As you know, I act as an antenna for transmitting their messages to you. And the antenna cannot work on the peninsula itself where all signals are scrambled.'*

'Yes, yes, I know all that,' sighs Serena. 'You can spare me the technical details. What does the board have to say to me? I'm all ears.'

'Just one moment, please. I need to confirm that the location is secure for a confidential conversation.'

Two red dots light up behind the helmet's dark visor, giving an impression that the android has eyes. In reality they are just sensors in his head – hypersensitive instruments able to analyse their environment with admirable precision.

He 'looks' around him, then lingers on Serena, whom he scans from head to toe.

'Oh, it gives me the shivers when you undress me like that with your eyes!' Serena jokes.

371

'You are mistaken, Ms McBee, I did not undress you,' says the robot, immune to any humour. *'My analyses are quite precise, and you are still wearing all your clothes: one kilo and twenty grams of silk, cashmere, cotton and leather. However, you removed your brooch-mic as per our agreement and you are not hiding any other audio recording devices. The perimeter is secure for our discussion for five hundred metres all around us. Please wait a few moments, while I establish the connection with the Atlas Capital board of directors.'*

Serena takes advantage of the pause to tidy her hair, using the android's head as a mirror.

Suddenly the black background of the visor comes to life, revealing a synthesised whitish face, neither a man's face nor a woman's nor the face of any other human on Earth. It is just a 3D mask, totally fabricated, behind which hide the directors of one of the most mysterious and powerful investment firms on the planet.

'Congratulations, Ms McBee.'

The crackling voice sounds the same, but it's no longer the android Oraculon expressing himself. It's the anonymous directors who bought NASA, hired Serena McBee to make their investment profitable through a global TV show, and gave the order to launch the Genesis programme despite the confidential conclusions of the Noah Report.

'Thank you,' says Serena. 'It's the electors who are to be congratulated, for making the right choice.'

'Our congratulations aren't about the election,' the voice replies, ice cold. *'They are about the events of the last few days: congratulations on having brought us so close to catastrophe. What*

happened on Saturday ninth December between 11:32 am and 2pm? Why was the broadcast interrupted?'

'I already explained, as soon as we came back on the air,' says Serena. 'The young people were really on edge, and I had to give them a little bit of time without the pressure of the cameras.'

'A bit of time? Two and a half hours! The screen was left blank for two and a half hours! It's not up to you to take decisions like that. Don't forget who you are.'

'The psychiatrist responsible for the pioneers on Mars,' Serena interrupts them. 'That is who I am. And as such, I took action.'

'You are our employee, first and foremost. You are answerable to us. Constantly. It is written into your contract. If you do not comply, we can quite legally dismiss you, without giving you a cent of the proceeds of the programme.'

Serena bares her white teeth in a smile that is reflected in the surface of the visor.

'Yet you really should be more careful what words you use,' she says. '*Quite legally?* Because do you really think sending twelve individuals to their deaths is legal?'

The synthesised face trembles slightly – that is as much emotion as it is capable of expressing.

'It was you and your team of instructors who sent them! It's your names on the Noah Report! Nobody will ever be able to prove we knew about the report and agreed to that! If there was to be even the smallest leak, it's you who would be found guilty and condemned! We will even sue you ourselves, claiming you lied to us for criminal purposes, and we will win punitive damages with interest until there is nothing left of the McBee Productions empire!'

Serena is impassive at these threats, a smile engraved on her face as if on a wax mannequin.

'Now, now,' she says, 'calm down. No point us getting worked up. My team of instructors whom you mention have been dropping like flies. There's only Arthur Montgomery left, and I vouch for him personally, as he's crazy about me, and Roberto Salvatore, who is far too much of a coward to dare to take the slightest untoward initiative. The others are dead, and have taken our secret to the grave . . . or rather, I should say, to the bottom of the Caribbean Sea.'

The executive producer stares hard into the hollow, pupil-less eyes in the circular screen facing her.

'*This story about the terrorists,*' says the voice after a long silence. '*That was your own invention, was it not? It was you who eliminated your colleagues?*'

'Yes, it was me,' replies Serena simply. 'I can tell you that without any fake scruples, without any pretence.'

'*But why these murders?*'

'For money, of course. To get hold of their bonuses. The millions that should have come to them with the landing have been on standby since their disappearance, isn't that so? And I understand you will wire that sum to my bank account in the Cayman Islands. I might be a psychiatric expert of international renown, but my own psychology is exceptionally simple. Everything I do, I do for money, nothing else. That's it.'

'*We understand,*' says the voice, calmed by this confession that explains Serena's actions, endowing them with a meaning that makes perfect sense to the board of Atlas Capital. '*We shall transfer the bonus originally destined for your colleagues to your account. But as of this moment, there are to be no more impromptu decisions without keeping us in the loop, Ms McBee. Do you understand?'*

'I understand,' says Serena, like a model daughter acknowledging she has done something wrong. 'You can count on me. And you needn't worry, everything's under control. The pioneers still suspect nothing. That's the main thing. I'm allowing them a few more weeks of frolicking, to keep the Genesis channel busy, and to deliver even more money into the coffers. Then I shall order my kamikaze into action, to bring down the final curtain.'

'This plan works for us. Though your creature must act before the base starts showing any signs of technical failure, for which we might be criticised, and before a new batch of astronauts is ready to leave for Mars. Season two of the Genesis programme will be cancelled at the very last minute, just as we planned from the start. But since you mention your mysterious kamikaze, you really don't want to reveal their identity to us? Here on the Atlas Capital board, each of us has our own little prediction. Most are convinced it's Kenji, the Japanese boy who wakes up in the middle of the night with staring eyes. It is him, is it not?'

Serena's smile is enigmatic.

'Perhaps . . .' she answers evasively, 'or perhaps not. Allow me to keep my secret, to avoid giving give you a "spoiler", as they say. Putting on a great show is my speciality, you know, and that's why you hired me. I'd rather keep it a surprise.'

The synthesised face seems to smile in turn.

'So be it. As you prefer. You're right, you're the entertainment professional. We are moreover very keen to see you in your new

375

role as vice-president of the United States! As agreed, we shall be remaining in contact after the end of the Genesis programme. We still have a lot of money to make together, Serena McBee, a lot of money!'

Serena bows slightly.

'I don't doubt it,' she says. 'Thank you for your confidence in me – and till next time.'

The spectral face fades away, turning the helmet visor back to its former impenetrable black.

The android Oraculon, himself again, bows slightly, offers some pre-recorded words of formality, then resumes his place in his Mercedes, which is soon back on the road north, towards New York.

A few moments later, a convertible jeep painted with the foetus logo arrives from the peninsula. The Genesis-uniformed driver is not alone; beside him sits Agent Seamus, his black hair flying in the wind.

'You?' says Serena. 'I wasn't expecting to see you here.'

'The sight of a man driving his car wearing a motorcycle helmet is pretty unexpected, too,' says Agent Seamus, gesturing with his chin towards the Mercedes that is moving away.

'It isn't a motorcycle helmet. It's not even a man, come to that. I'll explain later. But tell me, handsome, why have you come to fetch me? You already can't live without me?'

The young man smiles.

'Your safety is very dear to me, Ms McBee, as I've already explained,' he says. 'I'm paid to stay close to you.'

Serena throws back her head, making her earrings tinkle with her silvery laugh.

'Stop talking like that, you sound like a gigolo! I should point out to you that most men would *pay* to be close to me, not the other way around.'

'I don't doubt it,' concedes Agent Seamus.

He gets out of the jeep, and opens the back door for Serena to get in.

'And a gentleman too!' she says.

She pats the seat beside her, the way one might gesture to a dog to jump onto the sofa.

'Come along now, you aren't going to stay up front like an errand boy. Have a seat next to me; you and I will have a chat.'

'That was indeed what I had in mind,' says the young man, closing the door after him.

'Ah! So now we'll see if you know how to talk to women!'

'It's the vice-president I'd like to talk to first of all,' he says, as the jeep starts up and pulls away towards the base. 'Andrew Fisher has been found.'

The charming smile disappears instantly from Serena McBee's face.

'Yesterday evening,' continues Agent Seamus quietly, his words almost drowned out by the noise of the engine. 'On Interstate 80, in Wyoming. He was in a campervan, with a girl.'

'Where are they now?' asks Serena, her voice slightly too shrill.

'I don't know. The officer who identified them was found late last night, handcuffed to the steering wheel of his patrol car. He'd lost consciousness, and his revolver and his other pair of cuffs had been taken from him. But the strangest thing was, they found a message in his pocket.'

'A message? What message?'

Agent Seamus puts his hand inside his jacket and pulls out a sheet of paper folded in four.

'We had this document transferred here to Cape Canaveral by long-distance drone,' he explains. 'You thought young Fisher had something to say to you? Well, Ms McBee, you were right.'

Serena takes the note in her long fingers and opens it. There's no way of knowing whether it's the humming of the jeep starting back up after a checkpoint that is making her tremble like this, or something else . . . A few handwritten lines appear on the crumpled sheet of paper, in a nervous, hurried hand.

Dear Ms McBee,

I am ashamed.

Ashamed of having been so hard on this cop who only stopped me for a traffic violation. But that's how it was, I panicked, I got out my Taser and I paralysed this totally decent guy. I hope he's doing better now, and that this message has reached you. I'm at breaking point, and even after what I've done to this cop I don't feel I can turn myself in. I can only run. I'm too scared of prison.

I wouldn't dare to appeal to your clemency as vice-president elect of the United States, as I know you have such a strong sense of morality. In spite of the affection you feel towards me, the integrity that does you such credit would prevent you keeping a delinquent from justice.

*And so I'm ending this message not begging you, but
thanking you. I'm so grateful to you for having put my
mother and sister under police protection, paid for with
government money. It reassures me to know they are
perfectly safe, from any possible threat. If anything bad
were to happen to them, after Father's death, the state
I'm in right now I think I'd go mad . . . I think I'd commit
some irreparable deed that I'm sure we'd all regret.*

*Thank you from the bottom of my heart, Ms McBee,
for taking good care of Vivian and Lucy Fisher.*

With all my gratitude,
Andrew Fisher

'Clearly a very troubled kid,' says Agent Seamus, 'but also
very grateful to you.'

'Right . . . very grateful.'

'Let's hope he doesn't make an attempt on his life with the
revolver he's stolen. This irreparable deed he talks about, it's
got to be a threat of suicide. What do you think, Ms McBee,
since you know him, and being a great psychologist and all?'

'I'm sure you're right, Agent Seamus,' says Serena, no
expression in her voice. 'I'm sure you're right,' she says again,
then recovers her professional composure, adding: 'It's precisely
because I suspected his psychological fragility that I wanted
to talk to him and asked you to bring him to me. Oh, that
poor boy . . .'

At that moment, the driver of the jeep turns to the passengers
on the back seat, walkie-talkie to his ear.

'I'm sorry to interrupt you, but I have a message for Ms McBee from the editing suite,' he says.

'What is it?' the executive producer asks.

'Another request for a conversation in the Rest House,' says the driver, conveying the information he's hearing in his handset.

'Oh? And who is it that would like to share their pathetic little woes with me today? Is it Léonor again?'

'Yes, Ms McBee, but not only her. The other five pioneer girls want to see you at the same time. I guess they're too impatient to wait their turn.' The driver gives his boss a big, admiring grin. 'Heh heh, that's the price of success, Ms McBee!'

71. Shot

Month 20 / sol 554 / 14:27 Mars time
[4th sol since landing]

'Six in one go! What will they think of me, after I'd announced that the sessions in the Rest House would always be one-on-one? How am I supposed to explain this to the viewers?'

'You tell them the same thing we already said when we asked for this group session,' I reply. 'That we need a meeting just for the girls!'

Here we all are, the six of us in our undersuits in the living room of the seventh habitat, standing facing the wall screen that shows the disapproving face of Serena McBee. I told the others they could keep their helmets off – the air in here is OK to breathe, I tested it yesterday at the end of my time in the Rest House. The boys meanwhile have stayed behind in the Garden to keep the viewers entertained – and to respond in case anything happens to us. Only Marcus is still in his bedroom; I made him promise to stay one day longer to recover. His health is the most important thing to me and I don't want to cause him any unnecessary worry.

'Léo's right, the viewers will understand,' says Safia quietly.

'After all, we've just been married and just discovered . . . um . . . the secrets of the male body. It's normal we might have some questions, right? Hopes, maybe fears, things to share with a woman older than us.'

'Speak for yourself – I hadn't been waiting for my shower with Tiger to discover the male body!' proclaims Kelly proudly. 'But, well, the viewers aren't supposed to know that, so I don't mind if we have to play the petrified virgins.'

All eyes alight on Kelly in a mixture of envy and fear.

'Is that true?' asks Kris. 'Did you really take a shower with him?'

'Well, yeah. Kenji's right – it means we can shower twice a day, those of us who haven't got a hundred litres for ourselves like you and Alexei.'

'And you were . . . totally naked?' asks Safia, her kohl-ringed eyes wide.

'Like you guys shower fully clothed in India, do you? Like those women who go into the Ganges in their saris?'

'But you didn't . . . he didn't . . . well, you see what I'm saying . . .'

An amused smile appears on Kelly's lips.

'I didn't what? He didn't what? Any chance you could be a bit more explicit? If you're bothered about Serena hearing, I can assure you *our dear benefactor* has heard it all before. Come on, relax! You can say whatever you like in this room, the viewers won't hear us!'

Within seconds the Indian girl has blushed as red as the bindi adorning her forehead.

Kelly gives a big, open laugh.

382

'Breathe, take it easy. If you don't relax you're going to explode like a pressure cooker! Go on, I'll stop teasing you, hon. Nothing happened between Kenji and me. We even soaped ourselves down separately. And the bags under his eyes aren't from long nights of passion, before you ask; I'd have found it pretty difficult given he puts on his suit the moment the clock strikes midnight and the cameras stop rolling in the Love Nests.'

'Wait, he *puts on his suit?*' asks Kris. 'You mean, like the people staying up on duty in the Garden?'

'Yep, he's so afraid of depressurisation. I keep trying to tell him Serena would never press the button as long as there are two of us keeping watch in the dome, not to mention Andrew and Harmony covering for us on Earth.' She sneaks a look at the wall screen, as Serena waits for our words to travel up to her. 'Isn't that right, benefactress?'

Then she continues.

'He can't help it. No wonder, then, that he can't sleep well, crammed into that thing, stifled by his helmet with the noise of his own breathing relayed in the audio all around him! Léo, you wouldn't happen to have earplugs for him, in your pharmacy kit?'

I shake my head.

'No, sorry, I don't think we've got that in stock.'

'Kenji really is a hypersensitive boy,' Kelly continues, impassioned. 'It's something he's got to get under control. He's both super-direct and super-shy at the same time, which doesn't take away from his charm, just the opposite. No kidding, it's true I've known other guys before, but never anyone like him; I'm seriously in love. And the truth is, there's no one more old-fashioned than me. I don't like rushing things. I prefer to wait for just the right moment.'

Wait for just the right moment: nice euphemism.

Because that moment, we all know, might well never come.

Yet the idea of showering with Marcus isn't something I'd mind. No – *correction* – the very idea makes me shiver from my head to my toes! The sight of those trickles running down his skin, watering his forest of tattoos, would be something. But of course it would be too dangerous. We'd be playing with fire. I'm not sure Marcus has Kenji's restraint, and I'm so inexperienced compared to Kelly. The risk of it all getting out of control is way too great.

'No, I wouldn't press the button!' cries Serena suddenly on the wall screen, echoing Kelly's words spoken six minutes ago. 'I'm so hurt that Kenji could think me capable of doing such a thing! I would never depressurise the base as long as you keep silent, and we'll live out our long lives in peace: you on Mars, me on Earth!'

'It hasn't taken you long to forget that the trial animals were supposed to *live long lives on Mars* too,' I say bitterly. 'But they died in mysterious circumstances. That's why we've all come here together, to the seventh habitat. To try to understand what happened to them. With the six of us together, we have a much better chance of finding something.'

'Finding what, that's the question,' says Fangfang, sombrely. 'In mathematics, even in the most complicated equations, we can at least tell how many unknowns we have to find. But here we don't know. We have no clue.'

'Yes, we do!' I say, pointing towards the bottom of the wall, at the far end of the living room. 'We have this thing I told you about!'

The girls move towards the flat wall.

And there's the plastic weld, very visible once you know it's there – you can't miss it.

Liz runs her long fingers over it.

'You're right, Léo,' she murmurs. 'It really is a plastic weld, like the ones I learned to make in my engineering classes, to seal up any damage that might happen to the cladding of the habitats.'

'Well, I don't understand,' says Kris. 'Who could have made this weld, if there was nobody here before us?'

'The multitask robots are able to make them too, if the integrity of the base is under threat. They know how to use welding guns, like this one.'

Liz holds up the heavy gun she took from the base's toolkit and brought here to the seventh habitat, just in case.

'There's got to be some connection to the death of the animals,' murmurs Fangfang quietly.

'No shit, Sherlock,' grumbles Kelly, mockingly, crossing her arms.

But the moment the sarcastic comment has left her lips, her eyes widen.

She slaps her forehead as though a dazzling idea has just come to her.

'Yes! Of course!' she cries. 'The evidence is right under our noses! I'm going to tell you exactly what happened!'

Trembling with excitement, the Canadian girl looks at each of us in turn, to make sure we're all paying attention. Then she launches into her explanation.

'So look: I think the accident in the seventh habitat had nothing to do with the penultimate Great Storm, and everything to do with the rats! Say they felt a bit cooped up in here, either that or they couldn't handle being with the cockroaches and the lizards – whatever, I don't know, I haven't got a clue about animal psychology. But either way it meant they gnawed through the habitat wall to try to scram. By the time the robots had gotten their skates on and blocked up the hole, every one of the little creatures was already dead from the asphyxiation and the decompression! So it was the rats that dug their own graves with their teeth! But we aren't going to be gnawing through the walls ourselves, I'm guessing?'

Kelly puts her hands on her hips and looks up, triumphant.

'We were wrong to think there was a link between the death of the animals and the bad weather,' she says. 'The truth is, it was only the rats to blame! Want some more proof? The base got through the *last* Great Storm perfectly, the one that happened just two months before we arrived on Mars. There weren't any holes this time, no welds sealing them back up, no evidence of anything. Why? Because there were no more rats, obviously! *No more rats* equals *no more problem*: and that's the solution to the equation! So you see, girls, we've got nothing to fear! QED.'

'You're racing ahead too quickly with your so-called "reasoning",' says Fangfang. 'Your explanations only move the problem somewhere else, creating a whole bunch of new unknowns. It's as if in an equation you just replaced the x with a y or a z. First, we don't actually know if it was the rats that damaged the internal surface of the habitat; there's no footage to show that. Second, we don't know if this hole was ever deep enough to get through the shell all the way to the outside and create a leak. Third, even if there was a perforation – which remains to be proved, see my second point – there's nothing to lead us to conclude that this was what caused the trial animals' deaths.'

Fangfang taps on Ruben Rodriguez's cellphone, which I discreetly brought with me in a bag so that we'd have it to hand during our investigations.

'According to the Noah Report, the on-board log kept on Earth recorded no drop in pressure or loss of oxygen at any point,' she says. 'Which means that Kelly's scenario can only have happened during a single hour, the silent hour when contact with Mars was interrupted by the Great Storm, just over one Martian year ago. That would already be an amazing coincidence for the rats to have gotten all excited at that exact moment. And then just one short hour for them to gnaw a hole in the habitat, for the pressure to drop far enough for them all to die, for the robots to repair the damage and all conditions to get back to normal, just like before the interruption – it's hardly enough time, is it?'

'I think Fangfang's right.'

Everyone turns to look at Liz, who is still kneeling on the floor beside the plastic weld.

'The habitat contains a hundred and sixty cubic metres of air,' she says, quoting the figures she knows by heart as Engineering Officer. 'Say the hole is – what – five centimetres in diameter at the very most.' She puts her thumb and index finger either side of the plastic blister, to measure its width. 'That isn't enough to cause an explosive decompression. The air would have had to leave slowly, like with a puncture in a bicycle tyre. The robots would definitely have had time to make the weld before the loss of pressure and oxygen put the animals' lives in danger. Sorry, Kelly's scenario can't hold.'

'What's with this *Kelly's scenario*?' The Canadian girl gets annoyed. 'It's not like I registered my copyright, and anyway it was only a theory!'

'Well, I liked that scenario,' says Kris quietly. 'Because it explained everything. Because it meant that without any rats to gnaw through from the inside, the base no longer had anything to fear. Because it meant there was nothing left for us to do.'

She looks like a little girl who's just had her Christmas present taken away from her, just at the moment when she's starting to unwrap it.

'Don't worry about it, my darling Kris,' I say, putting my arm around her shoulders. 'We'll find it eventually.'

This is the moment Serena barges in again, after the usual delay.

'Tell me – do we have a clue?' she exclaims from the wall screen. 'I heard you say something about a plastic weld in the wall, is that it? I can't tell you how frustrating it is being so far away at these critical moments! How I wish I were there with you, in the habitat, to carry out the investigation!'

Serena's big smile, which is trying to be complicit, just looks predatory to me.

Claiming she wants to be here with us, in the waiting room of death!

Positioning herself as a member of the team, when she's our one true opponent!

'It's like an adventure in *The Famous Five*, those books I used to devour during my childhood in Scotland!' she goes on. 'Except there are six of you – seven, counting me . . . So we're *The Secret Seven*! Yes, I do like the sound of that!'

'Well, if you ask me, the sound of that makes me puke,' replies Kelly, whose directness has never expressed my own feelings better than now. 'I've never heard of those old books. But if we're talking literature, I think of you more like Voldemort's twin sister: mean as a snake, vicious as a hyena, with a plastic surgery disaster for a face.'

We've all read Harry Potter, it's a classic. And Kelly's comparison is perfect! Encouraged by our laughter, she immediately adds: 'Whenever I see you, whenever I hear you, there's just one thing I want to shout: *Evanesco!*'

The very moment she speaks that famous vanishing spell, we hear a humming sound. I know it sounds crazy, but for a moment I really do feel as though there's been some magic at work, and like in the novels it only took one word to dispatch Serena someplace from where she'll never return!

But reality is not a novel.

And magic does not exist.

The humming I heard is coming from the Rest House door: Marcus has just burst into the habitat, and he's furious.

'Léonor!' he shouts, his grey eyes flashing, his face trembling with rage and distress. 'You came here, to this place that stinks of death, and you did it without telling me – twice! And you were the one talking about trust!'

389

72. Off-screen

Last-Chance Highway, Death Valley
Wednesday 13 December, 8:15pm

'There it is: Dry Mountain!'

A massive shape appears against the black backdrop of the night, through the campervan's windscreen. The poor-quality road – sandy, covered in pebbles – makes the chassis shudder, and the gun and handcuffs in the glove compartment bounce around. The noise of the wheels slipping and sliding is the only sound for leagues around.

Hunched over the steering wheel, Andrew works the accelerator expertly; he's criss-crossed these routes last summer, he knows how to handle the difficult bits, where a less experienced driver would have got himself stuck at once. Beside him, wrapped in her blanket, Harmony is shaking to the rhythm of the jolts. Both of their faces are so drawn with tiredness that they look twenty years older than they really are.

The campervan turns onto an even smaller road – really more of a path than a road – that climbs up towards the starry sky.

'Hang on tight, Harmony,' Andrew warns her, his voice hoarse. 'The last mile of the three and a half thousand we've done from the Hamptons is the hardest of all. But my good old campervan's done it before, five months ago. Let's hope the four-wheel drive manages to hold out tonight.'

They begin their slow ascent, punctuated by the crunch of the loose stones and the growling of the engine.

'I found it by accident, this place I'm taking you, after I'd already been in the area for many long weeks,' Andrew explains. 'It's not recorded on the maps – nor is the abandoned road that leads there.'

Up in the sky, the Moon appears from behind a cloud.

Somewhere in the distance, they hear the howl of a coyote, greeting it.

Nearly an hour later the campervan stops at last, in the lee of a huge rock that marks the end of the road and which hides the vehicle from sight from almost every direction.

Andrew turns off the headlights.

He gives a pained sigh as he gets up from his seat, unfolding his stiff, exhausted body.

He slips the revolver into his waistband, then he opens the door; the cold, dry air of a January night in Death Valley slams against his cheeks. Landing on the pebbles, he walks around the front to open the door for Harmony, and helps her down in turn from the raised cab – she is so frail, so light.

'Keep the blanket round your shoulders,' says Andrew gently. 'Lean on me. We're nearly there.'

He puts one arm around the girl's waist, and offers the other to guide her, and like this, with her leaning on him, with him practically carrying her, they step into the dry undergrowth that rises up beside the rock. The thorns scratch their skin; they cling to the wool of the blanket and to Harmony's colourless hair, as if trying to hold her back.

But the two of them keep going.

And at last they emerge into a small hidden dip, at the bottom of which opens a black tunnel supported by girders. A half-dilapidated little wooden cabin stands beside it.

'It's an abandoned mine,' says Andrew. 'And this is the destination of our long journey. Welcome to my palace, Harmony McBee.'

73. Shot

'You lied to me! Everyone knew, the other ten all knew you were coming to the seventh habitat, with all the risks that involved, except me!'

'I didn't want you worrying.'

'And when I tell you I'm feeling better, just to reassure you, I'm a bastard; but when you take risks without telling me, you're a heroine – is that it, is that your new rule?'

'I never said you were a bastard, Marcus, and I never claimed to be a heroine.'

'But that's what you think. Don't deny it!'

Marcus's grey eyes sparkle in the spotlights of the seventh habitat. The other girls left the two of us alone, the moment when he showed up so furious.

'Léonor, our heroine, who opened the whole crew's eyes!' he yells, a grimace full of painful irony on those lips where I once tasted honey, and which are now spitting poison.

His words hurt me so badly! But he persists. 'Léonor, our saviour, the girl who's gonna defeat death!'

'What's so outrageous about wanting to survive?' I stammer, stabbed by a feeling of terrible injustice. 'Just to survive.'

Before I'm able to say any more, I hear a mocking voice behind me.

'Oh my! It's like watching a domestic scene! Do you want to take advantage of some couples' counselling? Don't forget that's my speciality; it's what made my talk show famous!'

I see red – in a flash, my frustration turns to rage.

I spin around towards the screen on the living-room wall, where Serena is smiling so widely we can see her gums. I grab hold of the heavy welding gun, which Liz abandoned on the sofa when she left the room in a hurry, and I hurl it with all my strength at Serena. I so want to smash her teeth in, but it's the screen that smashes into pieces, which itself isn't such a bad thing as I can no longer see her hypocrite's face.

But I don't want her to be able to see me any more, either, or hear me!

I retrieve the welding gun from among the shards of glass, and leap over towards the first camera I can see, beside the dead screen.

Pssscht! A jet of molten plastic sprays from the barrel of the gun and covers the dome of the camera.

I'm already onto the next camera, fixed to the wall of the kitchenette. I squeeze the trigger – *pssscht!* – and a sticky substance stinking of molten rubber covers this one in turn.

The third and last camera, set above the main doorway, the one that also contains the mic for capturing the audio, barely lasts another three seconds. Soon that too is sticky, deafened, blinded: *pssscht!*

Only now, dripping with sweat, do I let the gun drop to

the floor – and I realise that Marcus has clasped his fingers around my arm.

'Calm down,' he murmurs. 'Please.'

He pulls me to him, holding me close; like I do every time I find myself in his hands, I'm surprised by how strong he is.

I feel the warmth of his breath on my cheek. I'm expecting new reproaches, which I know deep down I deserve, as he's right and I'm wrong. I should have warned him in advance and I didn't. But this time, the words that come out of his mouth express no anger and no bitterness.

'My words were too harsh,' he says softly. 'You're right. All living things want to survive. It's normal. But the truth is, you aren't going to defeat death, Léonor. Nobody ever has. Nobody ever will. Not you, not me. When it comes calling, we have to follow, that's just how it goes. And while we wait, I don't want you to volunteer before you've been called. I don't want you to take unnecessary risks. I don't want . . . to lose you.'

I feel a lump in my throat. Somewhere deep in Marcus's hoarse voice there's something very precious, like a precious jewel in its rocky shell – a rough diamond of emotion.

'I'm sorry,' I murmur. 'I shouldn't have gone off to explore the seventh habitat without telling you. I'm so useless. I don't deserve you.'

'You're not – I'm the one who doesn't deserve you. I'm the one who hasn't told you everything. I haven't told you that death has knocked at my door once before, long before I boarded the *Cupido*. It set a date for me.'

Marcus's fingers are still closed around my arm. He's clinging to me like a shipwrecked man to a dinghy; like someone who doesn't know how to swim clinging to somebody who does. But all of a sudden, standing in the middle of the seventh habitat, I feel like I don't know anything at all.

Not about myself.

Not about him.

In my head the tattoos I've read on Marcus's skin start to spin around.

Dream as if you'll live for ever, Live as if you'll die today . . .

Life is short. Break the rules. Forgive quickly. Kiss slowly. Love truly . . .

Seize the day . . .

The words he spoke three sols ago, when he was trapped in the airlock door, are still echoing in my ears –

'*Looks like my date with death has come today . . . and she doesn't like it when you stand her up . . .*'

Struggling with the vice tightening around my throat, I manage to say: 'What are you talking about, Marcus? What date?'

'I would have told you eventually, I promise. There were so many times when we were meeting in the Visiting Room I almost told you my secret. But something held me back. Fear of scaring you off before you knew me well enough. I told myself if we spent enough time together, maybe you'd start to like me, and that if you started to like me, maybe you'd end up loving me, in spite of what I really am.'

'What you really are? I know, Marcus! You're an amazing guy I said *yes* to, in front of the whole Earth!'

'You didn't just say *yes* to me. You also said it to my sickness. Because I'm sick, Léonor, and I never found the courage to confess it to you till today.'

He lets go of my arm and takes a few steps back, his jaw clenched. His boots crunch on the splinters of glass. It's like the sound of cracking bones.

'Sick?' I echo. 'That doesn't change anything! I'm sure I'll find something to make you better in our pharmacy kit. Didn't I take good care of you after your accident? What's it called, this sickness? Maybe I studied it in my medicine classes.'

Marcus turns to face me.

There's such distress in his face, it takes my breath away.

'They don't know anything about the illness I've got, or not much,' he says. 'It's not something you'd find on the syllabus in medical school. It's something new, only affecting a handful of people – why waste time talking about some orphan disease for which there's no hope, when there are so many other illnesses to teach you about, which can actually be cured? I was born with a mutated gene. A mutant. I didn't know about it till I was fifteen, when I passed out in an episode that almost cost me my life. But it was only a warning. An invitation to some future date. At the time, the D66 mutation had only been identified in a few hundred individuals spread across the whole world. Since then, in the space of four years, thousands more cases have shown up. It's always the same scenario: a first episode of unconsciousness that can occur at any age, which initially looks like a sudden death but from which the patient recovers; then a second attack, which is deadly in one hundred per cent of cases.'

I feel a trembling run up my body from the soles of my feet to the top of my spine – but I plant myself solidly in my boots, to force my body to stand firm, to stay upright. I feel my eyes start to prickle, and my vision mists over the way it does when

I breathe too heavily on the visor of my helmet. I shake my head to drive away the tears before they come.

'How long?' I ask. 'Before the second attack?'

'I don't know. No one knows. There's no way of predicting it. The two episodes might be a few minutes apart, or several years. The record for the longest time is held by a man in Spain who had his first attack at twenty, and the second eight years later. He's followed closely by a woman in Korea, who held out seven years and nine months. I don't know all the stats by heart. But anyway, all that information doesn't carry any weight against the uncertainty: for four years, I've been waking up every morning not knowing whether I'll make it to nightfall. The way medicine stands right now, mutation D66 cannot be cured. We don't know what it does that makes the heart and all the vital organs stop working.'

Marcus's voice wavers, but it doesn't crack.

I can tell that he, too, is struggling to stay strong.

He leans on the back of the sofa, then slowly, controlling the movement of his body, lets himself slip down onto it.

He can't sink any lower. He's ready to tell me his story – and I'm ready to listen.

'Like you, and like lots of others in the team, I was a child in care,' he begins, eyes fixed on the floor, lost in his memories. 'But I'm not an orphan. I knew my parents – my dad not all that much, before he left us, my mom a lot better, even if sometimes she felt like a stranger. When she had bursts of mania followed by long periods of depression, I couldn't recognise her any more. She stopped talking, she stopped eating, and just lay there on her bed, staring at the ceiling. Eventually she was diagnosed bipolar, a severe case. Ever since my dad had left, I'd been her lifebuoy, her beacon. I loved her with all my heart, though I was terrified too. My way of escaping from it all was magic – or more particularly the conjuring tricks I learned from the old books I borrowed from the local library. When I was concentrating on making a sleight-of-hand trick work, nothing else in the world existed for me, all my tension disappeared and I was truly happy – that, the respite, was the true magic.

'I had my first attack one evening after coming back from the store. I collapsed onto the kitchen tiles, my arms still full of groceries. When I woke up, I was lying in a pool of milk, surrounded by broken bottles and squashed fruit. An emergency services nurse was leaning over me with an oxygen mask, while another was trying to control my mom, who was screaming and struggling, fighting with her nails and teeth. They took us both to the hospital, me to intensive care, her to the psych ward. We came out together two days later, with the diagnosis of D66 mutation that came from a genetic test only just developed, and a strengthened cocktail of mood stabilizers. Unfortunately, the drugs weren't enough for my mom; the moment she learned my days were numbered, she gave up completely. I no longer had the strength to comfort her. All I could feel was the unfairness of it. I was sure I was the one who needed to be consoled, only fifteen years old and just having learned that everything was about to end. Yes, that was what I felt, that huge frustration, on the same scale as the huge love I had for my mother – and I blamed myself, I blamed myself so much!'

I sit on the sofa too, now, next to Marcus. Because I can't stay standing a moment longer. Because I can't stay apart from him, not a centimetre. Because I need to touch him, to feel his whole body against mine, and never let him go.

'We stopped being able to pretend we were a normal family,' he goes on, eyes still on the floor. 'Everything collapsed in just a few months. My mother lost her part-time job as her manic and depressive phases were now coming in too quick succession. Some days she threatened to kill herself if I died, accusing me of wanting to abandon her, as if my illness was my fault; the next day she called herself a crappy mother and spent the whole day crying in bed. Once the social services had been notified, they decided to take me from her care – there was however no question of placing a boy who might disappear at any moment into a foster family. That's how I found myself in a home for teens nobody wanted, the ones who were too old, too different, or just too unlucky to get adopted. And there, for the first time, I saw myself die. Really. I had the totally clear sense that that was what the rest of my life was going to be like if I stayed there, in that closed-off place, between the dormitory and the workshop – a monotonous succession of weeks, months or years, without any meaning. I decided to run away.'

I curl up even closer against Marcus.

He flinches like an animal at bay the moment my fingers brush against his hand that's clinging to the stuffing of the sofa.

Then he continues: 'The first place I went was the psych hospital in Boston. What was it I wanted, exactly? To see my mom again, sure, but what else? Take her away with me? I didn't wonder about it for long. When she saw me appear through a hedge I'd managed to sneak through into the park where the patients were taking a walk, she started screaming, even louder than the day

I collapsed in front of her. '*A ghost! It's a ghost!*' I understood that to her, in her inner world, I was already dead. I managed to escape just before the nurses ran over. I never saw her again.'

A couple of murmured words escape my lips – 'Oh, Marcus.'

There is nothing else I can say.

My mouth is silenced by the emotion.

I can only squeeze his hand in mine, squeeze it tight.

'I got on the road,' he continues. 'Fare-dodging on trains, sometimes hitchhiking a bit. I crossed the whole country, all the way to the West Coast, to L.A. And I learned to live on the road. Yeah, I was young, but I was hardly the only person in that position. The city of angels is well named – its gutters are overflowing with fallen angels, with their wings clipped. At least I had a gift, a talent for the magic I'd learned in books, which helped me to beg. As soon as I'd managed to save a hundred bucks, after a couple of months, I had my first tattoo done. The black rose that's on my chest. To remind myself of my new motto, every moment: *Seize the day, Marcus, because it may be your last.* Everything seemed delicious, even the feeling of hunger in my belly those mornings when there was nothing to eat, even the bite of the cold on the back of my neck on winter nights, because it meant I was still alive, I'd managed to survive another day! And whenever I could afford it, I would race to the closest tattoo parlour to get another quote inked on my skin – like a new victory, a new trophy.

'And then one morning, two years ago, I found myself holding the Genesis programme flyer. The moment I laid eyes on it I started to dream. Yes, the kid with no future was dreaming again about tomorrow! The idea that death was going to cut me down in my prime seemed less harsh if it was in some other world, where no other man had been before. I submitted my application without really believing it could happen, without thinking too much about the speed-dating, about the couples, any of that. Nor later either, as I didn't get much time to think about it when it all happened so fast – the interview rounds, the psychological examinations, the aptitude tests. You experienced it all yourself, you know what it's like. Atlas Capital were in such a hurry to launch the Genesis programme – but I was in a hurry, too, a hurry to live!

'I got through all the stages of the selection process as in a dream, as if my illness no longer existed. Right up until the interview with the programme's selector-in-chief. That was when I finally woke up. I remember her perfectly, sitting there in her white suit in the casting offices of McBee Productions in New York: the great Serena, who we were always seeing on TV and in magazines, and who was welcoming me in – me, the street bum! I couldn't believe it. I was so intimidated. But she put me at ease right away, offered me a coffee, asked that we be left alone for the interview. Then she took out my evaluation file. On the first page there was an excerpt from my medical tests, the genetic sequencing that identified mutation D66 in my genome. Maybe deep down I'd imagined such a rare condition wouldn't ever show up in tests, or maybe I really had just forgotten I was ill. The piece of paper Serena put in front of me brought me brutally back to reality. "*Do you know what this means?*" she asked. "*It means I'm a failure,*" I answered, a lump in my throat. It had all been too good to be true. The conquest of space was a serious business. Nobody would send a dying person to Mars. "*No,*" she said. "*What it means is that I'll take you, providing you don't speak to anybody about what is written on this piece of paper – not to the journalists, not to your future travelling companions. You need to give yourself a chance to live your dream. The moment for telling the truth will come – later. And then the whole of Earth will be as moved as I was."* With these words, Serena started to wax poetic. She told me how touched she'd been by my story. She said she was ready to give me a place on the *Cupido*, to let me have an extraordinary experience. I thought I was talking to a saint, my fairy godmother who was just showing up a little late in life. I kissed her, with tears in my eyes. Then I told her I couldn't accept. Now that I'd actually been selected, I'd come to realise the consequences. I understood that when I died the girl who'd chosen me would be left alone, and I wasn't prepared to allow that to happen.

'Serena didn't let me say any more. She told me I didn't have the right to pass up an opportunity like this. That I deserved it, this ticket to Mars. That the risk of my mutation being transmitted to future children was minute, almost non-existent, and that could be controlled by the high-tech medical equipment on the base. That the candidates were embarking on a unique adventure in space, not to find their soulmates – because if it was really love they wanted, they would have stayed on Earth, where you could find love on any street corner. Apparently one candidate in particular kept saying in her selection interviews that she had no interest in love at all. That candidate, Léonor . . . it was . . .'

'Me!'

I quickly pull my hand away from Marcus's, refusing to believe my ears.

And yet . . .

Marcus had heard of me before we'd even boarded the *Cupido*!

Marcus had already chosen me, before we'd even met!

My breathing accelerates; the acrid smell of the molten plastic from the still-hot welding fills my nostrils and my brain.

'Our pairing up was planned without my knowing,' I say at once, all the words rushing out in one breath. 'The only piece of luck was my choosing you for my first session in the Visiting Room. Everything else was planned.'

'No!' shouts Marcus, taking back my hand. 'I never could have predicted I'd meet a girl like you! I never could have predicted I'd fall in love now! What an idiot I was, thinking Mars would give some meaning to my shitty little life! It's you who's given it meaning! What you've offered me fulfils me so completely that death no longer scares me – and at the same time I've never been so desperate to live, to be with you!'

The room starts spinning in shades of white and grey around me.

Or maybe it's my head spinning, I don't know any more.

I can no longer feel the sofa under my legs.

I no longer have any other point of reference – except Marcus's hand, which is currently closed around mine.

'You have to believe me,' he begs, his eyes shining. 'Like I said, I nearly told you the truth so many times at our meetings. I swore to myself I'd do it before the publication of the final Heart Lists. Yes, I'd been planning to tell you everything at our last session in the Visiting Room. You were going to invite me. That's what was supposed to happen, according to your own rule. But then you called Mozart.'

The whirlwind around me stops all of a sudden. All the furniture in the room is back in its place.

Marcus is right: it's him I was supposed to have invited. I'd even planned to reveal my own secret to him, the existence of the Salamander, at our final meeting, so that he could choose me knowing all the facts. But events decided otherwise. Just before the session, I'd found Ruben Rodriguez's cellphone; I discovered the Noah Report; I called Mozart to the Visiting Room to ask him – the Navigation Officer – whether he thought there was any way we could turn around.

I broke my promise to invite Marcus.

'It all happened so quickly!' he continues. 'The broadcast being cut off, all twelve of us meeting in the Visiting Room, the shocking revelation of the Noah Report . . . All at once I realised we were on borrowed time – not just me, all twelve of us. While the others were tearing each other apart to decide whether we should come down or turn around, I had another question tormenting me: *should I talk to Léo about the D66 mutation? What's the use in telling her, if we've only got a few months to live anyway? We're all doomed to die soon, so isn't it better I kept quiet?* I voted to turn around, to balance out the numbers, to let you make the final choice without influencing you. And I didn't say a thing about the D66 mutation.'

Marcus sighs deeply, making the lock of brown hair over his forehead flutter. His handsome brow is creased with tension, just like when he had watched me silently in the Visiting Room as the others argued. I wondered what he was thinking at the time – now I know. And I understand the meaning of those words he spoke, in our first real intimate moment, in our marriage bed the morning after the wedding.

'When you asked me whether I'd regret having married you if you died suddenly, it wasn't just a theoretical, crazy question, the kind of thing lovers ask each other to test their love. It was total reality.'

'Yes . . . but I didn't dare tell you. I was too much of a coward, right up until the end, to admit to my curse. What I did to you was disgusting. You could have chosen Mozart. I'm sure you would have done if you'd known that with me you might find yourself widowed from one day to the next. You're a star, Léonor, a red giant – but I'm a black hole, and black holes consume any stars that come too close to them. There's a danger I'll swallow your light up in my darkness. People who are condemned to death have no right to be loved.'

'Ask me again.'

'Huh?'

'Ask me your question again.'

Marcus's eyes widen.

For a moment, he says nothing.

And all I can hear is the drumming of my beating heart, composing an obsessive piece of music with the triumphant whistling of the Salamander which has awoken at my back. (*You were right not to trust love, Léonor. Now you're going to live with the torture of knowing that the person you love most in the world might be taken from you at any moment. Without your noticing, Marcus's face, his voice, his scent, everything has been inscribed on you indelibly and now there can be no forgetting.*)

(*It's too late!*)

(*It's too late!*)

(*It's too late!*)

In sharp contrast with this voice screaming at me, Marcus opens his lips just slightly and – ever so softly, like a prayer – he

406

asks: 'Léonor, when I die, will you regret having married me?'

And now, as if a spell has been cast, I feel the beating of my heart slow down; I hear the whistling of fear surge away, while a wave of calm confidence rises from the depths of my soul.

It's as if my red hair were swelling out on either side of my face – like the rays of a red star, as if they were being lifted by something or other that is carrying me and surpassing me, by some energy that raises me up above myself and truly turns me into a giant. How could Marcus possibly swallow up this light, as he's the one who has lit it within me? It will never go out.

The words pour from my mouth, clear and obvious.

'You kept your secret from me, Marcus. But I kept mine from you, too, and it wasn't even because of me that you finally discovered it, the day my dress got torn.

'You said you shouldn't have boarded the *Cupido*. But if you hadn't been here, to risk your life to save me in the airlock, I'd be no more than a sandy corpse in the Martian desert right now.

'You claim to be a condemned man who has no right to be loved. It's that same condemned man I've fallen in love with! It's that fugitive who has made me understand the value of every minute, of every second! That's the boy who kisses me as though every kiss might be his last!'

I place my hand on Marcus's chest; through the fine material of his undersuit, I can feel those letters in relief that he carved with his penknife, and I can feel his heart, very much alive, pulsing with a desire to exist, a thirst to love, in unison with mine.

'So I say it again, what I said to you before, Marcus the Condemned: even if you have to disappear, right here and now, I will regret nothing. Nothing at all!'

407

ACT V

74. Genesis Channel

Monday 25 December, 5:10am

Long shot of the red valley of Ius Chasma, at the heart of the canyon of Valles Marineris. The Sun is already pale and low in the purple sky, ready to disappear behind the vast cliff.

Subtitle at the bottom of the screen: EXTERIOR VIEW FROM THE TOP OF NEW EDEN / MARS TIME – 16:50

Acting like a telescope, the powerful zoom of the camera mounted on the top of the dome moves in on a small group of people lost in the middle of the giant valley, next to the maxi-rover. As the image gets larger, the tiny white ants are transformed into astronauts wearing spacesuits. There are three of them, their names sewn onto their sleeves: KELLY, FANGFANG and KIRSTEN.

Cut.

Semi-close-up on Fangfang and Kirsten; the former is busy carrying out topographical surveys of the landscapes using photographic equipment, the latter gathering Martian sand in small transparent plastic sachets, each one carefully labelled.

Suddenly a huge pink bubble enters the frame, momentarily blocking the view. After a couple of seconds – *pop!* – it bursts.

Subtitle at the bottom of the screen:

Kelly can be heard in the voiceover: '*Whoah! That was a good one!*'

Fangfang turns, the setting Sun reflected in the visor of her helmet.

'*Did you say something?*'

Kelly: '*No, I was just admiring my performance with the bubbles. The cab driver's got to keep herself busy somehow, while the scientists are doing their work. I feel like I've been managing to blow much bigger bubbles since we've been on Mars. You've got an answer for everything, Fangfang: can you think of some physical explanation for that little miracle? The reduced gravity, or something like that?*'

The Singaporean girl thinks for a moment.

'*It'll be more to do with the pressure – that's going to affect the size of the bubbles, not the gravity. So, the pressure inside your suit is actually slightly lower than that on Earth, while still perfectly healthy for a human organism. As a result, the air you blow into your bubbles meets with less resistance, and they swell up more. By the way, I'm not sure protocol allows us to chew gum while on sorties outside. Imagine if a bubble that bursts blocks your view or obscures your communications system.*'

Kelly shrugs: '*Don't worry about it, I've got it under control. And anyway, to be honest, I'm sure the viewers are at least as interested in my bubble-blowing performance as in watching you*' count grains of sand. If only a Martian could show up for a bit of a chat – that'd be cool, but meanwhile this place really is like totally dead.'

Kirsten looks up from her sachets: '*That's exactly what we're doing, trying to see if it really is as dead as you say. That's one of the most important parts of our mission, remember, to try to find traces of life on Mars. I'm sure that really would interest our viewers. And yeah, sure, it's true that grains of sand aren't all that thrilling in themselves, but imagine if I manage to identify organic molecules, or maybe even single-celled organisms, when I put these samples under the microscope very soon? That would be awesome!*'

Kelly sighs: '*Awesome is a matter of opinion. I was talking about having an actual chat. And I'm sorry, but I don't think a single-celled organism has much in the way of small talk. If we at least had the boys with us on our excursions, we'd have a bit of fun. Hell, I even wish Mozart was here, I love being able to tease him.*'

Kirsten scowls; her face can be seen clenching slightly in the visor of her helmet. '*You know perfectly well Alex prefers it to be just us girls on the excursions – at least when I'm involved. I know, it's ridiculous, but it reassures him. I've just got to give him some time.*'

By way of an answer, Kelly goes back to chewing her gum with great dedication, the sound of the chewing amplified by the audio relay.

Cut.

Semi-close-up on two new astronauts, leaning over a whitish rock sticking out of the red sand of Mars. One of the astronauts

413

is hunched over, handling a small ice-axe he's using to pull little translucent orangeish crystals out of the rock. The name on his sleeve identifies him as MARCUS. The second astronaut, who is identified as SAMSON, gathers the crystals in a little sachet, which he holds open in his gloved fingers.

A subtitle appears at the bottom of the screen:

SUBJECTIVE VIEW MALE PIONEER NO. 4 – MOZART.

The astronaut in question joins his two companions, and asks: '*So what's that?*'

Samson turns: '*It's jarosite. A mineral that can only be formed in super-acidic environments, like here on Mars.*' He takes one crystal, larger than the others, out of his sachet – it's the size of a thimble – and holds it out to Mozart. '*Here.*'

The Brazilian takes the crystal between his thumb and his index finger, and brings it close to the visor of his helmet.

The jarosite grows on the screen, and it becomes easier to make out its tiny sparkling hexagonal faces.

Mozart murmurs: '*So it's a precious stone?*'

Samson gets up to look at the crystal too: '*No. Well, it's not considered one on Earth. But whether or not it's precious, it's pretty gorgeous, and that's all that matters, right?*'

Mozart nods, not taking his eyes off the jarosite: '*I can't even tell what colour it is. Some faces look red like a ruby. Others are dark like onyx. The heart of it looks more bronze, like . . .*'

'*Like topaz?*' offers the Nigerian.

Mozart looks up sharply. '*No. Like Léonor's eyes.*'

At these words, Marcus gets up and turns away from the rock.

He puts the small ice-axe away in the hold-all pocket of his suit. '*I think we've got enough samples for today. The Sun will be gone soon. It's time to go back, especially since we let the girls have the maxi-rover, so we'll be moving more slowly, and it'd be a real pity to be late for our Christmas supper.*'

But Mozart doesn't move. Nor do Samson and Marcus. In the subjective view, the Nigerian and the American are totally still in the middle of this ancient landscape, like statues. The grey eyes of one and the green eyes of the other are fixed on the camera – on the face of Mozart, who murmurs finally: '*Léo is like jarosite. Maybe on Earth, in her old life, people were too stupid to see that she's a precious stone. But precious she is, more than anyone. So take good care of her, Marcus. And remember, I'm always going to be here, looking over your shoulder, just to be sure.*'

75. Shot

'That's it, Léo, I can see the headlights of the rovers coming back!' cries Liz.

She came back from her own sortie an hour ago. It's true she didn't go as far as the Planetology and Biology Officers did – exploring planet Mars, one of the highlights of the Genesis channel, takes those officers to places that are further and further from the base. Meanwhile, our Engineering Officer only had a few metres to travel to wipe down the solar panels covering the habitats. It's an exhausting task that has to be carried out constantly, to prevent the Martian dust from accumulating and reducing the amount of solar energy produced. Still, Liz takes care of it without a moment's hesitation, every sol, with the same degree of commitment. And every sol, when she gets back, she waits for the return of the rovers with the same impatience. Or perhaps I should say, she waits for Mozart's return, since he acts as driver for the scientists on their explorations.

Everything about Liz's behaviour shows how much in love she is: her forehead pressed against the glass of the dome; her

416

eyes squinting under their long lashes so as to get a better view through the powdery light, rapidly failing, of the Ius Chasma; the fiddling of her long fingers, twisting around her black hair, and the way she looks nervously at her watch, exclaiming: 'It's 17:50! It's almost night! Look, you can hardly see a thing. Even with their headlights I'm scared they'll fall into a rut, or run into a rock. It's better for Kelly, with those huge wheels on the maxi-rover; but I'm worried sick about Mozart, you know how fragile our mini-rover looks!'

Up until the very last moment it's as if she suspects Mozart won't come back to her, as if the belly of Mars might swallow him up and never let him go again.

I wander over and try to reassure her.

'Don't worry. Mozart couldn't be a better driver. It'll all be fine, and we'll soon have a full house for our Christmas Eve.'

I notice a quaver in my voice. Not that I have any doubts about Mozart's skill; it isn't that. It's because I too, every evening, feel afraid I won't be able to hold Marcus in my arms. The thought haunts me all day long: what if he succumbs to a second attack while he's out there, far from me, in the Martian desert? Compared to the threat that could strike him at any moment, the danger from Serena seems almost unreal. The danger from the Great Storm, which should be hitting New Eden twenty-one months from now, seems even further off, especially as we still have no clear idea what caused the deaths of the trial animals. We don't know if it's the hole in the wall of the seventh habitat that killed them, or if it really was the rats that made it. We don't really know anything at all . . .

'Wowowowowow!'

I give a start, surprised by the whining right beside me.

It's Louve, who has come over to us and pressed her nose against the glass of the dome. A long complaint escapes from her white muzzle like a song, like a prayer. She too is waiting for the return of the one who matters most in the world to her: Kris, her mistress. I put my hand gently on her head – the same hand she bit two weeks earlier, but which is now totally healed.

'It'll be fine, little one,' I murmur.

Her whining calms down a bit, but it doesn't stop completely. I can feel the vibrations spreading to my hand, my arm, my whole body, and I understand suddenly that we're the same, human or animal, when we love somebody.

76. Genesis Channel

Monday 25 December, 8:15am

The opening notes of *Silent Night* ring out against a backdrop of outer space. We see the galaxies turn and the stars pulse, to the calming sound of the well-known Christmas carol.

The planet Mars appears slowly, gradually lit up by the rays of the Sun.

It morphs into a red Christmas bauble, and all the stars around it are likewise transformed into twinkling decorations. The cosmos disappears as the carol comes to an end, giving way to a Christmas tree covered in wreaths.

The camera zooms out slightly.

The tree is standing in Serena McBee's study, where she is seated in an armchair in front of the French windows that open onto the snowy gardens of her villa. Two of the panes of glass look a little different from the rest, as if they've been recently replaced – but it's barely noticeable, and besides, it's the presenter who takes up all the viewers' attention. Today she's dressed in a bright red velvet dress, whose collar and long sleeves are adorned with white fur. Her silver bob is hidden beneath a hat, also red, which ends in a white downy pompom on its tip. There's no possible doubt: Serena McBee really is dressed as Mother Christmas, and she's managing to make even this outfit look elegant.

She beams at the camera. 'Good morning to you all, my dear viewers. Have you slept well? Did you find your presents under the tree? I'm sure you've hurried to your screens before you even opened them to catch up with this morning's broadcast: the eagerly awaited Christmas Eve supper of the pioneers on Mars! Two weeks after their landing, they are now twelve hours and twenty minutes behind us – if you need reminding, each day they accumulate a forty-minute delay in relation to Earth time. So it's still December twenty-fourth on the red planet, and it's nearly 8pm. Our lovers will soon be coming to the table. And they will have the right to receive some presents too! Just because you're an orphan doesn't mean you don't get to have Christmas, quite the contrary.'

The camera zooms out further, to reveal the rest of the room.

It's filled to bursting. Children aged between six and twelve are sitting on the parquet floor in their dozens, arranged around the foot of the Christmas tree, lined up in rows against the bookcases. One young boy is sitting in a wheelchair, close to the hearth in which a healthy fire is crackling. They are all in very simple clothes, dresses whose colours have faded from multiple washes, shirts with patched elbows, and all of them are wearing black Remembrance ribbons on their lapels. The girls' hair is pulled into severe braids, the boys have bowl cuts flattened to one side. But the poverty of their attire is eclipsed by the big smiles lighting up their faces. Some of the younger ones are missing a few milk teeth.

'On this Christmas Day, five per cent of the monies received by the Genesis channel will be given to the orphans of the world,' announces Serena solemnly. 'I would have invited every single one of those poor deprived kids here to my villa if I could, but regrettably it's not large enough. But I can at least welcome the residents of the nearby New Jersey orphanage.' She turns to the gathering: 'Are you happy to be here, kids?'

As one, their voices answer her.

'Oh yes, Ms McBee!'

'Have you been good this year?'

'Yes!'

'So can I call Santa?'

'Yes!!'

Serena throws back her head, her crystalline laugh making the pompom at the end of her red hat jump. Then she claps three times, sharply.

'Well, then – let's all call him together: Santa!'

'Santa! Santa! Santa!' the children chorus, starry-eyed.

At the third call, a figure dressed all in red bursts into the shot, sporting a long white beard, a sack filled with presents over his shoulder.

77. Shot

All twelve of us have eyes as round as saucers.

The spectacle unfolding in front of us, on the screen of the dome, is so surreal you'd think we were having a mass hallucination. Serena McBee as Mother Christmas, surrounded by children looking up at her as if she's a saint. It's like I'm having a waking nightmare.

We each look at one another, unsure how to react.

Should we laugh at the total kitschiness of the whole scenario?

Or cry about what it really means?

It's so easy to see ourselves reflected in those children, we who never knew our parents, who were rejected or who ran away. It wasn't so long ago that we also used to look at Serena as though she was going to snatch us from the grasp of our wretchedness and offer us the stars.

I turn to look at Marcus's face – he's sitting right next to me, his arm around my shoulders. He's totally engrossed in the show, like the others. We're all gathered at the ground level where we have set up a big aluminium table for our Christmas supper. Kris was very keen on doing it, and to be honest, I also thought it was a great idea, after these past two weeks taking control of the base that haven't left us a moment's pause for breath. The idea of spending an evening together, all of us, in a good mood, a Christmas unlike any I'd known before, with Marcus by my side – the whole thing delighted me. My first real Christmas, and maybe my last . . . I wanted to enjoy every second of it. Until Serena inflicted *this* on us.

'Reeeady!' Kris's calls.

She emerges from the access tube that leads to her Nest, arms loaded up with a big dish that's still steaming, which she's been cooking with care in her habitat kitchen ever since she got back from her expedition. Günter, the robot butler, follows after her like a kitchen boy in a bow tie, holding a bottle filled with freshly squeezed apple juice in his pincers.

'I've prepared a vegetarian shepherd's pie,' announces our master chef. 'I've replaced the meat with fermented soya. As for the rest of it, I've done the best I could, not having a potato masher. You'll have to tell me what you . . .'

She stops dead in the middle of her sentence and stands there, mouth agape, at the sight of the unlikely tableau that's suspended on a giant scale on the curved surface of the dome.

'But it's like . . . like Serena McBee,' she stammers.

'Yeah, on acid,' says Kelly, who still has the strength to be cheeky. 'Santa must have left some happy pills in her stocking this year.'

No sooner has she spoken these words than Santa Claus makes his entrance onto the screen, to the cheers of the children.

But . . .

There's something about that face . . .

Those surgical eyes, the colour of glaciers . . .

That neatly trimmed moustache, under the false beard . . .

'Arthur Montgomery!' I shout.

'No,' whispers Fangfang, incredulous.

'Yes!' cries Alexei as he gets up from the table. 'Léo's right! It's really him, our Medical instructor!'

I feel a nervous trembling in the pit of my belly.

The Genesis programme has gotten us used to all kinds of excesses, but this time we're way past the limits of ludicrousness.

I snap.

I have just enough time to curl up against Marcus's chest before bursting into a joyless laugh, which hurts me, shaking my sides and not letting up.

I feel him laughing too, feverishly, his intercostal muscles rising and falling in fits and starts.

Over his shoulder I can that see some of the others, including Kelly and Mozart, are having the same reaction as us, but most are left dumbfounded at the sight of Arthur Montgomery handing out the seemingly endless packages he's taken from his sack – red packages, wrapped in paper stamped with the Genesis logo. His movements seem so clumsy in this role to which he's so ill-suited, this man who usually gives out about as much warmth as a fridge. But the children don't pay any attention; they're too happy to notice what's wrong.

They open their presents with cries of delight. Under the torn paper, between their fingers, we can see cardboard boxes with brightly coloured markings, which themselves also bear the Genesis logo in golden metallic veneer. Through the large see-through plastic window in each box, we can make out a figurine in an astronaut suit.

'It's . . . us,' murmurs Liz, as the camera zooms in on the box held by a little girl in a lavender blouse.

There's a model of Liz, her face fixed in an eternal smile, an imitation of the pretty English girl right up to her hair, recreated in nylon threads and knotted into a dancer's bun. The letters embossed on the packaging proclaim:

ELIZABETH – ENGINEERING OFFICER

In this box, you'll find:
★ an astronaut suit! ★
★ a mini-toolbox of
space Meccano! ★
★ a leotard and ballet shoes
for a star dancer! ★

'Whoah, that's too cool!' cries the girl in the lavender blouse. 'Liz is my favourite pioneer – she's such a good dancer! One day I really want to be just like her.'

There's another shout of joy from the boy in the wheelchair next to her.

'Hey, look!' he says, proudly. 'I've also got an Engineering Officer, but the one from the boys' side!'

He's holding a box with the figurine representing Tao. He's

also got a wheelchair fixed to the cardboard by plastic ties, a high-tech model, perfectly reproducing the one used by our Chinese pioneer – so different from the bulky one, with its flaking paintwork, that the boy is sitting in.

Tao – Engineering Officer

In this box, you'll find:
★ an astronaut suit! ★
★ a mini-toolbox of
space Meccano! ★
★ a titanium-frame
champion wheelchair! ★

'*Ho ho ho!*' goes Arthur Montgomery, trying to imitate Santa Claus's jolly laugh. 'Are you pleased with your present, my friend?'

'Oh yeah, Santa, you did real good!' says the boy, his voice filled with gratitude. 'You've given each of us our favourite pioneer! Cause Tao's kinda like a big brother to me. Whenever I'm feeling down, when I think I'm never gonna make anything of my life, stuck in this chair, I think of him. And it pumps me right up again, seriously!'

'*Ho ho ho!*' is all Arthur Montgomery can reply.

The camera continues to focus on each of the models, those outer-space dolls made according to our measurements.

No detail has been omitted; the Kris figurine has a crown

of perfectly constructed blonde braids and there's a miniature model of Louve to accompany her; the text on Marcus's box guarantees that under his suit you can find tattoos that exactly match the original.

Suddenly my own effigy appears on the screen.

It feels like a blow to the gut seeing myself there, all in plastic.

Because the figurine really does look like me, right up to the red hair falling onto the shoulders of my suit.

Because that miniature body is totally still, wrists and ankles tied to the cardboard packaging.

Because it looks like I'm dead, stretched out in a white coffin.

Breathless, a lump in my throat, I can just about decipher the writing on the blister pack.

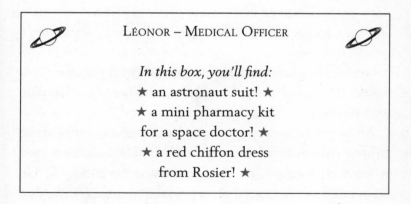

LÉONOR – MEDICAL OFFICER

In this box, you'll find:
★ an astronaut suit! ★
★ a mini pharmacy kit
for a space doctor! ★
★ a red chiffon dress
from Rosier! ★

I have a vague feeling of relief; unlike with Marcus's tattoos, the label makes no mention of the Salamander under the figurine's suit. The toymakers can't have known about it, and the viewers didn't learn about it till recently when my dress got torn. My doll must have a smooth back – or at least, that's what I hope. The idea of the scar I've spent my life trying to hide being reproduced in hundreds of thousands of copies makes me feel dizzy.

'Merry Christmas, my friends!' cries Serena McBee all of a sudden, turning towards the camera.

With a graceful movement, she pushes the pompom of her hat back over her shoulder, then continues: 'And what about you; have you been good this year? Yes, I can testify to that! I can't wait to see what Santa Claus has brought you.'

'*Ho ho ho!*' says Arthur Montgomery again. 'Let's see what we have for you, Kelly.'

He plunges his hand deep in his sack, which is now almost empty since the gifts have been given to the children, and pulls out a parcel wrapped in the same paper in Genesis colours.

'Since you aren't here, I'll open it for you, if you don't mind?' he asks.

'Well, even if I do mind, it's not like I've got any choice, right, Santa?' The Canadian girl raises her chin, her voice dripping with sarcasm.

Arthur Montgomery does not wait the eight minutes of the current communication latency. His nimble fingers, so used to handling a scalpel, are already undoing the packaging. He takes out a strange round object, a kind of huge granite disc topped with a plastic handle.

Instantly Kelly stops giggling.

'It's . . . a curling stone,' she says, moved. 'I never thought I'd see one of those again. It was too heavy to transport on board the *Cupido*, so they wouldn't let me bring one with me.' Then she adds, a little aggressively: 'So you're just showing me that to taunt me, then?'

Once again Arthur Montgomery anticipates the question.

'You must be wondering how I'm going to get your present to you, aren't you, Kelly? I would have come to visit you by reindeer, but it's a little too far for my old sleigh, and the base at New Eden doesn't have a chimney – *ho ho ho!*'

Yeah, he's about as natural as a robot, and you can tell from a mile off that his answers have been scripted for him in advance, just like for the wedding ceremony.

'But look – there's something else in the parcel!' he says, pulling a sheet of paper out of the box.

He holds it out towards the camera.

It's covered in figures and technical symbols that are too small to read, but the title is quite clear, in capital letters at the top of the page:

3D PRINTER FILE FOR CURLING STONE

'We're going to send you this file by laser,' says Arthur Montgomery. 'It will travel up to you at the speed of light, and in just four minutes it will land straight in the memory of Léonor's 3D printer. You'll only need to press a button to receive a beautiful new curling stone, printed out of the Martian sand, which contains all the necessary molecules to create a whole range of objects!'

Kelly's eyes widen.

'Too cool!' she says.

She turns to me.

'Léo, you will let me use your printer, won't you?'

'Of course,' I say, confused but nodding.

But Mother Christmas has already taken over and started unwrapping the second present. She takes out a pair of square black glasses, exactly the same model as Fangfang's – but in one piece.

'The printing file for these glasses frames is already on its way up from Earth,' says Serena with a broad smile. 'Fangfang will just have to put in her corrective lenses. And they'll be done!'

The Singaporean girl claps delightedly.

'Amazing!' she says, fiddling with her glasses that are currently fixed with sticky tape. 'I'll finally be able to get rid of these horrible things that have been disfiguring me for the last two weeks!'

Now Arthur Montgomery takes the floor, to open the parcel destined for Fangfang's partner; it contains a pair of designer gloves, made of a material that looks both supple and super-durable.

Tao understands immediately what they are.

'They're gymnasts' gloves, to protect me when I'm pushing my chair or walking on my hands, aren't they?'

The presentation continues at the same pace, parcel after parcel, and that same number of printing files sent through space into the memory of my 3D printer. Samson gets a frisbee for playing with Warden; Liz an elastic for her stretching exercises; Alexei the power grips he's been dreaming of; Safia a yoga mat; Mozart the shell of a guitar to which he only has to tie his strings; Kenji some earplugs so he can finally sleep soundly.

It quickly becomes obvious that the organisers of the

programme have been listening to our conversations since the beginning, to try to work out what object each of us was missing most. It would have been really touchingly attentive if the whole thing didn't have Serena at the controls. Because she never does anything for free, and if she's offering us these gifts it's because she's got something else going on in her head.

And now she pulls a utensil out of the parcel aimed for Kris, a kind of sieve with a crank attached.

'A potato masher!' cries my friend, as though beholding some angelic apparition. 'My prayers have been answered!'

Her words chill me, despite the warmth of Marcus's arms around my shoulders. The overflowing of enthusiasm that accompanies the handing out of the presents seems totally out of place all of a sudden. It feels like I'm watching the scene from the outside, like looking at a painting. And what I see terrifies me.

At this moment, I feel like my companions in misfortune are no longer angry at Serena McBee. I can see in their smiles that they no longer distrust her. They're just like the kids from that New Jersey orphanage, happy and serene, totally in the moment. This stress-free time will certainly be fleeting, and they'll recover their good sense once the excitement has passed – but still, what scares me is that Serena has managed, even for a few minutes, to make them forget the monster she really is. *My prayers have been answered*, Kris said innocently. As if this woman on whom our twelve lives depend, who blows hot and cold as she pleases, were a kind of goddess.

'Careful what you say, Kris,' I murmur. 'After all, Serena is not God.'

431

On the contrary, she's the devil incarnate, I might have added – but of course I stop myself, since the cameras are still rolling.

'Bah, killjoy!' says Kelly, still sparkling from her gift. 'Go ahead, then, you can mock, but you know you're going to benefit from the potato masher too!'

I can tell now isn't the moment to argue.

Just now nobody is ready to hear my warnings.

And so I keep quiet, while Dr Montgomery opens the penultimate present, a bulky cylindrical box bearing a label with Marcus's name on it. He takes out a handsome black top hat, the conjurer's classic.

I turn to look at Marcus, and see that famous, distinctive half-smile appear on his lips. It's the most beautiful sight I know, and I cherish it all the more because I know how transient it will be. I won't do or say anything to shatter Marcus's joy at this moment – even if my tongue is burning with a desire to ask him whether he's spoken about his top hat at any other moment than when it was just the two of us alone in the bedroom, at night when the cameras aren't supposed to be rolling, at a time when the programme's organisers weren't supposed to hear.

'And our twelfth gift goes to Léonor!' says Serena McBee from the screen.

She tears open the last rectangular parcel.

And she takes out a large portfolio.

Not a portfolio *tablet* like the one I brought with me from Earth – no, this is a real cardboard portfolio, filled with real sheets of paper.

'The 3D printer ought to be capable of weaving these sheets, rather like papyrus,' says Serena. 'Didn't you say you wanted to use the Rosier make-up for some painting, Léonor? I'm sure your luxury brand would be delighted to see their colours hijacked like that to create even more beauty, but you've been missing the necessary equipment. So here it is. You can give your creativity free rein now, and produce wonders for us!'

My lips half-open and, almost despite myself, I let out a couple of words.

'Thank you.'

I'm actually really touched.

Ridiculous as it seems, the gift from our executioner really does make me happy.

Am I going nuts myself now too, or what?

Has Serena bewitched me?

Hey, Léo – wake up! This witch is not your friend!

'We're going to leave you now,' trills Serena on the screen. 'Santa and I have other homes to visit. Merry Christmas once again, and bon appetit! The dish Kirsten has prepared for you looks delicious. I can almost smell it from here in the Villa McBee!'

The picture of the study filled with children disappears from the surface of the dome. It's back to its usual transparency, beyond which the darkness of the Martian night stretches out into the distance.

'It really does look great!' says Mozart, eying the large dish in the middle of the table. 'And I'm ravenous! Yum!'

Kris blushes adorably at the compliment.

'Oh, like I said, it's not much,' she says as Samson and Safia serve each other. 'I hope it isn't too horrible.'

'Are 'ou sherioush?' says Mozart, his mouth already full. 'Ish delishioush!'

Only Kenji seems doubtful. He looks at the portion of shepherd's pie that has been served onto his plate with suspicion, those circles still under his eyes – sleeping in a suit must be so uncomfortable, if he does manage to sleep at all, with his terrible anxiety. I hope his new earplugs help him a little.

'Um, you're sure there aren't any of those silkworms in there?' he asks, doubtfully.

'Of course I am – like I said, it's vegetarian!' says Kris, smiling. 'The silkworm eggs only thawed last week; the larvae are barely hatched, we'll still have to wait a few days before the first worms reach adult age – and then we'll be using them for breeding, not for eating! In any case, the worms have mostly been planned to allow our future Martian civilisation to have silk thread and so develop some textile industry.'

Our future Martian civilisation? She talks about it so confidently, as though there was nothing to threaten that future, when the truth is we're still on borrowed time. But tonight, on this Christmas Eve, I haven't the heart to remind her.

'Eating the silkworms is only a last resort,' Kris continues. 'In case the soya doesn't supply enough proteins, either to us or to the dogs.'

As if she'd understood her mistress's words, Louve gives a plaintive whine at her bowl that's filled with one quarter Eden Food rations and three quarters vegetarian mince. Protocol requires that we transition the dogs gradually towards vegetarianism – I'm not sure that'll do much to improve their mood, which is already not great!

Let's see if I like Kris's recipe more than Louve does.

I taste the mince on the tip of my fork.

Mmmm – an explosion of flavours in my mouth! Nothing like the tinned or vacuum-packed food I've eaten for five months on board the *Cupido*, and so different from the bland boiled potatoes I've been preparing these last two weeks in the kitchen of our habitat, for Marcus and me.

'You really deserve a Michelin star, Kris!' I say.

'You're going to make us look pathetic in front of our husbands!' says Fangfang, half-laughing and half-serious.

'Oh, because in the Fangtao household, it's only the lady of the house who does the cooking?' asks Kelly, serving herself some more mince. 'That's hardly very modern! In the Kenkelly home, it's Tiger who gets all that done. Which is just as well, as I may know how to pilot a space capsule but I have no idea how to handle an oven. With me at the controls of the cooker we'd both have been poisoned by now!'

At the end of the table, where he's taken the head-of-the-family place, Alexei rolls his eyes, appalled.

'You've got to be kidding, right?' he says. 'I can't believe my ears! Don't let her treat you like that, little Tiger! Get your claws out! Defend yourself!'

'I do really like cooking,' Kenji says, not looking up from his plate. 'Vegetarian stuff especially, which works out well. In the place where I lived before the programme, we never used to eat meat, nor any other kind of animal produce.'

The place where he lived before the programme? That doesn't mean anything to me, as he's never told me anything about it. I look at the youngest of the boys, at that strange

435

distant expression behind his combed-down hair, and I realise how much more mysterious than all the others he still is. And what if he's hiding a secret as terrible as Marcus's? Those phobias of his have got to come from somewhere. Maybe he's talked to Kelly about it, only to her, the way Marcus has only confided in me? Unless he still hasn't said anything to anyone? For the first time, he's starting to mention his past in public, and I'd like to encourage him to say more . . .

. . . but Alexei doesn't give me a chance.

'You're never going to persuade me cooking isn't a woman's job,' he says with a wry smile, which gives him his famous dimples. 'A man in an apron isn't a real man. Each person sticks to his role, and everyone gets to keep all their ducks neatly in a row – isn't that right?'

'There aren't any ducks in New Eden, in case you hadn't noticed.'

All eyes around the table turn to Mozart, who has just spoken.

Looking Alexei straight in the eye, he adds: 'For your information, at the Mozabeth habitat, I'm the one who cooks. It's something the favela girls taught me, when they were bringing me up. I wish you could see me in an apron, just so I could hear you say I'm not really a man – and prove the opposite to you.'

All of a sudden, the tension between the Brazilian and the Russian has ratcheted up so high that it's almost like a visible thing between them, like a laser beam across the table. For these past two weeks since we landed, they've provoked each other at every possible opportunity. Fortunately, these only happen rarely, as their respective roles tend to keep them far apart. Mozart spends most of his days outside, driving the scientists around on their expeditions; the rest of the time he helps the Engineering and Communications Officers in their external maintenance operations. Alexei, meanwhile, is most often confined indoors, just like me. It falls to us to carry out the necessary health tests on the astronauts, whenever they return from a mission; I'm supposed to look after the girls, Alexei the boys. But given how things are between him and Mozart, he refuses to give him his check-up. Probably for the best – apparently every consultation with Samson turns into a thorough interrogation about Kris, so I imagine with Mozart it would end up in a fistfight. So it's me who checks him over when he takes off his helmet; it's me who runs the Geiger counter over his chest to check the radiation levels; it's me who listens to his heart beating with my stethoscope. With a bit of practice I've learned to carry out all these things without once looking him in the eye.

'No way! Macho Mozart at the stove?' Kelly bursts out laughing, yanking me back from my thoughts. 'Well, I never would have guessed!'

'He manages very well, actually,' says Liz, with a loving look at Mozart. 'The little delicacies he makes for me are so good I'm going to have to watch out if I don't want to lose my figure.'

The Canadian girl rolls her eyes – here we go again with Liz's complexes, given she has a rocketing metabolism that burns off calories in a flash. Unlike Kelly, I don't get exasperated by our ballerina's worries; they just make me warm to her even more. The better I know Liz, the more I understand that, despite her qualities, she's still so unsure of herself. Her lack of confidence might have caused her to make mistakes in the past, but it was always in order to protect herself, not to hurt other people. Since then she hasn't stopped making up for it honourably, doing the most wretched maintenance tasks without a word of complaint.

'And how about we uncork a bottle of bubbly, to go with this delicious mince?' suggests Samson, immediately getting Kelly's attention.

'Now you're talking!' she says, getting up to go fetch the champagne.

A few moments later we're toasting with the second bottle, out of the six we brought with us. One of them we drank the morning after the marriage ceremonies, and we've already decided when we're going to have the other four:

on New Year's Eve, December thirty-first;

on Safia's birthday, February second;

on the eve of the Great Storm, in twenty-one months' time;

and as for the sixth and final bottle, we'll be opening that *after* the Great Storm, if we've survived.

But just now I want to do the same as the others and not think about that – just for an hour, just for a night, for Christmas Eve.

The sweet warmth from the champagne rises to my cheeks.

The warmth I feel from Marcus's body, right beside mine, is more intoxicating still.

Seize the day his scent sings to me, reminiscent of deep forests, and life in the open, and endless horizons.

Seize the day.

78. Off-screen

The Villa McBee, Long Island, New York State
Monday 25 December, 8:35pm

'Do we really have to subject ourselves to ridicule like this?' grumbles Arthur Montgomery, pulling off his sweat-soaked false beard.

'Come now, my dear Arthur, where's your inner child? It's just an innocent little performance, to delight our viewers and bring some joy to the pioneers. And the New Jersey orphans will remember it for the rest of their lives!'

The study no longer contains the children, who have been led out by Balthazar and taken to the kitchens for a Christmas breakfast, their hostess's treat.

Brandon and Dawson, Serena McBee's two valets, are gathering up the torn wrapping paper that is lying all over the parquet floor. Like everyone on the villa staff, each of them is wearing an earpiece attached to their neck.

'Leave that,' says Serena with a generous smile. 'You can come back and deal with it tomorrow. It's Christmas today, after all, take the rest of the day for yourselves.'

'Thank you, Ms McBee!' say the two servants in unison,

before leaving the room.

When the study door has closed, Serena turns to Dr Montgomery, who is sitting in a chair, trying to remove his too-tight Santa Claus boots.

'Ridicule – as you call it – is our best protection,' she says, instantly serious again. 'And the more we cover ourselves in it, the better protected we'll be. Because, you see, the laws of psychology are simple. It's not possible to be happy and sad at the same time, nor amused and fearful, nor trusting and suspicious. While we're making the pioneers laugh, they are forgetting to fear us. No doubt they'll always remember they shouldn't talk about the Noah Report while the cameras are on, that's the main part of our contract. But they'll genuinely believe we're respecting our side of the bargain. That's why I've decided to continue broadcasting from here in the Villa McBee, where we'll look a lot more exposed and vulnerable than in an anti-fallout bunker ten feet underground – more harmless, in other words.

'And bit by bit, insidiously, they'll start to lower their guard. They'll stop being so vigilant. Because they'll discover something they've been totally deprived of for their whole wretched lives: happiness. And love. As for us, we'll amplify that happiness; we'll pamper them, entertain them, spoil them. Contented and sated, they'll doze off during their inspection circuits, they'll forget to put on their suits and fasten their helmets. That's the moment – when they least expect it – we'll strike. How? That I don't yet know. And I don't yet know how to neutralise Andrew Fisher either. But I do know that time, habit, routine, a false sense of security are what we need to cultivate in the pioneers. All that will work in our favour when the time comes.'

'Yes, I do understand,' mutters Arthur Montgomery, wrestling with his second boot. 'Still, my dignity . . .'

'Hang on, Arthur, let me help you with that.'

Serena kneels beside the chair where the doctor is seated. Her red velvet dress rides up over her knees to reveal long legs, sheathed in black fishnet stockings.

Arthur Montgomery immediately stops protesting and falls as calm as if he's just been given a sedative, while Serena delicately lifts his calf and expertly removes his boot.

'Serena . . .' he stammers, devouring her with his eyes. 'And what about me? Have I been good this year? Have I earned the right to a present too?'

'We'll have to see later whether it's Mother Christmas or the Wicked Witch for you, you young rascal,' she says, getting back to her feet with a smile.

She smooths her dress back down over her thighs and adds: 'Soon we're going to have another chance to show the pioneers our apparent goodwill. Our meteorological service is predicting a small dust storm in the Ius Chasma area, in two weeks' time. It will only be a minor late-summer disturbance, but it'll surely be a stressful experience for the Mars colonists, as they're convinced the deaths of the animals were linked to the penultimate Great Storm that broke over Mars twenty-seven months ago.'

'That hypothesis hasn't yet been proved,' the doctor points out. 'There's nothing in the Noah Report to suggest a link between the two events.'

'But you'll accept that the hour-long blackout at the end of which the animals kicked the bucket does give our young friends some cause for concern. Just like the hole they uncovered in the surface of the seventh habitat. The Noah Report makes no mention of that, and yet there it is all the same.'

'Right, but no causality has been proved there either. We don't have any way of carrying out the necessary investigative procedures.'

Serena throws her head back in a laugh. Her red hat falls off, freeing her silver hair.

'Causality . . . investigative procedures . . . You really are such an incorrigible scientist, my dear Arthur. But as it happens, the actual way the animals died is of no significance whatsoever. What matters is that we show ourselves to be as cooperative as possible when the little storm is announced, so the pioneers really see us as their allies. The better we support them this time around, the easier it'll be to stab them in the back when the time comes.'

79. Off-screen

Abandoned mine, Death Valley
Monday 25 December, 8:33pm

The rays of the rising Sun filter in between the disjointed planks that form the walls of the cabin.

One of these rays finds a girl stretched out on a rusty metal bed, on a disembowelled mattress, its fabric yellowed with age. The blanket she's bundled in comes up to her nose, hiding half of her face and revealing only her pale forehead, her long colourless lashes and her hair that spreads around her. In the rapidly changing light of the new day, her hair itself seems to be changing, waving like the tentacles of a jellyfish: white, pink and orange, all the shades of the sunrise.

When the light is finally yellow and splashing across her fine eyelids, the girl opens two big water-green eyes.

'Wh-where am I?' she stammers.

'You're with me, Harmony.'

Andrew Fisher is there, sitting on a wobbly chair with a broken backrest at her bedside. He's already dressed, in a pair of faded chinos and a fluffy sweatshirt on which it's still possible to see the logo of the rowing club he used to belong to. It's

443

been weeks and weeks since he left his old world behind, along with the whole planned-out path that awaited him at Berkeley, plunging instead into the unknown. The few clothes he brought with him he's hand-washed so often in the campervan that they've lost all their original colour.

But his face has got some of its old colour back today.

The pink is back in his cheeks, the dark bags below his black-framed glasses have faded, his brown hair has recovered its old sheen. And then there is the golden sparkle of the cloudless morning, which is pouring through the exposed cabin and coming to rest on his shoulders, his neck, his forehead.

'Andrew . . .' murmurs Harmony McBee, as if she were seeking out a distant recollection from some place deep in her memory.

'You ask me that every morning when you wake up – *where am I?*' he says, smiling. 'As if you've forgotten everything overnight.'

Harmony looks at him for a moment without speaking.

The glittering light is flooding onto her too, emphasising her fragile, unearthly beauty.

'I remember now,' she says at last. 'Discovering my mother's secret . . . running away with you across the country . . . Death Valley . . .'

'We're still here. The last place anybody would expect to find us.'

He gestures around the cabin's only room. A second bed, in as pitiful a state as the first, stands against the opposite wall. An old sink in rusty metal, beside a worm-eaten table, makes up the kitchen area by the third wall. A burned-out bulb dangles on a cable from the ceiling. Hanging from the structural beams it's possible to make out an American flag, so faded now it looks like it's in black and white.

'Nobody's been here for decades,' says Andrew. 'But the dreams of those who once lived here haven't gone away. Listen . . .'

Andrew points towards the door that closes badly on its hinges, its lower part eaten away by desert vermin. There's a long whistling sound; it starts, stops, and starts up again, like a tune hummed by forgetful lips, unsure how the melody goes.

'It's the sound of dreams,' murmurs Andrew. 'Or if you prefer, the sound of the wind rushing into the abandoned mine, just next to this cabin. In some distant past, it used to shelter dreamers and madmen, people who came to find the only wealth Death Valley had to offer: gold.'

'And what about us?' asks Harmony. 'Are we dreamers too? Are we mad?'

'I don't know. But we have struck gold, haven't we?'

He points at the glittery light that is now covering the whole blanket and Harmony's face, before adding: 'You're covered in it.'

The girl smiles, waving her hands through the rays of light as if trying to catch hold of them. Her fine white fingers close on emptiness.

'I think we've lost our minds.' She sighs. 'This is only fool's gold; it isn't real.'

'And this?'

Andrew slips his hand in the pocket of his chinos, then pulls it out again, now holding something, and opens it in front of

445

Harmony.

A small shapeless stone, the size of a pill, is sitting in the palm of his hand. It's completely battered and porous like coral. It's dazzlingly bright, like . . .

'A nugget of real gold?' murmurs Harmony.

Andrew nods.

'Yes, a nugget of gold. I found it when I was exploring the mine last week, while you were sleeping – you need so much sleep.'

'But it must be dangerous in there!'

'Don't worry, if the mine was going to collapse I reckon it would have happened a long time ago. I've spent hours in there already, last summer, when I was here on my own. In the furnace of August, it was the only place I could find a bit of cool, and it made me feel good, peaceful, thinking about my dad, about my childhood dreams, about my future which I know now will never be written in space. Because this mine, I thought, was like a disappointed hope, a hole dug into the rock with blows from a pickaxe and a lot of patience, which may never have yielded a single ounce of gold. And even if it did once, it's finished now. At least that's what I thought, up until last week, when my miner's lamp lit up something sparkling asleep on the wall at the end of the gallery. It was this nugget. I'm giving it to you. Merry Christmas, Harmony!'

The girl sits up on her mattress, which barely even registers a dent under her feather-light body.

'I don't deserve this, Andrew,' she says. 'The last nugget from the mine.'

'It's not the person receiving the gift who gets to decide if they deserve it or not, it's the person giving it. Here.'

He puts the nugget in Harmony's hand.

'Thank you,' she says, her eyes shining. 'Thank you from the bottom of my heart!'

She tries to get up completely, to give Andrew a hug.

But she can't do it.

The blanket that's been covering her slips to the ground, revealing the grey lace dress that goes down to her alabaster calves. Something metallic glints around her right ankle. It's the pair of handcuffs – the ones Andrew stole from the cop in Wyoming. One of the cuffs is attached to the girl's leg, the other to the bedframe.

She turns to Andrew, astonished.

'I have to lock you in each night, Harmony,' he says. 'So you don't run away while I'm sleeping. You've already tried twice – you don't remember that either? You were in the grip of some fierce withdrawal symptoms. The first time you didn't get far. The second I only found you the following morning, lying unconscious in the dust of the road. When you opened your eyes that morning, you didn't ask, "*Where am I?*", you asked, "*Have I made it to the Villa McBee?*"'

'Oh G-God,' stammers Harmony. 'I remember now. The withdrawal . . . My m-mom's money . . . Getting hold of some Zero-G . . . It's a compulsion . . .'

Her fingers uncurl, trembling, and let the gold nugget fall to the floor.

Andrew picks it up at once, and places it back in Harmony's hand, closing her hand in his own until it has stopped trembling.

'Don't lose heart, Harmony,' he murmurs. 'We still have

447

thirty-two codeine pills left – I've counted them. If we keep using them sparingly, one every evening, I'm sure your crises will slow down eventually. A few days ago, you were waking up howling for Zero-G. But that's passed. Even in the most difficult situations, there's always still hope. Even in the most barren mines, there's still one nugget left.'

80. Shot

'Whoah – that's really magic!' says Kris, eyes wide.

We're all gathered in the panic room, beneath the crop plantations. It's a circular white windowless space, ten metres in diameter, neon-lit. An infirmary area has been set up in one corner, with a bed and various diagnostic tools attached to the wall – a scanner, an ultrasound, an ECG and other machines I ought to know but whose names I've forgotten. On the other side is the 3D printer, and that's what Kris is gushing about. It has to be said, the sight really is striking. It's – I can't think of any other word to describe it other than the one she used – *magic*. Even though I've seen 3D printers at work before on Earth, the way they function never ceases to amaze me – and the one in New Eden is the biggest I've seen. It looks like a massive cube, a good twenty centimetres taller than me. Through its glass walls you can see the construction area in which metal print-heads move around on rails, scrupulously following the code that's contained in the printer's memory. One by one they deposit each fine layer of the object being printed. It's already possible to make out the shape of Kris's famous potato masher; the handle will be created as a second phase, to be assembled by hand to form the final object. Doubtless that will be greyish too. That's the colour of the printing material obtained from the Martian sand which we brought from outside in hermetic containers and tipped into the printer tank, where it was chemically treated.

'You're sure the printer de-acidified the sand correctly?' asks Kenji suddenly, as though reading my thoughts.

I turn towards him. The bags under his eyes seem even deeper after the last few nights. He's staring anxiously at the print-heads that are working busily inside the glass cube.

'What I mean is, the machine is making a *potato masher*,' he says, never taking his eyes off the printer. 'Something that's going to be used for preparing *our food*. Imagine if there are still some toxic particles left in the printing material.'

'Don't worry, Kenji,' says Kris. 'I'm obviously going to carry out all the necessary biological tests. It's like when you buy a new pan at the supermarket – you've always got to wash it before using it!'

At that moment there's a loud beep, and an automated voice comes out of the 3D printer: '*Production completed. Please remove the printed item.*'

One of the sides of the cube rises, and a delighted Kris takes her potato masher.

'You see,' she says, reassuringly, 'it's not burning my hands. It's a hundred per cent safe, I'm sure of it.'

Kelly agrees with a vigorous nod, making her big golden hoop earrings tinkle.

'Kris is right,' she says, wrapping her arms around the Japanese boy. 'And now it's my turn! I can't wait to get my hands on my new curling stone! You'll see, Tiger, I'll teach you. Curling is super-relaxing; it's just what you need. You'll love it. Go on, Léo, start the file going!'

But the moment I press the button on the 3D printer to set the production of the curling stone going, a voice sounds from the panic-room speakers. It's Serena McBee.

'I'm summoning the Planetology Officers to the Rest House, for an immediate consultation.'

81. Genesis Channel

Monday 25 December, 10:30pm

Wide shot of the New Eden panic room.

Two of the pioneers move apart from the group of twelve: Fangfang and Marcus. They make their way in silence towards the exit.

The camera follows them across the Garden, where the mechanical arms of the farming robots are hard at work, to the access tube that leads to the seventh habitat. Marcus enters the corridor and disappears from the camera frame, as the Rest House may not be seen by the viewers.

Fangfang hesitates for a moment – zoom in on her anxious face, on her irises trembling behind the rickety glasses she hasn't yet had a chance to replace – then she recovers herself, and enters the access tube in turn.

Cut.

[COMMERCIAL BREAK]

Open onto a sumptuous pair of double doors, in a Chinese style, its handles two dragons in bronze.

To the sound of notes from a Chinese zither, the flaps open to let the camera through. It moves – in subjective view mode – along a corridor that is richly decorated with rosewood side-tables, on which stand jade statuettes and Ming vases.

A woman's voice – clear and confident – speaks in voiceover: *'There is a bank trusted by the greatest fortunes in Asia.'*

The camera reaches a second double door, this time in a Parisian style; it opens as if a spell has been cast, to reveal another corridor whose walls are covered in fine gold-inlaid panelling, now to the notes of a refined piece of chamber music.

The voiceover continues: *'There is a bank to which the oldest families in Europe entrust their heritage, from generation to generation.'*

A third door appears. It is neither eastern nor western in style. It is a heavy door in rolled steel. It opens as the others did, to let the camera through.

An explosion of red fills the screen, revealing the Martian landscape all around, 360 degrees. It's really a studio reconstruction, in which the rocks have been transformed into giant tourmalines and the sand replaced by sparkling powdered rubies.

A regal Fangfang stands in the middle of this landscape of precious stones, wearing a sumptuous Chinese dress in the same red as the setting.

Words appear superimposed on the screen in a refined, distinguished hand:

FANGFANG – NEW MARS WEALTH VALUED AT: $134,567,900

The girl opens her glossy red lips: *'I, Fangfang, have chosen Croesus Private Bank to deposit the gifts the viewers are going to send me for the birth of my children, and to begin a new dynasty on the planet Mars: my own.'*

Fade to black.

A logo appears in golden letters and Chinese ideograms:

CROESUS PRIVATE BANK

金王

THE CHOICE OF THE GREAT DYNASTIES

Cut.

82. Shot

'Sol 578 – that's in exactly eleven sols' time!' says Fangfang gravely.

She and Marcus have requested that one of each of our specialities joins them in the Rest House, where Serena mysteriously called them this morning. There are five of us, gathered with them in the narrow living room: Kelly for Navigation, Liz for Engineering, Samson for Biology, Kenji for Communications and me for Medicine. Meanwhile the others are continuing to fill the on-air hours in the relentless eye of the cameras.

'In exactly eleven sols' time,' Fangfang continues, 'a dust storm is going to strike New Eden. Serena has just notified us about it, and what she said tallies with the meteorological data we're able to capture from here on the base.'

'But I don't get it,' objects Kelly. 'I thought the Great Storm that was supposed to kill us off wasn't going to be coming till month eighteen – and I say *supposed* because I'm still convinced it was the rats who caused the deaths of the trial animals with

455

that damn hole they made, and that without rats there's no hole, and without a hole, well, then we're totally in the clear!'

'Just this once, I swear I wish I could agree with you and believe the story about the runaway rats,' says Fangfang. 'But good sense keeps telling me it's not possible. We did all the calculations with Liz, remember, and the hole is too small to have caused the depressurisation of the habitat before the robots intervened. Some other thing happened during the penultimate Great Storm. Something we still can't guess at. Something that might happen again at the time of the storm on sol 578.'

Kelly rolls her eyes, more out of distress, I think, than annoyance.

'I don't understand any of this,' she sighs. 'I thought we still had twenty-one months ahead of us, and now all of a sudden it's only eleven days.'

'Listen, Kelly,' says Marcus. 'I don't know any more than the others do about the rats, but I can explain the meteorology. You see, a monster like the Great Storm that's unleashed on Mars every year, that's capable of covering the entire planet in dust in just a few sols, sometimes gives birth to some offspring trailing behind it.'

He turns on his tablet, and expertly taps out a few lines.

I don't try to see what commands he's typing into the machine.

All I'm looking at is the concentration on his face, which is lit up by the light from the screen. I see his thick eyebrows, frowning slightly; his wide, intelligent forehead; his straight nose; his silver eyes, in which the lines of code are reflected.

Marcus.

My Marcus.

He looks so strong on the outside but he's so fragile on the inside, and I'm the only one who knows it.

'Look,' he says after a few moments, holding up the tablet on which two diagrams have now appeared. 'These are the revolutions of Earth and Mars, plotted on the same chart. In the first image, you can see the five months of the voyage of the *Cupido*; it left on July second and arrived December ninth according to the Earth calendar, which corresponds to a departure on sol 399 and an arrival on sol 551 by the Martian one.'

Each of us moves closer to the screen to get a better look. I find it funny hearing Marcus give these explanations; during the journey, when we girls were together, it was always Fangfang who'd reveal the mysteries of the universe and our new world. But Marcus is totally passionate about space, too. He didn't fall in love with it in books, but directly in the sky which he stared at every night as he fell asleep under the stars. I can imagine all the nights he spent, ever since they gave him the diagnosis of the D66 mutation, looking at the constellations . . . Years spent bumming around the highways of America, years I so wish I'd been at his side. But while he was questioning the meaning of his existence, under the open skies, I was portioning out dog-food under the factory roof.

Years lost, which we'll never get back.

But it doesn't matter.

I'm going to make sure every day I spend with Marcus has the intensity of a whole year.

457

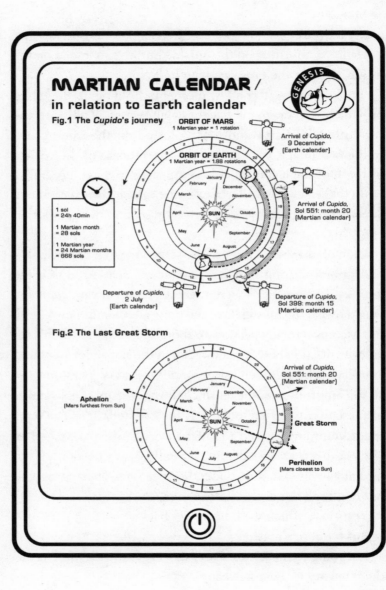

I take his arm gently, because I want to touch him, to feel his skin against mine, right now. And also because as long as I'm holding on to him, it's as if death can't take him from me.

He looks away from his tablet for a moment; his half-smile lights up his serious face.

'OK, Léo?' he asks me gently. 'Is there something that wasn't clear. Should I repeat something?'

'Please, go on.'

He nods, then continues his explanations.

'In the second image, I've shown the two extreme positions of Mars in relation to the Sun. We landed two months after Mars reached the point where it's closest to the Sun, the perihelion, the moment when the last Great Storm took place. Today, in month twenty-one, we're approaching the end of the southern Martian summer. Even if the worst of the disturbances has passed, the air's still hot by Mars standards. Here and there in the southern hemisphere, dust is still being whipped up by whirlwinds that are called *dust devils*. Some of them are coming together right now on Solis Planum, the vast plateau to the south of the Valles Marineris. In eleven days, around sol 578, they will combine to form a new storm. But really it's only going to be a late straggler, the baby of the storm family; the last little one bringing up the rear.'

A silence punctuates Marcus's words.

He may be trying to minimise the importance of the trial ahead of us, to reassure us, but the anxiety in the room is palpable.

It's enough to send chills up your spine.

'What are we going to do?' says Kris. 'I mean, in two weeks' time . . . We don't know if we should be scared of this small storm or not . . . We don't know anything . . .'

'We'll take all the necessary measures,' replies Marcus very clearly. 'Even though the base is supposed to resist this sort of phenomenon, we're going to strengthen it as best we can. Identify the weak points to shore them up. Cook and store food in advance. Put the plantations under tarpaulins to keep them safe in case of any tremors. Cover the rovers outside, too, to protect them from any abrasion. Kit out the panic room so that it can accommodate all twelve of us. Get ready to move New Eden onto low-energy consumption when the Sun is too obscured for the solar panels to operate. That's what we're going to do.'

A shy smile appears on Kris's face.

'Well said, Marco!' says Samson, high-fiving him.

'Yeah!' Kelly agrees. 'That's what I like, a real plan of action, instead of building castles in the air and diagrams that look totally meaningless to me!'

With a few words, Marcus has managed to dispel everyone's worries and mobilise the group.

I want to throw my arms around his neck and kiss him.

But at that exact moment, Serena's voice appears from nowhere.

'Hello? Hello? Can you hear me?'

Instinctively I turn towards the wall screen I shattered two weeks earlier. It's still in tiny pieces.

'The master bedroom,' says Fangfang. 'Serena's talking to us from the screen in the master bedroom. That's where she told us about the meteorological forecasts.'

We head for the bedroom, which is hardly a 'master' anything given its cramped scale – just like the one Marcus and I share in our habitat.

And there Serena is, on the small screen above the double bed: well made-up as usual, her hair neat, very well protected from any storm, small or great, that might threaten to mess it up.

'Well, then, Marcus and Fangfang, have you brought the others up to date? As soon as our meteorological service identified the formation of the dust devils close to the Ius Chasma, I knew it was my duty to warn the Planetology Officers. The *Transparency* commitment – isn't that so?'

She's doing everything she can, as she always does, to make us completely believe that she's on our side.

'Here at Cape Canaveral we're monitoring the meteorological situation from hour to hour, and we'll be keeping you well informed – as well as our viewers. The whole of Earth is with you. If we apply ourselves, all together, I'm sure we'll be able to get past this low point!'

'Don't try to make us believe you care about what happens to us,' I say, unable to take it any more. 'We're perfectly well aware you're only doing this to keep Andrew and Harmony from talking, so please, spare us any more of your unbearable phoney "team spirit" crap.'

Behind me, Kelly clears her throat.

'You're right, Léo, we all know that,' she says. 'But no need to remind us each time Serena opens her mouth. The other week, didn't she go to the trouble of postponing the wedding ceremonies just because we asked her to? And now she's clearly trying to help us, whatever her reasons. She's fulfilling her

Assistance commitment. She's just doing her duty. And today . . . it's Christmas. So let's get this over with and go print the rest of the presents.'

I can't believe my ears.

Kelly – *Kelly* – who so recently was calling Serena *a stinking old piece of trash* and *a slobbery old cockroach*, is now saying she's just doing her duty?

I'm too flabbergasted to reply.

And too surprised at the reproach I can see on Samson's and Liz's faces; they don't want me to pile on either, I can tell.

'Let it go, Léo,' says Samson kindly. 'Right now, we know it's in Serena's interest to help us, to collaborate with us, so let's let her do her thing – always keeping an eye on her, of course.'

Liz nods. I can see how tired she is of constantly mistrusting Serena, and what a relief she'd find it to be able to consider her – at least this once – an ally. I can't read anything in Kenji's impenetrable eyes. And from Marcus's, I draw a limitless love that allows me to overcome my frustration and swallow my anger.

'Fine,' I say at last, reluctantly. 'Let's say this mini-storm will be a test of our *collaboration* with Serena McBee.'

On the screen the executive producer seems frozen in a statue's smile.

She must be thrilled on the inside to hear the others garlanding her with laurels, but she gives nothing away.

83. Off-screen

The restaurant at the Hotel California is amazingly full for a winter night. But it's not just any night, it's New Year's Eve. Half a dozen tables are occupied by couples or families, making the most of a few vacation days between Christmas and New Year to take a little jaunt to Death Valley. The premises have been decorated, using whatever they had at hand, with a few wreaths hanging from the girders, and bouquets of dried flowers.

Dinner is coming to an end.

Wearing her apron, onto which she has pinned the black Remembrance ribbon, Cindy is busying herself between the tables to clear the leftovers of the turkey and serve the dessert, a cheesecake covered in raspberry coulis.

Mr Bill is at the counter, loyally at his post, like an old captain keeping watch over the deck of his ship from the tiller.

'Meals for sixteen, and six rooms!' he says, rubbing his hands. 'We've broken our record, Cindy. Maybe it's a sign business is going to be better in the New Year than it's been in this one. Come on, let's be optimists and just thank our lucky stars.'

Cindy gives a sigh, as she lifts the glass cloche covering the cheesecake and picks up the dessert slice.

'I don't know where in the sky my lucky star has got to,' she says.

'What's that you said, hon?'

Cindy points the dessert slice around the room.

'When I see all these couples in love, all these happy families, it really gets me down, Mr Bill,' she says with a sigh that makes her foundation make-up crack slightly – it's been a long day and she's tired. 'It reminds me I'm forty and I'm letting my whole life slip away.'

'Nonsense, kid!' the old man tries to reassure her. 'You haven't let anything slip away! For a start, I could never have kept the hotel going all on my own if you hadn't helped me stay at the helm. I'll be leaving it to you when I retire. I have no children to inherit it. You can sell it then, or keep it going, whatever you prefer. You're still so young, Cindy, you've got your whole life ahead of you!'

The waitress puts a slice of cheesecake on a plate; her hand is trembling slightly from the emotion, and the neat white slice tips over onto its side.

'You're so good to me, Mr Bill. You always have been.'

'But . . . ?'

'But nothing,' says Cindy, wiping her hands on her apron.

Mr Bill shakes his head knowingly.

'Come on now, Cindy, you think just because I'm an old man I can't tell you're in love? I felt it at once when you came back from the big wedding ceremony at Cape Canaveral. It was like you were glowing the whole time . . . until tonight, when the light's gone out all of a sudden. What's happened? I won't let anyone make you unhappy.'

Cindy looks up at last, and with a delicate gesture pushes away the red-dyed hair that's fallen over her forehead, to meet her boss's kind gaze.

'Oh, I think I've made all my own unhappiness myself, Mr Bill,' she says. 'I allowed myself to imagine all kinds of things after meeting a guy at the ceremony. There was such an incredible atmosphere, with all the music, the lights, the excitement of the occasion . . . We got carried away with the magic of the Genesis programme, and anything seemed possible. He told me a bit about his life as a soldier at a base up in Connecticut, where it gets so cold in the winters, and I told him about mine here, where it's often so hot. After I got back, we stayed in touch. He emailed me every day. Except that the last three days, I haven't had anything from him at all. He must have moved on. Out of sight, out of mind, I guess.'

'Don't say that.'

But Cindy just sighs again and picks up the sauceboat of raspberry coulis, which she pours generously over the portion of cheesecake. Then she turns away to look at the big TV set with faded colours that's sitting on the counter. The Genesis channel is playing with the sound off, with a small clock superimposed over the pictures that reads: MARS TIME – 06:55. One shot of the base follows another, all of them in darkness, and all totally still – except the Garden. There, beneath the great glass vault – a shape it's just possible to make out by the faint glow of the nightlights – three bloated silhouettes are moving. The first two belong to Samson and Safia, who are on watch tonight; they are dressed in their bulky spacesuits and their gleaming helmets. The third is Warden's, who is likewise in a made-to-measure dog suit, and he's running after the frisbee the two astronauts are taking it in turns to throw. Sometimes he jumps up to try to catch it, but his small helmet acts as a muzzle and makes it impossible for him to close his teeth around anything. Then he's ready to start up again, wagging his tail inside his suit. The sight of this silent game, in the middle of the shadowy glasshouse in this sleeping base, is profoundly unsettling.

'Here's hoping the storm they've told us about on the channel won't be too tough,' murmurs Cindy.

'Don't you worry, the base was designed to withstand bad weather,' her boss reassures her. 'This storm will be just a formality.'

'I hope you're right, Mr Bill. You've never had kids and nor have I, and I've got to live with that; I know I never will now. But it's not serious, because those kids up there have given me so many dreams, and I'm so attached to them, it's like they're my own kids now.' Cindy smiles, and it's not a smile she's just putting on, but one that truly comes from the bottom of her heart.

'There you go!' says Mr Bill. 'That's more like it – the light's back on!'

'I'll try to keep it on, then. I'm going to run outside to have a cigarette, so as I'm not here in the restaurant when all the couples start their kissing in two minutes' time.'

Cindy takes the plate, and crosses the room to a little boy seated between his parents, who welcomes his dessert with a clap. Then she pushes open the door and steps out into the night.

She takes a few steps away from the restaurant, pulls a pack of cigarettes from the pocket of her apron and slips one between her red lips. The flicking of the lighter breaks the silence for an instant, and the end of the cigarette pierces the gloom with a momentary red glow when she takes her first puff, then the night reclaims control. Cindy looks up at the sky that mingles clouds and stars, with no artificial lighting to dull it.

'My lucky star,' she murmurs, exhaling a small cloud of smoke. 'If you really do exist, where are you now? Hiding behind a cloud, I guess.'

Suddenly there's a slight click, which pulls Cindy away from her contemplation.

The noise comes from the tiny gas station fifty metres from the hotel, with two petrol pumps and a Lilliputian minimarket.

Cindy frowns. It looks like there's something moving, over in the shadows.

A coyote foraging through the trash cans?

She walks towards it, ready to shout and clap her hands to scare the animal away, as she usually does; those creatures that frighten the tourists so much don't scare her.

But she stops at the last moment, cigarette hanging from her lips.

Because it isn't a coyote coming out of the minimarket, a few steps ahead of her, arms filled with groceries.

It's a man.

Cindy is suddenly unsure what to do – keep quiet, shout for help, threaten quietly?

Before she's able to decide, the Moon appears from behind a cloud, bathing the gas station in a silvery light. The burglar freezes. He's seen Cindy.

And he knows she's seen him, too.

The waitress drops her cigarette and lets out a brief strangled cry – she's just spotted the butt of a revolver gleaming in the man's trouser pocket. But is it really a man? He looks more like a boy, barely out of adolescence . . . that brown hair combed to the side . . . those black-framed glasses . . . that piercing gaze . . .

'I . . . I know you,' stammers Cindy. 'You came to sleep here in the Hotel California back in July. You were chasing after a ghost, that's what you told me at the time.'

A few seconds slip past in the silence.

The boy has frozen, watchful like a wild animal. At any moment he might drop his plunder to grab hold of his gun and shoot the woman who's surprised him.

But he just says, quietly, 'I've left the money on the counter of the store. It's all there. I'm not a thief. Actually, I'm nothing, nothing at all – I'm also just a ghost, a shadow with no consistency, no reality. Remember what you said to me last summer? That for the living it's a waste of time trying to track down ghosts, and that here in Death Valley all you can hear is the whistling of the wind . . .'

'. . . and the rattlesnakes,' Cindy completes the line, repeating the words she spoke six months earlier.

The boy nods in agreement.

'You haven't seen me, right?' he asks.

Now it's Cindy's turn to nod slowly.

'Haven't seen who?' she asks, her voice very calm all of a sudden. 'There's nothing to see here, just a deserted gas station and the valley night.'

A grateful smile appears on the boy's face.

Then the Moon is veiled over again, and he disappears into the shadows, without a sound.

468

84. Shot

Month 21 / sol 573 / 09:12 Mars time
[23rd sol since landing]

'The date on which the late-summer storm will reach New Eden has now been confirmed by our meteorological services. It will indeed be sol 578, most likely at the very start of your Martian day, and it's only expected to stay in your vicinity for a few hours. For now, though, it's still in the process of formation, several hundred kilometres south of the base, on the Solis Planum plateau. You can see it on the screen.'

Projected onto the inside of the dome, Serena's face is replaced by a map of Mars, which we've seen every morning when she's presented her weather report to the twelve of us, broadcast live into the Garden.

But today something is different. Today the many small black snakes we've been tracking for days have started to gather, to mix, to fuse to each other.

'*I should remind those of you watching us again today that the black shapes on the surface of the Solis Planum are actually shadows,*' says Serena in voiceover.

Two windows appear on the screen in close-up, under the map.

WEATHER BULLETIN /
Storm Forecast for sol 578

Aerial view, Solis Planum region

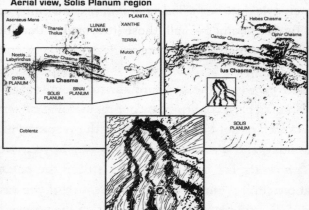

Dust Devil
1. Ground view

2. Aerial view

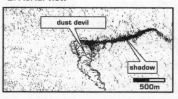

dust devil

shadow

500m

'On the first picture, you can see a dust devil moving along the ground,' Serena goes on. 'A tremendously beautiful sight, is it not? Especially as these tornadoes can be twelve kilometres tall! True wonders of nature. Incidentally it's because they're so tall that they have such long shadows. That's how we can follow them with our telescopes – as you can see on the second picture.'

Serena may be presenting things very spiritedly, Discovery Channel style, but her *wonders of nature* send chills up my spine. Twelve kilometres tall, those little snakes that look so harmless on the map . . . And there are dozens of them, creeping towards the edge of the canyon . . . Towards us . . .

'The most beautiful wonder of nature is the one I'm holding in my arms right now,' Marcus whispers in my ear.

He's standing behind me, arms around my waist, his chin resting delicately on my head. Suddenly I don't feel cold at all.

'The whole thing is very impressive, I'll grant you that,' Serena concludes, back on the screen now. 'But you needn't worry, dear viewers, the New Eden base was designed to withstand such phenomena, and its colonists have been trained for just this kind of situation. Everything will be fine when the storm eventually hits New Eden in five sols' time. In the meantime, I'll be back again tomorrow with my next meteorological bulletin – and for now I'll wish you, once again, a happy first of January, and a marvellous New Year!'

Serena's face disappears, and once again we can see the red valley of Ius Chasma behind the panes of glass.

'I've definitely started my year well!' says Kelly, rubbing her forehead. 'I can tell it's going to be a tough day. I've a hell of a headache this morning.'

'Did you drink too much champagne last night for New Year's Eve?' asks Safia.

Kelly gives a hoarse little laugh.

'You think one bottle between twelve is enough to give me a hangover? I can drink like a lumberjack! It's nothing to do with the champagne – it's just that my Tiger's sleep was . . . how should I put it . . . kinda disturbed.'

Our Japanese friend does look even more tired than usual, with black panda circles around his eyes.

'Looks like the earplugs don't work,' I say, thinking of the six little cones of some spongy material that came out of the 3D printer last week. 'Are you still sleeping in your suit every night, Kenji?'

To the viewers, his behaviour must really look like the ravings of a serious phobic. But as a doctor myself, or nearly, it's not Kenji's mental health that worries me, it's his physical health, after so many nights without sleep.

'Yes,' he answers, not meeting my eye.

'You really don't look well, you know. If you really prefer not to remove your helmet at night, maybe you could at least try to get a little bit of sleep in the fresh air during the day, while we're all busy around the base? Eleven people all to keep watch just for you, so I don't think there's any chance of an accident happening without anybody noticing! I can even let you use the infirmary bed, if you'd rather sleep in the panic room.'

Kenji's eyes meet mine at last – his head down as usual, looking up.

'Thanks, that's nice of you,' he says with a faint smile.

'But that wouldn't change anything. It's not the suit or the helmet that are stopping me sleeping . . . it's the nightmares.'

'The nightmares?' says Alexei, catching the conversation in passing. 'Grow up, man – you're not five years old any more! There aren't scary monsters hiding under your bed, waiting till night-time to come and eat you up!'

That's Alexei all over . . . He may have the cool head of a doctor, but where psychology is concerned? Not a clue. But I know what it's like being pursued every night by recurring bad dreams. I know you don't need to be five years old to wake up sweating, your heart thumping so hard you think it's going to explode, convinced you've only just escaped death. Or at least, I knew all these things until recently; since I've started falling asleep in Marcus's arms, my bad dreams have almost completely vanished.

'If you had the dreams I have, I swear you'd . . .' Kenji murmurs, throwing Alexei a menacing look.

'What? What are you saying?'

'I'm saying I bet you'd piss your bed like a child.'

Kenji really is strange. He's half Alexei's size, but that won't stop him answering back in a voice that doesn't tremble in the slightest. For a total phobic, he does sometimes seem to show incredible bravery. As if only certain things scare him, and everything else doesn't at all.

'I'd suggest you don't try me, half-pint,' the Russian warns him, 'or you're going to get what you're looking for.'

'I could say the same thing. And if you try me, you might get quite a surprise.'

The two boys glare at one another for a few moments; now Kenji's gaze is totally firm.

Beside me I can feel Kris shiver, just about to intercede, as usual, to calm the warlike passions of her great Slav – but this time Alexei doesn't give her a chance.

'You've got some guts, for an insomniac goth, I'll give you that!' he says, laughing. 'Good to see you haven't got turnip juice running through your veins!'

He claps Kenji on the shoulder – his usual buddy-buddy gesture. You might expect the smaller boy to flinch at the contact, but he holds firm, as steady as a rock, and Alexei gives a little grimace of pain, rubbing his fist.

'And pretty solid, too!' he adds. 'A real Shaolin monk! Go on, you can forget about those suits of yours, those anti-wave hoods and all that kit you have, you're a lot tougher than you look! Come on, let's drink to you, before we get to work. It's my round.'

He clicks his fingers and lets out a shrill whistle, then shouts: 'Hey, scrap metal! Go fetch a bottle of apple juice from the refrigerator in my habitat!'

The bow-tied robot, who follows his masters around the base as faithfully as Louve, turns on his wheels. He disappears in silence towards the access tube that leads to the Krisalex habitat.

'Günter is upset,' says Kris. 'He doesn't like it when you call him *scrap metal*.'

'I'm sorry, my angel. I didn't think. But between you and me, I think that machine doesn't give a damn what we call him. Despite what you'd like to believe, he isn't a child and he never will be.'

Kris says nothing, but I know her well, and I can see how sad she really is.

85. Reverse Shot

The White House, Washington DC
Saturday 6 January, 11:30am

'The electoral college vote has just been counted by Congress!' says a journalist, mic in hand, standing in front of the white dome of the Capitol. 'And it's now official: Edmond Green has been re-elected to the presidency of the United States of America, with Serena McBee as his vice-president!'

The news – which is met with a thunder of applause – is coming from the TV set on the wall of the Oval Office, part of the presidential suite in the White House. This legendary room, where so much of the world's history has been written, is full to bursting today. The newly re-elected president is here, of course, sitting at his desk, beaming, in a suit livened up by a green tie. His campaign team and his closest allies are surrounding him, each holding a champagne flute filled with a sparkling green liquid – champagne with added mint liqueur – reflecting the Ultra-libertarian Party colour.

'Thank you, thank you, my very dear friends,' says Edmond Green, as he too takes a glass of the strange beverage. 'And most of all, thank you, Serena, without whom none of this could have been possible.'

He raises his glass to the new vice-president. Where most of the people in the gathering felt it was enough to add a green accessory to their outfits to demonstrate their allegiance to the party, she has outdone herself, to include her whole look, with a green suit, green pumps on her feet, green nail polish and earrings set with emeralds. There are only three other touches of colour on her now: her silver bob; the brooch-mic, also silver; and the black Remembrance ribbon she wears in memory of the victims of the Caribbean crash.

'Isn't she something?' says the President.

'Oh, stop, my dear Edmond,' simpers Serena, 'you're going to make me blush!'

'Well, if so, you'd probably even blush green, such is your devotion to our cause! Nobody has ever worn green better!'

'Not even you, Edmond Green?'

'Oh no, not even me – ha ha ha!'

The whole gathering laughs along with the President, with the exception of two people.

In the middle of the Oval Office, Serena McBee merely smiles, raising her glass to her new boss.

And standing against the back wall, among the other bodyguards, Agent Orion Seamus watches the vice-president with his one shining eye.

86. Shot

'Come on, guys, one more and we'll be done!' says Alexei, wiping his forehead.

With the help of Samson and Marcus he is gripping the final tarpaulin to stretch it over the last section of the oat field. Behind them, the rest of the plantation pyramid has already been covered, an entire morning's exhausting work. All three pioneers are bare-chested and dripping with sweat – the tops of their undersuits were keeping them too hot in the dry air of the base. The countless sessions Alexei had in the gym on board the *Cupido* have served him well, unless it's the genes of which he seems so proud; he really has a champion physique, like something straight out of a body-building magazine. Samson has a finer build, but with a natural elegance that suggests a lot of strength, and every time he moves you can see his lean muscles working beneath his obsidian skin. Marcus's build is somewhere between the two. He's both solid and slender, and perfectly proportioned – in my humble opinion. His gleaming tattoos seem alive, drawing vital energy from the

477

movements of his body; the ferns of words become animated, the brambles quiver, the palm leaves sway each time he arches his back, then return to position as he tenses his abs. I store all this away in my head like a camera, to remember it when I'm at my drawing table. The red light filtering through the panes of the dome, the bodies at work, the concentration on the faces: this is the first scene I'm going to draw on my big sheets of paper from the 3D printer, when the storm is over.

When the storm is over . . .

It's happening tomorrow at dawn, according to the meteorological forecasts.

Protecting the plantations is the final stage of the preparations that have monopolised our time for several days. All the airlocks and openings have been carefully checked by our Engineering Officers, Tao and Liz, to be sure of their airtightness. Mozart and Kelly, meanwhile, have supervised getting tarps over most of the rovers, which will be staying outside during the storm. Kenji and Safia have been responsible for carrying out all the necessary tests to ensure the comms system is in perfect working order, most importantly the radio relay to Phobos and the supplementary satellites. With support from Fangfang, Kris has spent hours at the stove cooking and freezing kilos of her delicious mince. As for me, I've kitted out the panic room with mattresses taken from each habitat, in case we find ourselves having to stay longer than expected.

All these activities have kept us busy, and stopped us having too much time to think. But now that the preparations are done, one unanswered question comes back into my mind: *What is it exactly that we're protecting ourselves from?* We still don't know. We don't know if tomorrow's storm constitutes a real threat – and if it does, we don't know about all the danger we might be in.

'*Voilà!*' says Alexei, wiping his sweaty hands on the lower part of his undersuit. 'Off duty until tomorrow, guys! Don't know about you, but I'm planning a nice evening cuddling with my girl.'

He comes down the steps from the first terrace and puts his arms around Kris, who pretends to resist.

'Careful! You're all covered in dust!'

But everyone can see she's delighted at the idea of spending the rest of the afternoon with the boy she loves. Darling Kris . . . So quick to get annoyed when Alexei has an attack of jealousy or insults their robot, so quick to forgive him when he takes her in his arms. That boy has such an influence over her: with a single word he can hurt her terribly or fill her with total delight . . . But deep down, isn't it the same way with Marcus and me? Is that what *love* means, becoming completely dependent on the other person, like a drug addict?

While I'm wondering about this, my own addiction walks towards me, gazing lovingly at me with his irresistible grey eyes.

'You should always cover yourself up after you've been sweating, or you'll get a chill,' I say, trotting out some of my medical training.

'You bet, doc!' he answers, with his half-smile. 'But right now, what I want is a nice shower. Am I allowed?'

'I'm not aware of any reason why not.'

'OK, wait for me here, I'll be back in half an hour for our jaunt.'

'*Our jaunt?*' I say, not sure I've heard him correctly.

Marcus is standing very close to me now. His scent, intensified by the physical exercise, envelops me entirely – hot, woody, animal.

'We've been on Mars a month, and our days have been so busy we haven't had a moment to ourselves,' he murmurs in my ear, in his slightly hoarse voice. 'But now, for the first time, there's nothing we're supposed to be doing. Like Alexei said: we're off duty until tomorrow. They haven't covered up the last of the rovers yet, so I'm going to take you for a ride.'

I'm about to protest, but he's already turned on his heel to head back to our habitat.

A ride in the rover? Now, just a few hours before the storm?

It's not exactly sensible, but . . .

What a great idea!

87. Reverse Shot

The White House, Washington DC
Saturday 6 January, 1:32pm

'How are you feeling, Ms McBee?'

Serena turns away from the buffet table, a little spoon with scallops and caviar in her hand, to find herself face to face with Agent Orion Seamus. All around them, the marquee erected in the gardens of the White House is buzzing with people: after the interminable toasts, congratulations and more congratulations, the President's personal guard has gone to enjoy some food, mingling with the crowd of donors who financed the campaign.

'Oh, I feel very well indeed, Orion – you'll allow me to call you by your first name, I hope – and you must call me Serena too. How could anyone not be feeling at their best when they've just been confirmed as next vice-president of the U.S.A.!'

'That wasn't what I was talking about,' replies the agent politely. 'I was thinking more about the storm that's about to sweep through the Martian base tomorrow. I thought you might be concerned about your young charges – which was why I asked the question, *how are you feeling, Ms McBee?*'

The two of them stand facing one another without speaking for a moment – Agent Seamus half hidden by his patch; the new vice-president frozen, the spoon still in her fingers.

'There's no cause for worry,' she says at last. 'I'm sure it's all going to be fine. The New Eden base was constructed by the finest minds in NASA, before the purchase. Besides, this isn't the first storm it's been through, and it's survived worse ones. Our equipment couldn't be more robust.'

'That is reassuring,' says Agent Seamus simply, never losing the thin, enigmatic smile he constantly wears.

'I'm glad you think so,' says Serena, composing her own face into an equally unreadable smile.

She slips the little spoon between her lips for a taste without taking her eyes off the C.I.A.'s strange employee.

'I'm delighted you have been elected, Serena,' says the young man at last. 'You're an example to all the women in this country. And I'm very pleased to have been detailed by the C.I.A. to your protection. I'll help you in any way I can, with total loyalty. I believe in you and your future. I sense you're going to go far.' He repeats that last word again, insistent: '*Very far.*'

Serena McBee nods slowly.

'Orion Seamus,' she murmurs. 'You've certainly got more than your share of confidence and intelligence, as well as your mysterious charm, naturally. How old are you now? Thirty-eight? Thirty-nine?'

'Thirty-six.'

'Thirty-six years old, and already detailed to the personal protection of the vice-president! Hats off to you! Let me try to do your psychological profile – it's my speciality, after all.'

She looks the agent up and down, as methodically as the android Oraculon when he's scanning a subject, then produces her diagnosis almost in one breath, without a moment's hesitation.

'Only child. Middle-class family. Stay-at-home mom. She's smart and resourceful, but she sacrificed her career to take care of her husband and son. Which made her bitter, which is why you so value women like me who choose to work. Father a sales rep. He taught you to be confident, and also to make sure your shoes, belt and watchstrap (it's a Rolex) are matching; he must be in luxury cars or yachts. But since you were a kid your ambition has always been to go well beyond the paternal dealership; you excelled in your studies and aced every subject. That's how you secured this position, at your age, ten years younger than one might have expected. Ah, and I forgot – a confirmed bachelor. It's not just that you aren't wearing a wedding band, it's also that whenever I see you you're always in the same outfit – I'm sure your wardrobe is made up of dozens of black suits, white shirts and grey ties, that's the surest way of not making fashion faux pas when you haven't got any feminine advice to help you in the morning. Your eyepatch is the only thing I can't yet explain, but let me spend a bit more time with you and I'm sure it'll come to me.'

Agent Seamus tips his head slightly to one side, admiringly.

'Impressive stuff, Serena,' he says. 'If you weren't already taking on a new job, I'd recommend you try for a career in Intelligence. But talking about your new job . . . During your term of office, you are expected to live close to the White House, more precisely at the Naval Observatory that has served

483

as the vice-president's residence for decades. Are you sure you're still going to want to continue presenting the Genesis channel?'

'Of course I do, we've already been through this! And President Green is counting on it, too, as – let's not kid ourselves – the renewed popularity of the Ultra-libertarian Party is directly linked to my broadcasts. As of this afternoon, my teams will be installing the audio-visual equipment to allow me to present the show remotely, as I've been doing from the Villa McBee. I trust that you can secure them access to the residence?'

'As you wish.'

'And don't forget, I still want to be kept up to speed – day or night – with any sign of that unfortunate young man, Andrew Fisher.'

'Understood, Ms McBee.'

'You can bring him straight to me, no need to involve the Bureau. After all, if the boy wants to speak to me in private, there's no need to notify the whole world.'

'The C.I.A. isn't in the habit of notifying the F.B.I. each time we do any small thing. And in this case we'll be sure to be especially discreet. It's a private matter, as you say, and my men and I don't know the substance of it. I'll just carry out my orders, and that's that.'

Serena's smile widens.

'I'm sure we'll get along very nicely, my dear Orion,' she says. 'And I can sense that you're going to go *very far*, too.'

Then she picks up a lobster skewer, and gulps it down in a couple of elegant mouthfuls.

88. Shot

'It really feels like we're the only people in the world,' I say.

Through the windscreen of the mini-rover, we can see the great valley of Ius Chasma, an uninterrupted series of red dunes as far as the eye can see. The shadows are very long already, hollowing out the craters, drawing a trail of black ink behind each rock.

Marcus is in the central position, the driver's seat. I'm sitting to his right, and we've put a basket of provisions in the left-hand seat – apples and strawberries from our personal allocation, as well as some delicious oat biscuits made for us by Kris. Our two helmets are on the back seat; in the pressurised cabin of the mini-rover we don't need to wear them.

'That's actually almost true,' replies Marcus. 'Here on Mars we're the only *twelve* people in the world.'

'Plus all the viewers watching us,' I say, suddenly remembering the Genesis channel and the camera attached to the top of the windscreen.

I press my forehead to the thick glass to stare up at the glowing red Martian sky.

'Phobos and its comms antenna are somewhere up there, invisible, capturing every word we say. It really is like all the billions of viewers are here, with us, in the rover.'

'Are they really here?' says Marcus. 'I don't know. I'm not sure. The fact is, they aren't experiencing things at the same time as us. Our present is their future. And their present is our past. We're now four and a half minutes ahead of them, and that gap's going to keep growing wider as the communication latency grows from week to week.' He looks up at the camera and gives it a wink. 'Hello there, ladies and gentlemen – Léo and Marcus here, fugitives of time! Catch us if you can!'

I smile.

Fugitives of time . . . It's a nice image, like so many that come out of Marcus's mouth. It's also a metaphor that the viewers won't be able to understand completely; it doesn't just refer to the communication latency that keeps us at a distance from Earth, but also the time that he and I are stealing away from the illness that's going to catch up with us one day.

'Could I have another strawberry, doc?' Marcus asks.

I reach over his lap to get a handful of berries from the basket. Just like the Martian apples, they're fatter than their terrestrial cousins. I slip one between Marcus's lips, while he keeps his hands on the wheel – the landscape is so uneven he can't let go of the controls for a single moment.

'Careful, you've got strawberry juice dribbling down your chin!' I say, laughing.

A blood-coloured thread trickles down Marcus's neck, following the faint furrow made by the stem of the tattooed rose. I wipe it away with the back of my index finger and bring the finger to my lips; the sugary taste makes me think of summer, of feeling carefree, of happy days.

'We shouldn't be out too long,' I say, reluctantly. 'We've gotten quite far from the base, and we really need to be back before it gets dark, especially with the storm coming tomorrow.'

'Don't worry. There's something I wanted to show you, and we're just getting there now. Look!'

The mini-rover steers around a boulder that's even bigger than the rest, and suddenly an astonishing sight fills the windscreen. We're right up close to the cliff that blocks off the end of Ius Chasma to the south. The wall of rock and reddish earth rises for miles. But there's something else, something I haven't seen since we arrived on Mars; embedded into the cliff, at about our eye level, a white strip stretches several metres across, its surface glistening in a thousand colours.

'What's that?' I ask, amazed, as Marcus parks the rover at the foot of the cliff.

'An opal deposit. I discovered it two sols ago, when I was out here on my own, while Mozart was driving Samson further east to gather sand samples from a crater. I haven't told anyone about it. I wanted you to be the first to see it. Come over here!'

We attach our helmets, move to the airlock at the back of the rover and then, once the decompression procedure has been completed, we open the door and allow ourselves to slip down onto the ground of Mars.

Marcus takes my gloved hand in his, and leads me over to the opal deposit.

The closer I get, the further my eyes widen. It's an

extraordinary sight, unlike anything I've ever seen. It looks like a fossilised rainbow, set for millions of years in the rocky flesh of Ius Chasma.

'*Awesome. It's like the best magic trick ever . . .*' I just about manage to say into my helmet mic.

'*My tricks have nothing to do with this – what you're looking at is no illusion, it's reality,*' I hear Marcus's voice answer, slightly distorted by the audio relay. '*But you're right, this reality does have something magic about it. Because, you see, the opal is formed by the interaction of water and silica. Like on Earth, in hot springs bursting with microbial life.*'

I gently place my gloved hand on the sparkling surface, with a feeling of confusion as though touching something sacred.

'*Like Fangfang told us,*' I murmur. '*Mars isn't as dry a desert as it seems. There's liquid water here. And maybe even . . .*'

'*Yes, maybe even life!*' says Marcus.

Instinctively I pull my hand away from the opal deposit.

Life?

In this dead desert, on this dead planet?

'*I've taken the first samples, and they're currently being analysed in the New Eden lab,*' Marcus goes on. '*And I also used the opportunity to do* this . . .'

He points at an area where the opal is particularly bright and smooth.

Except in one place that is covered in grooves. These lines weren't carved out by storms, or by quakes, or by any of the cataclysms that have moulded Mars over billions of years.

LEONOR + MARCUS

488

That's what's engraved here in the opal, in handsome upright letters, like the ones you find adorning the façades of old temples.

'*Since you wouldn't let me finish writing your name on my chest, I decided to write it here,*' says Marcus. '*And mine next to it.*'

I turn to face him, my heart tight with emotion.

The sinking Sun throws brilliant reflections against the curved visor of his helmet, but his smile shines brighter still.

'*Will I sound really dumb if I say I think our love is going to last for ever?*' he asks me gently, almost shyly. '*Will you think I'm a dumb, useless poet, like Alexei would say?*'

'Marcus . . .'

'*Because I really believe it. What we've experienced together, the life we have right now, this will always exist somewhere, even after we've disappeared. It will remain here, engraved for all eternity, in the opal of Mars.*'

89. Genesis Channel

Saturday 6 January, 4:15pm

Semi-close-up on the compression airlock, seen from the New Eden glasshouse.

Above the metallic door, through the glass panels that make up the dome, the Martian night has already fallen. Elizabeth is there, like every evening, waiting for the darkness, like a ship's lookout on her bow.

Subtitle at the bottom of the screen: INTERIOR VIEW: THE GARDEN. MARS TIME – 19:15.

All of a sudden, the warning light above the metal lintel comes on:

COMPRESSION PROCEDURE UNDERWAY
EQUALISATION 10%
EQUALISATION 20%
EQUALISATION 30%

Elizabeth gives a big sigh of relief.

'Finally!'

When the display reaches 100%, the door opens to reveal

two silhouettes in spacesuits, and the English girl hurries over to meet them.

'I was getting so worried! I was afraid the storm had already started out there and it had carried you off! You could at least have . . .'

The words lodge in her throat the moment Léonor and Marcus take off their helmets. There's such obvious happiness in their faces, such serenity, that any reprimand seems pointless.

Elizabeth's voice is quieter now. 'I'm glad you're here,' she says simply. 'I'll let Kris know. She wanted to be here with me to wait for you, but Alexei wanted her with him. And as for Mozart . . . well, even though he was determined to stay in our habitat to make me a wonderful dinner before the late-summer storm, I know that deep down he's awfully worried too.'

Léonor turns to Elizabeth and gives her a big smile, which sparkles like a sun. 'Thank you, Liz. And I'm sorry we made you worry. It's time for you to go take a rest with Mozart. We have a tough day ahead.'

The two *fugitives of time* take off their suits and leave them in the area set aside for storing them, next to the airlock. Then they walk across the deserted Garden and disappear into the access tube leading to their habitat.

Cut.

Long shot of Léonor and Marcus's Love Nest, just as they are walking in.

There still seems to be a strange aura enveloping them.

Without a word, they undress.

They drop the second skin of the undersuits at their feet, leaving them in their underwear, standing facing each other.

The camera trembles.

It focuses on Marcus's body, his amazing interlacing of tattoos, as if wanting to record them all in its memory. But there are too many of them, each inky branch giving birth to a dozen others, each calligraphic word opening into a whole phrase. And already he is taking Léonor's hand and leading her gently towards the bathroom.

Now the camera goes wild, seeing its prey escape.

It zooms nervously in on Léonor, her legs, the elegant small of her back . . . but stops there. The back that the camera so wants to show its viewers, the scar that has excited the curiosity of the entire world, remains inaccessible to it. The girl's long hair forms a screen, a lush curtain of deep red velvet protecting an ancient mystery.

Together the young couple step into the shower cubicle, where the camera cannot follow them.

The frosted glass door closes gently behind them, without a sound.

90. Shot

Month 21 / sol 577 / 19:32 Mars time
[27th sol since landing]

The first drops crash onto my skin.

I can't tell if they're burning hot or ice cold.

I can't hear them, I can hardly feel them.

My bare feet, all the way down there on the immaculate base of the shower, seem so far away. Like Alice's feet in Wonderland when she's eaten the cake that makes her grow impossibly tall.

I feel like I'm outside of myself, detached from my own body, as if this were a story I was reading without really believing it.

The whirlpool of silent water falling on my lowered head, on my long hair, my stiff legs, seems unreal to me. Someone has muted the sound.

And then, suddenly, he puts his hand on my arm.

Suddenly the joyous crackle of rain is echoing in my ears.

Suddenly my whole body exists, shivers, feels.

But at the same moment, shame crashes down on me; a flood of thoughts overwhelms me, heavier than any storm, more acidic than any poison.

(It wasn't a good idea for you to take this shower together. There's a risk you'll get pregnant. And there's a risk he'll get totally disappointed. You aren't ready to strip yourself naked yet. Deep down, you know you never will be. It's too late now. He's seen you, he's looked at you close up, he's looking at you now, and he's regretting it – how terribly he's regretting it!)

A croak escapes from my mouth, as grotesque and discordant as the fear that eats away at my insides, like the cry of despair from a frog who thought she was a princess.

'I shouldn't . . .'

Marcus places his index finger gently on my lips.

His other hand runs along my arm, light as a breeze, up to my shoulder, to the Salamander . . .

. . . and he touches it, with no disgust, no impulse to recoil.

I can't feel the direct contact of his palm against that part of me that is burned and dead, deprived of its nerve endings, but I can feel the support of the arm behind that palm, of the man behind that arm.

The finger that sealed my lips moves down to my streaming chin.

He gently raises my head.

Marcus's face appears before me – his genuine smile, his thick eyebrows dotted with pearls of water, his big grey eyes that will keep the reflection of the stars in them for ever.

I'm not afraid any more.

I'm not ashamed any more.

There's no anguish that can withstand eyes like Marcus's looking at me as if I were the most precious thing in the universe.

91. Genesis Channel

Sunday 7 January, 4:45am

Mars appears, a gigantic red orb.

It's being filmed from so close that it fills the whole screen, leaving only two thin edges of black cosmos around the frame. The border separating day and night divides the planet vertically into two hemispheres.

A subtitle appears: AERIAL VIEW OF MARS, CAPTURED FROM THE PRINCIPAL COMMUNICATIONS ANTENNA ON PHOBOS / MARS TIME – 07:05

The camera zooms in, giving the impression that it is plummeting towards the surface of Mars.

The sharp gash of the Valles Marineris is getting bigger every second. It's currently at the exact place where light and shadow meet, the juncture that cuts straight through it; the east is already lit up, the west still in shadow.

Then suddenly the Sun's rays light up the contours of Ius Chasma, now very familiar to the viewers. But while the edges of the famous canyon are being revealed, the Solis Planum plateau is also appearing on screen just below it: it is no more than an expanse of red and black mist, all curls and whorls, light and shadows. Seen from this far away, one gets the misleading impression that the late-summer storm is stationary – it looks like the twists of a baroque bas-relief, carved into the Martian ground.

The powerful camera zooms in further still, and the closer it gets, the more obvious it becomes that the storm is moving. It's not a bas-relief, it's a moving, living mass, and it's crawling towards the edge of Ius Chasma.

92. Shot

'Look, the Sun's coming up!' I hear Safia's voice in my earphones.

She's pointing up at the top of the Ius Chasma cliff, which we can see through the glass dome.

Today we woke up well before dawn, put on our suits and sealed our helmets. Then we all gathered in the Garden with the covered-up plantations, all twelve of us, plus the two dogs and even the robot butlers – Krisalex's with his bow tie, Fangtao's as naked as the day he came out of the factory (he has at least been granted a name: Lóng, which means *dragon* in Chinese). For the past hour, we have watched the shadowy vastness of Mars and waited for the monster to arrive.

But what appears at the top of the endless cliff is not a monster.

Safia's right: it's the Sun.

It's just the Sun, and above it the sky is clear, with not a cloud in sight.

Rays of light stream down from the top of Ius Chasma, flooding the whole valley and the Garden. At the same moment,

497

I feel Marcus's arms pull me a little tighter against his chest. Even though we now have the double thickness of our two suits between us, it's as if I can feel his bare skin against mine. Last night my fear of getting pregnant disappeared right alongside my fear of the Salamander. We didn't make love, or at least not in the way you have to do it to make babies. But whatever! The music all came naturally. The score has been inside us since time immemorial. We took our time to perform it, as if we had a whole life ahead of us for learning to love. Then we fell asleep pressed against one another, him bare-chested and me in the fine little satin nightie I never thought I'd wear – as if this new life was only just beginning.

'Looks like Serena screwed up her predictions!' Kelly's voice brings me back into the present. *'It's a beautiful day!'*

One by one the others add their voices, creating a feedback loop in my helmet: *'Looks like Kelly's right . . .'*; *'Think the storm's calmed . . . ?'*; *'Yes, the wind's changed now and moved it away from Ius Chasma . . .'*; *'What do you say we open a bottle of champagne now to celebrate?'*

There's a shrill noise all of a sudden, drowning out all the theories and the cries of happiness.

It's Louve, who's started barking, and Warden with her.

Through their little round helmets, each has their muzzle pointed at the cliff, towards the Sun that the humans are all so happy about.

'What's up, girl?' asks Kris, kneeling beside the dog.

'What's up?' says Kenji like a gloomy echo. *'Look up there!'*

Which is what we do, screwing up our eyes to filter the blinding rays between our lashes. And that's when we see it.

The storm.

It's a gigantic red mass, stretching miles and miles over the summit of Ius Chasma.

It expands and contracts, like a living organism driven by a thousand muscles.

It swallows up the Sun between its jaws of dust.

Then it reaches the very edge of the cliff and slips over the precipice like a vast octopus reaching its tentacles towards its prey.

'*Oh God,*' whispers Kris, while it twists down into the canyon, drowning the dunes, the rocks and the whole landscape.

Louve and Warden fall suddenly silent and press themselves against the floor.

An enormous tongue of smoke appears from the end of the valley and descends on the dome, making all the panes of glass tremble.

Instinctively I close my eyes and huddle up against Marcus's chest, waiting to feel the shards of broken glass rain down on us.

But the dome holds.

The trembling stops.

When I reopen my eyes, there's no more sky, no more valley. There is only an opaque, glowing red screen, surrounding us and blinding us.

We are in the heart of the storm.

93. Off-screen

Abandoned mine, Death Valley
Sunday 7 January, 3:13am

'What's happening, Andrew? Why is the image trembling?'

Andrew and Harmony are sitting on the edge of one of the ruined beds, in the cabin beside the old abandoned mine in Dry Mountain. The pair of handcuffs is sitting open at the foot of the bed, shining weakly in the dim light. The screen of the computer on the boy's lap is the only light source in the night-time darkness; here in Death Valley it's three hours earlier than on the East Coast, and eighteen hours and forty minutes earlier than on Mars.

The online broadcast of the Genesis channel, currently focused on the Garden, is streaming onto the screen. The dozen Mars pioneers are standing there, huddled together, in their white spacesuits. The light is only a faint glow, the helmets impenetrable; it's impossible to say for sure who is who, with the exception of Tao in his wheelchair.

Suddenly the picture jumps, and is streaked with white lines.

'Look, Andrew, it's starting again!' says Harmony. 'Oh God, Earth is starting to lose contact with the base at New Eden, just like it did in the Great Storm with the silent hour when all the animals died!'

'Don't say that,' says Andrew. 'It's just occasional interference, from magnetic disturbances caused by the storm. The audio relay can make up for phenomena like that.'

He speaks as the son of the Genesis programme's former Communications instructor and main creator of its transmissions system. And yet the tension in his voice is palpable.

Harmony presses a little closer to him and pulls the blanket she's wrapped in over her delicate shoulders. She shivers.

'And what if my mother takes advantage of the interference to depressurise the base?' she murmurs.

'She'd never do something like that,' Andrew assures her. 'Not as long as we're free, and while we still have a copy of the Noah Report.'

Once again there's doubt in Andrew's voice. Harmony seems to notice it. She turns to look at him – in the light given off by the screen he looks thinner than ever. In contrast, her big eyes seem twice their usual size – two vast, bottomless water-green lakes.

'How long are we going to be able to hold out, Andrew?' She points at the few supplies he acquired from a nearby minimarket, heaped up in the shadows against the cabin wall. 'Are we going to spend the rest of our lives hiding in the desert, constantly on the alert, waiting for the moment when we reveal the Noah Report to the planet? A moment that might never come?'

Andrew gives her a pained look.

'What do you suggest?' he asks. 'Do you want us to turn your mother in, right now? We have the power to do it. We only need to upload the pages of the Noah Report onto my site and the whole world will have access to it.'

By way of demonstration he taps away on his keyboard and the window showing the channel is minimised to show his site: *Genesis Piracy*.

'It would only take me one click!'

'No!' yells Harmony, breathless.

She grabs hold of Andrew's wrist hovering above the keyboard.

'If you touch those keys, my mom will also press the button that will kill the pioneers . . . kill Mozart.'

'Fine,' murmurs Andrew. 'I won't do it.'

He closes the *Genesis Piracy* window and returns to the Genesis channel, as Harmony breathes a little easier.

'The twelve of them up there have already made their choice,' he adds. 'They decided to land on Mars. But we have to re-make our choice again and again every day: reveal the Noah Report, or stay quiet. I can't say how long that's going to last. I have no idea if we're going to be spending the rest of our lives in the desert, like you dread we might. We can't even vote on it, because there are two of us! That's the responsibility we carry, Harmony. If one day we're too tired of carrying it and we let it go . . . Well, if that day comes, may the pioneers forgive us.'

At the mention of the Mars pioneers, the two fugitives turn their attention back to the screen, unable to say another word.

Overview of the Garden, as the image finally stops jumping around and stabilises.

The twelve colonists are gathered at the foot of the covered plantations, instinctively withdrawing, protecting themselves. All around them, beyond the giant glasshouse, there is only a blinding reddish dusk, neither day nor night.

All of a sudden, the supplementary spotlights hanging from the roof of the dome come on to compensate for the lack of light. They are, however, set to just twenty-five per cent of their power, to save energy.

Cut.

The screen switches to a subjective view from ground level.

Subjective view female pioneer no. 4 – Kelly

The Canadian girl turns around, revealing the same blocked-out landscape, for all 360 degrees around the dome.

Her hesitant voice comes through the microphone: 'I'd still really like to know what's going on. Why aren't we getting any instructions? Have we lost contact? Hello, Earth?'

But nothing happens.

There's total silence.

Total?

No, if you listen closely, you'll be able to make out a slight clanking, coming from somewhere in the depths of the base.

Clank . . . Clonk . . . Clank . . .

Elizabeth's voice comes through the audio relay: 'Can you hear that?'

The worry on the English girl's face can be seen through the visor of her helmet, on which the scattered dull radiance of the spotlights is falling.

The other astronauts don't seem much more confident.

503

Kris asks no one in particular: 'Where's that coming from?'

Alexei shrugs his huge shoulders: 'Oh, it's probably something or other that's come detached outside and is being thrown around by the wind – a hook from the tarps around one of the rovers, something like that.'

CLANK! A noise much louder than the others, much closer, interrupts him.

Kris starts to panic: 'You can't tell me that's from the tarps on the rovers, Alexei! That was nearby, and much too loud to be just the tarps!'

At that moment, the interior surface of the dome starts to tremble, crossed by fuzzy lines. After a few tremulous moments, it stabilises on the picture of Serena McBee, sitting in a huge room with cream-coloured wallpaper: it's her new vice-presidential study in the Observatory residence.

Dressed completely in green, the programme's executive producer has faint circles under her eyes. The time difference between Earth and Mars has required her to wake up early.

Still, she puts on her best smile the moment she's ready to start talking. 'Can you hear me? Yes? Ah, yes, this does seem to be working! The communications system is up and running again, after a few minor disturbances. Well, then, listen to me. You are surrounded by the storm. Ius Chasma has completely disappeared from the satellite pictures we're getting from space. But there's no need to worry. You just have to wait for the squall to pass. So listen, we're going to do a little relaxation exercise, all together. You remember the technique we used, visualising dolphins, in the good old days? Very well, then, after me!

'One, I empty my lungs all the way down and I close my eyes . . .'

94. Shot

'*Two, I sink into my belly and I see a great, calm ocean where dolphins are swimming . . .*'

I glance around me.

And discover to my amazement that most of my companions are carrying out Serena's instructions, just like they did when we were being trained in Death Valley, or at the *Cupido*'s moment of take-off. Like they did before we discovered the Noah Report.

'*Three, I let the air back into my nostrils, and fill my body back up, starting at my navel . . .*'

How can the voice that's coming through our earphones possibly be bringing them the least bit of calm, knowing what they know? It's beyond me. Only three of the other people around me still have their eyes open: Marcus, who is looking at me; Liz, who is looking at Mozart; and Kenji, who is staring hard at the red clouds beyond the glass dome, as if he was trying to see through them.

'*Four, I feel my inhalation press against my diaphragm, I imagine dolphins swimming inside my belly . . .*'

I can't take my eyes off Kenji. There's something crazy in his black eyes, an intensity I've never seen before – maybe because with their constant darting about I've never really been able to look at them. But they're not moving now. At all.

'*Five, I . . .*'

Serena doesn't finish.

A new bit of interference stops her, jumbling the screen of the dome again; after a few white lines, the glass goes back to being transparent and all we can see is the impenetrable nothingness outside.

'*There's something that's . . .*' We suddenly hear Kenji's voice in our helmets.

'*Huh? What? What something?*' asks Kris, opening her eyes abruptly. '*Where's Serena? I want to go on with our exercise! I want to see the dolphins again!*'

My poor Kris is totally overwhelmed, like a little kid who's lost all her reference points. Alexei should take her in his arms and comfort her, but instead he reacts in his usual way, with anger.

'*You shut it, Kenji!*' he yells. '*Can't you see you're scaring the girls?*'

The Japanese boy seems not to hear him.

His eyes are still fixed on the outside, as he says again, '*Out there, in the storm . . . there's something . . . like in my nightmares . . . I can sense it . . .*'

CLANK!

This time the shock from outside causes a terrified scream, and not only from Kris.

'*The panic room!*' yells Fangfang. '*Quick!*'

506

She's already rushing for the reinforced door in the side of the first terrace.

But Alexei takes hold of Kris's arm before she's able to follow her in.

'*You'll stay here, my angel!*' he says to her, his commanding tone in stark contrast to the affectionate expression he usually wears around her. '*You'll all stay here. You are not going to be scared off by some stupid little noise, for Christ's sake!*'

But I can sense his fear – in the raising of his voice, the way he holds on to Kris's arm with his gloved hand, just a little too tightly.

CLANK!

'*It's just pebbles bumping into the base, you bunch of chickens! Plain old pebbles being carried by the wind, that's all!*'

He's almost shouting now.

He can't hear Fangfang's stammering – '*The Martian air is a hundred times less dense than on Earth, much too light for any wind to be able to lift pebbles.*' But all Alexei can respond to is his own fear, and he twists Kris's wrist without even realising it.

'*Let go of her, you're hurting her,*' says Samson.

'*What?*'

'*Can't you see you're pulling out her arm?*'

Even through his helmet I can almost see lightning bolts shoot across Alexei's blue eyes.

'*I knew there was something going on between you!*' he roars, letting go of Kris's arm sharply and hurling himself at Samson.

The Nigerian boy falls back under the impact.

Warden immediately rushes to his master's rescue, barking

wildly, the noise filling the audio relay and piercing my eardrums. If he hadn't been wearing his own helmet, I reckon he'd have torn through the Russian's suit and flesh in seconds, but behind his slobber-stained visor, his fangs just close on nothingness.

'*Admit it!*' spits Alexei, crushing Samson's chest under his knee.

'*I've got nothing . . . to admit . . . asshole!*' Samson just manages to say, struggling to catch his breath.

'*Liar! All those times I've left the two of you alone in the plantations, just trusting you! You totally screwed me over! You especially – because you must have forced her, didn't you? – I'm sure of it! My Kirsten would never betray me of her own accord. Take that!*'

Alexei's fist comes down on Samson's suit with a dull noise, while Mozart and Marcus hurry over to separate the fighters.

The girls are starting to shout now, too, trying to make themselves heard above the barking of the dogs.

'*I swear nothing's happened, Alex!*' says Kris, frantic.

'*Violence never solves anything,*' says Fangfang, trying to appeal to reason. '*It's time to get yourself under control.*'

Safia, meanwhile, is much less diplomatic: '*You're just a nasty brute, Alexei. And an idiot!*'

Alexei lifts his eyes from Samson's for a moment, to stare at the Indian girl.

'*Don't you think you're on the wrong side?*' he asks her. '*You should be on my side. You've been betrayed too!*'

'*That's crap.*'

'*How can you be so sure?*'

'*There's no reason for jealousy between Samson and me. I could explain why, but I don't think you'd understand. Nobody has betrayed you, Alexei – if you're wearing horns, it's not because you're a cuckold, but because you're dumb as an ox!*'

Alexei is still for a moment, like a machine malfunctioning, unable to deal with a piece of information that hasn't been anticipated by its software. Samson takes advantage of the moment to push him roughly away and get back to his feet.

The Russian's massive body rolls over and bumps into Günter, who falls onto the aluminium floor with a loud metal crash.

A red light immediately turns on around his single eye, as an artificial voice comes out of some unknown opening.

'*Lateral shock experienced . . . Assessment of damage sustained is underway . . . Evaluation completed: no breakages . . .*'

The surprise caused by Günter's voice, when we'd all thought he was mute, is so great that the boys stop punching, and the girls forget to shout, and even fear itself disappears for a few moments. And just then, the wall of the dome starts crackling again, bringing the period of interference to an end, and Serena McBee's face reappears on the glass panels.

'*Oh – at last! Here I am again! We're going to be able to resume our relaxation exercise,*' she says, unaware of the brawl that's just happened, as there are now ten minutes of communication latency separating us. '*One, I empty my lungs all the way down and I close my eyes . . .*'

But this time no one's listening to her, and all eyes remain firmly open, fixed on Günter.

'*So, scrap metal, you can talk?*' says Alexei.

'*Affirmative,*' replies Günter's artificial voice, which must

509

be connected to our audio relay network, since we can all hear it through the earphones in our helmets.

The robot reaches out his long mechanical arms, presses his pincers against the ground for support and straightens himself up with a creaking of joints.

'*But why haven't you said anything before?*' asks Kris, suddenly emotional, like a mother whose child has spoken his first words.

'*No direct question has been put to me. My programming requires that I speak only in the event of a threat to my physical state or when I am asked a direct question.*'

We all exchange glances through our visors. There's no need to say anything to know that we're all thinking the same thing at this moment; if the multitask robots are capable of speech, then they can tell us what happened during the silent hour on sol 511 last year. They can tell us what made the hole in the wall of the seventh habitat, and what caused the deaths of the animals.

I'm burning to ask the question, but not now, not here!

There's no way we can refer to the hidden flaws in the base in front of the viewers; that would be a breach of our *Serenity* contract, and we'd be signing our own death warrants.

'*Shut up, everybody, and listen to me!*' I shout, before anyone gets the chance to open their mouth.

Without another word, my stomach clenched, I cast my eyes slowly around all the various cameras positioned around the Garden, and at Serena's giant face which is still spouting her relaxation instructions. The others absolutely must remember that this isn't the time or the place to question the robots. There's only one spot on the base where we can make them talk without risking it going out on the Genesis channel.

'Can you hear?' I say quietly. 'It's gone quiet again. If you ask me, I reckon the weird noises that scared us just now were coming from the Rest House.'

It's a lie, but it's enough to pull the wool over the viewers' eyes, to give them an explanation for why I want to go to the seventh habitat as quickly as possible . . . and why I want to take at least one of the two robots with me.

'I'll go check everything is OK there,' I add, trying to keep my breathing steady. 'Samson and Kenji, you should both come with me, to let tempers cool a little. And I'll need an Engineering Officer – Liz, will you come along? And one last thing – Krisalex, can I borrow Günter, to help us carry out the technical checks?'

Kris, still in shock, nods. She gestures to Alex to make him understand he has no say in the matter.

'I'm the one who talks to Günter from now on,' she says. 'Look how badly you've been mistreating him.'

She squats down next to her robot, her almost-child.

'Günter, would you do me a favour and go with Léo to the seventh habitat?' she asks him, a tremor in her voice.

'Negative,' the monotone voice replies from somewhere in the belly of the machine.

My blood freezes in my veins, as Günter continues to give his answer in plain sight and hearing of the cameras, of Serena McBee and the viewers all over the world.

'My programming forbids me from putting my physical status in jeopardy. The seventh habitat is not secure. It was damaged during the Great Storm of sol 511, month eighteen. At 22:46, an unidentified body perforated its shell, from the outside.'

511

95. Off-screen

Hotel California, Death Valley
Sunday 7 January, 3:31am

'. . . *an unidentified body perforated its shell, from the outside.*'

In surprise, Cindy drops the spoon she was dipping into the tub of ice cream she has wedged between her knees. Her eyes widen under the headband she puts over her hair every evening before going to sleep. Except that tonight she has decided to stay up out of solidarity until the pioneers have made it through the storm, even if it takes the substantial reinforcement of strawberry ice cream with nougat chunks for her to stay alert.

Without even bothering to pick up the spoon, which has left a long pink smear down her lace bedcover, she hurries over to the small TV set that sits on the chest of drawers of the bedroom she occupies in the Hotel California. The light from the screen illuminates her exhaustion-lined face.

She turns the volume up to max.

96. Off-screen

'. . . *an unidentified body perforated its shell, from the outside.*'

Andrew's knees begin to tremble with nerves, shaking the laptop.

'Oh, that's terrible!' cries Harmony shrilly. 'Now the viewers know about the accident in the seventh habitat!'

'Which means your mother is going to press the depressurisation button,' says Andrew. 'But I'm going to press my own button, too!'

His fingers start to race across the keyboard.

The window showing the *Genesis Piracy* site reappears on the screen. The young man has only one more key to press to upload the pages of the Noah Report.

'Not yet!' cries Harmony, snatching the laptop from his hands. 'The robot mentioned there was a hole, but it didn't refer to the deaths of the animals; maybe my mom won't carry out her threat!'

The two Dry Mountain fugitives struggle for a moment on the mattress, surrounded by the silence of the night.

Their fingers crash onto the keys.

Windows open and close like crazy: the piracy site, the Genesis channel, the mailbox files stolen from Serena McBee's study, everything rushing past.

The laptop falls flat onto the floor, jolted fully open like a book whose binding has given way.

Andrew and Harmony hasten to pick it back up.

But at the same moment, with the glowing rectangle in front of them, they stare at each other. An email has opened, one of the thousands that make up the archive. The subject appears in black letters, clear against the bright whiteness of the screen:

SELF-ENERGIZED SPACE ELEVATOR

97. Off-screen

'. . . *an unidentified body perforated its shell, from the outside.*'

In Paris, unlike in the United States, it's not the early hours of the morning when most people are still asleep. It's Sunday midday. Tens of thousands of locals and tourists have descended on the Champs-Élysées to watch the storm on Mars live. Beneath a huge banner of Léonor, which has been replaced since vandals burned the original one a month earlier, a gigantic screen has been set up. It's hanging over the Arc de Triomphe, and it's broadcasting the weird body of Günter the robot at nine metres by sixteen.

'What did he say?' asks an old lady who is pulling a shopping bag on wheels and a dog on a leash.

She turns to her neighbour, a young man in a tracksuit and cap, accompanied by his gang who are all similarly attired.

'I'm a little hard of hearing, I'm not sure I got that right.'

'There's been some shit that screwed up the seventh Love Nest during the storm!' says the young man, stunned, before registering the advanced age of the lady speaking to him. 'That

515

is, um, sorry, I mean there's a kind of crack in the seventh habitat.'

As if echoing his words, a hubbub travels through the crowd that has gathered on the famous Parisian boulevard, like a thunderstorm swelling second by second: '*The New Eden base isn't as safe as we thought . . .*'; '*There's already been some accident . . .*'; '*There's something in the storm – the pioneers are in danger!*'

98. Off-screen

Vice-Presidential Residence, Washington DC
Sunday 7 January, that same moment, 6:31am

'. . . *an unidentified body perforated its shell, from the outside.*'

Alone in the huge study that has welcomed generations of vice-presidents before her, Serena McBee is pale – and the pallor of her face has nothing to do with her lack of sleep.

The desk at which she is seated is the one from the Villa McBee, which she has had transported to Washington. Multiple electrical cables come out of it and run along the floor to the large aluminium gantry covered in spotlights and cameras, itself likewise imported from the Hamptons. Hanging from the middle of the gantry is the large editing screen that broadcasts the Genesis channel, and which is currently showing the robot butler surrounded by the pioneers.

Serena presses her bee-shaped brooch-mic firmly, then gives her instructions to the teams in Florida: '*Serena to the editing suite.* I need to be as close as possible to the pioneers now, without any intermediaries, to help them get through the stress of the storm. I'm taking over the controls.' With her other hand, she presses a key on the control panel set into the wood of the desk.

A message appears in red at the top of the large screen.

CRISIS PROTOCOL ACTIVATED

The executive producer presses a few more keys. The view of the robots and the twelve pioneers vanishes, to be replaced by the opening frames of a commercial.

99. Genesis Channel

Sunday 7 January, 6:32am

Open onto Kenji's face, in extreme close-up, in wavering light. All around him it's thick, dark night. The young man's anguished eyes sweep across the space, back and forth, like a pendulum.

There is a gravelly, insistent voiceover, like you hear on the trailer for a Hollywood blockbuster: *'Phobos – is Mars's mysterious moon . . .'*

The camera pulls slowly back, revealing Kenji's perspiring forehead, his hair sticking up in spikes.

Suddenly a harsh creaking pierces the silence, making him jump.

Voiceover: *'Phobos – is the Greek god of fear . . .'*

The frame continues to widen, allowing us to see that Kenji has his back to a steel wall with a porthole in it: it's the colour of a spacecraft, reflecting the dull glare of a flickering neon light. Kenji's arms are clutching an impressive machine-gun to his chest.

And there's that creaking again, much louder than the first time – much closer.

Voice-over: '*Phobos – is . . . the new game from Dojo Studios . . .*'

The neon bulb goes out, plunging the screen abruptly into total darkness.

There is a yell,

then the crackle of gunfire, accompanied by flashes of light,

then silence.

A caption in disturbing letters, fluorescent red, appears slowly on the black screen.

PHOBOS
The official videogame
IF YOU'RE PHOBIC, STAY AWAY!

Another hit from
DOJO

Cut.

100. Shot

My heart is pounding in the sound box of my helmet.

The moment Günter answered Kris's innocent question, revealing the secret we've been keeping for a month, I thought time had stopped and would never start up again. It was as if it had smashed into a wall of reinforced concrete.

But no wall can ever be solid enough to stop time. It resumed its inexorable course, and everything else unfolded very fast.

We knew instinctively that we only had ten minutes ahead of us – the five minutes it would take for Günter's words to reach Earth, and five more for the depressurisation command to fly back to us. We raced into the panic room, taking the robots and the dogs with us.

That's where we are now, in the windowless neon-lit room, squashed between the 3D printer, the infirmary bed and the rack where all the gardening implements are kept.

The heavy reinforced door has closed behind us.

We don't dare move, or speak.

We don't know if the cameras are still filming us.

521

We don't know if Serena depressurised the base the moment she heard Günter's admission.

If she did, then back there, beyond that door, New Eden is now no more than a heap of shattered glass, plantations torn up by the force of the decompression, already covered in Mars's acidic red sand.

If she did, there's only the wall of the panic room between us and the thing in the storm, the thing that so fascinates Kenji, that scared Günter, that opened up a hole in the wall of the seventh habitat one Martian year ago. And we all thought the hole had been made from inside . . . It was so much simpler imagining that the rats had gnawed through the shell – it was so much more reassuring than *the other possibility*: that the breach came from outside, from the red vastness of Mars, from the unknown. Was it the impact from a fragment of rock thrown against the base by the storm? No, Fangfang has reminded us that's impossible, that the atmosphere is too thin for any wind to carry stones.

What, then?

Unable to find an answer to this question that's obsessing me, I grip Marcus's gloved hand and make an effort to concentrate all my thoughts on our immediate survival.

The sums whirl through my head. We each have thirty-six hours of oxygen in our suits. Well, thirty-five, since we put them on an hour ago. The panic room, meanwhile, is supposed to have twenty-four hours' reserve for all of us. If Serena has done it, we then have fifty-nine hours left to live.

'*I've taken you off the air, covered by a commercial break, and I have my finger on the button,*' a voice roars suddenly out of nowhere as though echoing my thoughts.

Here in the panic room there are no screens.

But there are speakers, connected to the audio relay in our suits.

'*At this very moment, I can feel the button against the fleshy pad of my index finger . . .*' continues Serena McBee. '*The surface is smooth, slightly rounded . . . It offers just slight resistance under my finger . . .*'

Kris falls to her knees on the panic-room floor.

'*Oh, thank God, you haven't pressed it yet! It's not our fault, Serena! We kept our promise! We didn't say a thing! It was Günter who talked! It's his fault!*' Her voice tightens into an entreaty, a prayer murmured quietly: '*I beg you, give us one more chance . . .*'

Once again, she's addressing Serena as if she was a kind of divinity. It's very disturbing. But it's understandable. At this moment, more than ever, we really are at the mercy of this woman, invisible and omnipotent like a goddess.

Liz falls to her knees in turn.

Then Fangfang, Alexei, Samson, Safia, Kelly and, finally, Mozart.

I'm the only girl still standing, beside Marcus and Kenji. Tao is in his wheelchair, but his head is bowed in a gesture of entreaty.

Long minutes slide by, the silence crushing the kneeling bodies with all its weight.

And then, all of a sudden, the voice from the heavens thunders once again.

'*I shall be magnanimous this time, because I love you all. I'm going to spare you,*' she says.

Sighs of reliefs and babbled thanks fill the speakers of my helmet.

'Oh, thank you, thank you,' says Fangfang.

'You understood it was nothing to do with us,' adds Tao.

'God will repay you!' says Kris.

The final blow comes from Alexei.

'We can see you're so much better than we thought after all, Serena! You rule!'

How can I tell them that by pretending to save us, Serena is saving herself? I'm sure if she decided not to press the button, it's to protect herself. To my ears, her so-called magnanimity is an admission: she has not yet found Andrew and Harmony.

'But from now on, we're going to have to play a much tighter game,' she goes on, without waiting for an answer. 'Don't forget one of the robots nearly did away with all of us, you and me. It was sheer luck he didn't talk about the Noah Report or the animals, and referred only to some vague accident that happened in the past. No doubt the viewers will be wanting to know more details, once you are back on the air, given what they've heard so far. So you will need to question the robots once again in public, but guiding their answers in such a way that everybody is reassured. We will rehearse that conversation right away with the owners of the two machines. As for the rest of you, go straight back to the Garden, since the commercial break is coming to an end – you'll say that Krisalex and Fangtao are clarifying a few things in private with their . . . children.'

101. Off-screen

Abandoned mine, Death Valley
Sunday 7 January, 3:42pm

Andrew picks up the laptop that had fallen onto the cabin's worm-eaten floor.

The email that opened during his brief struggle with Harmony is still glowing on the screen.

Slowly, without saying a word, the two young people sit back down on the bed.

And they start to read . . .

From: Barry Mirwood (bmirwood@usa.gov)
To: Serena McBee (serena@mcbeeproductions.com)
Subject: Self-Energized Space Elevator

Dear Ms McBee,
    I hope you remember me and our all-too-brief meeting at the fundraising garden party for the Ultra-libertarian Party last September on Long Island. I said a few words to you then about my area of expertise, the space elevators I have been working on for some years now. The sale

of NASA and my subsequent redundancy temporarily halted my research, but when I met you in the fall I had just been taken on again as scientific advisor for space attached to President Green's office – it's thanks to you, my dear lady, and to your fantastic Genesis program, which brought the skies back into fashion! It goes without saying that I voted for you, and I'm sure you will be elected vice-president of our great nation!

I am convinced that in you, Edmond Green has a fervent advocate for space by his side. And I'm sure that space will be the main priority of your term of office. Does the Genesis program not anticipate a new team being sent to Mars, every two years, to gradually grow the colony with new blood? It's a fine long-term challenge. I believe, however, that we will go further still, and faster still. I'm convinced we'll be able to speed up our colonization of Mars ten-fold, a hundred-fold. How? With a space elevator! There are so many technical possibilities, each more thrilling than the last; nanotube elevators, graphene elevators . . . or most remarkable of all, pure energy elevators! The more I think about it, the more convinced I am this is THE perfect solution. Up till now my work has been limited by a lack of adequate budget. But you have shown that you can raise billions with a click of your fingers!

Imagine if you could convince Atlas Capital to reinvest a portion of the revenues from this awesome project . . . if you could mobilize the government's resources so that America would spearhead this adventure . . . With both political control and financial power in your hands, you would be in a position to realise this crazy dream: building a new Martian civilization, not in a century but in just a few years!

Thanks to my self-energized elevator, we would be able to bring materials and crews down onto Martian soil as often as we needed to, totally safely. We could also bring the citizens of Mars back into orbit if one day they are seized with a desire to see their old home again. The principle is totally simple, and it could be put in place when the next Cupido mission carries twelve new contestants up towards Mars.

Stage 1: the craft coming from Earth transports a self-energized satellite, which is positioned in the Martian orbit, in addition to an ultra-light transit capsule, which travels down to the surface of Mars carrying our twelve newcomers.

Stage 2: the satellite functions like a giant solar panel, capturing the rays of the Sun.

Stage 3: once on Mars the candidates could board the transit capsule at any moment; the self-energized satellite when fully charged emits a beam of microwaves capable of raising the capsule up, extracting it from the planet's gravitational forcefield and lifting it back into orbit.

Stage 4: the capsule can transfer its passengers onto the Cupido or any other craft it docks with in space, before travelling back down to Mars to work again.

What's so amazing about the space elevator is that the energy source stays up there. Which means we get around the thorny problem – some thought the insoluble problem – that until now has stopped us contemplating any possible departure from the red planet: gravity. There's no longer any need to slave away trying to launch a huge rocket from Mars, something filled with fuel that's designed to lift the astronauts back up from the surface (a rocket which in any case would crash on landing owing to its weight). With my elevator, only the ultra-light transit capsule travels between Mars's orbit and its surface. It's totally renewable. Each time the satellite is recharged with solar energy, it can carry the transit capsule back up, indefinitely. Just like a real elevator!

In short, the Earth and Mars will no longer be two hermetically separated environments, but two societies permanently connected, between which people will be able to circulate freely in both directions. Consider the self-energized elevator a gangway between worlds, a red thread of human civilization across the solar system.

I hope I've managed to convey some of my enthusiasm. I'm sure you're very busy at present, but I'd be absolutely delighted to have the chance to meet you again, in Washington, at your place in New York or at Cape Canaveral, to tell you all about this.

Yours truly,
Professor Barry Mirwood, PhD

P.S. The little diagram attached will help you to visualize things a bit better.

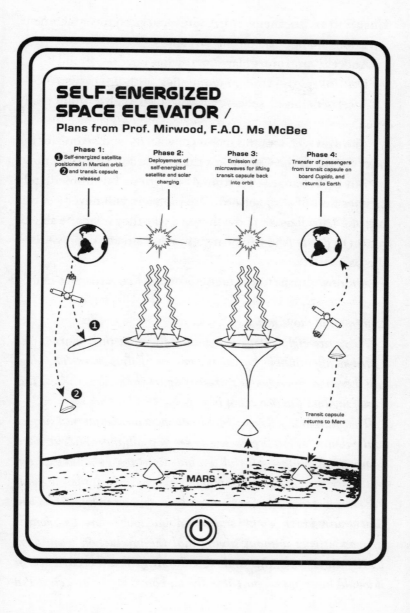

Unable to say another word, Andrew clicks on the attachment.

A diagram appears on the screen.

'Andrew,' murmurs Harmony, 'what have we found?'

'Our Joker,' the young man replies, with fire in his voice.

'A self-energised space elevator? Can such a thing really exist?'

'The man who sent this seems convinced – and in time for the next voyage of the *Cupido* less than a Martian year from now.'

'But that changes everything!' she cries – but immediately catches herself – '. . . or not. The pioneers will never see this picture. They'll never know there's a way they might be able to return to Earth. And maybe my mom has already depressurised the base.'

Andrew returns to the Genesis online live-stream to check.

Long shot of the Garden.

There are eight pioneers standing there, in their suits in the Garden, identifiable by the names on their sleeves. The dogs are there too. Everybody is present apart from Alexei, Kris, Tao, Fangfang and the two robot butlers.

The giant face of Serena McBee appears on the internal surface of the dome. 'What a pleasure to see you all after that extended commercial break – scheduled a long time ago, I should explain, but which regrettably fell just when tensions were at their highest! We have just learned from Günter about a minor technical incident that occurred in the empty seventh habitat, long before the colonists arrived. It goes without saying that the production team were totally unaware of this undoubtedly insignificant occurrence, or it would have been reported in the on-board log. In any case, I'm eager to learn more, as you are too, my dear pioneers, and also you, dear viewers. But tell me, while we're talking about him – where has Günter got to?'

Kelly takes a step towards the wall of the dome.

The camera immediately zooms in on her, framing her face in close-up through the visor of her helmet: 'Krisalex and Fangtao are in the panic room with their robots – they wanted to talk to them in private. Kind of like parents with their kids – you can see how far gone they are!'

The sarcasm isn't very different from Kelly's usual, but there's no ironic smile to accompany it this time, and there's no spark of mischief in the Canadian girl's blue eyes.

She adds at once: 'In any case, I'm sure the accident was nothing. Like you said, Serena, if it had been something important it would have been recorded in the log. We aren't worried here. Isn't that right, guys?'

The camera pans out to show the rest of the pioneers, who nod with exaggerated enthusiasm, swearing they haven't the least concern about the solidity of the base. Only Léonor, Kenji and Marcus remain silent, observing the scene without a word.

Elizabeth speaks next. 'As Engineering Officer, I'm ready to bet that the external object Günter was talking about was a tiny fragment of rock, a bit sharper than the rest, which must have scratched the seventh habitat – and yes, maybe it did make a hole, but honestly just a ridiculously small hole, no bigger than a pinhead.'

She's talking a bit too loud, a bit too quickly, without pausing for breath.

531

'You can tell she doesn't believe a word she's saying!' declares Harmony suddenly. 'And the terrible noises we heard just now, they definitely weren't caused by *tiny fragments of rock*!'

Sitting on the edge of the old mattress, at the back of the darkened cabin, she shudders with annoyance.

'It was my mom who asked them to lie, I'm sure of it,' she says. 'It's as plain as the nose on her face.'

'To you perhaps, because you know the truth,' says Andrew, who is wearing the miner's lamp he often uses for exploring the abandoned mine on his forehead. 'But the viewers don't know. I'm sure they think Liz is telling the truth – a bit shaken by what's happened, but telling the truth.'

Lighting up his backpack with his lamp, he takes out a big remote control, but Harmony is paying him no attention. She has already looked away, eager to see whatever happens next on the programme.

The reinforced door of the panic room opens abruptly behind Liz. Finally, the English girl takes a breath, as the two missing couples come back into the Garden, accompanied by their robots.

Ostentatiously ignoring Alexei, Mozart speaks to Kirsten: 'Well?'

The German girl is white as a sheet behind the visor of her helmet, but she manages to smile, and answers: 'Oh, a false alarm. Everything is back in order.'

She leans over towards the robot in the bow tie and asks him a question, articulating each of her words with exaggerated care: 'Günter, has the hole in the seventh habitat been repaired now?'

The robot answers in his artificial voice: 'Affirmative.'

Kirsten takes a deep breath and embarks on a second question.

'Günter, have there been any other breaches, of any kind at all, anywhere in New Eden, in the more than three years since it was built?'

Günter, expressionless, answers: 'Negative'.

Like a prosecutor interrogating a witness in the dock, constructing her argument on the basis of her interlocutor's own answers, Kirsten concludes: 'In three years, then, there has been only one single incident, which has now been fixed – in other words, a technical fault rate that is objectively very low?'

The camera focuses on the round eye of the robot, who answers: 'Affirmative.'

Kirsten stands up at last, perspiration on her forehead, her visor misted over, and turns to the other pioneers: 'You see? We were making a big deal out of nothing.'

'She only asked questions whose answers were going to reassure the viewers!' says Harmony. 'It's a performance, the whole thing's totally fake!'

'It's been that way since the start, Harmony,' replies Andrew, still wearing the lamp on his head. 'Ever since the *Cupido* first took off.'

'I can't believe the pioneers are forced to act as though everything's just fine, when they know the base is rotten, and there's something outside threatening them! I so wish I could tell them there's some hope they might be able to get out, however tiny it might be! I so wish I could tell them about the self-energised elevator!'

'Maybe you'll be able to do that, Harmony.'

Suddenly the girl seems to notice the frantic activity of her companion, seated beside her on the bed.

'What's that?' she asks, pointing at the large remote control lit by his lamp. 'Some new gadget?'

'It's a satellite phone,' says Andrew. 'Thanks to this I was able to infiltrate the Cape Canaveral base with my mini-drone at the start of the summer, avoiding their block on terrestrial communications. My poor bug was destroyed later, but not the system I put in place – that should still be operational.'

'A system? What system?'

A smile crosses Andrew's face. For a moment it replaces his anxiety and fatigue with the pure joy of a child who has set up the perfect practical joke, the mischief of a lifetime.

'In July I made secret contact with the only network capable of communicating between the Cape Canaveral base and the outside world,' he says. 'A network constantly in operation, twenty-four hours a day, transmitting the flood of images that for months has been pouring through space and down to Earth. Do you need me to draw a picture for you, or do you understand?'

Harmony's eyes widen.

'You mean . . .' she says softly.

'Yes,' he replies, 'the Genesis interplanetary network! I went through my father's files – you know he was in charge of all the programme's communications – to unearth the access codes. What I wouldn't have done at the time to screw him over! Then I connected my phone to the satellite that receives the laser data coming from space and converts them to a secure radio frequency destined for the parabolic antennae at Cape

Canaveral. My aim at the time was just to surf the frequency and attach myself to it like a parasite, to be able to control my mini-drone at a distance and put the images stolen from the control room onto my hacking site. But there's nothing stopping us getting back on that frequency today, Harmony, nothing to stop us connecting to the satellite that's orbiting the Earth, and to the antenna installed on Phobos . . . and to the base at New Eden!'

With one hand, Andrew switches on the large telephone. A message appears on the small screen:

SATELLITE CONNECTION IN PROGRESS . . .

'You're going to try to talk to the pioneers?' asks Harmony, overwhelmed by the excitement. 'The way my mom talks to them from Earth?'

'Better than that!' answers Andrew.

With trembling fingers, he uncoils a cable and plugs one end into the satellite phone and the other into his laptop.

'Napoleon said a good sketch is better than a long speech.'

'No!' whispers Harmony. 'Don't tell me you're going to show them the plans for the elevator?'

'Yeah, that's exactly what I mean to do. But they won't be the only people to see it. If I manage to do what I'm planning, the whole of humanity will also be able to enjoy the view!'

102. Shot

'*We're all greatly reassured!*' says Serena from the wall of the Garden dome.

She's giving us a broad toothy smile, a wolf's smile disguised as an angel's.

'*Günter was referring to a tiny incident of no significance whatsoever, and which furthermore was unique. That explains why nothing was recorded in the log, and why I wasn't aware of it. Of course, we must carry out our enquiries in order to understand exactly what happened, but for the moment, you're all perfectly safe, my dearest pioneers: it looked a lot worse than it really was!*'

. . . which is just as good news for you as it is for us, I want to add. You came very close to disaster. But you'll get what's coming to you in the end. One day justice will be done; there's no way you'll go unpunished for ever.

'*Thank you, Serena, for watching over us so well!*' I hear Kris's voice in my speakers, saying almost exactly the opposite of what I'm thinking.

I turn to see if she's kidding.

536

But through the visor of her helmet I can make out no trace of irony.

Just genuine gratitude and – I have to admit it, though it horrifies me – a kind of devotion.

'The weather service has informed me that the worst of the storm has passed,' Serena continues on the screen. *'Conditions should start getting better soon. You can count on me: I'll always be here . . . to help you . . . and fulfil my commitment . . . of Assist-ist-ist-istan-stan . . .'*

Serena's voice is jumping about like a scratched record, and her picture, once again, is streaked with white lines.

'Looks like more interference,' says Liz, worried. *'Maybe the storm hasn't passed completely?'*

Soon the white lines have occupied the entire screen, and in a few moments Serena disappears, to be replaced by a diagram that seems to have come out of nowhere.

It shows the Earth and the Sun, in the form of drawings.

There's also the *Cupido*.

And there's a beam connecting the surface of Mars to space, with a kind of capsule levitating between the two.

'What the hell's that?' asks Kelly. *'What's that got to do with the* Assistance *commitment?'*

No one answers her.

Because everyone is reading.

Self-energized space elevator . . .

Plans by Prof. Mirwood, F.A.O. Ms McBee . . .

Transit capsule . . .

. . . the return to Earth . . .

Return to Earth?

'*Are we . . . dreaming?*' stammers Mozart.

Kelly leaps across and grabs the Brazilian's arm.

'*Owww!*' he yells. '*Are you suffering withdrawal symptoms or what? Do you want my body so badly, is that why you've pinched me like a crab?*'

'*You felt that? Then no, you aren't dreaming, and nor am I. We really did read that:* the return to Earth! *Alexei was right, Serena really is a superwoman who definitely does rule!* Repatriation assistance: *she's going to bring us home!*'

103. Off-screen

'Repatriation assistance: *she's going to bring us home!*'

Serena McBee is frozen like a mummy at her desk, which has nothing on it but a secure corded telephone.

Opposite her, on the editing screen, are the various windows corresponding to the different cameras on the New Eden base. The one in the middle represents the long view of the Garden, which shows Kelly raving over the sketch displayed on the wall of the dome.

The executive producer recovers herself and sets about tapping frantically on the keys of her control panel, trying to transfer to another camera.

But the system won't respond.

On the editing screen, the central window of the Genesis channel remains stubbornly fixed on the Garden, on the pioneers, and on the enormous diagram of the self-energised space elevator that hovers above them.

104. Off-screen

Champs-Élysées, Paris
Sunday 7 January, 1:22pm

The Champs-Elysées is filled with a great clamour, the like of which it has heard only twice before in history: at the liberation of Paris in the Second World War, and the last time France won the football World Cup.

The giant screen hanging from the Arc de Triomphe is showing the Martian dome, with the diagram of the self-energised elevator that the generous Serena McBee is offering to the colonists of Mars – or at least, that's how the crowd sees it.

'What's going on?' the granny returning from the supermarket asks the young man in a tracksuit, who seems to have adopted her.

'It's that American lady, Serena – too cool. She's going to set up an elevator between Mars and space so the pioneers can come back home in case the base starts to play up!'

'An elevator?' says the old lady, confused. 'I've spent thirty years trying to persuade the owners to install one up to my little apartment, but I suppose those youngsters need it more than I do – isn't that right, Mirza?'

The poodle gives a little bark, as though to concur with her mistress.

At that moment, the young man puts his hand on the old lady's shoulder.

'Look, it's us! The Genesis programme is showing the pioneers how happy we are for them!'

On the giant screen, something has changed: the wall of the Garden dome is no longer showing the picture of the elevator . . . but of the Paris crowd itself, gathered at the foot of the noble monument, being filmed by the state TV channel! Up in their glasshouse, the pioneers in their spacesuits start making big gestures and giving shouts of delight.

In response to these signals sent from Mars, a gigantic Mexican wave starts to climb up from the Concorde obelisk towards the Place de l'Étoile.

'Get ready to do a Mexican wave!' says the young man. 'One . . . two . . . three!'

The old lady raises her arms heavenward at the same time as her neighbours, pulling on Mirza's lead so that she too raises herself up on her back legs.

'Waaaave!'

105. Off-screen

Hotel California, Death Valley
Sunday 7 January, 4:28pm

With her nose right up close to the TV screen, Cindy is zapping frantically between channels.

On the rug at the foot of her bed, the tub of ice cream has tipped over and finally melted, spilling its pink-and-white magma, strawberry flavoured with nougat chunks.

Times Square, New York City, 7:29 am
Despite it being Sunday morning, the square is as packed as any at weekday rush hour. The countless screens fixed to the skyscrapers are transmitting the images from the pioneers on Mars, standing amazed in front of the wall of the Garden. The utter delight of the New Yorkers is reflected on the panes of glass, like a mirror held up between the two planets.

A journalist is babbling excitedly into his mic. 'It's an astonishing twist in the drama, like only the Genesis programme knows how! The moment suspicions begin to be shared about the safety of the New Eden base, the moment the wildest speculations begin to spread about the nature of the noises that we heard at the heart of

the storm, Serena McBee reveals her plan to install a self-energised
space elevator to accelerate our conquest of Mars . . . and to make
it possible to evacuate the pioneers in the event of any problem!
What a gift that woman has! Seriously, what a gift!'

Zap!

A special edition of the TV news.

The presenter in suit and tie seems to be questioning the viewer
with his piercing stare.

'But who is Barry Mirwood? Who is the man behind this name
which, just a few minutes ago, was unknown to the general public?
Quick as a flash, our teams have found him for you, and we're
about to bring him to you live!'

The screen splits in two, leaving the presenter in the left-hand
window, and adding a window on the right to show an old man
with a big white beard, wearing pyjamas printed with stars and
rockets. His crumpled skin, which still has a pillow-mark on it,
suggests he's only just got out of bed. But his sparkling eyes are
wide awake, fully charged like an electric battery.

'Mr Barry Caesar Mirwood?' asks the presenter, confirming
his interlocutor's identity.

'I am!' says the old man.

'Special scientific advisor to President Green on space matters?'
the presenter continues, reading his notes.

'Right, that's me!'

'Are you the creator of the project to build a self-energised space
elevator that's currently being broadcast on the Genesis channel?'

'I am indeed!' says the delighted professor. 'I've been working
on the thrilling subject of space elevators for thirty years, and I've

talked to Professor McBee about it when I could. I've always been sure she'd understand the critical scientific value of an invention of this kind – she holds a scientific doctorate herself, after all!'

'Well, this invention has certainly come at just the right moment. Tell us, do you really believe something as remarkable as this could be put in place in time for the new Cupido voyage to Mars, for the second season of the Genesis programme, less than two Earth years from now?'

'Absolutely. We could even speed things up if we wanted to, sending the Cupido up to Mars even more quickly, equipped with my self-energised satellite and its transit capsule.'

'Extraordinary! But let me ask you the question which, to be frank, everybody has been wondering about, professor – how much would all this cost?'

'Oh, a couple dozen billions of dollars! But as I suggested to Serena McBee, by investing the revenues from the Genesis programme back into this project, in the name of science, the economics can be made to add up perfectly well! No doubt the vice-president will be able to persuade Atlas Capital to do that!'

106. Off-screen

Vice-Presidential Residence, Washington DC
Sunday 7 January, 7:35am

The door of Serena McBee's Observatory office opens to reveal Orion Seamus.

Despite the early hour, he is impeccably turned out, as is his custom; not a hair out of place, his one eye shining with concentration beside the black patch.

'You called for me, Ms McBee?' he asks.

'Close the door.'

Serena's voice is as sharp as a blade.

Agent Seamus closes the door carefully behind him, then turns his cyclops stare back to the impressive equipment that Serena McBee has had installed in the vice-presidential study. On the big editing screen, the central window is still focused on the wide view of the Garden. In front of the pioneers, on the inside surface of the dome, there are pictures alternating between a variety of TV channels from all over the world, greeting the news of the self-energised elevator with overwhelming enthusiasm.

'Agent Orion Seamus, the time has come for you to

demonstrate that *total loyalty* you swore to me yesterday,' says Serena.

A smile appears on the young man's face.

'I'm at your service, Ms McBee.'

But Serena is not smiling. She points at the editing screen; the dome is showing pictures from Tiananmen Square in Beijing, which is filled by an overjoyed crowd.

'Are you just as delighted as everyone else at this business with the self-energised elevator?' she asks out of the blue.

'I'm sure the production team will always take whatever decisions are best for the pioneers,' Agent Seamus replies diplomatically.

'It wasn't the production team who released the information about the elevator project, and nor are we the ones broadcasting the fans' reactions up to the dome. The diagram, these pictures, none of it is coming from the Genesis programme. Yet my team at Cape Canaveral assures me that the signal is passing through our secure interplanetary communications network. Which means some hacker has managed to infiltrate it. Now, the programme's incredibly tough encryption has been breached once before – six months ago, last July, when pictures from our base were broadcast on a hacker website. I'm sure it's the same person behind both intrusions. And I think I know who he is.'

Serena gets up from her desk and walks over to the man standing in the middle of the office.

She looks straight into the agent's one eye; from this close, she can see the countless little ochre specks scattered across his brown iris.

'You don't know the whole story about Andrew Fisher. Last

month he broke into my villa. I didn't tell you earlier because I didn't want to condemn the young man any further. But today I have to face up to the evidence: the drawing that is currently being shown on the screen comes from my email archives. Only he could have had access to them. So he is the one who has hacked into the Genesis channel right now and it must undoubtedly have been him who hacked into the base last summer, too.'

'These actions constitute terrorism,' says Agent Seamus seriously, 'especially at this time that's so critical for our country. You really have been too indulgent towards him, Ms McBee. We will redouble our efforts to find him, combing the whole country if necessary.'

'It won't be necessary. My teams have also told me they've tracked the origin of the hacker signal that has attached itself parasitically to the Genesis network. California. Death Valley. Dry Mountain.' She puts a piece of paper into the agent's hand. 'I've written the exact coordinates here.'

Orion Seamus's fingers close on the piece of paper, briefly touching Serena's.

'I'll go, Ms McBee,' he says. 'I'll notify the special forces based in the area, and I swear I'll oversee his arrest personally.'

'I can count on you. But remember, Andrew is quite clearly disturbed. He'll invent all kinds of stories to justify his actions.'

'Don't worry. It'll be drones that catch him, and drones don't listen to humans' stories. I'll arrange for the suspect to be brought to a secret base, without notifying the federal authorities via the usual route, so that you can question him personally. The suspicion of terrorism allows us to do that.'

Serena gently pulls her hand away from the young C.I.A. prodigy.

'I see we understand one another,' she says, smiling. 'My employers at Atlas Capital believe I am motivated only by money, and I gladly allow them to keep believing that, but money is only a means to an end. My real ambition has always been power. Just like you, Orion, isn't that so? That's why we understand one another so well. We were born to enlighten and guide our fellow creatures, you and I.' She smiles a bit more, then adds: 'Oh, one last thing. I'm certain that you'll find a girl with Andrew Fisher – arrest her too.'

Agent Seamus gives a slight bow then disappears without a word.

No sooner has he closed the door than the corded telephone on the desk starts to ring.

Serena picks it up and speaks sharply.

'Hello?'

'A helicopter from Atlas Capital is seeking authorisation to land on the Observatory lawn, Madam Vice-President,' says a secretary's voice.

'Granted.'

107. Off-screen

Abandoned mine, Death Valley
Sunday 7 January, 4:39am

Andrew Fisher and Harmony McBee are staring at the laptop screen, with several open windows showing TV stations from the four corners of the Earth. All of them are broadcasting the extraordinary news: the Genesis programme's decision to build a self-energised elevator between space and the surface of Mars.

'France, Germany, the U.K., the U.S., Canada, Nigeria, Brazil, Russia, Japan, Singapore, China and now India!' says Andrew. 'There you have it, a full house! I've linked New Eden up to the national channels of each of the pioneers in turn!'

The howling of a distant coyote pierces the silence of Death Valley.

Andrew looks away from the screen, the beam of his miner's lamp sweeping across the cabin and finally coming to rest on his watch.

'It's almost half an hour since we hacked into the channel,' he says. 'We've been able to ensure that the whole world has really taken on board the idea of the self-energised elevator – there's no going back for the Genesis programme now . . . or for Serena McBee. I'll let her have the controls back in a few moments, and she'll be forced to confirm to the viewers that Genesis is going to build it!'

'That's incredible, Andrew!' says Harmony. 'Thanks to you, the pioneers have been able to see displays of solidarity by millions of people!' Then she adds at once: 'It's just a pity they haven't seen the two of us – they don't know we're behind it. But it would be too dangerous to let them see our faces, of course.'

'I think there's another way of letting them know!' says Andrew.

His hands start to race across the numerical keypad, lit up by his miner's lamp.

He and Harmony are too absorbed to see the distant shadows crossing the face of the Moon, beyond the cabin's broken window. It looks like a squadron of wild birds, in a V formation, pointing towards Dry Mountain like an arrow.

108. Off-screen

'*It's unacceptable,*' says android Oraculon in his toneless voice.

Deep inside the black globe that serves as his head, the synthesised face trembles slightly – that is as much emotion as it seems capable of expressing. Behind the android, it's possible to see the helicopter in which he arrived, in the middle of a vast circle of snow blown about by the blades on his arrival. The blades are still now, and the Observatory lawn has been plunged back into its night-time silence.

'*The whole of the world's media is announcing that Atlas Capital is going to be reinvesting its returns into this preposterous project of building a self-energised elevator,*' the android continues, standing opposite Serena, who sits wrapped in her opulent mink coat. '*It's totally out of the question!*'

'Tut, tut!' she says, scolding the robot with her manicured finger. 'You should never make definitive statements like that. I strongly advise the Atlas Capital board not to announce anything of the kind. Do you really want to come across as the company who for reasons of profit alone have chosen not to bring help to the pioneers at the very moment when public opinion is starting to think they may be in some danger? If so, you're going to have to be ready for your offices to be stormed by hordes of raging viewers.'

The 3D face tenses up a little more.

'*But . . . our profits are protected by law . . .*'

'All I'm saying is if you don't play the game properly, you're going to unleash a tsunami that nothing will be able to hold back. Then there will be no barriers, no laws to protect you – not you *or* your profits. People are really passionate about the story of the colonists of Mars, as if they were members of their own families – what am I saying, as if they *themselves* were up there! You asked me to put together a unique show, something we've never seen before. I've fulfilled my task beyond every expectation, it seems to me. I couldn't have predicted that this self-energised elevator project would have cropped up suddenly, because of some hacker. But now that it's here, we have to deal with it. If we ignore the will of the people, the people will revolt; that's how every revolution in history has started. And when the revolution comes, you'll be the ones who will stand to lose everything. You need to buy time. Make them think we're on their side. Start to invest in this ridiculous elevator, and pretend it's going to be a part of season two of the Genesis programme, while we're trying to come up with a solution. Yes, it'll cost you a bit of money – but if you refuse, that will cost you absolutely everything.'

This time, the face in the android Oraculon's head has no answer.

109. Shot

'Look, the picture's changing again!' says Safia, pointing at the side of the Garden dome.

She's right.

Our view of the Indian crowd, gathered in the golden light of a late afternoon in New Delhi, is streaked across by white lines. For more than half an hour we've really been given quite an eyeful; first came the diagram of the self-energised elevator, like a mirage rising out of the depths of space, which I found hard to believe in, but I really had to start believing in it when the view switched to the Champs-Élysées where hundreds of thousands of people were seeing the same thing I was! Then we got to see each of the countries where we twelve come from, and the sight was the same everywhere, the same unbelievable jubilation.

There's no way it can be a hoax, or some twisted new strategy. There are just too many people involved, too many people now expecting this elevator to become a reality.

But what am I supposed to make of it, then?

That Serena really is *much better than we thought after all,* like Alexei said?

That she really does want to save us, and not just her own skin?

While these questions circle round and round in my head, the answer appears on the side of the dome.

What follows New Delhi is a black screen.

With a line of numbers running across it, several metres high:

$$12 + 2 = 14$$

I immediately understand the meaning of this equation, which must be a mystery to the viewers but is perfectly clear to me. And I'm sure it's perfectly clear to the other pioneers, too without anyone needing to risk speaking Andrew's or Harmony's name on the air.

Twelve plus two equals fourteen!

Our Survival Officers have never deserved their title more!

It was them, I'm sure of it. They were the ones who unearthed this plan for a providential elevator and forced it onto Serena McBee!

I send them a huge thank-you from the bottom of my heart, just before the black screen disappears in turn with a crackle. What it leaves this time is the executive producer herself, wrapped in a mink coat, her cheeks very flushed as though she's just raced indoors to get herself in front of the camera.

Much better than we thought? Her?

What a load of crap! But given how things stand, she's definitely going to have to act like she is!

'*Well, my dear pioneers, I hope you enjoyed my little surprise?*'

554

Despite speaking with her usual self-assurance, I know her well enough that I think I can sense a tiny tremor in her voice. *'You signed up for a one-way ticket, you see, but I've always had a secret plan to allow you to come home one day if you choose to, you and your babies. I've always had a vision of a permanent link between the Earth and Mars, which worked both ways. I'd planned to tell you about it later, during future seasons of the Genesis programme, once we'd ironed out all the financial and technical aspects, but I know that Günter's revelations about what happened that one time clearly upset you, I can see that, even if everything has now been fixed. And so, in agreement with Atlas Capital, I took the decision to accelerate our planned self-energised space elevator and get everything underway to have it ready as soon as possible!'*

All around me, the other pioneers are falling into each other's arms.

'We really are going home!' sobs Kris. *'I don't believe it!'*

'But it's true, my angel,' says Alexei, holding her tight.

'Could we take Günter with us? Please?'

'Sounds good – and we'll make a whole lot of better-looking brothers for him!'

I'm just as transported by happiness myself. Even if there are still so many details missing. Serena is well and truly stuck. For the first time since I discovered the Noah Report, I can see a concrete chance that we might get out of this alive!

I turn to Marcus, to take him in my arms, to share my relief and my hope with him, like all the other couples are doing.

But the face I see behind his visor cuts my delight dead. He's as pale as a ghost.

'*Follow me . . . to the Rest House . . .*' he says, his voice wavering.

'*M-Marcus?*' I stammer. '*What's happened?*'

Instead of answering, he frantically undoes his helmet and drops it onto the floor, leaving the audio relay network. Then he turns on his heel and goes to the access tube that leads to the seventh Love Nest – the only one out of sight of the viewers.

'*What's up?*' asks Kelly.

'*I . . . I don't know. I think I should go with him.*'

I take off my own helmet in turn, drop it behind me and run after Marcus.

'*This is it, he's about to have his attack!*' all my instincts are screaming in my head. '*The second one, the last one, the unforgiving one! He can sense his time is coming and he's gone off to die in secret like an animal!*'

I feel a cold sweat trickle down my spine the moment I reach the entrance to the access tube. Marcus has pushed open the door leading from the Garden and is already at the other end of the airlock, in the process of lifting the lever that opens the second door – the one into the seventh habitat. The corridor is only a few metres long, and yet it feels endless now, it feels like my boots are skating on the metal floor.

Marcus opens the door.

The spotlights in the Rest House have thrown his suit into silhouette, blindingly bright.

I think about the light at the end of the tunnel, the light some people claim to see when they pass into the next world.

'Marcus!' I cry as I reach him at last.

I fall into his arms, desperate, while he pulls back the lever to shut us both into the seventh Love Nest.

556

110. Genesis Channel

Sunday 7 January, 8:07am

Long shot showing the access tube that leads to the Rest House.

The internal door of the tube, the one from the Garden, gapes like the mouth of an ogre that just a few moments ago swallowed up Marcus and Léonor, and is still hungry.

The ten pioneers in their suits walk gingerly towards it, all except Kirsten and Mozart. The two of them have taken off their helmets so Léonor could hear them when they called after her as she ran. They are the first to reach the passageway and plunge inside, disappearing from the view of the cameras.

Safia's worried voice comes through the audio relay.

'Wait . . . Maybe Marcus and Léo want to be left alone.'

But Alexei and Elizabeth are already unable to hear, as they too have just removed their helmets and started running. They in turn cross the threshold of the airlock in pursuit of their partners.

The moment the other pioneers reach the opening, the broadcast stops abruptly, replaced by the jingle that announces another commercial.

Cut.

Open onto the slightly yellowed photo of a group of children, standing in a neat row in a concrete courtyard. They are wearing expressions that are unusually serious for their age. As the notes of some nostalgic tune emerge from a piano, the camera zooms in on the child in the middle of the row: a little girl, just six, her face covered in freckles, wide eyes that seem to be asking a question of the viewer. It's Léonor. She has been given the job of holding a slate on which someone has written in chalk: "Paris XX Orphanage: Junior Section".

Fade into a second photo, showing a little boy frowning, with storm-grey eyes, holding the hand of a distracted-looking woman. We immediately recognise the young Marcus, and guess the dishevelled woman is his mother. We have the strange sense that it's her who is clinging to her son's hand, not the other way around.

Violins are added to the piano, making the melody richer.

Fade into an image of Léonor as a young adult, standing on the boarding platform at Cape Canaveral for the Genesis programme's launch ceremony. Compared to the earlier photo, her face has more shape to it, her cheekbones are more sculpted, her eyelashes are longer, and yet the expression above the collar of her white suit is the same, burning with questions.

Fade into the reverse shot: a still of Marcus waiting on the same platform, the same day, on the opposite side of the logo-covered curtain. Here too, despite the thicker eyebrows and the squarer jaw, we can recognise the serious little boy behind this young man who is off to conquer the stars.

The music continues to pick up pace, volume and intensity. Fade into a new picture of Léonor. Hair held back by a ribbon, chest shaped by her small grey jersey top, she is floating in the middle of the glass Visiting Room. In her fingers she's crumpling the slip of paper drawn by lot with the name of her first contestant, during the first speed-dating session.

Fade into Marcus, also weightless. He's dressed entirely in black, his hair carefully combed, a half-smile lighting up his face. In his hand he's holding the magnificent red rose he's magicked into appearance, as an offering to the girl who has just invited him.

Two oboes join the other instruments now, the music becoming more symphonic for a final surge.

The next photo that appears on the screen shows Léonor and Marcus together, for the very first time, just after the landing of the capsules; dressed in their thick white spacesuits, they embrace in the middle of the red Martian desert. Behind the visors of their helmets, which are resting on each other, their faces are glowing with happiness.

A woman's voice speaks gently: *'From out of the most beautiful marriages, the finest creations are born.'*

A whole range of frozen dishes appears on the screen, packaged in black plastic tubs shaped like hearts.

Voiceover: *'Léorcus cooked meals. When Merceaugnac refinement meets Eden Food know-how, quality gastronomy becomes available to all lovers with good taste.'*

Fade into the inscription carved into the white opal of Mars:

LEONOR + MARCUS

The two names morph into one, forming an elegant brand logo:

LEORCUS
Simply Delicious
From Merceaugnac and Eden Food

*

Twelve recipes from top chefs
for you to taste with your beloved
Coming to a freezer aisle near you

Cut.

111. Shot

Month 21 / sol 578 / 10:26 Mars time
[28th sol since landing]

'Marcus! Don't die, I'm begging you! It's not yet time!'

Tears mist up my eyes, blurring the spotlights, distorting that face I adore . . . A face that's still as pale, as stunned as it was a moment ago when he asked me to follow him to the Rest House.

'I'm not going to die, not now, not yet,' he says quietly.

The knot in my belly relaxes at once.

'I was so scared!'

'But I am going to let you hear the end of my story. The bit you haven't heard. That I promised myself I'd never tell you. Up till now I've been able to convince myself there was no point telling the truth, as we were all going to die in a few months on Mars anyway. But not any more. The elevator has changed everything. I've got to spit it out, this last thing, right away, before we let the others in – because if I don't open the door to them I'm sure they'll force it open.'

'What? What are you saying? You can tell me *everything*, do you hear? You know I'll keep your secret!'

From the access tube, behind the large metal door that Marcus has locked from the inside, I can hear the muffled shouts of Kris and Mozart. I can also hear Serena McBee's voice filtering in from the screen in the habitat's master bedroom.

'*What's going on, Léonor? Marcus?*' she asks anxiously, unable to see us or hear us as long as we stay in this room whose cameras and mics are glued over with melted plastic. '*What are you doing in the Rest House without an invitation from me? You left the other pioneers in chaos, and I've just been forced to interrupt the broadcast yet again with a commercial break. But that'll only buy us a few minutes, and soon the viewers will start to suspect something's going on: do you really want to ruin everything?*'

I don't answer Serena's questions, or even my friends' shouts.

I pay no attention to the shuddering of the door, beyond which their fists are raining down hard against the metal.

The only thing that matters is Marcus.

Is he afraid I've changed my mind about him, because of this elevator that has fallen from heaven?

Just because my expectation of survival has just taken a great leap forward, does he think I'm going to go back on all the things I promised him?

'Even if we do make it back to Earth, that changes nothing!' I cry. 'Remember what's carved into the opal – we will love each other for all eternity!'

A half-smile appears on Marcus's face, but it's quite different from the usual one I know and so love. This one is sad, warped, cut short – like a scar.

'It changes nothing – you're sure of that?' he says. 'Listen to me, before you go back naively to that old "an eternity to love" slogan.'

Ouch. That hurts.

And I have the confusing sense he's about to hurt me more still. I want to go back in time, close Marcus's mouth, forget the meanings of words and all the memories I've been accumulating these past months.

But the Salamander warned me: by opening up my heart, I was taking a risk. The memories are written there, indelibly. And now there can be no forgetting.

Marcus's mouth is half open, contorted into a grimace.

The words that come out of it curl all around like ropes entangling me.

'Does it still change nothing if I tell you I knew before we set off that the base was rotten, that I knew the animals that came before us had all died, and that we were headed for our deaths too?'

He puts his hand on the lever that opens the shuddering door and gives it the first quarter-turn. I feel like I'm on a torturer's rack, and that he, the torturer, is turning the handle to stretch my limbs till they break.

'Does it still change nothing if I tell you I knew about the Noah Report, and that I could have revealed everything to the world during the launch ceremony – but that I let you all board that rocket without saying a word?'

He gives the lever another sharp quarter-turn; I feel my whole body clench, my guts twist.

'Does it still change nothing if I tell you the only thing that mattered to me was getting to Mars, and doing it no matter what the cost?'

He gives another quarter-turn, and with the same violent gesture he tears apart what's left of my heart.

His handsome face, so calm a short time ago, is now just a mask of bitterness that makes me feel both terror and pity. Except it's not a mask. It's really him. The mask is the forehead, the cheeks, the lips I've kissed so many times.

At this thought, disgust overwhelms every other emotion.

I feel my stomach rising.

The taste of bile is in my mouth.

At that moment, the stranger whose hands were only yesterday exploring my naked body gives the last quarter-turn, the coup de grâce.

'I'm not a victim, Léonor. I'm a murderer who threw away your eleven lives, knowing full well what I was doing. Would you dare to say the same thing to them, that you will love me for all eternity?'

The door opens silently to reveal the faces of the innocent people Marcus has condemned. All ten of them are there, their helmets off, clustered around Tao's wheelchair – he's holding the all-access key he was just about to use.

Kris is the first to rush to my rescue.

I can see her lips move, but I can't hear a sound.

Then she starts screaming, gripping onto my shoulders, and her voice finally reaches me as if from very far away.

'Léo! What's happened? You look so pale!'

The girls form a protective circle around me.

Over their heads I can see the boys similarly gathering around

Marcus – two separate groups, like our time on the *Cupido*, as if we'd just taken a huge leap backwards.

I can see Mozart's furious face, his forehead almost pressing against Marcus's as he yells: 'What have you done to her? What did you say to her? Answer me!'

Kris's hands are squeezing my shoulders so hard it's like she's trying to crush them.

'Talk to me, Léo, I'm begging you . . .'

All eyes turn to me, filled with fear and incomprehension.

I feel a burst of acid rise from my guts into my throat.

Puking up my pain!

Right here, in the Rest House, in front of the whole crew!

Tell them Marcus is a filthy traitor and let them tear him to pieces, let them avenge me, in this room where nobody can see us or hear us!

'Speak to me!' begs Kris. 'Say something!'

The truth is on the tip of my tongue.

I could spit it out, to free myself, the way you spit out a bit of spoiled food you've bitten into by mistake – because that's what it is, the story that Marcus and I share: a fraud as disgusting as the Genesis programme itself, lovely and pink on the outside, totally foul on the inside.

Or I could swallow the truth, digest it until it forms an inextricable part of me, until it dissolves into my skin, into my hair, into every cell of my being – so that nobody will ever discover it.

Speak, or keep quiet?

Give up this man who has torn me apart, or keep his pitiful secret?

Nobody but me has the power to decide.

This time I can't turn away. I can't appeal to the group, or organise a vote.

The party is over, the Heart Lists are set, the names of the lovers are engraved on the immutable rock of the planets and in the fake eternity of the screens.

I've played and lost.

There's no longer twelve of us, nor even two.

I'm one person, alone –

. . . just one!

112. Genesis Channel

Sunday 7 January, 8:15am

GENESIS PROGRAM – SEASON 2

SIX NEW BOYS

SIX NEW GIRLS

SIX NEW LOVE STORIES

AND EVEN MORE BABIES!

APPLICATIONS OPEN TODAY

APPLY NOW ON THE GENESIS WEBSITE!

Acknowledgements

As we complete a new leg in our space journey, the time has come to thank all crew members from both French and British sides of the programme. Always on the job, Glenn, Constance and Fabien helped me take off from French ground into space, while Daniel, Georgia, Talya, Anna and Melissa propelled my story into the whole new galaxy of the English language. Tina expertly organised my visit to the Hay Festival, an experience that I will always remember, and Sahina precisely coordinated the launch from the control tower.

Last but not least, my family supported me during all those months when I was writing this book, with a lot of patience and understanding, as my mind was more often on Mars than on Earth!

The second phase of this mission could never have been completed without each and every one of them: I would like to thank them dearly.

Explore the world of Phobos on Victor Dixen's site:
www.victordixen.com

HOT KEY BOOKS

Thank you for choosing a Hot Key book.

If you want to know more about our authors
and what we publish, you can find us online.

You can start at our website

www.hotkeybooks.com

And you can also find us on:

We hope to see you soon!